Return of the Dragon

By

Sam Ferguson

This is a work of fiction. All of the characters, organizations, and events portrayed in this book are either products of the author's imagination or are used fictitiously.

Return of the Dragon

For my son Connor.
Hard times won't last forever.

Other Books by Sam Ferguson

Tales from Terramyr

The Dragon's Champion Series

The Dragon's Champion
The Warlock Senator
The Dragon's Test
Erik and the Dragon
The Immortal Mystic
Return of the Dragon

The Netherworld Gate Series
The Tomni'Tai Scroll
The King's Ring (Coming Soon)
Son of the Dragon (Coming Soon)

The Dragons of Kendualdern
Ascension

Other novels:

Dimwater's Dragon

Jonathan Haymaker

CHAPTER ONE

Al left his warriors in the antechamber and hustled alongside the dark-haired guard. The gray walls of stone were streaked with stark lines above the burning torches held fast to the stones by brackets of brass that had long ago lost their luster. The hallway leading away from the antechamber was long, roughly fifty feet before another door of brown, aged wood broke the monotony of the dark stone. To Al's right, the door was propped open with a sandbag and inside he saw several pairs dueling with wooden swords. Al stopped briefly to survey the room. There were seven rings drawn in sand with white chalk. Two warriors dueled inside each ring while others waited along the outer rim. The swords *click-clacked* with each strike and parry as the officers barked out instructions or criticism. Each warrior was dressed in light linens, with a heavy armor of leather covering their vital areas and extending down below their groins. They also wore crude helmets with metal face guards. The officers observing them wore their full battle dress. Highly polished plate mail with a sword of steel at their hips and a plumed helmet tucked under an arm.

"This way, my lord," the guard insisted.

Al nodded and hurried along.

"Commander Nials has been drilling the men every day," the guard said. "King Mathias has already ordered some of our troops out to the east to deal with the Tarthuns, but then I suppose you know about that."

Al nodded, but he didn't offer any details. If the last several months had taught him anything, it was the value of discretion. So many had proven false that he had no inclination to talk at length with anyone unless he had to. Commander Nials had to know the details of his message, but this guard did not.

The two of them turned left at the first intersecting hallway. The floor abruptly descended five stairs and then extended out straight again. Here again, there were no windows. Only sconces lit the way. There were, however, many more doors lining the hallway. Every ten yards there was a set of doors. Some were closed, others were open. Al glanced inside to see barracks. Bunk beds of wood with hide blankets covering the mattresses. None of the open rooms were messy, all were clean and properly kept. The beds were well made and the floors oft swept.

Another intersection and the two of them turned to the hallway on the right hand side. Al climbed up a short stairway and then the guard opened a large set of double doors. The sunlight broke through with alarming brightness and heat. Al shielded his face and his irises painfully contracted.

"Again!" a booming voice shouted.

Al peeked around his arm to see a large man swinging a heavy flanged mace from a leather thong looped around his wrist. The man was obviously an officer, but he was not dressed as the others had been. He wore wool trousers with a leather girdle over them. A thick pad of wool was lazily draped over a wooden chair behind him, along with the chainmail shirt and heavy metal pauldrons. The man moved through the ranks and formation of spearmen practicing a phalanx drill. Al watched the bald officer and took note of the several purple scars across the man's back.

"This is Captain Hitage, he trains all of our spearmen," the guard told Al as he gestured with his hand to hurry along.

The bald officer turned and regarded Al with a questioning stare. He flipped his mace up into his palm and then promptly turned to address his men. "Run it again," he bellowed.

The men marched in perfect cadence with each other. A large phalanx twenty columns wide and at least thirty rows deep.

"He is training for Tarthuns?" Al asked. The dwarf king knew that a slow moving phalanx was not the best device to employ against a horde of galloping, agile horse-archers. Then again, it might be a decent defense against the orcs in the south. Perhaps Al would suggest moving Captain Hitage to Ten Forts.

The guard didn't bother to answer Al's question. Instead he led Al around the courtyard and in through an open set of double doors on the opposite side. They walked through a short hallway and then ascended a winding stairway to the third floor of the fort. The two of them stopped in front of a large oaken door.

Another guard stood there, blocking the way with a halberd. Like the soldiers Al had already seen, this guard was dressed in red linen with armor over the top. His helmet was fastened under the chin with a leather strap.

"King Sit'marihu to see Commander Nials," Al's escort stated dryly.

The guard at the door nodded and pushed the door into the chamber.

Al moved in after him.

"Commander Nials, sir, King Sit'marihu seeks an audience with you, sir," the door guard shouted.

Al looked across a short, rectangular room to see a large man standing at the window. He stood staring out, with his hands clasped behind his back. He turned to reveal a tanned face and strong, brown eyes. Instead of armor, he wore a simple black tunic and brown linen trousers tucked into black leather boots. A longsword hung from his belt and swung widely as Commander Nials turned to regard Al.

"So, the dwarves have emerged from their dark hole to join us in the sunlight I see."

Al bristled and stopped in the middle of the room. He folded his arms and locked eyes with the commander. "*I* have been above ground more than most men," he said evenly.

Commander Nials grinned slightly. "I meant no offense," he assured Al. "I received word from King Mathias that you have lent your warriors to the Middle Kingdom."

Al nodded. "I have done my fair share of splitting skulls as well," he put in.

Commander Nials eyed the dwarf and then nodded. "I don't doubt it." The large man looked up to the guards and dismissed them. Then he turned and gestured toward a small table off to the side of the room. The two of them moved to sit.

"Wine?" Commander Nials offered.

Al shook his head. "I'll get straight to the issue at hand," he began. "Orcs have besieged Ten Forts."

"Ah," Commander Nials said. "Well, with young Finorel as commander, that spells disaster if the orcs are organized."

Al held up a hand. "Mercer commands the troops at Ten Forts."

Nials arched a brow and his lips drew taught over his face. He narrowed his eyes on Al and silently waited.

The dwarf king sighed. "I wasn't there for the change in

command, but from what I understand, there were quite a few traitors to the crown at Ten Forts. Finorel was among them."

"Was?" Nials probed.

"Apparently he died in his dungeon cell after Mercer imprisoned him." Al leaned forward. "I myself delivered five hundred warriors to Ten Forts, but it isn't enough."

Nials scoffed. "What do you mean? Have the dwarves gone soft, or have the orc tribes united?"

Al glowered at Nials. "The tribes have united." Nials' smirk vanished and he straightened in his chair. "The orcs receive reinforcements by the hundreds, sometimes thousands, while the troops at Ten Forts struggle to fend them off."

"I am afraid I have to cut you off," Nials said abruptly. "I can see you are here to ask for reinforcements, but I have none to give."

"None?" Al repeated. He jabbed a finger at the window. "I saw the troops down there."

Nials shook his head. "New recruits, all of them," he explained. "There isn't a soldier in the bunch that has more than a few weeks experience with a weapon. The only veterans I have are my officers, and even those are thinning."

"What happened?" Al asked.

Nials sighed. "King Mathias called us into action. Kuldiga Academy was ruined in battle, Lokton Manor was destroyed by a marauding horde, and then Valtuu Temple was destroyed by a large dragon. Events like that tend to make a king rather nervous. I am only here because I have the fresh recruits to train. All of my veterans have been called out. Some have gone east to the Tarthuns. Some have gone to set up camp near Valtuu Temple and defend the nearby villages there. Others have been stationed around various regions in the Middle Kingdom. You may not know, but some of the nobles have also turned traitor to the crown lately. So, King Mathias has called for martial law. My men have been sent to bolster, or outright take over, the garrison of every town and village with a large enough population to pose a threat north of here."

"So you have none to send south?" Al questioned again. His voice broke in the middle of the question and his head sank down to land in his upturned palm. "The dragon is dead, that much I know for sure. However, there is no way for me to know how much longer Ten Forts will hold against the orcs."

Nials nodded. "You will have to send the request directly to King Mathias. I have no authority to send the freshies even if I wanted to." Nials paused and pointed to Al, leaning in close. "And, just to be clear, I *don't* want to send them out. They aren't ready for battle yet. Certainly not against orcs."

Al dropped his eyes to the floor and drew his brow in tight as he stroked his beard. There wasn't time to go north to Drakei Glazei. Even with the cavedogs it would be days, weeks, before they could get there and back to Fort Drake, not to mention they would only then be able to march south, and who knew how long it would take to prepare the army for such a journey. The dwarf king rose to his feet.

The two locked gazes again as Al brought his eyes up to meet Commander Nials' brown orbs.

"I am not one for speeches," Al said. "Words bore me. I am a dwarf, and we are people of action. The orcs are battering down the gates as we speak. We sit here in your fine fort and you have wine at your disposal. Meanwhile, I have friends and kin under the barrage of arrows, and they go for want of food and bandages. We need men, and we need fresh supplies. We need it now. The orcs aren't going to wait for the new recruits to finish their training. There isn't the time to teach them the perfect way to march or the proper way to polish their dress boots. If they can hold a spear, or help shore up defenses by digging ditches, they are fit for the fight. Commander Nials, this is one of those battles that history will remember. Thirty years from now they will either praise your name for having the common sense to make the right decision, or, if you stay here to train your men and leave mine to die, then orcs will sit around this very room and drink to your name and call you fool." Al folded his arms and set his jaw as he watched the man bristle in his chair. "Which is it to be?"

Nials cleared his throat and glanced back to the window. "Are we that bad off?" he asked.

Al huffed. "I wouldn't be here if we weren't."

Nials nodded. "I suppose every now and then an officer must change the orders as the battle takes shape before him." He rose to his feet and stuck out his hand. "We'll march south. I'll send a pair of messengers north to King Mathias. The rest of the men will be ready by tomorrow. Given the recent transfers we have set up quite the efficient system for packing out. We'll take every last recruit we have, and marshal our wagons as well to see if we can't get some extra food and bandages down to Ten Forts."

Al let out a sigh of relief and took Nials' hand. "Thank you," he said. "You are a good man."

Nials scoffed. "I am a demoted man," he said. "Or, at least I will be once the king hears of my insubordination. So this army in the south better be as big as you claim it is."

"Oh, there will be more than enough fighting to take your mind off the king, I promise."

*****

Salarion waited for the silvery quarter moon to fall back behind the thick curtain of clouds again. She wanted to avoid confrontation, if possible, as she stalked along the stone corridors of Ten Forts. The raucous, raunchy orcs were busy filling themselves with an unconscionable amount of wine and ale in the courtyard outside. Through a window she watched as one of the drunken fools climbed up onto a religious shrine, squatted over the top and attempted to defecate over the edge. The buffoon slipped and fell to the ground, landing head-first on the stone pad below and putting a quick end to his debauchery.

The nearby orcs laughed and threw dirt and food at the corpse.

"Orcs," Salarion said. Occasionally she found one of the creatures to be tolerable, but she had never found a group of orcs that she liked.

She moved through the shadows in the corridor. It followed the line of the outer wall facing the south. Piles of rubble and the smell of fresh dirt mingled with stains of blood along the floor and walls gave her an idea of just how bad the fighting had been. As if she hadn't already figured that out by seeing the large pits on the north filled with heaping piles of dead men and orcs when she had arrived a couple days before.

Watching those piles burn almost made her question her mission.

The orcs had spilled oil over the piles and set torches to them as if it were nothing more than lighting a camp fire. There was no ceremony for the dead, just the cold dismissal brought on by war.

It was smart, she knew, to deal with that amount of bodies in such a way. It would keep the living army safe from disease and filth. It still felt wrong. Even for a dark elf, there were codes of ethics.

She snaked through the corridor until she reached the central keep. She paused near a window to inspect the courtyard. She expected more of the same foolishness she had seen before, but was surprised to see a somber gathering of orcs instead. They were dressed in their armor, standing neatly in perfectly formed columns and rows. Beyond them was a raised platform of wood, with a ladder leading to the top. On the platform was a bed of kindling and branches, with a white shroud over the form of a body. An orc climbed to the top of the ladder and turned to address the others.

"This man was the commander of this fort," the orc began. "He sacrificed himself so that his men could survive." The orc held his arm out and a large torch was tossed up to him. "He fought with the honor and courage of an orc, and so he will be honored in death." He held the torch up into the air. "He was lame, and had only one good leg, still he fought against us. He managed to slay seven before losing his own life." The orc turned and set the torch to the bed of kindling. Sparks popped and crackled as the flame took hold. "Honor the honorable," he shouted.

The gathered orcs in chorus shouted, "Honor the honorable."

"Maernok," Salarion whispered under her breath. He was one of the few that she found tolerable. She could only hope he would be reasonable tonight. Rather than watch the rest of the ceremony, she took advantage of the distraction. She crept out into the night, skirting the outside of the courtyard and slipping into a window in the main keep. The dark elf quickly identified the commander's chambers and moved toward it, assuming that Maernok would have claimed them for himself.

She was wrong.

Inside lay another orc upon the bed. Books were strewn about the floor. Chests and drawers had been flung open and left in disarray. She didn't bother entering the room. This orc had nothing to offer her. She moved back out into the main hall and melded into the shadows at the back of the chamber.

Fifteen or twenty minutes passed. Several smaller groups of orcs came in and disappeared down the hallway at the other end of the hall. Another ten minutes came and went before Maernok entered the hall.

The orc rubbed a weary hand over his face and sighed. He moved over to a long table situated against the far wall. He retrieved his sword from upon it and then made a direct line for the room where Salarion had just seen the other orc sleeping.

No sooner had Maernok vanished into the bed chamber than Salarion stole her way across the main hall to listen at the doorway.

"What do you want?" one of them said.

Salarion slowly snuck a peek around the doorway. Maernok was standing with his back to her right next to the bed. The other orc was moving to sit up and grumbling to himself.

"I know you want to take command," Maernok said.

The other orc stopped. He looked up to Maernok and then glanced over to the foot of his bed where a sword was propped between the wall and the bed. Maernok held up a hand.

"I haven't come to fight you for it," he said.

"Then out with it," the other orc barked.

"It's yours," Maernok said. "I am leaving tonight. I have unfinished business."

"Gilifan?" the other orc asked.

Maernok laughed. "I guess we can each see the other's true motivations, can't we? Yes, I go to settle an old score."

"What of your tribe?" the other orc asked. "No chief can abandon his tribe."

"If I return, then I resume command of my tribe," Maernok said. "If I fail to return, then you assume control of them, along with the others."

"You would trade the glory of conquest for the life of a human wizard?"

Maernok turned, obviously finished with the conversation. "It was never my dream to unite the clans and lead a campaign into the Middle Kingdom."

"Khullan smile upon you," the other orc offered.

Maernok set a rolled parchment on a round table and slid his ring off a thick finger and placed it next to the paper. "This will show the others that I leave command to you. Fight well."

Salarion slipped back into the shadows a moment before Maernok marched by her. She carefully circled around the chamber and out through a window on the opposite side of the hall. Once in the courtyard she saw only a handful of sentries, all sitting near a smaller fire with a pot of potent coffee hanging over it. Knowing they would be unable to see her as their eyes would be blinded by the fire and unable to penetrate the surrounding darkness, she walked openly and approached Maernok. The gate to the south was open, and she exited only a few yards behind Maernok.

She followed him as he took the road to the south. Salarion stepped silently, stalking the large orc until they reached the burnt trunks that had been a lush forest before the siege of Ten Forts.

"Maernok," she called out.

The orc wheeled around with a dagger in hand. His eyes searched for her, but could not find her. Salarion had moved to meld with the shadows between the burned trees and ash-covered ground. It was the perfect camouflage to hide her in the darkness.

"Who's there?" Maernok growled. "If you are sent to kill me, you will find it is not an easy task."

Salarion circled around him and stood five yards behind him. "If I wanted to kill you, you would already be dead."

Maernok spun around again and his eyes narrowed on her. "Dark elf," he spat. "For what have you come?"

Salarion smiled wryly. "I hunt the same man you do," she answered. "You and I have a common enemy."

"Then why don't you go and slay him?" Maernok pressed.

Salarion's smile faded. "As much as it pains me to say it, I don't think I can succeed on my own."

Maernok huffed and slid his dagger away. "Then leave the fight to me and be off," he snarled.

"You need my help," she pressed.

The orc shook his head. "I don't want your help."

"Do not succumb to the same mule-headed traditions that plague the rest of your men-folk. Even you have to know that you cannot defeat a necromancer with a sword."

"Orc courage will defeat the meddler's crafts."

"Your pigheadedness is going to get you killed."

Maernok stepped up to her and exhaled his hot, musky breath

onto her face. "I don't want your help."

"Gilifan is protected inside an old fortress buried within a mountain. He has mercenary guards and a host of soldiers at hand. Furthermore, he has a dragon egg and is working feverishly to hatch it. You will not come within a hundred yards of him, and your family will never be avenged." Maernok cocked his head at her and emitted a deep, throaty growl. Salarion figured the orc was deciding between joining with her, and killing her. She pulled the onyx box out to show Maernok. Its humming, violet light danced in waves around the cube.

"Magic," Maernok hissed.

"I have here a powerful shield that can get you close enough to kill Gilifan."

"Then why don't you use it?" Maernok asked.

Salarion nodded. "I intend to do just that, but I need your help. In an instant she flicked her left hand up to Maernok's throat. She was so fast that the oaf couldn't even flinch before she rested the edge of her curved dagger against the taught skin covering his neck. "If I wanted to kill you, I could very easily have done so." She jumped away from Maernok in a flash and disappeared into the burned trees again to make her point. The orc's shoulders jerked back reflexively and his hand went for his blade.

"What trickery is this?" Maernok snarled. "None have ever lived after threatening me in such a manner."

"None except Gilifan," Salarion pointed out. Maernok turned in the direction of her voice but she had already circled around him again. "He managed to slay your entire family and you have yet to do anything about it."

"I was bound by the oath," Maernok said. "Until his debt had been repaid there was nothing I could do."

"I wonder how Gilifan will use you," Salarion said as she moved to yet another place. Maernok was now turning frequently, scanning the darkness to find her.

Salarion emerged from the trees and stood directly before him again. She placed the box on the ground as well as her dagger. "I offer you help. The magic I have can help us infiltrate the fortress. More importantly, it will even the field of battle."

"There is more glory to be won if the battle is tipped in an opponent's favor," Maernok said.

"Yes, I have heard the orcish proverb before. It is oft recited before some orcish commander leads his warriors to an ill-fated and unnecessary death."

Maernok folded his arms. "I am done talking. Either get out of my way or pick up your weapon."

"Very well," Salarion said. "If you won't accept my magic, then at least allow me to tell you where he is."

"He is in Demaverung," Maernok asserted.

Salarion laughed aloud. "I take it you missed the fiery eruption then? What about the clouds of ash, did you not notice them?"

"He survived it," Maernok explained simply.

"He caused it," Salarion replied evenly. "He does not hide there anymore. Now, are you interested in what I have to say?"

Maernok exhaled and began walking. "Fine. Tell me where he is, and accompany me if you must, but keep your magic to yourself. I will have no part of it."

Salarion smiled devilishly and picked up her items. "Come, we have a long road ahead of us. Gilifan lies in a mountain fortress near Pinkt'Hu."

CHAPTER TWO

"Who did you say informed the king about this place again?" Captain Benbo asked.

Faengoril looked up from what he was doing and smiled. "A trapper. His name was Fariche, or Ferris, or something like that. King Sit'marihu said that they crossed paths as he was heading east with Gorin, Peren, and Lady Arkyn and the trapper was headed west."

"And he said water had flooded the village that had been out here, right?"

Faengoril nodded. "Our job is to make sure Tarthuns don't come through it. King Sit'marihu and King Mathias already discussed the plan and we are just following orders."

"Did the trapper mention Tarthuns before?"

Faengoril nodded impatiently. "Yes, after the floods came there was a battle and they wiped out the trading post that was nearby. It was just a scouting party, but it was enough to destroy everyone but the trapper. That's why we are here, to make sure no one else comes through it."

Captain Benbo moved next to the large rock that Faengoril was using as a table and looked down. A few other officers gathered in close as well.

Faengoril observed the schematics drawn on the parchment before him. The others watched him as he traced his fingers over the drawing. As ordered, his dwarves had scouted every inch of this new pass, and mapped it out with the accuracy only a dwarf could manage in such an underground cavern. He studied the map several times before he finally looked up from the large, flat stone in front of him.

"What of the scouts?" Faengoril asked.

"They report an army of Tarthuns moving toward us. The Tarthuns number several thousand. They should reach the cave within three days."

Faengoril nodded. "Will we be ready by then?"

One of the officers stepped forward and pointed to the

several circles drawn into the map. "I have positioned some of our strongest dwarves at these locations. They will dig in shifts so that the process is continuous. We will be ready in two days, well ahead of the Tarthuns' arrival. We will be able to bring the entire cavern down and block them off."

Faengoril shook his head. "No, I want to draw them in."

"Sir, there is no need to expose ourselves to unnecessary risk. If we seal off the pass, we can avoid a costly battle."

Faengoril grinned wide and his fiery eyes sparkled under the torch's flame. "And leave the Tarthuns with the option of traveling to the north where Grand Master Penthal is already engaged in battle? No. We draw them in, all the way into the cave. We station volunteers at each of the trigger points we have identified, and then we bring the cavern down on top of them. We number five hundred strong. If we work in shifts to dig at the trigger points, then we should only need fifty to volunteer for the final shift."

"That is madness," Captain Benbo chimed in. "The cave is three and a quarter miles long, so in theory it could hold the entire Tarthun army, but there are choke points along the way, not to mention the half-mile long lake at the opposite end where they will be entering from. They would almost surely have some of their soldiers exiting the cave before the entire army made it inside."

"So we divide our forces," Faengoril said. "We have two hundred dwarves prepare defenses out here. Then, when the Tarthuns exit they will be forced back into the cave. If a few stragglers have not yet entered the cave, it won't matter. The bulk of the enemy force will be trapped inside."

"That would work," another officer spoke up. "We are already building escape tunnels for each dwarf that has to activate the cave in. We would just have to hope that none of them are discovered before they can trigger their area."

"We can wall them in the day before," Faengoril said. "We could also create a few traps inside to slow them down. Let's not make anything so overt that they might understand the cave has been manipulated, but let's dig a few pits and slicks that the stream inside the cave can hide and that way their attention will be on the ground, and not the walls. Even if they did have the time to gaze at the cavern, I doubt they would perceive our handiwork anyway." Faengoril pointed to a trio of spots on the map and drew larger circles with a red pencil. "We could dig a few larger holes here, at these points. The water from the stream will make them into death traps."

The officers all saluted and broke out from the group. Faengoril remained with the map, rehashing the strategy in his mind several more times. He knew it was risky, but if they prepared well and managed to camouflage their work, then they would be able to execute the plan without suffering any casualties. After all, the Tarthuns were nomadic horse-men that relied on their skill as archers. They would be completely out of their element inside a cave.

Over the next two days Faengoril oversaw the preparations personally, picking up a pickaxe himself on several occasions. He kept his engineers close, making sure that each trigger point was being adequately prepared, and ensuring that each escape tunnel would be sufficient to enable the brave volunteer to escape without being crushed in the cave-in. The commander alternated between each of the trigger points and then moved on to inspect each trap. He was more than pleased by the depth and span of each hole and jagged trench cut in the stone. Water from the overflowing stream pooled into each crevice, hiding the true depth and creating the perfect obstacle for blundering horsemen who would almost certainly be relying on torches for light.

"I have to admit, this might work," Captain Benbo said as they surveyed the last of the pits.

Faengoril nodded as he watched the dozen dwarves who had dammed off a portion of the stream in order to finish digging their pit without getting caught in the water themselves. It was pitiless work, but the commander was certain it would be worth it in the end. "Of course it will work," Faengoril said. "Come, I want to inspect the entrance now."

The commander smiled wide as they made the long trek through the winding, gently sloping cave. Faengoril led the other officers around the northern bank of the half-mile long lake in the cavern. A great hole in the east let in daylight from above. It was a beautiful sight, albeit extremely dangerous. Even after days in the cave and working around it, there was no way for any of the engineers to estimate the lake's depth. The banks dropped off sharply into what appeared to be a liquid abyss. "It must have taken some time," Faengoril said as he pointed to the lake. The officers with him surveyed the dark water as Faengoril swept his hand out toward the west. "The water comes in from the east. Our scouts say that there is a stream out there, most likely from runoff. It bored its way through the soft limestone on that side of the mountain and then began flowing into this chasm. No way of knowing how many years it took to fill this pool. I would guess at least centuries, though." Faengoril stopped and held both arms out wide to the side. "Don't even ask me how long the overflow has been flowing downhill toward the west. That process must have also taken many, many years. In the end, the water destroyed the mountain and created this tunnel. It meant the end for the trading post nearby, and provided an alternate route for the Tarthuns in the east."

"Why would horsemen come through here?" one of the officer asked. "I mean, they can't bring their horses down that entrance slope, the animals would never make it."

"They have a large army heading north. There have already been skirmishes with Grand Master Penthal and the knights of the Lievonian Order. The Tarthuns would use this underground passage to sneak around and catch the Lievonian Order on both sides. Once they have a foothold in the Middle Kingdom, they would be able to launch an assault on Drakei Glazei directly. With our forces split across the kingdom, we can't afford to let the Tarthuns accomplish that."

Faengoril motioned for the officers to follow him the rest of the way around the lake. They came to the entrance and a few of them starting laughing and pointing at the new waterfall.

The commander smiled and bowed proudly. "After the other fortifications had been ordered, I led a group of twenty dwarves to this slope under the entrance. We tunneled behind the water that entered the cave from above in the east, creating a waterfall in place of the slope. The drop is twelve feet tall, and the slop above it is steep enough that a simple slip could spell death for the unwary coming through. This will slow them down of course, but better than that, it will make it nearly impossible for them to retreat even if they should discover our trigger points farther in the cave."

"You aren't afraid that it will scare them off?" Captain Benbo asked.

"Always the pessimist," Faengoril grumbled. He shook his head and folded his thick arms across his barrel-like chest. "No. The only other way for them is to go north through the normal pass, but that is blocked by Grand Master Penthal. They would do better to risk losing a few men here than to travel northward."

"The Tarthuns will be here sometime tomorrow," Captain Benbo said. "We should finish making ready."

Faengoril nodded. "I have two scouts up at the entrance. They will alert us when the army draws near. The last estimate put them at the mouth of the cave by tomorrow afternoon. Let's go back."

The others cheered and a couple of dwarves made falling noises and mimed breaking their backsides. Then they retreated back around the large lake and into the more narrow part of the cave.

All of the dwarves ate well on that second night. They posted the watchmen and then they slept.

The scouts woke Faengoril just after dawn. The bleary-eyed commander yawned and slipped his feet over the boulder he had been dozing upon. "Are they here?" he asked.

"The Tarthuns have made camp at the base of the mountain on the eastern slope," Midger said.

"What are they doing with their horses?" Faengoril asked. That very question had been keeping him up most of the night. Knowing that the Tarthuns needed their horses, he wondered if they might have found an alternate path over which to take the animals, thereby bypassing the cave altogether.

Midger shrugged. "Most of them have been corralled in a large area the Tarthuns partitioned off with pine trees they felled last night. It looks as though this group is preparing to finish the journey on foot. They have spears and bows, and have put large packs on many of the warriors."

Faengoril scratched his head. "If we could scatter or kill their horses, the Tarthuns would be even more helpless."

Midger nodded knowingly. "We counted seven thousand Tarthuns in all. However, it looks like several hundred of them are actually going to stay behind with the horses."

Faengoril tugged at his beard. "I would wager they either go north, to augment the forces embattling Grand Master Penthal, or perhaps they will take the horses south and come through Hamath

Valley."

Midger shuddered. "If they come through the south, they will be destroyed by the curse."

Faengoril turned a fierce eye on the scout. "Only if the ghost stories are true, Midger, otherwise they have a clean opening to the southern area."

Midger smiled condescendingly and turned to the other scout. "Well of course they are true, sir," he said. "Everyone knows of the vanishings in Hamath Valley."

"Bah," Faengoril snarled. "I never believed it. It's just a story they tell to keep people away." The scouts looked to each other, but they let the point drop. Faengoril reached down and fastened his belt. He had undone it during the night in an effort to get comfortable. He never could sleep with the buckle digging into the bit of stomach that overlapped the belt. He then stretched and jerked his head to the side, cracking his neck. "How long till they enter the cave?"

"They haven't begun the hike up the slope yet. We did see some that looked like they were preparing to scout the cave, though, just before we made our return. Given the size of the group and the items they are carrying, I would say we should expect the first of them just after noon. Otherwise, I would say that the Tarthuns are going to make camp at least for another night."

Faengoril frowned. "Why make camp at the base of the hill?" he wondered aloud. "I don't like it."

"Sir?"

"If they are making camp, then perhaps they are not fully decided on going through the cave. Maybe they are considering riding around to the south through Hamath Valley." The commander reached up and stroked his beard. He knew that if they rode quickly, it would only take a few days longer to go around to the south. It was time they could easily make up once they were inside the Middle Kingdom compared to walking on foot from here to the north to fight Penthal's forces. Not only that, but they would be deadlier with their horses. "We need to make sure they want to come through the tunnel."

"Sir, they wouldn't survive in Hamath Valley," Midger said.

Faengoril shook the notion away. "I do believe in dragons and magic, but I don't believe in a ghost army that can destroy seven thousand Tarthuns," he said. "I would rather see to that myself."

"What should we do?" Midger asked.

"If I sent the engineers with you, could you cause a rockslide?"

Midger shook his head. "Not one that would reach the Tarthuns. Maybe we could hit part of the corral they made, but it would only break the barriers and scatter the horses at best."

Faengoril snapped his stubbly fingers. "That's it!" He then ran around the boulder and picked up a bit of paper. "Midger, you will take this to Captain Benbo. I want him to create a series of barriers inside the cave. We are going to place dwarves with crossbows at each one. He will send a handful of engineers with you, and you will help them find a position from which they can create a rockslide."

"If we cause a rockslide, the Tarthuns will retreat away from the cave," Midger pointed out.

Faengoril shook his head. "No. You and the other scouts will go down and attack the horses tonight. I saw a patch of Rot-blossom growing a short ways from here. I can have it turned into a potent poison. You'll put it in the animal feed. Afterward, you can use crossbows to kill some of the horses and try to create a stampede. Then the engineers will drop rocks down on top of them. Whatever horses the Tarthuns save will then be killed with the tainted feed."

"What if we are discovered?"

Faengoril shot Midger a stern look and shook his head. "Don't get discovered." Faengoril then went back to scribbling on the paper. "I will lead a group of dwarves out to the mouth of the cave and while everything else is happening, we will rain arrows down on the Tarthun camp. The goal here is to make them think our force is much larger than it is, and get them to follow us as we retreat."

"I understand," Midger said. Had Faengoril looked up, he would have seen the doubt written across the scout's face, but he didn't bother.

"Good. Get to it."

The two scouts disappeared without another word.

It wasn't long before Captain Benbo was approaching, eyes angry and face flushed. Faengoril had expected resistance from him. None of the other officers had come to support his objection, however, which meant that despite Benbo's blustering, the other dwarves would be busy fulfilling Faengoril's orders.

"Exactly what do you think you are doing?" Benbo gruffed.

Faengoril leaned back against the boulder and folded his arms. "Answer me this, Benbo, why are the Tarthuns setting up camp?"

Benbo threw his hands up in the air and angrily waved the question away. "What difference does it make? Maybe they are tired of marching, so they are going to wait for a couple days before coming into the cave. Maybe they are coming in the morning."

Faengoril remained calm and pushed off the boulder to walk closer to Benbo. "Or perhaps they haven't decided whether this pass is sufficient for them. What do we do if they skirt around to the south and then ride upon their horses up from Hamath Valley? We won't be able to engage them then."

"We can't engage them now!" Benbo snarled. "There are seven thousand of them, or do you not understand arithmetic?"

Faengoril took in a breath, letting the slight roll off his back. "If the Tarthuns go south, we lose. If they turn back and then go north through the pass, we will lose."

"I thought you said they were sure to come through here?" Benbo reminded him.

Faengoril nodded. "I was. I made a mistake, but we can solve this riddle easily by making the choice for them. We kill and scatter their horses. They will be too enraged to think clearly. They will see *us* as the threat. If we show enough force, perhaps they will even think we intend to invade the eastern wilds."

"Stonebubbles," Benbo growled. "What dwarf in his right mind would leave Roegudok Hall? He would have to be more than daft and crazy to want to fight for the eastern wilds too. They won't fall for it. I say our best choice is to stick with the original plan."

The commander shook his head. "This isn't your call, Benbo."

The dwarf clenched his jaw and folded his thick arms across his chest. His icy blue eyes bored into Faengoril's own as if to spear through them. Benbo shook his head in disgust. "You won't be happy until we are all dead."

The commander shook his head. "I ask only for volunteers.

All others who do not wish to take part in the new plan can remain with you, outside the cave."

"What, now I am not good enough to include in your plan?" Benbo shouted.

Faengoril smirked and socked Benbo in the shoulder. "You are better than good enough," he said. "That is why I want you outside. If things go sour, then I need to make sure my warriors are in good hands."

Benbo's demeanor changed instantly. His gruff, forceful exterior broke, giving way to a frown of concern and a nervous stutter. "Y-you better not- you better not be planning a suicide mission."

The commander smiled. "This isn't the time to suddenly start caring about me," he said. "Besides, no one really plans on such missions. However, I can see the odds as well as anyone else. Despite your earlier comment, I am fairly good at arithmetic. That is precisely why this must be done. We cannot allow the Tarthuns to change their mind now. If I could move the mountain to bury them, I would. But I can't, so I must make sure they come into the mountain. The best way to do that is to take away their horses."

"So what shall I do?" Benbo asked.

"Just send the men to do as I asked on the orders. Ask for volunteers to man each barricade. Have at least twenty or thirty exit the other side of the cave so that once the horses are loosed and the rockslide hammers them, then there are enough to make the Tarthuns want to chase them into the hole."

"Even if the plan succeeds, the Tarthuns will likely send scouts after us first," Benbo pointed out.

Faengoril nodded. "That is true. However, if we are convincing, then perhaps we can suck them all into the cave."

The dwarf commander spent the next several hours preparing for the fight. Volunteers moved in and out of the cave. Some were digging and building the rock barriers inside, while others were getting into position to fight. A relay chain of scouts was set up on the other side of the mountain, keeping close watch on every move the Tarthuns made.

Fortune was with the dwarves, for no enemy scouts came to the cave that day. They were able to make all of their preparations without being discovered. Better than that, the surprise attack just before the next dawn went off without a hitch.

Before the sun rose, Midger came running toward Faengoril. The dwarf commander was already awake and dressed. He hadn't slept a single wink that night. When he saw the scout, his heart jumped and his stomach twisted. Only when he saw the smile on the dwarf's face did he understand that all had gone well.

"Sir, the corral has been destroyed. We managed to kill a few score of the horses with our crossbows. Several hundred of them actually stampeded up the mountainside and were crushed by the rockslide that followed after we snuck away. The rest are scattered off in every direction. Many ran through the Tarthun camp and it caused a great commotion."

Faengoril smiled wide. "What of the poison?"

Midger nodded. "There were many feeding barrels. It looks as though the horses were set to graze on the grasses, but we made sure to poison each barrel we found."

"Good, good," Faengoril said. "Whatever horses they recover will likely be led by their riders to the barrels in order to comfort them."

"The Tarthuns sent a dozen men to attack, but we slayed them. They sent another fifty, but we all regrouped at the mouth of the cave and fought them off. We had the high ground, so we didn't lose a single dwarf."

"Excellent," Faengoril said. "Did they come into the cave?"

Midger shook his head and his smile disappeared. "No. They did send a force maybe two or three hundred strong up toward us, and we retreated at that point. We paused at the far edge of the lake, but they only came in as far as the waterfall and then they turned around."

"What about the fake orders? Did you plant them?"

Midger nodded. "We left a single pack just outside the mouth of the cave. It had the fake orders and the map showing the route through the pass to the north."

"Good, good. Now they will think our strategy was to circle up behind them. Combine that with the loss of horses they suffered and they will surely come after us. We have maybe a few hours at best before they send a scouting party after us. It is time to get into positions."

CHAPTER THREE

Faengoril moved to take his place just inside. A group of cavedog riders were waiting for him. Each of them wore grim, yet determined faces. It was obvious to him that they had heard how many Tarthuns were coming. Still, if any of the twenty riders feared the day, none of them showed it upon their faces.

The commander went to the front of the group and clambered into his sturdy leather saddle. The horn of polished brass stuck up and he took hold of it while he turned in his seat to offer a final word of encouragement to his men. "We are not called upon to slay each Tarthun with our sword this day, though Ancients know we certainly could if we wanted to!"

The men chuckled and smiled to each other. They all knew it wasn't true, but each of them acted as if it were *exactly* correct.

"We are few in number only because our brothers will cover our retreat. Our job is to wait until the Tarthuns have lodged themselves just deep enough in our cave so as to be stuck here. Then, we harass and pester them to make sure the rest of the savage mongrels follow in after them. On my mark, we will attack. The twenty-one of us will be able to maneuver easily in the cave while the Tarthuns are imprisoned by their own numbers. When I give the order we all fall back, pulling the enemy further into our trap. Once we are at the cave's exit, I will blow my horn and the engineers will bring this place down around the enemy's ears."

The riders smiled wide, but none of them said anything. They all knew the possibility of Tarthun scouts, and shouting would create echoes.

They urged their cavedogs onward. The giant lizards, though bulky and very heavy, padded silently through the cavern. As the riders passed by defensive barriers where the others were hiding in larger groups, armed with crossbows and throwing axes, the groups would all offer nods and salutes.

When the riders finally reached the last bend, just before the large underground lake, they halted. Faengoril dismounted and crept around the rock wall just enough to enable him to use his spyglass and check the entrance.

White light broke the darkness from the opening, creating a faint rainbow over the newly-fashioned waterfall. For a moment he thought the tunnel was clear, but then he saw a pair of tanned legs slipping and sliding down the slope. Faengoril repositioned the spyglass to get a better look. The man was covered with a loincloth, and wore a pack slung over his left shoulder while his right hand gripped a bow. He wore no armor, and his head was shorn. The dwarf commander smiled to himself. The Tarthun's lack of armor would make him an extremely easy target.

He slipped back around the wall just enough to signal with his fingers that one person was coming down into the cave. Then he poked back around the corner to watch. The Tarthun slowly approached the edge and looked for an easy way down.

He slipped.

Schnap! Even the waterfall was not enough to drown out the noise of splitting bone.

Faengoril winced when the Tarthun's right leg broke below the knee and the man hollered out in pain. A moment later two more Tarthuns came rushing down. The three of them communicated with their hands at first, but after a few minutes of inaction the injured man started shouting at the other two.

Faengoril held his left hand out to make sure that none of his warriors moved. He was not about to give away their position yet.

He watched the trio blunder around for a while longer until another pair of Tarthuns came down the entrance. These two wore simple leather armor, and held spears in their hands to help steady themselves along the slippery path. They appeared to converse for a minute or two and then the newcomers disappeared up and out of the cave.

Faengoril feared that perhaps they had decided the path was too treacherous, but he needn't have worried. Soon a large group appeared. They quickly created a ladder out of ropes and scaled down the waterfall. They hoisted the injured scout out from the cave and then the massive march began.

Fifty Tarthuns descended the chute, each successfully navigating the waterfall, and setting up a defensive perimeter on the far side of the lake. A few of the men ventured into the water, only to turn back once they realized it dropped off and would require them to swim the width of the lake.

After about ten minutes there were so many Tarthuns in the cavern that the group had to push forward around the lake toward the waiting dwarves.

Faengoril lost count, but he estimated the number were close to one thousand. He put away the spyglass and moved back toward his riders. He signaled with his hands that it was time to prepare. Each of them pulled up a crossbow and nodded back to him. The commander mounted his cavedog and counted silently to himself. He wanted the approaching group to come close enough that they wouldn't be able to fire their own bows before the dwarves managed to get within range to attack.

The footsteps echoed over the lake and through the cavern. Flickering, dancing orange light played upon the walls. Faengoril's own heart beat furiously as the adrenaline coursed through his veins.

"Ancients preserve us," he whispered. Then he charged around the corner with a crossbow in each hand. The twenty riders followed after him.

He rounded the corner and leveled his weapon. He pulled the trigger. A second later a score of bolts flew from behind him. Twenty-one Tarthuns fell to the stone floor, a couple of them tumbling into the lake. A series of shouts erupted from the large group. Faengoril smiled wide. The group was stuck with the cavern wall on one side and the deep lake on the other. They were only able to stand about fifteen men shoulder to shoulder. It gave the dwarves the advantage.

The cavedog riders managed to reload and fire once more before they collided into the oncoming Tarthuns. Spears and axes glanced off the dwarves' armor as the giant lizards snapped out with their powerful maws and ripped legs out from under nearby Tarthuns.

Faengoril dropped one crossbow, tied to the saddle horn with an iron chain, and pulled a short battle axe. He deflected a spear and turned with a savage swing to the Tarthun on his left as his cavedog lunged up and bit a hunk out of the Tarthun on the right. The man cried out in agony and fell to the ground with only half of his midsection still intact.

Then, before the Tarthuns could encircle the dwarves, the

cavedog riders turned around and fled. They fired their crossbows and took down another two score before disappearing around the bend. The echoing chorus of footsteps grew to a great cacophony. Shouts and yells followed after the dwarves. Faengoril led his riders fast as he could to the next bend. Then they dismounted and hid behind their cavedogs as they leveled their crossbows. The enemy came into view and the dwarves fired. This time only a few Tarthuns were hit as some of the shots went astray. This stretch of the cave was wider than the stone bank next to the lake so the Tarthuns fanned out. That was a mistake.

Several fell into the deep pits dug by the dwarves days before. Those who weren't drowned or killed by hitting their heads on the stone as they fell were trampled by the unstoppable horde. Others tripped in the trenches, snapping ankles and legs like twigs.

Faengoril and the others fired three more volleys. By that time the Tarthuns organized and pulled bows out.

"Now!" Faengoril shouted. They leapt atop their mounts and made haste to escape around the next corner. A flurry of arrows crashed into the stone behind them. A couple arrows hit one of the riders, but they glanced off of his armor.

The dwarf commander had his group halt right on the other side of the curve. He wanted to surprise the Tarthuns as they rounded to follow. Faengoril signaled for everyone to dismount again. They did so, leaving their lizards in the Tarthuns' path as they ran a few yards off and prepared their crossbows.

The first row of Tarthuns came around the corner. They never saw the dwarves hiding in the dark before the cavedogs tore them down. Startled, the second row tried to run backward, but the pressing throng pushed them into the cavedogs' waiting jaws. Faengoril whistled, calling the cavedogs back. Then the dwarves fired their crossbows to cover their mounts as the animals rushed back to them.

Enraged, the Tarthuns shouted and fired their bows. This time, one of the cavedogs went down with several arrows riddling its back. The rider was able to double-up with another dwarf.

"You steer and I will shoot!" he shouted. The group raced down the cave, firing their crossbows and trying to duck clumsy arrows as they hurried toward the next bend, which also was narrower and would bottleneck the invading enemy.

Luckily, even with the torches the Tarthuns were unable to clearly identify their targets when they aimed their bows. The dwarves, on the other hand were just as comfortable in the darkness as they would be on the open fields. Almost every crossbow shot hit its mark.

They continued on like this for several hundred yards, stopping at turns or behind rock outcroppings to antagonize the horde. The Tarthuns were playing right into their hands. They had already passed two of the trigger points, and there was no sign that the Tarthuns were slowing.

As the riders ran out of their crossbow bolts, they rounded the first defensive blockade. The dwarves there not only prepared their own shots, they tossed new quivers to the riders.

When the Tarthuns came into view they were met with a wall of biting steel teeth flying through the air. Shouts and shrieks filled the cave. The Tarthuns grouped into formations and fired back. The dwarves ducked behind the blockade, waiting for the arrows to stop so they could fire another volley. The arrows *plinked* and *tinked* off the blockade, bouncing over the dwarves or back up the cave. The arrows came incessantly. Faengoril looked to the others and realized that the Tarthuns were rotating their shots in order to keep up a steady volley to suppress the dwarves.

Unfortunately, he didn't realize this until it was too late.

The arrows stopped right as Faengoril started to shout his order, but he never got the chance. No sooner had the arrows stopped than a wave of Tarthun warriors leapt over the barricade, hacking down with their spears and axes. Faengoril caught a spear in the chest. The point didn't pierce his armor, but the force of the blow knocked him to the ground. Faengoril's lizard snapped its jaws around the attacker's leg at the knee. The bone crunched amidst a spray of blood and then the real fighting began.

"Footmen out!" Faengoril shouted. "Drop the ceiling!"

This was the order to spring a trap that had been set at this first blockade. A lever clicked off to the side and a series of pikes and sharpened branches dropped down from the ceiling, angled at the oncoming enemy. Each of the points had been crafted to stop just a few inches above a dwarf's height, thus placing it squarely in a Tarthun's chest without hindering any of the dwarves as they retreated from the first blockade.

The anguished screams blotted out all of Faengoril's following orders. The riders stayed with him, firing their crossbows from a few yards beyond the pikes and shouting at the dwarves on foot to get out of the cave as fast as they could.

Many dwarves fell, but most were able to escape. The riders picked up the last few stragglers and made a dash for the next blockade.

The next station would afford them better odds, Faengoril knew. The dwarves there had fashioned fake walls and rigged them to create miniature cave-ins. This time he knew to trigger the trap shortly after the arrows began flying.

As they cleared the next set of traps, the other dwarves were already standing atop the next blockade and aiming over Faengoril and the other riders. The crossbows began firing before Faengoril and the others reached the blockade. The dwarf commander cast a glance over his shoulder and saw the Tarthuns close on their heels. Many of them slipped and tripped in the trenches and pits still, but the horde as a whole was moving much faster now, infuriated by the dwarves' assault.

Arrows flew back. Two riders went down as arrows found their mark between the plates of armor and also stabbed through their lizards. Still, they couldn't stop until after they rounded the blockade. Faengoril ordered the riders to fire their crossbows again. Now it seemed as if the Tarthuns were unstoppable. They went down by the dozens, but each corpse only barely hit the ground before being swallowed in a wave of angry Tarthuns.

A pair of dwarves fell from the blockade, looking like pincushions as they hit the stone with a plethora of arrows protruding from their chests. Faengoril cursed the Tarthuns and ordered the next retreat.

A stout dwarf at the far end of the blockade pulled a heavy lever with the help of two more dwarves. A flash of sparks blasted out into the cavern as rocks exploded out from the walls and crushed a huge number of the enemy.

Even that was not enough to stop them.

Faengoril grabbed a pair of warriors and shoved them forward as he ordered the retreat again.

The riders stood their ground, firing crossbows until their quivers ran dry. Then they turned and brought up the rear. Arrows rained down all around them. Faengoril was hit a few times, but they were glancing shots that ricocheted off his armor. The next bend in the tunnel was closer, and soon the dwarves were out of range.

The group raced toward the third and final blockade which was near the mouth of the cave. Faengoril shouted to the dwarves to run and abandon their blockade. None of the dwarves moved. Instead they clambered atop the blockade and prepared to fire.

"Run, you stubborn fools!"

The thundering Tarthuns rounded the corner. Their torches illuminated the cavern. The dwarves atop the blockade waited for a few moments longer and then fired their deadly bolts. Arrows pelted the retreating dwarves from behind, spurring them faster through the cave.

Only when Faengoril passed the edge of the blockade did the other dwarves turn to retreat. They all coursed out over the shallow water. There were no trenches or pits dug here. They had actually worked to level this area somewhat in order to facilitate their own escape.

"We won't make it out," one of the riders called out.

Faengoril turned to see the Tarthuns were only about forty yards behind them. At that moment an arrow sailed just by his face and sunk deeply into the base of his cavedog's neck. The animal went down and Faengoril tumbled across the wet stone, barely able to stop himself. A second later a pair of hands reached down and plucked him up by the armpits. Two riders flanked him. Each one held one of Faengoril's arms, half dragging him out of the cave as he furiously pumped his legs as best he could until finally the two riders maneuvered close enough to sit him behind of them.

As they hurried out from the cave, Faengoril noticed that the Tarthuns were slowing down. The cave was narrowing again, forming a natural bottleneck and the dwarves were much better equipped to navigate the treacherous path in the darkness.

A few minutes later Faengoril hopped off the back of the cavedog as they emerged from the cave. A group of dwarves ringed the exit, spears and crossbows at the ready just in case any enemy Tarthuns escaped before the cave-in.

Faengoril reached down to his hip for the horn. His stout fingers only grasped an empty chain where the horn had previously been attached.

"Blow the horn!" someone shouted.

Faengoril sprang into action. He yanked the nearest rider from his mount and charged into the tunnel. "Spear!" he called out.

A nearby soldier tossed his spear to Faengoril.

Faengoril urged his cavedog as fast as its four legs would carry it. The shallow water splashed up and the beast's mighty tail swished side to side.

"Come on, run!" Faengoril growled. He rounded the nearest corner, scouring the stone floor for the gold encrusted horn. The thundering footsteps were growing ever closer. The orange and red light of the many torches grew brighter upon the walls. Still, Faengoril could not see his horn. If it had broken from his belt when he had fallen, there would be no way he could reach it in time. If it had fallen even farther back during battle, then the cave-in would never be summoned. The plan would fail.

His army of several hundred could not possibly hold off seven thousand at the cave's entrance.

He rounded a bend and saw the first couple Tarthuns sprinting around a corner roughly one hundred yards away. His heart sank. Two of the Tarthuns stopped and knelt as they drew back their bowstrings. Their torchlight pierced the darkness enough for them to spot him. They took aim.

Just then a glint caught his eye. There, off near the wall sat the gold encrusted horn. He pushed his cavedog toward it.

Arrows sailed toward him. He hunkered down and tried to cover his lizard, hoping his armor could protect both of them. One arrow sailed by harmlessly, and the other bounced off his back. Faengoril smiled, but his mirth was short-lived as row after row of Tarthun rounded the corner. A dozen archers now knelt, spanning the breadth of the cave. A dozen more stood behind them with their bows. The chances of reaching the horn were slim at best. Faengoril took a mental note of where the horn sat, and then watched the archers as he charged on.

Bowstrings snapped into place and arrows took flight. Faengoril let out a hopeful shout as his cavedog galloped forward. A second volley of arrows followed the first. Black streaks filled the air in the cave. Then, at the last second the dwarf commander leapt from his mount, tucking and rolling across the stone toward the wall.

The squealing shriek emitted from the cavedog he had just betrayed pained him, but he knew there was no other way. He didn't bother to look back at the arrow-riddled animal. There was no need. He sprinted for the horn and blew long and hard. Cracking and exploding rock shattered out around him. A great rumble shook the ground. A volley of arrows struck all around him. A few bounced off his armor, but there were a few points that found his flesh.

He groaned and leaned back against the wall. He put the horn to his lips and blew one more long, loud blast. He knew the trigger had already been sprung, but he wanted the dwarves outside to hear him, and know that all had worked out in the end.

Rocks crumbled all around, and Faengoril closed his eyes and waited for the mountain to take him. It was a fitting death for a dwarf.

*****

Lepkin leaned heavily on the spear shaft. His heart pounded in his chest and his shoulders ached with fatigue. His forearms burned and cool, stinging sweat dripped into his eyes. He clumsily wiped the liquid away and surveyed the forest around him. Bodies littered the ground. The smell of blood filled the air. Some of the fallen were eerily propped against a tree, or tangled in a bush. Human bodies mingled with those of orcs and goarg. It had not been easy, but they had triumphed over the latest group of skirmishers sent to pursue them.

He looked down, letting his eyes follow the spear he leaned upon until it abruptly disappeared into an orc's chest. Fright and anger were still painted upon the orc's twisted features. Instead of anger, he felt pity and sorrow for the corpse beneath his feet. For a moment he wondered whether the orc had a wife. Perhaps she was safe back at home, with a young orc growing within her belly. Even without a wife, the orc most certainly had a father and a mother.

Lepkin sighed and yanked his spear free of the orc. He turned away from the dead orc and pushed the empathy out of his mind. It was dangerous to allow such feelings to control one's mind, Lepkin knew. The orcs sought conquest. Lepkin wanted only to protect and defend his homeland. There was no allowance for forgiveness. The enemy had to be driven back. Despite all of the lessons he had given to Erik to the contrary, Lepkin would need to put away his mercy. Now it was time to be a dragon at heart, and not just in form.

"Master Lepkin," a voice called out from nearby. Lepkin looked up to see Virgil Gothbern, one of the dragon slayers. "Shall we put the orc heads on spikes to deter them from following us?"

Others nearby twisted their faces in disgust. Lepkin paused for a moment and considered it. It was a brutal tactic, but it had its place on the battle field. Still, Lepkin knew it was not a tactic that would stop the orcs.

"In order for a monster to frighten a man, there must be a heart within the man," Lepkin answered. He shook his head. "Such ploys have little, if any, effect on the orcs."

"We should do something," Virgil pressed.

Lepkin nodded. "I agree." He gestured to the men around and then pointed up at the nearest tree. "Let's clear a swath of forest. Drop every tree from this one to five hundred yards north. Then we move east and west to create an open area."

"We don't have the time," one of the soldiers commented.

"The orcs are done for today. If there is another raiding party we will be more ready for them than if we just continue to flee northward without preparing the field a bit in our favor."

"How far out to the east and west?" Virgil asked.

Lepkin folded his arms. "One thousand yards in each direction from where I stand. We will fell and limb each tree. Then, we will pile the logs along the southern edge, forming a loose wall of logs between us and the orcs. The branches we will pile at the outer base of this wall."

"That would only slow them a little," Virgil pointed out. "Goargs could easily skirt around the sides of such a construct."

Lepkin nodded knowingly and turned to glance over his shoulder. "That is why when the piles of branches are set in place we are going to light them. We are going to burn the forest to the ground. The orcs may be fierce, but they can't walk through fire."

Murmurs rose up among the soldiers, but Lepkin clapped his hands and pointed to the men. "Use axes if we have them, or swords if you must, but get the job done. The clear band will give us enough time to move northward before the fire spreads around the gap we will create."

Lepkin wasted no time pulling a battle axe from a fallen orc and moving to the large aspen tree. The first swing broke the bark and wedged the blade inside the moist wood. He wiggled the axe back and forth to free it and then took another swing. This time bits of wood exploded out. The others realized he was more than serious and began their work as well. The chorus of *chip-chop whop-whack* played through the forest as the army cut through the trees. Each one that fell was cleaned of its limbs in minutes and then whisked away to form part of the two thousand yard wall.

The men toiled until the light had vanished from the sky. They had cleared most of the area and were all exhausted. They set watchmen and ate their supper, which consisted mostly of berries and mushrooms gathered from the forest during their flight away from Ten Forts.

Lepkin went without any food. There was little to go around, and he refused to eat unless all the others were filled first. He rested with his back against the log wall and let sleep take over his body. It hardly seemed like more than a blink to him before the first rays of light played upon his face and woke him.

He moved slowly, still achy from the day before. Others in the camp were beginning to stir as well. Lepkin was thankful that the night had been peaceful. As for the day, there was no guarantee that another band of orcs wouldn't show up at any moment.

Lepkin stood and walked into the clearing. He surveyed the swath of clear-cut land carefully and then moved to a still-burning camp fire. He put some more wood into the fire to keep it going and then woke the soldiers nearby.

"Get up, wake the others. We will set fire to the forest now."

The soldiers nodded and sprinted off through the camp. Before long, Virgil approached.

"Will we have enough buffer to protect us from the fire as we continue our retreat?" He asked.

Lepkin nodded. "We should be alright. Have them light the fires every ten feet along the wall. Once a good blaze is going, then we make haste to rejoin with the others in Stonebrook."

Within minutes the crackling flames were taking hold of the branches and logs piled against the forest. The flames began to spread to nearby deadwood along the forest floor and expand out to the south. Smoke rose up into the sky and logs popped and creaked as the orange and red flames consumed them.

The soldiers quickly gathered their belongings and made their way northward as the fire furiously roared south. No orcs would be able to follow them until the blaze had run its course.

CHAPTER FOUR

King Mathias stroked his long, white beard and looked out over the assembly hall. Rows of wooden seats were filled as noble families streamed in. Senator Mickelson sat to Mathias' right, ticking off names on a long list as people arrived.

King Mathias noted Lady Lokton and her man-servant were in attendance. She was dressed in a flowing yellow gown, though she made the effort to cover her face with a dark veil. She nodded slightly to him. The old king returned the gesture and then continued to watch as people filtered in. To his delight, most families were represented in the meeting. He even saw Lady Cedreau enter the meeting hall. She stopped briefly to speak with Lady Lokton, and then the two of them sat down together.

"I would not have imagined they would wish to speak with each other," Mickelson commented as he ticked off House Cedreau on his list.

King Mathias cleared his throat and leaned over so as to keep his comment between the two of them. "Both women have seen their houses torn apart. Where men might continue to uphold a feud between houses, women have more sense than that when presented with outside dangers. That is why both houses have pledged their warriors to my service. When this is over I doubt they shall ever speak to each other again, but until then I dare say that House Lokton and House Cedreau will unite against every enemy that threatens either house until we have restored peace."

Mickelson didn't respond. He shrugged and went back to his list. After the doors were closed, the guards moved in to block the doors. Two more remained in place behind King Mathias, as Mickelson insisted.

"I do not see Lord Finorel," King Mathias said. "Did you mark him down as present on your list?"

"No, sire," Mickelson responded. "I have no members of House Finorel or of House Hischurn, though we did not expect any from the latter."

"Not after Dimwater dealt with them some time ago, no,"

King Mathias put in with a short nod. He rose to his feet and Senator Mickelson banged a smooth, round stone on the arm of his chair to call for silence. The room fell quiet immediately.

"Noble families of the Middle Kingdom, I bid you welcome." He paused to take in a breath. He was not as readily able to make speeches as he once was. Still, his eyes scoured the crowd before him, searching for those who were yet loyal to the crown. "Thank you for answering my summons. As you are all aware, all things are not well in the Middle Kingdom. Dark times have come to us, and now I call upon you to uphold your oaths. Each noble family sends their young sons and daughters to Kuldiga Academy upon reaching their fourteenth birthday. Some study the magical arts of wizardry, others become great historians and philosophers, some are taught to become knights, while others earn the skillful title of healer. Each apprentice takes a vow upon entering Kuldiga Academy to serve the Middle Kingdom. Now I evoke that promise." Mathias paused again. None stirred. No one whispered. All eyes were upon him. "One thing I should make abundantly clear, I know of your petty squabbles and fighting to make a claim for the throne, but as I live and breathe this day, none of you shall have it."

Now the murmurs started. King Mathias looked to Senator Mickelson and gestured to the stone in the man's hand. Senator Mickelson banged the stone upon the solid arm of his chair and called for silence.

"None of you should lament this decision, for the throne never belonged to any of you in the first place," Mathias said. "The throne is destined for my son. Are there any here to claim to be of my loins?" He paused again and waited. He could feel some of the angry, hot stares boring into him, but he did not care. Today was not a day for pacifying the nobles. It was time to draw a line, and see who would abide on the correct side. "I have chosen an heir, one who is like my own son. This man is also the lawful heir, and the throne will pass to him. Those of you who know the law, understand that I speak of Master Lepkin. The Keeper of Secrets has ever served our kingdom faithfully, and he is free of the same pettiness and jealousy that plagues all of you."

King Mathias stepped away from his throne and down three steps to the main level of the audience hall. "Now that this matter has been settled publicly, and beyond disputation, let us move on to the subject for which I summoned all of you. I have called up our armies and sent them throughout the Middle Kingdom. Mostly, I have stationed them in the northern parts between this city and Fort Drake. We are threatened by Tarthuns from the east. Even now they are attacking. Grand Master Penthal of the Lievonian Order has bolstered our defenses in the northeast. However, a new pass has been discovered also. Tarthuns are expected to attack there as well. King Sit'marihu has taken it upon himself to see to securing that pass." Mathias stopped and sighed.

"Worse still," he continued. "Old enemies have risen again. Blacktongues scourge our lands. A dragon has destroyed Valtuu Temple. Wizards and warlocks plague our people. Lokton manor was destroyed by an army of fiendish brutes led by a warlock who had been masquerading as Senator Bracken. He was defeated and slain, but not before Kuldiga Academy was overrun." King Mathias shook his head. "Many of you know all of this already. Your sons and daughters escaped from the Academy, were taken down to Fort Drake and then helped on their way back home to you. I need not waste more time explaining the gravity of the situation." He turned to Mickelson and extended his bony, weathered hand.

Senator Mickelson reached behind his chair and produced a simple staff made of cherry wood. He quickly moved to Mathias and placed the staff in the king's hand.

King Mathias turned and tapped the staff on the ground. "The Blacktongues are being rooted out of the Middle Kingdom. Others who would see chaos, or use the dark arts within our borders are also being hunted. What I ask of you is whether your house has any warriors to spare. If yes, then line up on my left. Senator Mickelson will make a list of how many you can send. On the morrow, I will announce where the soldiers are to be sent." He held a finger up in the air. "Let me be clear. I am asking for any who have completed their training, and all who serve and are of fighting age. If, however, your house has none to spare, then assemble on my right. I will hear your justifications and decide whether I can send further aid to you. I know many of you watch over hamlets and villages, and may not have the strength to send me additional soldiers as well as maintain the safety of your own subjects."

He tapped the staff on the stone floor. "Make your choice

now." King Mathias turned back toward his throne so he could sit and watch while those present formed into groups on either side of the hall. Senator Mickelson worked quickly to record names and numbers from each house volunteering to help. The guards in the room ensured that the lines were as orderly as possible. Once Mickelson had finished with a particular noble, the guards would allow that person to exit the hall.

The whole process took well over an hour before Mickelson finished with the houses volunteering support. After they had all departed, there were ten nobles remaining in the audience hall.

Lord Millard was the first to approach the throne. "My King," he began with a deep bow. "Please do not think me a coward, or unfaithful. As you know, I have a small village to protect within the borders of my land. I have, including men of fighting age, two hundred spears to command. As my lands are in the north eastern region of the Middle Kingdom, I have already sent all but thirty of my men to aid Grand Master Penthal." He reached into his pocket and produced a small parchment. "I have a letter of thanks from Grand Master Penthal to verify my account." He offered the letter up.

Mickelson took the letter and transferred it to Mathias' hands. The king opened it and read its contents quickly. Then he nodded.

"All is well, Lord Millard. Thank you for your service, and your forethought."

The next person to come forward was Lady Lokton.

King Mathias arched a brow at her. "Why do you stand before me?" he asked. "You have already offered every able-bodied man in your service, except for Braun, whom I insisted should stay with you. You have no need to explain yourself to me."

She nodded and smiled. "I come for her," she said as she gestured with a hand toward Lady Cedreau.

Lady Cedreau came forward, her dark hair falling over her face as she bowed low.

"You come to intercede on her behalf?" King Mathias asked.

Lady Lokton nodded. "I do."

"Lady Cedreau, many of your house were among those who fought with the warlock masquerading as Senator Bracken, do you deny it?"

Lady Cedreau kept her head bent to the floor as she shook her head and said, "I do not deny it."

King Mathias sighed and looked to Lady Lokton with his tired, yet fierce eyes. "These men killed those who served you. They destroyed your home. Yet you stand here and ask for a pardon?"

Lady Lokton bent down to a knee beside Lady Cedreau. "My king, it was not under her order that these things happened. Allow her to explain, and I believe you will see her in the same way I do. She is no enemy to the kingdom, nor to me."

King Mathias cleared his throat. "Such an exoneration from one so terrorized warrants a hearing indeed," he said. "Speak, Lady Cedreau, and I will decide your fate."

"My house fell into disarray after my husband and child died. Many would no longer listen to me. They yearned for vengeance."

"Why did you not inform me of their actions?" Mathias pressed.

"Because my eldest son, Eldrik, was stolen from me by a coven of witches. It is they who charmed him, and helped him persuade those of my house to follow him and join the warlock of whom you spoke."

"And why have you not sent word to me before now?" Mathias asked.

"Because after the battle at Lokton manor, my son went missing. I hunted the witches, and killed two of them, but I have been unable to find the third, or my son. I fear for him more than anything else in this world. I came only when I received your summons. I knew then that I had run out of time to find my son."

"How did you receive my summons if you were out in the countryside hunting for your son as you claim?"

"My bodyguard remained at my home. I gave him a spell through which he could contact me if needed. He took the summons from your messenger, and then called upon me with the spell."

"But you are not of noble birth," Senator Mickelson said. "You only attained that after marriage with Lord Cedreau. How is it that you know of spells?"

Lady Cedreau paused, and then stood slowly. She held out her hands, palms facing up to show she wasn't hiding anything. "In my youth, I had been taken in by the witches. I had been one of them.

When I met Lord Cedreau, I forsook the dark arts, and did not use them again until the witches betrayed me and stole my son." Tears ran down her face, and her lower lip quivered. "He is all I have left in my life. All I ask is that you allow me to continue looking for him."

"Witchcraft is a serious crime," Mickelson said as he glared down his nose at her. "You have fully admitted to it, and must be—"

"Senator Mickelson, be quiet," King Mathias said. The king rose and moved in close to Lady Cedreau. "Answer me truthfully three questions."

Lady Cedreau nodded. "Ask anything."

"Have you killed using witchcraft?"

Lady Cedreau nodded. "I have killed two witches, but no other human have I harmed intentionally. The only other time I sought to use magic upon a person was to heal my own womb, as it was dry."

King Mathias pressed on. "If the witches charmed your son to join with the warlock, then the coven must have known the warlock. Had you any knowledge of him?"

Lady Cedreau shook her head. "I knew of others, but in name only. The only warlock I saw in person was an old hermit who dealt with spiders and frogs within a dark cave. He helped our coven decipher old writings, but there was no connection to the warlock who masqueraded as Senator Bracken. I had no knowledge of him, or his plots, until after my family was entangled in his web the same as House Lokton."

"Is your son a threat to the Middle Kingdom?" Mathias asked.

Lady Cedreau hesitated. She closed her eyes, holding them shut for several seconds before finally nodding her head as tears fell. "As long as he is under a witch's charm, he is a danger indeed. That is why I was hunting the last witch. I fear for him. He is a good man, but his will is not his own."

King Mathias nodded slowly and reached a hand out to Lady Cedreau's shoulder. "I have no son of my own," he said. "I don't know the pain you feel inside, but I think I understand it. Go, find your son, but when you find him, take him away from here."

"My liege," Lady Lokton interjected. King Mathias silenced her with a glare and then looked back to Lady Cedreau.

"It is not out of spite that I say this," he explained. "Feuds run long and deep. Lady Lokton may have forgiven you, but others will blame you. Many perished in that battle at Lokton manor. If you find your son, take him far away. Go east, across the mountains or go west across the sea. Begin anew some place where no one else knows either of you, so as not to overshadow your family."

Lady Cedreau nodded. "That is most generous," she said.

King Mathias turned to Mickelson. "Ascertain the value of House Cedreau's holdings. Set the sum of gold aside from the treasury and take possession of the deed and title." Senator Mickelson nodded. King Mathias turned back to Lady Cedreau. "When you are ready, return here, or send your servant. I will give you the value of your holdings so you may have means wherewith you can rebuild your lives."

Lady Cedreau rushed in and fell upon the frail king's shoulders. "Thank you," she whispered. "It is more than I deserve."

King Mathias pushed her away gently and looked into her eyes. "May the Ancients, and the Old Gods, guide your search. Go."

Lady Cedreau turned to leave.

"Lady Lokton, stay a moment," King Mathias said. He walked close to her and took her hand. She rose to her feet and then Mathias brought her by the hand to Senator Mickelson. "Transfer the deed and title to House Lokton. Lady Lokton will now assume all of House Cedreau's holdings."

"My king, I cannot accept this," Lady Lokton said.

"You have no house," King Mathias replied. "It is a fitting recompense for the destruction brought to you. My only regret is that I cannot restore your husband to you."

Lady Lokton fell silent and looked to the floor.

"See her out," Mathias told Mickelson. The senator set his list on the throne and walked Lady Lokton out of the audience hall.

King Mathias retrieved the list and then turned to ease himself down into the throne. He glanced at the list and then he looked up to the nobles remaining in the hall. His features turned hard and cold. He knew these men. He knew none of them had any excuse for withholding support. He beckoned the first man forward.

"Come Lord Roeper," King Mathias said. "Why have you not volunteered your help?"

Lord Roeper, a portly man with a red beard and bald head bowed from the waist up and then straightened himself. He spoke in a nasal voice. "Our holdings have not produced a great crop this year, sire. I am afraid we need all of our men in the fields to tend what we have."

King Mathias scoffed and pointed a bony finger at Roeper's bulbous belly. "You could stand to forego a meal or two to ensure the women folk in your holding have enough food to fill their own plates with."

Roeper's eyes went wide. "Sire, without the men in the fields, the women would have to tend the crops. Who would tend to the looms that produce our textiles?"

King Mathias shrugged. "Who cares?" he asked pointedly. "I am faced with war and all you can think of is how you will fill your belly and your purse."

Lord Roeper's mouth opened and closed as if he was trying to speak, but nothing came out. He threw his hands up in disgust and turned his back on King Mathias.

"Escort Lord Roeper to the adjoining hall," King Mathias instructed one of the guards. "List all able-bodied men in his service and then I will decide where to send them along with everyone else."

The guard moved without a word and grabbed Lord Roeper by the arm, twirling him around and moving him out of the audience hall.

"Lord Brenigan, I see that you are also unwilling to share your strength with the kingdom. What is your excuse?"

A short man with a gray circle of hair ringing his liver-spotted head stepped forward. He held a green felt hat in his hands and dressed modestly in a forest green tunic over a simple pair of black trousers. "My king, it is not that I am unwilling. As you know, I have lands that encompass the region north of Kuldiga Academy. We were attacked, and our lands were pillaged, by the same forces that attacked Kuldiga Academy. I sent messengers, but they were cut down. We have been unable to get any communication to you."

"I thought you had a wizard in your house?" Mathias pressed.

Lord Brenigan looked to the floor. "My cousin had sided with the warlock. I had no idea of his involvement until after the battle at Kuldiga Academy. It is my suspicion that he is responsible for the army coming through my lands. I have but five men left who are whole. There are seven others who lie upon their beds with injuries too grave for me to attend to. Most of our women have been slain as well."

King Mathias' hard demeanor softened and he stroked his beard and sighed. "I misjudged you, Lord Brenigan. Go with this guard here, detail to him what you need and we will see what supplies and manpower we can send your way."

Lord Brenigan bowed his head. "You have my thanks."

The King grew weary of the ordeal, and his backside ached from the hard, unrelenting throne. He cast a gaze at the others waiting for judgment. "Do any of you have an excuse half as acceptable as Lord Brenigan, or are you all fat wastrels like Roeper?"

Lord Howgen held up his hand. King Mathias nodded to him. "Perhaps we can find some manpower to spare. We can go in the other chamber with Roeper and discuss options with Senator Mickelson."

King Mathias looked to his left and saw that Mickelson was indeed returned. He nodded and called out to Mickelson. "Take these men into the next chamber and ascertain what forces they can spare to help defend the Middle Kingdom. Don't let any of them pull the wool over your eyes either. I am going to my chambers." The guards behind the throne moved to follow the king as he rose from the throne and walked away, but he turned and gestured for them to stay. "Mickelson needs you more than I," Mathias told the guards. "Ensure that the nobles fulfill their duty without hassling Mickelson."

"By your command," one of the guards said.

*****

Gulgarin moved to the table and took the leather bracer in hand. He turned it over, admiring the image of the horse, the symbol of his tribe, and then placed it over his left forearm. He took his time fastening it into place. He wanted everything to look perfect when he stepped outside.

His officers had already gathered the orc tribes outside the main keep. Officers had priority and would be grouped in the courtyard. Lower ranking tribesmen would be lining the walls, stairs, or without the southern gate.

A platform had been erected near the main keep to allow him to address all of the orcs.

He looked down to the parchment Maernok had left. The fool. Willing to trade the glory for a simple wizard. Maernok's feats on the field of battle would be short-remembered in the minds of any orc who followed Gulgarin north to reclaim their homeland.

"I have united the tribes," Gulgarin said to himself as he took the parchment in hand. "Every tribe will now merge together, and move north as one." He breathed in deeply and closed his eyes. Such an accomplishment had not been achieved since the first orcs had sailed across the great waters to this land, in the time before humans came and created what they called the Middle Kingdom.

Gulgarin would be remembered as the orc who took back their home. He would be the orc who rid the land of the infestation known as humans. None of them would stand before him. "Even the dwarves will have no choice but to run and hide in their holes," Gulgarin told himself. He would take back what the dragons had stolen and then given to the humans.

The muscular orc exited the room and made his way across the large chamber to the exit. His steps echoed off the walls. He moved with purpose, and confidence. His cousin, Gersimon, stood at the door beaming from ear to ear. Gulgarin nodded to him and Gersimon opened the door.

Gulgarin passed out into the sun and was greeted by a sea of fully armored orcs. There was no cheering, no fanfare, only silence as they watched him ascend the platform and then turn to address them.

"Maernok has given me command of the field," Gulgarin stated. He held up the parchment and the ring. "He has decided to hunt the wizard known as Gilifan, to exact revenge for his family."

The orcs from Maernok's tribe cheered and shouted their approval.

Gulgarin nodded and smiled. "Yes, it is a worthy cause, but we have not come this far to turn back now," he went on. "Glory awaits us in the north!" A cheer went up from all the officers then.

"Maernok has faith in me to lead all of the tribes, united as one, to take back our home. We are not marching to Pinkt'Hu, or to any other single settlement. Our ancestors were driven south because they were not united. They were not strong enough to answer the humans blow for blow, but we are!" Gulgarin pounded his chest. "We will drive them into the seas and put them into graves. We will burn their houses and their storehouses. We will lay waste to their forts and destroy their beloved castle. We will exterminate them, and cleanse our ancestral homeland of the filth that has perverted it since the dragons came here and established Roegudok Hall. Then, when we are done, we will fill in the dwarves' hole and let them suffocate beneath the dirt under our feet!"

A great cheer went up that lasted for several minutes. Officers drew weapons and clapped them together. Those along the walls stomped their feet and waved their spears and axes. Gulgarin smiled. He could smell the victory even now. The imagined scent of human blood flared his nostrils and he looked out over the army before him.

A melody rose up above the din. It was soft at first, almost unrecognizable, but as it grew, more orcs ceased shouting and took up the chorus.

Long ago, in days of old,
Legends born, and stories told.
Alone he stood,
Fearless and bold.

His breastplate dented, the shine grown dim,
His sword he wielded, protecting kin.
Elshuapa, his might alone,
Vanquished evil, and built our home.

Our lands were taken, our heritage lost.
We take them back now, though high the cost.
Oh Elshuapa, march with us now.
As we pay homage, and keep our vow.

Off to battle, your sons are bold.
Off to recapture, those days of old.

The orcs repeated the song, the chorus growing as more and more took up the song. Gulgarin turned, seeing Gersimon climbing the platform.

"Isn't it glorious, cousin? This is what we have worked for."

Gersimon nodded. Then he pointed behind Gulgarin. Gulgarin turned to look and saw a great, thick wall of smoke rising to the north.

"They set the forest on fire," Gersimon said.

Gulgarin shrugged it off. "Let the trees burn. Soon their whole kingdom shall burn. Go tell the officers that they are to prepare the army. When the fire is done, we march north. Have them gather food and make wagons. The seasons will change soon, and the harvest will already be upon us by the time we reach the first settlement."

"By your command, King Gulgarin," Gersimon said.

Gulgarin's smile faded. He turned back to his cousin and then glanced out at the thousands of orcs still singing their battle hymn. His smile returned. "King Gulgarin, I like that."

"It has a good sound," Gersimon said.

"Go, make the necessary preparations." Gulgarin turned back to the orcs below and joined in the singing.

CHAPTER FIVE

Erik sat cross-legged in a small room of glass. The walls were so thick that they appeared green. The golden chandelier above shone brightly with magical crystals that bathed the room in warm light. He sat on the floor, which was also made of glass, and waited for the Immortal Mystic.

The glass double doors opened on silent hinges.

The Immortal Mystic entered. He was tall, maybe close to seven feet. His frame was slim, but not frail despite the age that so obviously tugged at the lines on his face and caused the skin around his jaw to droop ever so slightly. The long, white beard was neatly braided into a single, thick plait that hung down over the Immortal Mystic's chest. His eyes were a bright golden color, something that Erik found most intriguing. He had seen many different eye colors before. He had even seen Marlin's gray eyes that no longer had any iris at all, but never had he seen eyes that seemed to be made of gold before. The Immortal Mystic tucked each hand into the opposite sleeve of a grand, silver robe that was so long it covered the man's feet.

"Did you sleep well?" the Immortal Mystic asked.

"I did," Erik said. "I feel as though I have slept for days."

The Immortal Mystic smiled and nodded. "That is because you have," he explained. "You slept for a couple of weeks, actually."

Erik's eyes widened. "What do you mean?"

"Time has little meaning here," the Immortal Mystic said. "It exists, but we flow through it at a different pace than everything else outside." He held up a hand and moved in to sit upon his knees in front of Erik. "You needed your rest," he said. "I wanted to make sure you were fully rejuvenated before we began our training. Now that I know you have rested, we can begin in more earnest. Do not fear. The time invested in your recovery will be returned to us tenfold."

Erik nodded and let the matter drop. There wasn't much he could do about it in any case. His stomach growled loudly enough that the Immortal Mystic could hear it. Erik blushed at first but the Immortal Mystic waved the matter off and smirked.

"Do not worry, that is normal after such a sleep. As for nourishment while you were resting. This palace is able to sustain a body with a special kind of magic. You will find that not only is your mind more prepared for the training, but your muscles are none the weaker despite your sedentary state."

The glass doors opened and several men dressed in gray robes entered the room. They split into two lines, circling around either side of the room and silently turned to face Erik.

"Your training begins now," the Immortal Mystic said.

Erik turned to look at the men in robes and then looked back to the slender man kneeling before him. He expected some form of instruction, but he only was given silence. "What would you have me do?" Erik asked at last.

The Immortal Mystic frowned. "Must you still be guided along?"

Erik bristled and leaned back as he repositioned himself on the floor. It had been months since he had been in Valtuu Temple with Marlin for training. He had always had clear instructions before, even when he was given reading assignments by Al. He looked around the room and tried to guess what his task might be.

He closed his eyes and called up his power. He could feel the energy roll through him and then out into the room around him. The men that had entered the room all disappeared. Only the Immortal Mystic remained. The man smiled and nodded with approval.

"Very well. Now let's move to the next room." The Immortal Mystic rose to his feet with grace and speed that eluded even Erik. It seemed as though the man lived up to his title, and was not subject to age and decay as the rest of the world was. The two of them exited the small room and walked through the hallway. They passed several rooms, all of which were empty except for the chandeliers. There was no sign of anyone else in the palace.

A thought came to Erik then as he looked around. He hadn't seen Jaleal yet. Before he could ask the whereabouts of his companion, the Immortal Mystic turned around with a faint smile on his face.

"Your friend is on the upper level of the palace. I have

opened our library to him."

Erik nodded. The Immortal Mystic turned around and continued leading them through the hallway.

Mention of the library brought Tatev to the forefront of Erik's thoughts. The horrid sacrifice replayed in his mind and his heart fell heavy with sadness. He had managed before to hold the emotions at bay, except for the occasional sorrowful thought here and there, but not now. There was no longer any imminent danger nor treacherous road to travel and force his thoughts to focus. Now he walked in an empty glass palace, with only his thoughts as company. Tears filled his eyes. Waves of guilt washed over him.

He should have saved Tatev. Or maybe he should have encouraged the red haired librarian to teach him more, instead of cutting off his lectures whenever he could.

The Immortal Mystic turned around and placed both hands on Erik's shoulders. He leaned down, bringing his fiery golden eyes lower to meet Erik's gaze. "You must focus your energies, Erik," he said. "If you cannot control your mind, then you powers are nothing."

Erik nodded. "I...I...I lost a friend," he stammered. Tears fell from his eyes despite his efforts to choke them back.

The Immortal Mystic sighed and shook his head disapprovingly. "You have a lot yet to learn," he said. "Come, I will set a task before you here. Then you can rest for the day."

"I don't need to rest," Erik interjected. "It would be better to have something to take my mind off of it."

The Immortal Mystic shook his head. "No, it would be better for you to deal with it. For that, you will need silence and solitude." The slender man opened the door to a room and showed Erik inside. There in the room stood thirty men in six rows. They stood silently, watching Erik as he entered the room.

Erik turned around and looked at the glass wall. It was thick, but not so thick that he shouldn't have seen the men inside the room before the Immortal Mystic opened the door. Erik looked to the tall man, but the Immortal Mystic declined to offer any instruction. Erik nodded and called his power up. A few of the men disappeared, but to Erik's surprise others appeared for a moment.

The sudden appearance of new people startled him and he

lost his focus. Those who had appeared when he called up his power vanished again. Then, the remaining people in the room rushed toward him.

Erik remembered the trial where he had to ascertain which warriors would fight against him and called up his power again. In an instant he saw that not all who ran toward him had the intent to attack. Most were going to shield him, but three had other designs. Erik called them out, and immediately all the others formed a circle around him and kept the three would-be attackers at bay.

"Well done," the Immortal Mystic said. "For the most part," he added quickly.

Erik looked around the room and tried to focus his power again, but he never again saw the men who had appeared for a moment when he had first used his power. Perplexed, he turned to the Immortal Mystic for an explanation.

"When your mind is clear and focused, then so shall your power be," the slender man said. He waved his hand and then all of the other men in the room disappeared.

Erik was astonished. "None of them were real?" he asked. "I used my power, how could they have remained if I had tried to dispel the images?"

"How indeed?" the Immortal Mystic echoed. "Perhaps you should return to the first room and meditate. Try to work through your feelings for your friend, and understand the true trajectory that all beings are on."

Erik screwed his face and asked, "What does that mean?"

The Immortal Mystic wrinkled his nose. "If you are to take the place of the Champion of Truth, I cannot spoon feed you all of the answers." The tall man turned and left the room, leaving Erik both insulted and confused.

"*If* I am to be the champion?" Erik repeated after he was sure the Immortal Mystic was gone. "Am I not already the champion?" He reflected back to the confusing conversation he had had with Allun Rha. He exhaled impatiently and left the room to retrace his steps back to the first, smaller room that had been given to him for training.

As his feet carried him through the sparkling halls his mind gave room for the doubts to grow. Had he lost his power, or was the Immortal Mystic simply that much stronger than Marlin that his illusions were harder to dispel?

He tried to tell himself that he had slain Tu'luh, and done many other great things that most men could never hope to achieve, but then he heard Salarion's voice bringing him back down to reality. Erik had always had help. Dimwater and Lepkin had battled Tukai the warlock. Al had saved Erik from Janik, and had used a large portion of his life force to do so. When the dark wizard Erthor came to Valtuu Temple riding a twisted dragon, Lepkin and Dimwater led an assault to protect Nagar's Secret from falling to the Blacktongues. Al had ventured with Erik and saved his life countless times as Blacktongues assailed him at every turn. An entire army had stood behind him at Lokton manor. He may have slain the warlock by his own sword, but none of that would have been possible without the countless warriors who fought and died to give him that chance. Jaleal and the other gnomes had saved him from the giant spiders in the forest. A host of dwarves had helped him and the others fight Tu'luh when Valtuu Temple was destroyed. Tillamon had tricked and killed the shadowfiend pretending to be Patrical. Erik had ventured to fight Tu'luh on his own, but even then he had Jaleal with him.

He pushed through the glass door and went to the middle of the room.

He sat on the uncomfortable glass floor.

Then he let himself lie down and he stared at the thick, greenish ceiling above him. He could see shadows and light piercing through and reflecting off the glass, but that was all. There didn't appear to be any movement near him whatsoever. What had at first been breathtaking and beautiful was now cold, and hollow. He was alone is a gargantuan glass prison.

He was more frustrated now than ever he had been. Through every hardship before there had always been a shining hope to reach for. The promise of his power, or the strength of a dragon born warrior to lean upon had propelled him through it all in the beginning. Then, when those had seemed not enough, there was the Immortal Mystic. The one being in the realm who would know the answer to Tu'luh's riddle and show Erik how to defeat the four fireballs that would come to devour his world. The Immortal Mystic was promised to show him the wisdom of fighting on, when Tu'luh had presented an equally viable plan.

Where was the hope now?

The Immortal Mystic proved more austere than Lepkin had ever been. Not only that, but there were no answers yet. Erik had been met only with tacit approval, or outright displeasure, and this was only the first day of training.

Erik then reflected on the fact that he had been allowed to sleep for weeks. What kind of nonsense was that? All this time he was rushed around, walking, working, and fighting himself to the bone just to reach the ultimate goal. Now, with Nagar's Secret presumably in Salarion's hands and Lepkin holding off an orcish invasion, Erik was placed under a magic spell and made to sleep for weeks. How was that going to help?

"You left me there," a voice called out.

Erik jumped and propped himself up on his elbows. No one was there. He looked around and then shook his head. He closed his eyes, but quickly opened them when Tatev's face appeared in his mind. Erik tried to fight it, but the guilt flooded back over him. Tatev's screams filled the room and Erik placed his hands over his ears.

Those screams were joined by others. Scenes from the battle at Lokton manor came to Erik's mind. He tried to shut them out. He conjured up the image of Nagar's Secret, the book that promised to enslave all of the Middle Kingdom.

"I am fighting to protect them," Erik said aloud as he pressed his hands into his ears in an attempt to shut out the voices.

They would not be silenced.

Right or wrong, Erik's war had brought death. The images and faces of those he had known assaulted his mind until he was lying on his side on the glass floor, crying and shouting for the images to go away and leave him alone.

"Erik, why are you crying?" a voice called out.

Erik barely heard it. The screams of horror and pain were so loud he could focus on nothing else.

"Erik, I am here," a voice beckoned.

The voice was much louder this time, pushing the screams away. Erik turned and looked. He saw his father, Trenton Lokton, standing in the doorway. He was wearing his striped pajamas underneath his green and gold robe, and held a steaming mug in one hand and a pair of oranges nestled in his other palm. Erik wiped his eyes and blinked. The glass room melted away and in its place he saw his own room. He looked down and saw that he was on his bed, wearing pajamas and the sun was pouring in from his bedroom window.

"I thought you might want to follow me to the solarium," Lord Lokton said as he tossed an orange to Erik. "Perhaps we can discuss what happened yesterday."

Yesterday? Erik wondered to himself. He looked down and saw that his hands were bandaged. He flexed his fingers and felt the sting where the blisters and lesions had formed and then he remembered. The pull ups. Master Lepkin had ordered an impossible amount of pull ups to be done as punishment for breaking into Dimwater's tower.

Dimwater's tower! That was it. That was why Lord Lokton wanted to talk with him. Erik's stomach turned. He knew this was not going to be a pleasant conversation to have.

Lord Lokton stopped in the doorway. He turned and the oranges fell from his hand as he clutched at his stomach.

Erik froze when he saw the dagger embedded up to the hilt in his father's gut. Blood oozed out and spread through the pajamas around the dagger. Lord Lokton's eyes went wide and his mouth quivered. "What have you done?" he asked.

"I didn't—" Erik started but then his father fell to the floor and a man stood behind him cackling wildly.

The man wore black robes with shiny, purple trim on the sleeves. A long hood hung loosely over his face, covering his features. Strands of silver hair poked out from the hood like old, wispy snakes. A golden medallion in the shape of a triangle enclosing an open eye hung over the man's chest. The man held a long staff of wood in his left hand and pointed at Erik.

"I warned you. I warned you all. I said that you would destroy House Lokton. Your power is a dangerous one. I told you that the power would consume all living. Yet still you persist. Your father is dead, your house is in ruin. The Middle Kingdom is at war, and you still press forward. Can you not see that it is *you* who must be stopped?"

Erik fell back to sit on the bed, but he crashed to the glass floor.

The room transformed back to the empty, cold cell of glass.

"Tukai was right," Erik muttered. "I may not have killed my father, but I am the one who set him on his path. If not for me, Lokton Manor would still stand."

"Hogwash and horse-apples," a familiar, nasal voice called out from behind him. Erik jumped and spun around. No one was there.

"Who is there?" Erik asked, almost afraid to see who was visiting him now.

A hand materialized in the air holding a pair of gold-rimmed glasses.

"If only you hadn't left these, they could help you see the truth of it."

Erik recognized the voice now. It was Tatev. Just as he started to say something the hand vanished, and the Eyes of Dowr along with it.

"It's cold here, Erik. Why is it so cold?"

"NO!" Erik shouted. His eyes opened and he slowly understood that he had been dreaming all along. He was still lying upon the floor. His tears had formed a small puddle next to his face. He turned around to look at the door. It was still closed, as it had been after he entered the room. His father was no longer lying upon the floor, and there was no warlock in the doorway.

Darkness had fallen outside, which meant that now the chandelier inside the chamber created a mirror-like effect on all the walls so that no matter which way Erik turned, he saw himself. His red, puffy eyes and his guilt-stricken face.

Still, dream or no dream, perhaps Tukai's words were right. What if Erik would end up consuming all living with his power in his futile attempt to save them? After all, he didn't fit any of the visions that Allun Rha had seen of the Champion of Truth. Perhaps he was not the right person. Perhaps he was simply good enough to pass the tests, and with the help of others able to put down some of the enemies that sought Nagar's Secret. Would that mean that he couldn't conquer the final battle? Or perhaps he was too strong. What if his power was uncontrollable?

Goosebumps tightened his skin along his arms and shoulders. He scooted up to the nearby wall and rubbed his arms furiously. Then he remembered Tatev's words about being cold and the sadness hit him again. Tears would have streamed down his face, but he had no more to give. He dropped his head into his arms folded atop his knees and sobbed, going mad with grief and guilt.

*****

Aparen walked through the lush thicket and upon exiting found a large, emerald pool of water. Njar sat upon the grassy bank with his legs crossed in front of him. The satyr gestured for Aparen to sit near him. The young boy sat, with his legs stretched out before him so that they almost touched the reeds shooting up from the edge of the water.

"Today, I have a small lesson prepared for you," Njar said. "You must simply relax and watch."

Aparen nodded his head. "Very well, show it to me," he replied. His voice was neither eager nor uninterested. He was accustomed to Njar, and the goat-man's lessons, but he wouldn't go so far as to say he was completely comfortable with him yet."

Njar held out his left hand and his staff appeared instantly. He touched the head of the staff to the waters. The surface danced and swirled. Steam rose up and formed figures that waved and shimmered above the pool. "What is that?"

Aparen looked and beheld the form of a satyr. "It is a satyr," he said. "A being that is half man and half goat."

"Not precisely," Njar replied. Aparen screwed up his face and cast an impatient glance to Njar. Njar held up a hand. "I am not the offspring of some human who fell for a goat, that would be preposterous," he said. "I am a wholly separate being, created by Terramyr herself, as all of the Natural Races are."

Aparen nodded. "Yes, I remember."

Njar gestured to the water with his head. "Then name all of the Natural Races, let's see what you know."

"Satyrs, minotaurs, and centaurs," Aparen said.

"Very good," Njar replied. His staff touched the water again and several forms of each race sprung up from the mist. "However, there are many more. Can you think of any?"

Aparen thought for a moment. "Gnomes?" he guessed.

Njar nodded. "Here, let me speed this along." He tapped the water with his staff once more and the mists rose high over them. Njar laid back, folding his arms behind his head as he smiled and looked up at the images taking shape.

Aparen did likewise, watching the mist swirl into different shapes.

First it formed into a ball. Soon there were masses upon the globe.

"This is Terramyr," Njar said.

"It is round?" Aparen asked.

"You didn't know?" Njar asked astonished. Then he nodded. "That's right, you were an apprentice of the sword, the art of brute force and subjugation. Why would I have thought you should know anything important?"

Aparen reddened in the face, but he let the comment go. He knew the satyr well enough by now to know that the creature meant no insult by his words, it was simply an observation.

"The world is indeed round. The masses of land you see are continents. There are many of those, each subdivided into kingdoms, countries, and wastelands."

The globe grew to enormous proportions, capable of showing massive armies and other groups of peoples and creatures across the surface.

"There are so many," Aparen said.

Njar nodded. "This is just a representation, mind you," he said. "I haven't the space or time to show you all of the creatures upon the face of Terramyr, but hopefully this will give you incentive to seek balance." Njar held up his hand and the globe spun over until a large continent faced them. Nearly the whole of it was covered with a dense fog, and encircled by steep, jagged mountains that rose out of the seas.

"What is that large area?" Aparen asked.

"It is Terra's Navel. It is a lost continent that is hidden to the rest of the world. A dense fog surrounds it, and borders of impassable mountains seal it away from explorers. Its area is so vast that there are actually seas and continents within its covered borders."

"Where is it?"

Njar smiled. "That is the secret," he said. "For within Terra's Navel lies the life force of Terramyr. From that, the source of all life springs throughout the world. That is why it is hidden. When the Old Gods formed the world, they created a bond between

Terramyr and Hammenfein, the underworld or Hell if you prefer. When that bond was formed, Terramyr protected itself by creating Terra's Navel and hiding the sacred source of life."

Njar motioned with his fingers and the glob spun to show a continent off in the east.

"Do you see the large island to the northwest of the continent?"

Aparen nodded. "I do."

"That is Icadion's Footstool. It is thus named because the rainbow bridge that connects Terramyr to Volganor, the heaven city, used to rest there."

"Before the Old Gods abandoned the world," Aparen said with a nod. "I have heard of it."

Njar offered a half smile and then pointed to the continent before them. "Starting from the west and going eastward, we see a large kingdom built upon a lush plateau that is raised above the rest of the continent. This is where the first human civilization was established after the Old Gods created the continent. Going east across the lower plains, the forest and a large lake, which could pass for a sea, and then over the first range of mountains and over the large canyon that nearly severs the continent in twain, we come to Tanglewood Forest." Each place on the continent glowed slightly as it was named, helping Aparen trace his way across the continent as Njar spoke. Tanglewood Forest now glowed brightly with a golden hue. "This is the first home of the elves. All elvish peoples come from here, though they have spread over the globe just as far as the humans have.

"Now, moving on we pass over the Nahktun Mountains and pass into a wasteland that is shrouded in darkness every hour of every day. The creatures and abominations that live here would give an army of wizards more trouble than they are worth. Luckily, they are unable to sustain themselves in sunlight, and thus cannot spread over into neighboring lands lest the sun would burn them like chaff in an oven."

"What kinds of creatures?" Aparen asked.

Njar turned a fierce eye to him. "Creatures that shall not be named within my home." Njar then turned back to the globe. "Deep within this land lies Gaia's Tear."

"The volcano that connects Terramyr to Hammenfein,"

Aparen said.

Njar smiled pleasantly. "So, you are more than a sword-wielding brute after all."

Aparen sniggered. "And it is this connection that caused Terramyr to create the Natural Races."

Njar shook his head. "No," he said. "Many people think that is correct, but that is an oversimplification. When Gaia's Tear was created, the world formed Terra's Navel, to protect all life. However, it was not until the War of the Gods that Terramyr realized the danger it was truly in. When the Old Gods could no longer stay for fear of being overrun by Atek and his minions, they withdrew. Lysander, Icadion's most faithful son, remained behind, and has vowed to find a way to save the world and restore order, but none have heard from him in centuries. So, when Terramyr found itself in peril, and only the Ancients remained upon her face, she created the Natural Races. We were created in an attempt to protect the life source, and to spread balance throughout the world. That is what we still are trying to do. However, you humans are a greedy, selfish, and bloodthirsty lot. We are slowly losing the battle for the hearts and minds of Terramyr. Ultimately, it will likely boil down to a final war upon the heart of Terramyr."

Njar pointed his staff and the globe dissolved to form into several different beings. Njar explained each of them as they appeared.

The first image stood before them with a pointy hat atop a short body with a long beard and sharp, pointed ears. The image wore spectacles, and held a book in front of its face.

"The gnome. A short creature, usually averaging between two and three feet tall. They live for about six hundred years. They are highly skilled wizards, and love the forests. They are distrustful of all other races that were not created directly by Terramyr, but they can coexist with humans."

The gnome pushed its glasses up on its narrow nose and then disappeared. In its place appeared an extremely small, winged humanoid. Its body resembled a human in every respect, save for the butterfly-like translucent wings that kept it afloat.

"Fairies are an odd lot. They are fairly reclusive. They are incredibly small, usually only about six inches tall. They live in small glass-like towers they create by freezing the morning dew. Oddly enough, some of them choose to live with wizards or sorceresses as familiars. They tend to focus on scholarly research rather than seeking balance. They can live for as long as one thousand years."

The fairy blinked into nothingness and then appeared a chubby baby. At first it also had wings like the fairy, but then the wings disappeared. Aparen was stunned when the baby got up onto his legs and walked around. The misty image came down near Aparen and growled at him.

"Pixies are a troublesome bunch. They are similar in height to gnomes, though they tend to look more like oversized human toddlers than lean miniatures. This is their weapon, actually, as they often gain entrance into human homes or settlements by disguising themselves as babies and resting on a doorstep. If the town or family that finds the pixie does not meet the pixie's standard for what a good creature should be, then the pixie unleashes a flurry of spells and curses to lay waste to everyone around it." Njar paused and looked directly at Aparen. "To be clear, almost all other races are deemed unworthy by pixies, so they kill far more than they ever consider sparing."

"Where do they live?" Aparen asked. "Are there any around the Middle Kingdom?"

Njar shook his head. "We satyrs do not approve of pixies. Where we are in abundance, we try to run them out. We are immune to their charms and curses, so it is easy for us to rid an area of them. The only place where that is untrue is on the continent Prirodha, which lies far to the south of here. Some pixies do venture out on their own to curse and kill, but alone they are somewhat vulnerable, and eventually a wizard or witch-hunter finds and slays the rogue pixie."

The pixie wound up as if to spit on Aparen, but just before it succeeded, the image faded away. Out from the mist came an oddly shaped humanoid. He was maybe the size of a dwarf, but a little taller and not nearly as stout. His feet were large and hairy and his nose was long, with a slight up curve at the end.

"This is a Halfling. It lives for up to two hundred years. They are often referred to as Terramyr's forgotten race, as they have no real special abilities, and they are scattered about the world with no apparent reason. They are pacific, and prefer to run or hide rather than fight. However, one should not wholly discount them, they are very clever and can be mischievous if pressed."

The Halfling melted away and up floated the image of a large, muscular man that from the waist down had the body of a great fish with bright, hard scales.

"Mer-people. These are a wondrous creation. They can live up to three hundred years, and they live underwater with the fishes. Their whole purpose is to keep sea monsters in check, and so they are quite adept warriors, though, some groupings of mer-folk have been known to prey upon human ships or coastal settlements as well. They were originally created in Terra's Pool, which is a sea-like lake in the center of Prirodha. However, they have spread far and wide throughout the oceans in an attempt to claim all of the waters for our mother, Terra."

The merman dropped down to disappear into the water and up galloped several large horses that were half man. Each of them carried large weapons. One carried a great halberd, another a claymore, and the third wielded a mighty bow. Their images continued to gallop in place as if they were running down an enemy before Aparen.

"Centaurs are a special creature with the speed and agility of a horse and the upper body like a man's. They can live for as long as three hundred years, and they make fearsome warriors on the field of battle. They have nearly inexhaustible stamina and their speed is unmatched by even the best horses. Most of them disdain humans so much that they will kill any human upon sight. The centaur is a wise race, and does not identify with the greed and pettiness the humans are prone to. They also see human cities as blights upon the land that should be cleared away for Terramyr's health and continued prosperity."

The centaurs turned, galloping off into the distance as their images shrank away. Njar snapped his fingers and there appeared an exact replica of himself in the mist above them.

"You have already met quite a few satyrs. As you have come to understand, we do not seek to fight openly with other races. Many of us live in seclusion as we seek for balance and wisdom. Those of us who venture out into the world usually become merchants and traders. We can be quite shrewd when it comes to negotiations. We live for three hundred years on average, though there are a few of our kind that have lived as long as one thousand years."

"How old are you?" Aparen asked.

Njar grunted, but he said nothing.

The image above them mutated with a terrible roar. Its legs thickened and the arms grew muscles to shame any human warrior. The head flattened and then broadened, taking on the appearance of a bull. The image was several times larger than the satyr once it had finished shifting. In some respects, it was much larger than the centaurs that Aparen had seen.

"Minotaurs are not the abominable offspring of some deranged queen, as some tales might suggest," Njar said. "They were created by Terramyr as well. They are the strong guardians. They guard all of the most sacred places. As such, they don't usually venture far from their homelands. To do so would weaken their positions. When they are met on a battlefield, there is little hope for any who oppose them. They have even been known to put down rogue dragons. That being said, there have been some tribes that have broken off from their homeland in an effort to conquer nearby lands. When they do, it is a horribly costly campaign."

The minotaur flexed its muscles and bellowed out a mighty roar before fading away. The mists again began to take shape, but the next image was not anything Aparen might have expected. At first he thought it might be human, but then it grew too tall and the arms hung low below the waistline. Then, shaggy fur grew out over the body and the being had a lumbering gait as it walked around the air above them. It made short grunting noises and constantly looked over its own shoulder. It hissed once, revealing a mouth full of jagged teeth.

"What is that?" Aparen asked.

"This is the elusive, highly fabled, Yeti. I would explain their existence by calling them the forward scouts of the Natural Races. They inhabit the snow covered peaks throughout the world, though vastly more so within Prirodha. They attack exploration parties in order to prevent them from ever reaching the fortified settlements that the centaur and minotaur civilizations have made. Not much is known about the Yeti, even among the other Natural Races, other than they can be highly unpredictable. Like the pixies, they can become an extremely savage and bloodthirsty creature."

The image faded away and the globe returned, spinning slowly before them over the waters.

Aparen watched the globe and understood why Njar had brought him here. "In Kuldiga Academy, they never focus on geography." He pointed to the globe. "We never hear of the other continents, or the large oceans that I see here."

"Why is that?" Njar asked. His tone showed that he was not so much without understanding as he was helping Aparen come to the knowledge for himself.

Aparen pushed himself up to his elbows, propping his upper body and craning his neck around awkwardly to regard Njar. "We are on the covered continent, aren't we? The Middle Kingdom, and all the lands around it are hidden somewhere under that shroud."

Njar nodded. "The Ancients came here to form a protection. They have already lost their home world, and they know the risk posed to this one."

"So they formed the dwarves of Roegudok Hall to help them," Aparen guessed.

Njar nodded again. "In those days it was only the Natural Races, those of us created by Terramyr, and the Ancients and dwarves. It was a fairly peaceful time. Certainly there was mischief on occasion, but most understood that all of us had the same goals. Then, as eras passed, the orcs found this land. They were pushed out of other lands, hunted and driven out by the humans and elves from nearly every land they had possessed. The orcs found a way in through the mountainous barriers and then started making a home in the lands now called the Middle Kingdom."

"Why not push the orcs out?" Aparen asked.

"There were struggles," Njar replied. "But the orcs created mighty fortresses and strongholds. They even brought down dragons with their ferocity. Their strength pushed us out. It wasn't until the humans and elves found their way to the continent that the orcs were finally kept in check. Even then, all the humans could do was push them south. There was no full victory over the orcs."

"And then the Ancients created a pact with the humans," Aparen stated.

Njar sighed. "Humans had existed on the Ancients' home world as well," he said. "They had proven to be a great scourge that accelerated the end of their world. The Ancients thought it wise to court the humans that came to the Middle Kingdom, to try to guide them in better ways."

Njar halted the globe on the shrouded continent and whispered its name. "Terra's Navel." The clouds dispersed from part of the continent, just enough to show them the Middle Kingdom, the mountains to the east that separated them from the wilds where the Tarthuns roamed, the seas to the west, with the islands that Aparen had crossed, and the orcish lands to the south. "This land is more important than some war for territory," Njar said. "Everything that happens here has an effect on the rest of the world. To corrupt this land is to bring corruption to Terramyr. To purify it, is to cleanse the world."

Aparen pointed to the clouds. "Why not show me the whole of the continent?"

Njar shook his head. "I seek balance. To show you everything would tempt you beyond what is necessary to achieve balance. I show you this only so that you know why the events that unfold here are so important. Should Tu'luh be allowed to conquer the Middle Kingdom with his horrible magic, he could easily spread that influence over the entire globe. Countless peoples and nations will be subdued, and brought under his despotic rule. He would decide all matters of life." Njar sighed again. "Terramyr would be imprisoned by the magic as well, unable to live freely, as she ought to. Her life force would be under the dragon's chains." He turned to look at Aparen. "This is about so much more than one kingdom, or even all of the people and creatures in the Middle Kingdom. To lose this war is to die and lose the balance that lets us truly live. Life would be as a garden without the seasons. No renewal, no blossoms, only death and an eternal winter of decay."

"I have a question for you," Aparen said.

"Ask it," Njar replied.

"After the war is over, what would you have me do?" He shifted his body and moved to sit up. The globe dissipated and the mists fell back to the green waters below in the pool. "You offer me additional power, and have given me training, but I wonder what will happen once you have attained your goal."

"You still do not trust me," Njar said softly. "I can understand that. Your path into magic was not your choice, nor was it an easy ascension." Njar leveraged his staff to push himself into a standing position. "I cannot make the choice for you. Know only that no one controls you here. You are free to think for yourself. You are also free to observe me. I know that trust may not come as easy as that, but search your heart. You will see the truth of it if you meditate on it."

"That doesn't answer my question," Aparen said.

Njar smiled ever so slightly. "My greatest wish is for you to help restore balance. Use your powers to wipe this blight from the Middle Kingdom. If you can do that, without succumbing to the temptation of power, then I wish for you to find joy in your life."

"Where would I find that?" Aparen asked. He pulled his knees in close to his chest and stared out over the water. "My family is destroyed. *I* will no longer be a noble even if I do help fight against the dragon. There is nothing for me there."

Njar stretched his staff out to the water one more time. The mists rose up and formed into a lovely figure with long, flowing hair. It didn't take long for Aparen to recognize Silvi's shape. "There is still joy to be had, young apprentice," Njar said. "Perhaps you will not be able to remain upon Terra's Navel, but if you so choose, I know of a few routes out from this land. I could help you start anew somewhere else. With your magical skills, you could be anything you wish."

Aparen stared at the figure.

Njar laughed silently to himself and left the boy on the bank of the pool to think.

CHAPTER SIX

Lepkin stood in the drawing room at Tillamon's home. The town's guard was out scouting the nearby fields while the soldiers who had escaped with Lepkin were busy preparing lookout towers and building fences and barriers. Lepkin stared at the map before him. Stonebrook was not a large city by any means, but the terrain could be used to their advantage. A mile to the south of the settlement was the long waterway for which the town was named. The brook wasn't very deep in terms of water, but it was nestled at the base of a twenty foot chasm that spanned thirty feet across at its widest point and more than fifteen feet at its narrowest. The water flowed in a winding path from east to west for miles.

Walls, pickets, and towers were being built along the northern side of this chasm. The bridge that led out from the town and over the brook was seemingly left intact, but the supports had been sawn mostly through so that any significant weight would cause it to crumble into the chasm.

If Lepkin could defend the position until winter fell, then there was a much better chance that King Mathias could rally enough forces to push the orcs back down south of Ten Forts come spring. Still, without additional support there wasn't any obvious way to hold the settlement and keep the orcs from continuing north. Lepkin knew the townsfolk were just as busy as the soldiers. The men were either digging additional trenches, placing caltrops along the southern fields, or harvesting anything and everything that was ready to be stored in the cellars for winter. Some of the townsfolk had opted to flee north for refuge. The next obvious point would be Axestone. The waterway there was more formidable than the paltry creek to the south of Stonebrook. Not to mention Fort Drake was only a few miles to the north of Axestone.

Many of the officers had begged Lepkin to raze Stonebrook and fall back to Axestone for exactly those reasons, but he had refused. That would be giving the orcs more ground. He was not about to let the pig-faced savages stomp that far into the Middle

Kingdom.

Lepkin was going to make his stand in Stonebrook.

The few dragon-slayers who remained never wavered in their support for him. They were out there, right now, shouting Lepkin's praises and spurring the men to work harder to prepare the field. Without them, many soldiers would have undoubtedly fled.

Even still, some of the men had deserted. That much was obvious. Lepkin had slightly less than four thousand men left from Ten Forts. This including a mob of one hundred and fifty angry dwarves. The town guard added only another ten to that number. They were not entirely useless, however. Lepkin used the guards as scouts, and as liaisons with the local populace so as to make any martial law seem softer and more palatable. He wasn't sure the device worked, but he didn't see any obvious signs that it *wasn't*, so he continued.

For a moment, as he considered the situation he now found himself in, he wondered if this was anything like what King Mathias did from day to day. He knew it probably wasn't *much* like sitting on a throne, at least not during times of peace, but still he thanked the Old Gods that he had not been given the crown.

The door to the drawing room burst open and in came a heavily panting soldier, ripping Lepkin from his thoughts. Lepkin looked up and frowned sourly.

"I sent you northward for help yesterday, before the refugees left the town. How can you be back already?"

The soldier smiled. "Because help is already on the way."

Lepkin's brow drew in together and then his eyes went wide and his facial muscles relaxed momentarily before stretching into a smile. "All!" he exclaimed.

The soldier nodded. "King Sit'marihu rides along with his escort at the front of many soldiers. The commander of Fort Drake has come as well. I galloped ahead as fast as I could to deliver the news. They should be here by nightfall."

Lepkin slapped a palm onto the map and let out a short grunt of satisfaction. "That is the best news I have heard in a long time. How many are there?"

The soldier grinned and nodded eagerly. "There are five thousand recruits in all. Some of the Masters from Kuldiga Academy have joined in with them, though from what I was told most of the Masters have either returned to their own homes, or been assigned by King Mathias to other places. There are five thousand soldiers coming from fort drake. There are three thousand pikemen, and two thousand swordsmen."

"Recruits, did you say?" Lepkin asked.

The soldier nodded. "King Sit'marihu said that all of the veterans had already been transferred to other locations. The Tarthuns are pressing hard along the north eastern plain and Grand Master Penthal needed reinforcements."

Lepkin nodded. "Recruits are better than no help at all." He paused and looked down to the map for a moment. Then he looked back to the messenger. "You didn't mention any archers. Do we have any bows coming?"

The messenger's smile faded. "No, just pikes and swords."

Lepkin folded his arms and focused on the map. "Bows would have been useful," he said as he eyed the blue line that marked the location of the brook. In an instant, he solved the problem. "Go out and call the dwarves to me, now."

The messenger nodded and rushed out from the drawing room.

No sooner did the young man leave than Virgil Gothbern entered in. "Calling the dwarves in?" he asked. "I had them quarrying rock."

Lepkin nodded. "That will still come in handy. Listen, we have reinforcements coming, but no bows. I will need the dwarves to make catapults."

Virgil approached the map and looked down. "How many do we need?"

"As many as we can fashion before the orcs arrive," Lepkin countered.

Virgil shook his head. "Each catapult will need stones to throw, otherwise the effort is wasted.

Lepkin pointed to several places along the brook on the map. "If we can position catapults along the brook, we can keep the orcish archers at bay while we defend the line."

"The orcs will see the catapults," Virgil countered. "Unless we can camouflage them, I don't think the orcs will march up and ask us to rain stones on them."

Lepkin sighed. "We could position them behind haystacks,"

Lepkin offered. "It isn't a lot of cover, but we can't very well hide them in the bushes either."

Virgil snapped his fingers, "What about blankets?" he asked. "What if the women in the town made large blankets and dyed them to look like haystacks?" We could then throw straw over the blankets. Up close it would be obvious, but from far away it might not seem so out of place, especially since we have just newly erected towers and pickets."

Lepkin smiled and arched a brow. "That might work, for now. We'll start with that. I will also send for Marlin. Perhaps if my wife has recovered, then Marlin can come and use his magic to help us better hide the machines."

"Have you heard from them?" Virgil asked. His tone took on a friendly, sincere quality not found often among officers.

Lepkin nodded. "I have. The communications have been brief, but enough to know that she is beginning to mend, and they are both safe."

Virgil smiled. "That is good." The strong man pointed back down to the map. "How many catapults and blankets should we make?"

Lepkin shrugged. "We need at least ten if we are to make a dent in the enemy. Each catapult requires a crew of five to operate."

"Three to load, two to pull the bucket and then release," Virgil said. "Then there are the stones. If each catapult is to be effective, we will need many stones."

Lepkin said, "Each catapult crew can fire a stone roughly every three to four minutes. If the average engagement lasts forty minutes, then we will need ten stones per catapult per engagement."

"The quarry is on the north side of the brook, but it is set back about a mile, and out to the west a bit. It will take a long time to bring in fresh stone."

"So have the dwarves fashion the ten catapults. Afterward, they are to place twenty stones at each machine. This will give us what we need in the short term. Then, the hundred dwarves not operating catapults will fashion carts that the cavedogs can pull and form a supply line from the quarry to each catapult."

Virgil nodded. "If we ran two or three carts per machine, we could keep a steady enough supply coming in for ammunition. Any dwarf not operating a cart or catapult can then be put to work mining stone."

Lepkin nodded and then snapped his fingers. "See to it."

Virgil looked surprised. "But you just called for the dwarves to return here," he said.

Lepkin rubbed his face and took in a breath. "It's alright, just go out and put them to work. I trust you to convey the orders properly."

Virgil cocked his head to the side. "When was the last time you got any sleep?"

Lepkin waved him off.

"A commander needs sleep. The muscles feed on food, but the brain dines on sleep."

Lepkin scoffed. "I'm fine. Just go."

Virgil pointed to the sofa in the drawing room. "Just take a few minutes. If anything happens, I will personally come to wake you. We are preparing the field, and I will set the dwarves to the catapults. There is nothing else for you to do at this juncture, so get some rest." The dragon-slayer stared at Lepkin until Master Lepkin finally surrendered to the request and dropped back onto the sofa.

Even the mighty Lepkin had to admit how nice it felt to have a cushion under his rump and a sturdy yet soft rest for his back. He leaned his head back and barely heard Virgil's exiting footsteps before his eyes fell closed and his body gave in to sleep.

*****

Al led Commander Nials to Tillamon's home. The bulk of the soldiers continued on to the fields just south of the settlement and began erecting tents. Commander Nials and Al entered the large home and found a pair of soldiers standing inside.

"Lepkin is asleep," one of them said.

"Asleep?" Commander Nials huffed. "What kind of commander sleeps before sundown?"

A large man with ridged and spike plate mail entered the entryway from a side chamber. "The kind of commander who hasn't slept for days because he has been beating orcs to a bloody pulp," the soldier said.

"Commander Nials, may I introduce Virgil Gothbern," Al said with a smirk. "I'll let the two of you get acquainted while I go and speak with Master Lepkin."

Commander Nials wrinkled his nose and gestured with his hand for Al to move along.

Al chuckled to himself. "In the drawing room, is he?"

Virgil nodded. "The map is on the table. I hope you won't mind, but he has put your dwarves to work."

Al smirked again. "My kin can do any task he sets before them." He walked quickly toward the drawing room. His legs were a bit stiff from riding, causing him to nearly waddle as he moved along the hall. He found the door to the drawing room nearly closed. He pushed it open and moved in to see Lepkin splayed over the back of the couch. He wasn't quite snoring, but he was certainly breathing loudly thanks to his awkward position.

The dwarf king pushed the door nearly closed and then walked to the table. He studied the terrain of the map, and quickly understood Lepkin's hand-drawn symbols. "Catapults, fences, and trenches," the dwarf commented as he ran his finger along the map. "It's a start," he added with an approving nod. Al turned around to wake Lepkin, but found that the man was already staring at him from the couch.

"Ever the light sleeper," Al commented.

"It's a skill that has kept me alive," Lepkin replied.

Al nodded and moved to sit on the opposite side of the sofa. "I heard about Ten Forts, and Mercer. I am sorry."

Lepkin sighed and leaned forward, rubbing his eyes and then slapping his hands atop his knees. "Mercer died well, just as he would have wanted," Lepkin said. "Peren is gone, vanished from the battle field. He fought well, but no one has seen him since before the forts fell."

"Lady Arkyn?" Al asked.

"She is out along the perimeter, scouting for orcs."

"I noticed a thick haze to the south," Al said. "Did you use your dragon form to burn the forest?"

Lepkin shook his head. "We scorched the forest the old fashioned way."

Al's face turned sour. "I see."

"It was the only way to seal off our retreat. We were being

pursued constantly."

Al raised a hand. "I understand. I am not new to the devices of war. I just don't like seeing trees go to waste."

"Ironic, for a dwarf who spends his life underground," Lepkin replied with a half-smile.

"Except this dwarf didn't spend his life in the dark," Al reminded him. "I ran a blacksmith shop, in Buktah. That's all I wanted out of life, and I lived it well." His eyes lost their focus and his face grew long and sad. "I guess there isn't any use thinking about going back there now."

"I suppose not," Lepkin said.

"My apprentice died defending us," Al put in. "The Blacktongues found me and the boy, back when he was stuck in your body."

Lepkin nodded. Al had already mentioned that shortly after Lepkin had woken from his coma, but Lepkin didn't stop the dwarf from talking about it now.

"He was a good lad," Al said. A half smile flashed across his face. "A good man, I mean," he corrected. He slapped a hand to his face and leaned back into the sofa. "It's the quiet ones who surprise us the most, I think. No one would have called him a warrior by any means. He was a blacksmith. He had never known anything other than that his whole life. He was good at it too. He could have made a great smith. Still, never would have dreamed he would be the one to come out fighting against the Blacktongues." Water welled up in his eyes and he turned away from Lepkin.

"I'm sorry," Lepkin said.

Al nodded and wiped the tears from his face. "Me too," he said. "War is an ugly game, isn't it? It wasn't bad enough that we were fighting off warlocks who wanted to make us slaves, but now we have orcs trying to kick in our doors and take everything from us."

"They see it as their home," Lepkin said. "At least, that is what I choose to believe. Otherwise they are just monsters, blinded by their lust for blood and conquest."

Al shook a finger at Lepkin. "That is all they are! They didn't live here first, the dwarves did. They came and ruined everything. They stole what they could and killed whatever crossed their path. They aren't retaking their homeland, which is thousands of miles away on a continent covered in darkness. They should all go out to the sea and jump in, do us all a favor."

Lepkin nodded. "Well, I don't think we are going to be so lucky."

Al slapped his left hand to his knee and then pointed at the map. "And that is why I have taken a look at the map. I plan on sending those dogs down to Hammenfein as soon as they arrive here. They want to rule in Hell, and I am happy to send them there."

Lepkin rose and moved to the map. "I assume you saw the positions I had marked already?"

Al nodded, but he didn't get up. He didn't need to. He had memorized the map in its entirety. "I am sure your messenger told you, but I have a number of spears we can put at a few locations. There is a narrow spot in the chasm if you look about two miles east of the axis due south from Stonebrook. We could assign some there."

"I have a catapult there, so they can help defend it," Lepkin said.

"Yes, I noted. But why only ten?" Al asked.

"I wasn't sure when, or if, we would have support."

Al grumbled something about tall-folk that Lepkin couldn't quite hear before jumping off the sofa and coming over to the map. "We can divert some of the recruits we brought. I assume you have assigned dwarves to mine the stone?"

Lepkin nodded.

"And then what, have you tasked them with building carts to carry the stone for the catapults?"

Again, Lepkin nodded.

Al grumbled. "Thought you would." He jabbed a finger in Lepkin's side and then seized the pencil from the table. "Don't waste dwarves driving carts that any fool with two hands could do. Reassign the dwarves to create more catapults. I'll mark the best locations here, here, and here. Place two more in each of those three spots. Then, place one catapult here, here, and another here and here." Al stepped back and smiled. "There, I just doubled our fire power, and they are placed at the most advantageous positions. I'd like to see the orcs bring their bows within range to cover any of their footmen. It will be a slaughterhouse filled with orcish brutes!"

Lepkin smiled and held up a finger. "For the first skirmish, we want to bring them in close," he said.

Al screwed up his face and shook his head. "No we don't. We want to send them running as fast as possible."

"Hear me out," Lepkin implored. "We are in the process of designing camouflage for the catapults. We don't have the time to completely disguise them, but enough that we can lure the orcs in just close enough that running away will be difficult. The last thing I want them to do is spot our catapults from afar and skirt around the brook and come at us from behind."

Al shook his head again. "No, the worst thing would be if they bypassed us altogether."

"They need food," Lepkin said. "Winter is coming on soon and they will want to raid what they can in order to dig in. They will not want to fall back."

"Unless they dig in at Ten Forts," Al said.

"It's possible, but if they do that, then we can dig in here as well. The more time we have, the better off we will be."

Al growled. "And they know that too," he put in. "So they will come soon."

Lepkin gestured to the forest marked on the map. "I would wager that as soon as the forest is calm again, they will come north."

"Well then, I suppose it is time for me to find a pickaxe," Al said. "I should help my kin."

Lepkin placed a strong hand on Al's shoulder. "Do we have good men with us?" he asked.

Al nodded. "Commander Nials appears to understand what is going on here. He was reluctant at first, but he agreed to come here even though it disobeyed orders. He sent a messenger to Drakei Glazei of course, but he could still lose his job over this."

Lepkin shook his head. "King Mathias will see the wisdom in it. You can't ignore an invasion by the orcs. To do so is to commit suicide."

"The officers appear solid as well," Al put in. "I made an effort to study them on the march down here. I think we have as good of men as we could hope for." He smiled again and then pulled away. "I will rejoin with my kin and get the new catapults underway. You should go back to sleep. I'll tell Commander Nials to wait until tomorrow to call upon you."

Lepkin shook his head. "That wouldn't be right. Send him in at his earliest convenience. He has brought reinforcements, after all."

Al smiled the sly grin of his. "I know, I just thought it would be funny to see the look on his face, that's all. I'll send him in."

*****

Lady Arkyn sat in the tall, yellow grasses fifty yards north of the scorched earth and the burnt skeletons of the once mighty forest. The wind flew toward the northeast, bringing with it the smell of ash, and the unyielding heat from the stubborn embers and fires that still burned. In the last day, the smoke had thinned. Where before it was a black, dense wall of billowing heat and death, now there was only a gray haze along the ground highlighted by red and orange undertones. Ash and bits of burning wood flew up into the air only to fall several yards away from the forest. Every now and again a small fire would ignite in the grasses nearby. She didn't let it bother her, though. She had enough magic to cool the area around her and keep her spot unharmed.

Her eyes scoured the smoke and heat waves, looking for any sign of forward scouts. Most of the animals had already fled from the forest long ago when the blaze first began, but occasionally she still saw the odd hare or deer making its way out of the forest, or crossing from east to west in front of her. She marveled that even when they did come straight from the forest, they had no significant wounds upon their bodies. Singed fur and small blights, to be sure, but nothing severe. It was as if the animals had found places of refuge inside the blaze instinctively. Or, perhaps they had a magic all of their own. She liked to think that they did. It seemed to balance the laws of nature in her mind if she thought of animals that way, instead of simply as creatures of instinct and habit.

A long stem bent low in the wind and tickled her face. She pushed it away gently and then raised a bit of bread to her mouth and took a bite. She chewed the dry, stale morsel and then put the rest back into a small satchel that hung from her belt.

She sat there until well after sunset. Darkness fell over the land like a blanket, but it could not smother the lights from the fires. The orange and red spots played out their dance as the haze and smoke above blotted out the stars. Still she watched.

Nothing happened until shortly before dawn. It was faint at first, a movement that could have been nothing more than the shifting wind blowing a wisp of smoke between the burnt trunks in the forest. Her gut twisted with that primal fear and anger that only comes before a fight. She stroked a left hand over her bow. She was far south of the chasm and the brook, so waiting a bit would not endanger anyone else. So she let the stranger come closer.

A few minutes later she spied a second scout. She smiled. Orcs always worked in pairs when scouting, she knew. Now that she had found the second, she would be able to engage at will. An arrow flew and the second orc caught it in the eye. His body fell instantly, throwing ash and embers out around him. The first orc turned to run, but an arrow through the back of his left knee dropped him to the ground.

Lady Arkyn was up in a moment and sprinting across the blackened ground. She leapt atop the first orc and slammed her right elbow into the back of the orc's neck. A second blow with the handle of her dagger put the orc out cold. She seized the orc's sword and tossed it aside. She undid the orc's leather belt and then looped it around his elbows behind his back as tightly as possible. The orc's greenish skin stretched and turned white against the belt.

The she-elf moved along to the second orc. Her arrow was too far embedded into the orc's skull to be successfully removed. She reached under the corpse's armpits and dragged it to a pile of lumber that was still burning and then threw him into it. Any who found him would be left to assume he tripped into a fire. Unsatisfied with how the body looked haphazardly cast into the fire, she went to the nearest burnt tree and pushed it over on top. Now it looked like a burning tree had fallen onto him. That was better.

She went back to the first orc and slapped his cheeks.

The orc groaned.

She rolled him over with a push of her foot.

"How many orcs are with you?" Lady Arkyn asked.

The orc glared at her with burning eyes. "Foggd be!" the orc shouted.

Lady Arkyn reached down and ripped the arrow from the orc's knee. The orc grunted, but he did not overtly show his pain nor cry out. "How many orcs are there?" she pressed.

"Foggd be!"

Lady Arkyn sighed impatiently and pulled her dagger. She knelt down and placed the blade against the orc's neck. "Last chance," she said.

"Csinalja!" the orc shouted.

It was useless. Either the orc couldn't speak Common Tongue, or he was far too proud to fear for his life. Lady Arkyn ended the interrogation and then dragged his body to a ditch some three hundred yards away. She dropped the orc's body down atop seven other orc corpses.

"Stubborn pigs," she spat as she looked down upon all her other failed attempts to interrogate the forward scouts. She knew that soon the orcs would cease sending scouts. Soon they would march north in force. Until then, she was going to go back and sit in her spot in the grass.

*****

"Why don't they fight back?" Maernok asked as he swirled the ale inside his pewter mug.

Salarion pulled her left boot free of her foot and dumped the pesky pebble that had been bothering her onto the wooden floor. "They are afraid," she explained.

"Afraid?" Maernok echoed sarcastically. "I count seven men in the street right now and only two of the governor's soldiers. They should fight and keep their children safe rather than let them be taken to be sacrificed."

Maernok watched as yet another teenage daughter was loaded into a cart. Her hands were bound with leather strips. One guard moved to the front of the horse-drawn cart while the second secured the newest prisoner to the cart via a chain. "An orc would never be paralyzed by fear."

"Pinkt'Hu has been losing people for weeks now," Salarion stated dryly. "It was quiet at first. Then the governor moved on to accusing people of false crimes. Soon the ruse was abandoned altogether. Now, anyone who fights back is killed in the streets, their body either left to rot or hung from the nearest balcony for all to see."

"If they cannot fight, they should leave," Maernok said simply.

Salarion laughed and slid her boot back onto her foot. "Some have. Most can't. The Middle Kingdom was at war before the orcs came to Ten Forts. There aren't any cities that are unaffected by it. The lone traveler is doomed to certain death. Those who had money purchased their way out with merchant ships, but the rest are here, trying to keep their heads low and their children hidden."

"There is no honor to be found among them."

Salarion stood and moved to the window. "That is not entirely true," she said. "Would a wolf assume that a fish is without honor because it does not fight the bear?"

Maernok cast a glare at her. "Weak as the humans might be, they are not fish."

"Fear is a powerful oppressor," Salarion said. "Some are brave and fight back, but humans are easier to frighten than embolden. They are oppressed by shackles they place upon their own minds and hearts."

"And that is why they have no honor."

Salarion sighed. She turned to say something but Maernok cut her off.

"Orcs are born cursed. Before a baby orc takes its first breath, it is predestined to spend an eternity in the flames of Hammenfein. Such is our fate as assigned by the Old Gods of the humans. Yet, despite this, we fight. We raise our young to embrace honor and glory."

"That is because you are beyond hope," Salarion said. "And that is your blessing, not your curse. For the humans still hold on to hope, and it is that hope that strengthens their fear and holds them down. They know they should have hope, so when it is taken from them they are paralyzed, afraid of losing it entirely."

Maernok finished his ale and set the mug down upon the windowsill. "Then why not kill the governor and disrupt Gilifan's dastardly deeds here?"

Salarion nodded. "I have thought of the same thing, but it would not work just yet. We must wait until Tu'luh is bound to the new dragon."

"Why?" Maernok asked.

"While Tu'luh is a spirit, he will be able to sense our presence if we get too close. If we were to assassinate the governor, Gilifan would likely send Tu'luh out to find us. Better to wait."

"We will watch while people are led to slaughter?"

"What difference does it make to you? They are only humans, as you put it."

Maernok shook his head. "I only warred with the humans in order to earn the right to kill Gilifan. I see no honor in merciless killing. These people have not the strength to raise up swords in their own defense."

"An orc with a conscience?" Salarion teased. She moved to sit upon the bed. "How interesting."

Maernok eyed her from head to toe and then went to sit by the table in the room. "When Tu'luh is joined with the new egg, what is the plan?"

"What do you know of Nagar's Secret?" Salarion asked.

Maernok shrugged. "Never heard of it."

Salarion sighed and curled her legs up under her slender body. "To make it simple, it is a spell created by my father and Tu'luh. It is designed to bind the hearts and souls of every living creature so that they can be controlled. This is the power that Gilifan seeks. No one is immune to the spell."

"Then we should strike before he can use it," Maernok said quickly. "Even if Tu'luh's spirit is watching, if both of us go in then one of us can get to the wizard before it is too late."

Salarion shook her head. "It isn't that simple," she said. "To infiltrate the underground fortress I will need to use powerful magic to disguise us both. Using my magic will draw his attention. The only way is to wait until Tu'luh has been rejoined with the new hatchling. As for Gilifan, he will sense me when I approach, even if I use a disguise. He put a marker upon me the last time we met."

"If you already met with him, why didn't you kill him?"

"It's complicated," Salarion started. "But, I need Gilifan to use the spell in order for Nagar's Secret to be destroyed."

"You would let him enslave everyone?"

Salarion shook her head emphatically. "I altered the spell in a way that he will not detect. It will affect the spell's range and limit it to just a few square miles from wherever the magic is used. Then, after the first use, its range will diminish to only twenty or thirty yards."

"How could you do such a thing without him noticing?"

Salarion sneered slyly. "I am a dark elf, and the book is written in my language. I altered a couple of words, and that is all it takes. Then, once he uses it and it is discovered that the range has been limited, he will have no choice but to transfer the power to some sort of object like a staff or an amulet."

"So instead of being able to hide with the book in a far off mountain, you would force him to come out with the magic, thereby giving the humans a chance to take the amulet or staff and destroy it."

"Precisely," Salarion confirmed. "Otherwise the whole of the Middle Kingdom, the Eastern Wilds, and the orcish lands would be enslaved within the blink of an eye. I did something similar when my father first used the spell some centuries ago, but I did not hamper it enough. He was still able to use it from a great distance, and many battles were fought before the book was finally taken away from him."

"Still," Maernok pressed. "Why not gather an army to here and fight?"

Salarion shook her head. "If we alert Gilifan to our presence, or force him to run away as an army chases him, he will have more time to inspect the book. He needs Tu'luh to use the spell, but he could study the book in the meantime and discover my tampering."

"But we could destroy the egg too, and then there would be no more dragons."

Salarion folded her arms impatiently and shook her head. "Gilifan is able to lengthen his own life force, and he would either find a way to resurrect Tu'luh, or he would scour the world searching for a new host. Imagine if he traveled across the oceans and disappeared. How would we stop him then?"

"You are not very different from him," Maernok said after a moment. "You are willing to sacrifice all the people in Pinkt'Hu just the same as he is."

"I do it to save many more souls, whereas he does it to enslave them all," Salarion countered.

"The blood is still upon your hands," Maernok said. "How can you justify such a slaughter? It is not honorable."

"I am Sierri'Tai," she said curtly. "I am willing to do what it takes because I see the vast chasm of destruction that will engulf the world if I do not follow through with my plan. I will stop Gilifan, and I will break Tu'luh's power, but to do that requires sacrifice. Gilifan must be allowed to use the magic as quickly as possible so as to prevent him from discovering my manipulation. Then, as soon as he has Tu'luh resurrected we will strike."

Maernok shook his head. "But if none are immune, then we will be swallowed by the spell."

Salarion shook her head. "I have a charm that will render you immune to the spell," she said.

"Me?" Maernok asked skeptically. "What about you?"

Salarion frowned. "I do not have the strength to defeat Gilifan. I can use my magic to disguise us, and I will fight beside you for as long as possible, but it is you who must destroy the wizard."

"Why not use the charm yourself?"

"Gilifan is as wise as a serpent," Salarion said. "Long ago he put a mark upon me. He always suspected it was I who was responsible for my father's fall, but he could not prove it. Furthermore, he needed my help. So, we made a pact. I promised never to slay him by my own hand or by means of my magic, and he promised the same toward me. He thought he had the upper hand, of course, because he knew that I am not immune to my father's spell. He knows that in the end I will be turned by the curse." Salarion looked up to Maernok with her sparkling, violet eyes and smiled faintly. "When he uses the spell, then you must kill me. After that you will be on your own. For a time after using the spell, Gilifan and Tu'luh will both be weakened. If you can fight your way through the remaining mercenaries, then you should be able to defeat the wizard."

"If you altered the spell's range, you could escape," Maernok pointed out.

"Then who would disguise you and get you into the cave?" Salarion asked. "I am Sierri'Tai. I do what is necessary to achieve my goal."

Maernok nodded and the two sat in silence for a while. Then, as he let the thoughts sink in he gave one final question. "How do I destroy the magic once it has been transferred?"

Salarion smiled. "That is not easily done," she said. "The item must be given to the Champion of Truth. Only he will know how to destroy the magic."

"Who is that?"

Salarion laughed. "A boy," she said. "He is far in the east even now, preparing for the event. If you get the magical relic, make haste to the eastern wilds."

She didn't bother to tell the orc that he would also most likely die in the underground cavern. He was a seasoned warrior. Surely he already knew the odds were against them.

Maernok smiled and nodded as if he could read Salarion's thoughts.

"I accept your plan. It will be a good fight," he said.

CHAPTER SEVEN

Lepkin looked through the spy glass toward the south. The cool, late autumn breeze ran over his knuckles and frosted his breath.

"Can you see them?" Lady Arkyn asked.

Lepkin nodded grimly. "Just as you said. It appears they have brought their entire army north."

Commander Nials held out his hand expectantly. Lepkin gave him the spy glass. "Mhm, that is a nasty looking bunch of brutes."

"We are ready for them," Al put in quickly. "Thanks to your fire barrier we have had enough time to construct thirty catapults, instead of the twenty we had planned on. We have enough stone for several engagements piled behind each one and we have wool blankets topped with dirt and straw to camouflage everything. Let them come up."

Lady Arkyn cleared her throat.

Al blushed slightly. "And thanks to your arrows no orcish scouts discovered our secrets."

Lady Arkyn offered a smile.

Al rolled his eyes and turned for the ladder to climb down from the tower. "I will command the dwarves. We'll keep those dunderheads from crossing the chasm."

Nials turned and held a red cloth over the balcony. An officer down below signaled back and then ran down the line. Commander Nials turned back to Lepkin then and smiled. "It will be an honor to see the great Master Lepkin wield his mighty flaming sword."

Lepkin cocked his head to the side a bit and folded his arms. "I gave the sword to the Champion of Truth."

Nials frowned slightly and glanced down to the sword hanging from Lepkin's waist. "Well, I am sure you will manage in any case."

"In Mercer's absence, I have become the ranking officer for the men of Ten Forts," Lepkin explained.

Nials nodded and patted Lepkin on the shoulder. "Heroes belong on the field, not in towers. Leave the strategy to me."

Before Lepkin could reply Nials gestured out to the men below on the field. "We can't win this war if we are split betwixt three commanders. Let King Sit'marihu run the catapults with his dwarves, and I will command the men. You are a great warrior, but you are no general."

Lepkin bristled. Still, he knew that Nials was right. Lepkin could only muster a semi-polite nod before turning away. He stopped just before descending the ladder and looked back to Nials. The large commander was already turning back to face the oncoming orcs. "Commander Nials," Lepkin began. The man turned back to regard Lepkin.

"Yes, Master Lepkin?"

"I will take the remaining dragon-slayers along with Lady Arkyn. You can command the others, but I will be more useful if I have autonomy."

Commander Nials drew his bottom lip up and narrowed his eyes as he considered the notion. Finally he nodded. "I would expect nothing less," he said.

"Additionally, I will be in charge of Lady Dimwater and Marlin when they arrive."

"As you wish. Now, if you will excuse me, I have a field to command."

Lepkin nodded and descended the ladder.

He made his way back toward a smoldering fire pit nearby and spied Virgil Gothbern. The dragon slayer saw Lepkin approaching and rose to meet him.

"What are your orders?"

"How many dragon slayers do we have left?"

"We have four," Virgil said. "Except Jubal is still recovering from the wound that the orc gave him. So, we have three that are able-bodied, including myself. Eriem and Aelron have positioned themselves near the old bridge."

"Let's go," Lepkin said. "Do you know where Lady Arkyn is?"

Virgil nodded and pointed out behind Lepkin. Master Lepkin turned to see Lady Arkyn jogging toward them, her bow in hand and her quiver empty. "Where are we going?" Virgil asked.

Lepkin turned and sneered. "We are going to hunt officers."

Virgil shrugged and nodded. "Sounds pleasant."

The two waited for Lady Arkyn to reach them. Her golden

hair was kept in a neat braid that bounced with her steps. Her brown trousers showed smudges of dirt and blood and her wool top was torn on the side, revealing just a hint of her toned stomach as she ran.

"Take a few on your way back, did you?" Lepkin asked noting her quiver.

Lady Arkyn nodded. "A few forward scouts," she confirmed.

"Refill your quiver, and maybe get an extra one or two besides," Lepkin said.

Lady Arkyn glanced over her shoulder at the tower. "Nials assumed command, didn't he?"

Lepkin nodded.

"I thought he might," Lady Arkyn said. "He isn't one to share authority."

Virgil frowned and looked to Lepkin. "You gave him command of everyone? But, why? The men look up to you. They have been loyal to you, and they have broken their backs preparing the field for you."

"Not for me," Lepkin corrected. "We prepare the field to defeat the enemy. The more experienced commander has assumed control of the army. It is as it should be.

"What about the dwarves, do they agree?" Lady Arkyn asked.

"Al will remain in command of the dwarves," Lepkin replied. "Come, we are wasting time. I have charge over a select group, and I intend to sting the enemy where it counts." Lepkin pointed to Virgil. "Go and get the others. We'll be heading far to the east. We'll double back and then select orc officers to drop."

"Sewing confusion by cutting off the heads," Lady Arkyn commented. "I like it."

"Good, then go and get arrows."

*****

Lepkin, the three dragon-slayers, and Lady Arkyn all crept along through a thicket of briars and brambles. It was slow going, but they found if they stuck low to the ground there was enough space to maneuver without getting hung up on the thorns. The enemy marched only sixty yards away from them, marching slowly toward the chasm.

Commander Nials would wait until the orcs were close before launching the catapults. The idea was to surprise and catch as many orc warriors as possible. Lepkin, would try to circle around and aim for a few of the captains to further complicate the orcs' retreat.

"There," Lepkin whispered as he signaled for all of them to halt. "The one with the gold trim upon his platemail, riding the goarg. That is the captain for this grouping."

"I can take him now," Lady Arkyn said.

Lepkin shook his head. "No, let them pass by until the catapults launch. After the orcs have realized their mistake, then take him." Lepkin continued on slowly through the briars. "Virgil, you stay with Lady Arkyn, the rest of you come with me."

Lepkin, Aelron, and Eriem slithered over the dirt. The sand and grit scratched and scraped against their armor. Occasionally the brambles would shake as a thorn caught on one of them, but they were careful not to tug against the briars. Instead, they would stop and use their fingers to pry the thorn free. It slowed them considerably, but it didn't attract attention from the passing army.

As they neared the edge of the briars, they were forced to stop. A dozen orcs were peeling off from the main group and moving toward them. Lepkin signaled for the others to stop. They hugged low to the ground, hoping that their black armor wouldn't be visible through the brambles. Lepkin hardly breathed for fear of making noise. The heavily armored orcs approached, and then stopped short of reaching the brambles. They formed a circle and two of them removed backpacks and pulled wooden blocks and squares out.

Lepkin watched as they quickly assembled a field table and then slapped a map over it. He couldn't understand what they were saying, but he assumed that this group was tasked with finding an alternate route around the chasm. It was smart. Send the army directly in to draw all of the enemy out and make them reveal themselves while you send smaller parties out to scout the terrain for alternate routes. Lepkin assumed there was likely a similar group out to the west somewhere.

Master Lepkin slowly inched backward so he could whisper to the others. "When the catapults fire, we are going to kill these orcs."

Eriem and Aelron both nodded. The three of them crawled

and angled themselves so that they could emerge from the briars without too much difficulty. Then they waited.

It didn't take long before shouts rose up throughout the orcish ranks. These shouts were followed moments later by thunderous crashes. The stones beat upon the troops and dirt as great drums. Lepkin launched up, the other two joined him.

The dozen orcs quickly drew swords and axes.

Lepkin thrust his sword into the back of the nearest orc. Eriem cut the head off of an orc to Lepkin's left, spraying blood up and out over the table in the center of the ring. Aelron drove a dagger into an orc's face and then moved on to slay a second with a single thrust of his sword.

Lepkin used his leg to push the corpse from his sword. His left hand reached down and pulled the dead orc's axe from its hand and raised it up just in time to block a strike from his left. He brought his sword back in quickly, smashing it into the orc's armor, but it had little effect other than to cause a great vibration in his arm as steel collided against steel.

The orc came in with a left handed uppercut, but Lepkin spun away. The orc pressed the fight, running forward and swinging his axe in a sidelong chop. Lepkin ducked quickly and brought the axe in his left hand down at an angle against the orc's knee. A horrendous *crrrack* resounded from the orc's leg as the joint bent inward and the axe lodged itself inside. Lepkin brought his sword up and over his head, deflecting the orc's attack, then he stood and barreled his spiked shoulder up and into the orc's chest. The Telarian steel proved much stronger than the orc's armor. The spike pierced through, screeching and squealing as it pierced through the metal and found the flesh underneath. The orc grunted, and his limbs went weak.

Suddenly carrying several hundred pounds of dead orc, Lepkin was forced to fight awkwardly as another orc charged in before Lepkin could disengage himself. Lepkin wheeled around, presenting the dead corpse pinned to his shoulder as a shield. The charging orc was repelled as his own spear glanced off his fallen comrade. Then Lepkin pushed forward, driving his feet and using the corpse to bumrush the attacker. They all fell to the ground, but Lepkin pulled his legs in for momentum and swung from his waist, effectively rolling into a sideways somersault that at once disengaged his pauldron from the corpse and placed him within striking distance of the attacker's throat. He drew his sword across the orc's neck and ended his life.

A sword-wielding orc was already upon him, bringing his sword down in a massive chop. Aelron barreled into the warrior before the sword ever connected with Lepkin and the two flew off to land several feet away from Lepkin. A moment later a dagger ceased that orc's shouts and all twelve were dead. Master Lepkin rose to his feet and saw the mound of corpses around them.

"Grab the map," Lepkin said.

Eriem seized the parchment and stuffed it through the narrow opening at his neck to rest behind his chest plate. "We should move," he said.

Lepkin turned around to see massive stones raining from the sky. Upon impact, dirt and orcs were thrown for yards around each stone. The shrieks and shouts of those caught by the hulking missiles were nearly drowned out by the quaking *thawump* as each stone crashed down.

"Look there," Aelron said as he pointed up to the north.

Lepkin turned just in time to see the captain fall from his goarg. The beast had several arrows in it as well, but it showed no signs of slowing as it charged directly toward the three. Lepkin and the others quickstepped out of the way just seconds before the goarg growled and galloped through where they had just been standing. Its hooves tore up dirt and clods of grass as it ran on. The captain's corpse was stuck with its foot caught in the stirrup. Two arrows protruded from the small space between the helmet and hauberk and blood dripped from the captain's neck, painting a semi-solid red line in the dirt.

"She hit the artery," Eriem said.

Lepkin nodded. "Let's circle back.

The three of them ran around the other side of the brambles as fast as their armor would allow. Lady Arkyn and Virgil killed three more orcs that came at them after the captain fell, then they hacked their way through the briars and out to meet Lepkin and the others.

"Come on, we need to go," Lepkin shouted.

A group of nearly thirty angry orcs tore through the brambles after them. The five of them sprinted in a north-easterly direction.

They were too far out for the catapults, so they didn't have to worry about inadvertently being crushed by friendly fire, but that also meant they would need to handle the orcs on their own.

Lady Arkyn strung an arrow and in a single moment turned back to fire without losing step as she sprinted. The arrow flew straight and true, sinking through the slit in an orc's visor and dropping the orc instantly. A couple orcs that were too slow to evade the obstacle tripped on the corpse, but she knew that wouldn't stop them.

"We won't be able to outrun them forever," Lady Arkyn said. "They'll catch us by the ravine."

Lepkin knew she was right. "Keep using your arrows," Lepkin ordered. "Take down a few more and then we'll turn on them." Lady Arkyn broke off toward the west. "That isn't what I meant!"

"Keep going!" Lady Arkyn shouted.

The majority of the group continued on after Lepkin and the others. Lady Arkyn fired two arrows, slaying two orcs that were after her. She quickly set another arrow to her bowstring and stood her ground. An arrow through the neck killed a third. Four more sprinted toward her. She strung another arrow. They were thirty yards away. The arrow pierced through another orc's armor. The three remaining orcs were now twenty yards away as she fired another arrow. This one caught a lightly armored orc in the groin. It wasn't an instant kill, but it did take him out of the fight. She fired another arrow as the last two were ten yards away. The arrow sunk into an orc's skull.

She pulled another arrow as the last orc closed in. He raised a heavy sword over his right shoulder. Lady Arkyn had no armor. If she took a blow from that sword it would be the end. Her arm brought the arrow out of the quiver and over her shoulder. There was no time to string it. The orc was already swinging.

Lady Arkyn opened her left hand and let her bow fall. She ducked to her right, still grasping onto the arrow shaft. She somersaulted and twisted up. As the orc rushed by she stuck the arrow up through the opening between the orc's rump and the plate over the back of its left thigh. She plunged the steel tip deep into the orc's leg and then pulled down sharply, snapping the arrow shaft and tearing the wound as large as the narrow opening in the armor would allow.

The orc shouted out and fell to the ground.

Lady Arkyn jumped up to her feet. She launched onto the orc's sword arm and wrested the weapon free. The orc did not give up the fight so easily, though. He turned over and socked Lady Arkyn in the chest. Pain ripped through her bosom as the gauntleted fist mashed into her and knocked her to the ground.

She barely moved before the orc drove a dagger into the ground where she had been. She was up on her feet in an instant. She came down hard on the orc's arm with the sword she had taken from him, severing it at the wrist. The orc howled in agony and then Lady Arkyn drove the sword down through the orc's open mouth.

Breathing heavily, she quickly grabbed her bow and started taking aim at the group chasing Lepkin and the others. She aimed for the orcs with less armor, dropping them down just as quickly as her arm could work the bowstring. Soon she had thinned the orcs down to a manageable number.

Lepkin and the others turned suddenly and the clashes of metal and shouts of struggle preceded the hoots of victory as Lepkin and the others made quick, dirty work of the remaining orcs.

Lady Arkyn then turned to watch the main body of the orcish army retreating back from the barrage of stones. None of them wanted to stay on the field. As she scanned the army she saw a large orc sitting upon a goarg near the edge of the burnt forest. His gaze fell upon her and her skin shriveled into tight goosebumps.

The orc slowly raised his hands and started clapping at her. With her keen eyesight, it was easy to see the contempt and rage painted upon the orc's face. It unnerved her more than anything had so far. She set another arrow to her string and aimed up. She let loose. The missile flew up into a high arc before descending and dropping to stab the ground well short of the orc.

The orc smiled and drew his blade with one hand while he beckoned to her with the other.

"Lady Arkyn," Lepkin shouted from behind. Lady Arkyn turned to regard Lepkin and then turned back to watch the orc. The orc was already engaged in other business, shouting orders and barking at his soldiers.

"That's the chief," she said. "If we can kill him, we can cut the head off the snake."

"There are too many of them," Lepkin said as he and the others came close to her. "We could never get close enough to strike."

"No," Lady Arkyn said. "*You* couldn't," she corrected.

*****

A short while after sundown Lady Arkyn sat in the dining room in Tillamon's old house. The food was set but only a few people were at the table. Al and Commander Nials were among them, of course, but there were no others seated with them. Lepkin paced back and forth, mumbling to himself and fidgeting with his hands. He would take a few steps with his hands clasped, then switch to folding his arms only to shake his hands out a few moments later.

"Been a while since you've seen her?" Commander Nials asked as he poured himself a bit of wine. "A drink might calm your nerves."

Lepkin shook his head and continued pacing.

"At least have a seat, bean-pole," Al grumbled. "I have seen squirrels less active than you."

Lepkin stopped and looked at his hands. He smiled and then moved to sit. Two seconds later he was up out of the chair and walking toward the hallway that led to the front door.

Lady Arkyn giggled to herself. Al shot her a cross-eyed look and then shook his head as he followed Commander Nials' lead and poured himself a bit of wine.

"Excuse me," Lady Arkyn said as she stood up from her chair. Commander Nials rose up out of his chair as was customary, but Al remained in his seat and pressed the drink to his lips after offering Lady Arkyn a simple nod.

"Shouldn't one stand when a lady leaves the room?" Commander Nials asked.

"What's the point of being a king if you can't even sit on your backside when you choose?" Al quipped.

Lady Arkyn stifled a laugh. "It's alright," she told Commander Nials. "I have grown accustomed to this one." She jabbed a thumb in Al's direction.

"I think you should all bow whenever I enter or leave a room," Al continued. "I am a king, after all."

Commander Nials cocked his head to the side and glanced between Al and Lady Arkyn.

Lady Arkyn just shrugged and walked away, leaving the two to figure out for themselves who would bow to whom. She wanted to talk to Lepkin. She found him sitting on the front step outside.

"Nervous?" she asked.

"Is it that obvious?" Lepkin smirked.

Lady Arkyn shrugged and smoothed out her trousers before she sat on the front step next to Lepkin. "Funny how you can charge an entire army and exude nothing but confidence but then when your wife is a few minutes late you start pacing like a puppy."

"You've never loved someone before?" Lepkin asked.

Lady Arkyn smiled. "Twice, actually," she said. "I was married once, a long time ago."

Lepkin nodded, but he didn't say anything. His eyes were glued to the road to the north.

"Being half-elf I have a longer life span than most," she said. "I outlived my first husband, though it didn't help that he was caught by a highwayman."

Lepkin sighed and shook his head. "I am sorry to hear that."

The blonde-haired woman nodded. "It was a long time ago," she said. "It still hurts, but not as much."

"What about the second time?" Lepkin asked.

Lady Arkyn grinned and moved her hands up to fix her braid. "I fell for a young man on the battle field actually," she said.

"Not an orc I hope," Lepkin jested.

"No, it was you," Lady Arkyn said.

Lepkin knit his brow and his mouth opened for a moment before closing again. Before he could find any words to speak, Lady Arkyn started laughing out loud and slapped a hand onto Lepkin's shoulder.

"I'm sorry," she said. "I couldn't resist." She wiped a tear from her left eye and patted Lepkin's shoulder a couple times before setting her hands back in her own lap.

"Proud of yourself?" Lepkin asked. His tone had definitely changed to one of annoyance. Still, Lady Arkyn didn't let it bother her.

"I thought it might break the ice a bit," she explained. "When you have a hard subject to broach with someone it is easier to open with a joke."

"So, you thought it appropriate to tell me that you love me while I am waiting for my wife and unborn child?"

Lady Arkyn smiled and nodded. "That will make it all the more palatable for you when I say that I have actually taken a liking to Erik."

Lepkin arched his right brow and sighed. "This is getting tiresome," he said. He turned and locked eyes with her. Lady Arkyn smiled, but kept his gaze. After a moment she raised her own eyebrows and nodded twice to show him that the last bit had not been a joke.

"He's only a boy," Lepkin said quickly. "How could you fall for him?"

Lady Arkyn laugh and shrugged. "He has fought armies, warlocks, and even a dragon. I don't know that 'boy' is the correct term."

"He isn't of age," Lepkin said decisively.

"Not yet," Lady Arkyn said. "But he will be soon. I already said that life for me is different. I can wait a few years if I must." She leaned back on her palms and cleared her throat. "Many young women have their marriages arranged at similar ages. You, of all people, should know that."

Lepkin nodded. "You are speaking of Dimwater?" he asked.

"And countless others."

"So you are asking for me to arrange a wedding between you and Erik?"

Lady Arkyn shook her head. "No. I know he has been through a lot. When I saw him and Al…" her voice trailed off. "Well, let's just say that I saw what he has been through. I was at the senate hall. I was at Lokton Manor."

"You knew that was him?"

Lady Arkyn nodded. "I didn't tell anyone, but I could see that it was not you inside your body. You should have seen him then. You would have been proud. He is far more of a man than any give him credit for."

"What do you want from me?" Lepkin asked.

Lady Arkyn smiled and leaned forward again. "I want what

you have," she said. "I want to pace nervously when my husband is about to return from his latest adventure. I want to feel the bond the same as you and Dimwater. Only, I don't want to wait as long as you did of course."

"I can't make the boy love you," Lepkin said quickly.

Lady Arkyn nodded. "I know that. I have spent many decades searching for someone who could fill the hole in my heart. I have not found any I have felt comfortable with until I met Erik. I know he is too young now, but in a few years he won't be. Also, he is a Sahale, so I will not have to live with the pain of outliving him. All I want from you is your blessing."

Lepkin inhaled deeply and pouted out his lips as he reached up to rub his chin. "Answer me one question." Lepkin turned to look at her. His blue eyes were steady and warm, yet overwhelming at the same time. "What will you do if he does not return your love?"

"Then I should like to stay near him for a while. Even if things do not unfold the way I would like, there is a gravity to him that pulls me in. Maybe there will be another adventure after this business is done. If so, then I want to be at his side."

Lepkin scoffed. "After this I hope there are no more adventures."

"You have lived with the sword too long to hope for that," Lady Arkyn pointed out.

Lepkin frowned. "Not for me," he said. "When this is over I am taking Dimwater far away. We are going to build a home in a forest where no one can find us. All I want is a life of peace. When Nagar's book is destroyed, that is what I aim to have." Lepkin then turned away from her and nodded. "If Erik decides that he is happy with you, and you feel the same, then you have my blessing. After all he has been through, I wish for him to find peace as well."

Lady Arkyn smiled and leaned over to give Lepkin a peck on the cheek. At that moment the two of them spied Dimwater and Marlin. Marlin walked ahead of a small horse-drawn cart while Lady Dimwater sat near the front and held a hand over her belly, which was now starting to bulge out from under her dress visibly.

Lepkin jumped up and sprinted out to greet Dimwater.

Lady Arkyn watched for a moment and smiled wide. "Yep, that is what I want," she said as she watched the two jump into each other's arms. She imagined Erik, grown into a man and running to her the same way. Lepkin was more cautious about the idea, but Arkyn had seen the glances Erik had stolen when they were together. There was something there, if only a spark. Still, a spark was worth exploring. Lady Arkyn knew that life was too short, even for her, not to.

She stood and went back into the house, though she was not going to stay for dinner. She moved into the drawing room where she had left her bow. She grabbed it and began gathering her daggers and sword as well.

So as not to be seen, she left the house through a side window and jogged stealthily out from Stonebrook and into the night. Neither the dwarves nor humans saw her cross the chasm and make her way across the field.

The stars above her winked in and out of the clouds and haze from the forest. There was no sign of the orcish army. If not for the many bodies lying in the grass it might have been possible to forget the orcs had even attacked earlier in the day. There were no campfires, no forward scouts in the field, nothing. Large boulders littered the field, giving her easy cover as she made her way to the burnt forest. She crouched low behind a particularly large boulder and scanned the area. Once she was sure it was clear to proceed, she darted out to the nearest tree.

Lady Arkyn nearly toppled the burnt oak trunk by touching it. Black soot smeared across her palm and gray ash shot up from her footsteps. She leaned around the trunk and scoured everything around her. She sprinted to another trunk fifty yards away, pausing just long enough to scan for movement before running to a large mound of dirt and ash and hunkering down near it.

This time instead of peering around the side of her cover she closed her eyes and listened. Her half-elf ears strained for the slightest sound. The slight breeze, which she had only faintly noticed a moment ago, now seemed a mighty gale as her ears amplified every sound around her. She heard a rustling sound and looked up to see a pair of carrion birds resting on the sole branch left on a tall, mostly burnt pine tree. Still, none of the sounds alerted her to any enemy presence.

Satisfied now that the orcs had made a full retreat, she jumped up and made her way through the burnt forest. She ran for hours in the night. Her feet fell lightly upon the blanket of ash, making no sound as they stirred up little gray clouds around her ankles. Eventually she came upon a forward camp of orcs. There were only twenty of them, so she knew that the orc chief would not be found among them. A pair of goargs slept peacefully, each tied to a sword stabbed into the ground. It was a common sight with orcish scouts. One goarg per ten orcs. That left nine orcs to hold off the enemy while one used a goarg to warn the main camp. Using a sword to anchor the goarg made it all the faster to release the goarg from its tether and escape before an enemy could attack. Having twice the number of orcs and goargs as a regular scouting party meant that they expected to be chased when they routed.

Lady Arkyn entertained the temptation of killing the scouts. She knew that she could easily take five plus the goargs before any could raise an alarm. She pushed the notion out of her mind. She was not after a scouting party. She wanted that chief.

Even now she could still feel his smug, fierce eyes upon her. Goosebumps formed along her forearms just at the thought. She cast a glance back the way she came. If Lepkin had known what she was doing, he would have stopped her. Still, she felt confident. Where a group might fail, she could slip in undetected.

She pressed on, beyond the scouting party and deeper into the burnt forest. She walked for another two hours before arriving at a place where the majority of the tracks in the ash diverged from the southern direction. She studied each imprint, each indentation around her. There was no way to know which way the chief had gone. Hundreds, no—thousands, of tracks peeled out to the east while thousands more went due west. A third column of tracks double-backed south.

She looked specifically for goarg tracks, but that didn't help. There were several sets of those in each direction as well. Lady Arkyn sighed and sat upon the gray ash on the ground. Her ears twitched with the slightest of sounds as she closed her eyes and focused on the orc chief. In her meditation, she tried to imagine his march northward from Ten Forts. She conjured up the image of thousands of orcs before her. In her mind she watched them get pummeled by the catapults and scatter before her. A group of warriors slew a few officers, adding another layer of chaos into the commotion and through the chief's eyes she watched herself fire an arrow. It wasn't real of course, Lady Arkyn had no way to read minds, but she found the practice of imagining the enemy's perspective useful. It helped her arrive at a better idea of what the enemy might do, and where the chief may have gone.

"West," Lady Arkyn whispered aloud. "The pig-faced orc went west." Where else would he go? The fastest and best path around the chasm that held the brook was to the west. The chief must have taken a large force that way so he could circle back and flank the catapults. The other two massive groups were likely positioned defensively, hoping for a pursuit.

She rose to her feet and was about to take a step when a strange sound caught her attention. It was slight, almost inaudible even to her half-elf ears. There was a soft wheeze on the air accompanied by *pit-pf-pf, pit-pf-pf, pit-pf-pf.* She readied her bow and turned left. A gray wolf slowed to a stop ten yards before her. Its head hung low. Its body expanded and contracted quickly with panting, wheezing breaths. One leg was up, held defensively. The wolf looked at her with its yellow eyes and then began slowly limping toward her. It was then that Lady Arkyn saw the blood on its right foreleg. Still, despite its injury the wolf did not growl nor show hostility.

Lady Arkyn called out to the wolf softly. "Trouble with orcs?"

The wolf hung its head low to the ash. Before her eyes the wolf grew, expanding to the size of a large man. As the body transformed it lost its fur. Fingers grew out where the paws had been. The tail shortened. A man lay face-down in the ash.

"Peren?" Lady Arkyn gasped. She went to him and knelt next to his shoulder. The man's right arm had a deep gash though it down to the bone.

"My name is Rjord," the man said as he rolled to his left side and looked up at her.

Lady Arkyn's excitement was dashed when she saw that the man before her was not her friend. Still, she set her bow down and reached for a small pouch where she kept her bandages. "Be still and I will help you," she said. "Where are you from?"

"Ten Forts," Rjord said. "I am from Ten Forts."

Lady Arkyn screwed up her face. "I don't recall any werewolves stationed at Ten Forts," she said.

"Of course not," Rjord replied. "I am a shapeshifter. I have the ability to change my form into that of a wolf at times, but I am not a werewolf. I keep my mind at all times, and I choose when to transform."

"Shouldn't you be at Stonebrook then?" Lady Arkyn asked.

Rjord reached up and placed a weak right hand on her forearm. "There isn't any time. The orcs who found me are coming. They will be here soon."

Lady Arkyn looked out to the east. "How many follow you?" she asked.

Rjord shook his head. "After one of them hit me with an axe I didn't exactly stop to take count. I ran."

"They saw you transform?" she pressed.

Rjord pushed up and nodded.

Lady Arkyn peered into the darkness. Her senses didn't detect anything yet, but she knew that would soon change. "Orcs hate magic," she said. "They'll surely follow you. Wait here." She grabbed her bow and moved away from the wounded man, leaving a roll of bandages with him so he could tend to his arm while she moved to a better position.

She didn't have to wait long before a trio of orcs came into view. They were running at full tilt through the ash, stirring up great clouds of gray around them and breathing heavily. She let them get close enough to see Rjord on the ground. They redoubled their pace and sprinted in with their weapons ready. One of them whistled sharply.

That was what she was waiting for.

A large goarg galloped up from a little farther south. The rider upon its back held a great spear in his hands. Lady Arkyn jabbed four arrows into the ground with one more already against the bow string. In a matter of seconds all five arrows took flight. The first coursed through the goarg rider's neck. The second pierced the goarg's eye, sinking deeply into the animal's head and dropping the beast to crash through a thick layer of ash. The third tore through an orc's chest. The fourth and fifth arrows, however, sunk into the sides of the remaining orcs' knees. They fell to the ground crying out in agony.

Lady Arkyn sprinted toward them as quickly as she could. One of the orcs pushed up, but an arrow pierced his right shoulder and he fell back to the ground. The she-elf leapt over the first and landed on the second orc before he could move. Her boots drove the orc's face deep into the ash, muffling his shouts. She followed that with a quick strike to the back of the orc's head with the heel of her right boot, then she leapt over to the first orc, taking hold of the arrow shaft running through the orc's shoulder and jamming her knee into the small of the orc's back. The orc jerked upwards, arching his back. He opened his mouth to yell, but Lady Arkyn grabbed a hold of his throat and squeezed on the orc's windpipe. It wasn't enough to kill the orc, but it was enough to silence him.

Out came her dagger. The blade went up to the orc's neck and she whispered into his ear. "You chief is a coward. He ran from the field of battle."

"Foggd be!" the orc grunted.

"You will all die," Lady Arkyn said.

"Foggd be!" the orc repeated.

She knew then that this orc did not speak Common Tongue. If he did, he would have responded to the insults directly. She plunged her dagger into the orc's neck and dropped his now lifeless head back to the ash.

Lady Arkyn moved back to the unconscious orc. She grabbed his left arm and twisted it up behind his back as she positioned her knee directly in the center of the orc's spine. She used the dagger in her right hand to poke the orc's cheek until he woke up.

"Your chief is a coward," she told the orc.

"You are coward," the orc said. He wasn't fluent by any means. He struggled to find each word, but they emerged from his mouth with all the bravado and false confidence the orc could muster while the point of Arkyn's dagger pressed into his skin.

"Your chief fled the field, running home as fast as he could while he left all of you to die."

"Graa!" the orc shouted as he tried to squirm free. Lady Arkyn's grip on the orc's arm was surprisingly tight given her slight frame. The orc wiggled and wormed, pushing this way and that, but nothing worked. She held him pinned to the ground. "You die soon. Chief no run home. Chief go east around your coward catapults. Chief destroy human home." The orc then started laughing.

Lady Arkyn slit his throat. "East then," she said as she rose and cleaned her blade. "That saved me a lot of trouble."

"You're going after him?" Rjord asked.

Lady Arkyn nodded her head. "The snows will be here in a couple of weeks. If I can cut off the head before then, the orcs will be forced to turn back." She situated her bow onto her person and then beckoned for Rjord to join her. "Come with me."

Rjord shook his head. "I have no intention of going back. I barely escaped."

"There are some scouts up north," Lady Arkyn said as she gestured behind herself with her head. "You might want to go back into your wolf form. They have goargs."

Rjord huffed. "I'm not going north either," he said.

"You're leaving?" Lady Arkyn asked pointedly.

Rjord nodded his head.

Lady Arkyn's hand reflexively moved up to her quiver. There was only one punishment for desertion. Rjord's dark eyes pleaded with hers silently, but he didn't move to run. He held his breath, staring at her. Lady Arkyn's fingers grasped the cold, smooth shaft of an arrow. She knew what had to be done. Her arm pulled and the arrow slid free of its place. Rjord closed his eyes. She put the arrow to the string and pulled it back to the corner of her mouth. She stared down the arrow at the man. She drew in her breath and held it. Then she released her hold on the arrow.

No sooner had the string twanged into place than the arrow embedded itself deep in the ash and dirt next to Rjord's face. The man twitched, and then slowly opened his eyes. He slowly turned his head away and put a hand up to the red line where the arrow's fletching had scraped him. His eyes again looked up to her, but this time there was no pleading, only puzzlement.

"I guess I missed," Lady Arkyn said coolly. "Go on, get out of here."

"Why?" Rjord asked. "You owe me nothing. Why didn't you do it?"

Lady Arkyn sighed. "I fight enemies of the kingdom. I am not about to start shooting scared countrymen on the field. Go on." Lady Arkyn motioned with her chin out to the east. "If you see any able-bodied men, send them out here to us."

Rjord nodded. "I can do better than that," he promised. "Look for me after the snow falls."

CHAPTER EIGHT

Lepkin woke early in order to make breakfast for Dimwater. He pushed his way into the bedroom with his hips as he balanced a tray of eggs, fruit, juice, and bread in his hands. After he twirled into the room and nudged the door closed with his left heel he smiled when he saw Dimwater still sleeping on the bed. The large, round bulge from her stomach moved up and down with each breath. Marlin had said the child would be born sometime in the middle of the winter, another couple of months away.

He glanced to the frosted window and noted a few early flakes of snow drifting in to chase autumn away. He could only hope the premature frost would drive the orcs away as well. He moved in and set the tray on a small, round table. Then he picked up the table and carefully set it next to the bed.

"Smells good," Dimwater said with a groggy smile as she opened her eyes. She didn't bother looking at the food. Rather, she looked up to Lepkin. "It is good to be back with you," she said.

Lepkin sighed and smiled wide. "I am happy that you are no longer ill."

Dimwater pushed up awkwardly to a sitting position. Lepkin moved quickly to offer one arm for support and gently push her back with the other. "You had me frightened beyond what I can describe."

Dimwater smiled. "It was a curse," she said. "Something my father gave me some time ago."

Lepkin knelt beside her. "I am so sorry, for all of it," he said.

Dimwater shook her head and put a finger on his lips. "No, you shouldn't say that. We are together now. It may have taken us longer than we would have liked, and there have been some rough points, but I wouldn't trade it for anything."

Lepkin reached up and gently slid his fingers around her hand and pulled it away just enough so that he could kiss it. Then he leaned over and kissed her growing stomach. "Marlin said it is a boy," Lepkin said.

Dimwater smiled. "He will be big and strong, like his father."

She leaned over and kissed Lepkin on the cheek. "Now, what do we have? I am starving."

Lepkin laughed. He had already brought her two additional meals during the night. He knew better than to mention it though, so instead he uncovered the food and positioned the tray closer to her. She tore into the food, abandoning all etiquette as she ripped hunks of bread off with her teeth while she simultaneously poured juice into her mouth. She moaned something and closed her eyes and nodded. Somehow she gulped the massive bite down and then let out a burp.

"This is perfect, thank you."

Lepkin nodded and smiled.

"Any word from Erik?" Dimwater asked through a mouthful of eggs.

Lepkin's smile faded. "Not yet," he said.

Dimwater choked the bite down and took another gulp of juice. "He'll turn up," she assured him. "He always does."

Lepkin nodded and moved to the window.

"Tell me more of the orcs," Dimwater said.

Lepkin knew she was turning his mind away from Erik so as not to let him dwell on his worry about the boy. He had already recounted the battles with the orcs last night. He told her everything from Mercer's sacrifice, to burning the forest for weeks on end to slow the orcs, and even the most recent battle. Still, he obliged her. "There is nothing to report. The scouts have not alerted me to any new developments."

"Would Commander Nials inform you?" Dimwater asked. "I never liked him much. He always struck me as an arrogant sort with an eye only for his own glory and advancement."

Lepkin folded his arms. "I would have said the same before he arrived, but Al assured me that he disobeyed orders from King Mathias to reinforce our position here. So, I have decided to give him the benefit of the doubt."

Dimwater dove right into her eggs, shoveling bites in as quickly as she could while still maintaining some semblance of propriety.

"I suspect the orcs will be looking for a way to flank us, rather than charge us head on again. Al was thinking we could reposition the catapults, but Commander Nials doesn't want to divide them up. So we wait."

"What about Lady Arkyn?" Dimwater asked after she swallowed a mouthful of bread and eggs.

"Haven't seen her since you arrived last night." Lepkin shook his head and turned to lean against the window sill as he watched his wife finish the last few bits of food on her plate. "Shall I get more from the kitchen?"

Dimwater shook her head. "No, that was enough." She grabbed the last morsel of bread, used it to wipe up the yolk from the plate and then plopped it into her mouth. She chewed twice and then washed it all down with the last of her juice. "That was perfect." She swung her left leg out and then used both arms to help push herself up. "Still getting used to it," she said as she patted her protruding stomach.

"You should rest," Lepkin said. "Marlin is out helping the army. You should relax."

"I have had enough of that," Dimwater said. "I want to go for a walk outside. Let's see if we can't prepare a few surprises for those orcs."

Lepkin smiled. He loved her tenacity. It was good to have her back.

"You know what I could use more of though?" She looked down to the empty plate. "How about just another apple, oh, and maybe another roll."

"Sure," Lepkin said with a chuckle.

"And maybe one more glass of juice and a couple hard-boiled eggs for the road?"

"You baking a human in that belly, or a dragon?" Lepkin asked.

Dimwater shrugged. "Knowing us I suppose it could be either." She flashed a wry smile and then tapped her plate. "But seriously, we do have more food right?"

*****

Gulgarin stood near the fire. He frowned at the crystalline snowflake drifting down in front of his face. The others saw it too. Gulgarin didn't miss the nervous glances the officers shot each other. One of them even had the audacity to rub his shoulders.

Cowards. Gulgarin grimaced and turned away from them to look at the simple canvas tents set up in the ashen valley that had weeks ago been a lush forest.

"We do not have enough food, Chief Gulgarin," one of the orcs said from behind.

"We must turn back to the fortress," another put in. "If we leave now, we can avoid needless casualties from the early frost. We can dig in and build our strength. When the thaw comes, we will bring our swords to the humans."

Gulgarin took in a deep breath and turned around to face the officers. "With the few weeks that the forest fire gave the humans, what did they do?" Without waiting for an answer he picked up a gray stone and chucked it into the fire. "They built catapults!" The vein in his forehead stuck out like a grotesque snake writhing under his skin. "You now wish to cower down for months on end while the humans grow stronger?"

Captain Krelik stood from his position and pointed to the north. "The forest has been destroyed. There is no game here with which we can feed our troops. To bypass the settlement is impossible. Our soldiers cannot fight on empty stomachs."

"Then we do not bypass the settlement," Gulgarin roared. "We attack the city head on, and destroy every last one of their catapults."

"But to do that is suicide," Krelik said.

Gulgarin shook his head. "No. We will do what the humans did back at Ten Forts. We will send small groups to destroy the catapults. We can use our goargs and berserkers to flank the easternmost catapult. We can send small units under the cover of night. If they can reach the catapults, our losses will be diminished. Then, once the machines are destroyed, we will slaughter the humans."

"We will still have the winter to deal with."

Gulgarin shook his head. "Our lands are always cold," he replied.

"But not always covered in snow. Additionally, the deer and other animals have adapted to our environment. The animals here will not be as easy to find for food."

Gulgarin narrowed his eyes on the orc, giving the obvious signal that his patience was wearing far too thin for a drawn out argument. "We will occupy the city. We will live off of the food they have stockpiled for themselves. We can also use the road to venture north and raid smaller villages if need be. We will not let the humans rest through the winter. We will assail them constantly and drive them out of the land before us. For the glory of Khullan."

"For the glory of Khullan," the others repeated. Gulgarin saw the anger in Krelik's face, but the orc did not dare challenge his orders.

"Go, prepare the army," Gulgarin said. He then turned and walked a short distance toward his tent. Something caught his eye. A shadow, or perhaps movement. His fingers flexed, but he did not move his hand to his weapon. If someone was waiting for him in the tent, he didn't want them to know he was ready for them.

He strode confidently for the flap and slipped his left hand in and around the coarse canvas. He peeled it back. His eyes scoured the entire interior of the tent in less than a second. Whatever it was he had thought he saw, it was no longer there. The hairs on the back of his neck stood on end as he entered the tent and let the flap close behind him. He moved in. A red and yellow blanket covered the large wooden chair to his right, hiding the entire frame. The cot was made perfectly, as he had left it when he woke. His extra pair of boots stood at the foot of the cot. His war chest remained locked near the side of the cot. Nothing was out of place.

He pulled his sword free and drove it through the center of the cot. The blankets and fabric popped open as his blade slid down to stab into the ground below. He started to reverse his arm and pull the sword free but there was a movement from behind him. He released his sword and pulled a pair of long knives from his belt as he whirled around. The red and yellow blanket flew up and off from the chair, only the chair was gone. In its place stood a comely she-elf with a bow. The string snapped into place.

Gulgarin took the arrow in the chest, letting the strong mithril mail under his leather hauberk absorb the impact. He looked at the bow and smiled. "That weapon does not belong to you," he said. "Szelevo is an orcish bow."

The she-elf pulled another arrow and moved to set it to the string. Gulgarin lunged in headlong, tackling the elf to the ground. Her nimble, sharp elbows rocked his face and neck as he grappled with her. He tried to angle his knives toward her flesh, but no matter which way he turned, she seemed able to block his thrust. Gulgarin growled and struck down with his head. The elf slid away and landed two elbow strikes to his temple.

Gulgarin barely managed to block the elf's arm with his left forearm in time to stop a wickedly curved dagger from entering his own belly. Unfortunately, he did not stop the simultaneous knee to the groin. Another elbow strike smashed his nose and then he felt a fiery pain rip along the left side of his head. He roared out in pain and somersaulted away from the she-elf. His eyes widened when he noticed the blood splatter on the ground.

His left hand went up to the side of his head. The warm, viscous liquid met his palm in copious amounts.

"Looking for this?" the she-elf asked as she held up Gulgarin's left ear.

Gulgarin threw one of his knives, but the she-elf jumped to the side. She flung her dagger at Gulgarin in answer for his attack. Gulgarin tried to move out of the way, but the elf had guessed accurately which way he would flee. The dagger caught his right thigh a few inches above the knee. The elf ran for the bow that was now lying on the ground. Gulgarin reached out for his sword, tore it free from the bed, and whirled it toward the she-elf with all his might. The blade spun end over end. The she-elf managed to grab the bow and hold it before her to catch the sword. The blade cut through the bow, severing it in half and then biting into the she-elf's shoulder before bouncing out again to land on the ground. She groaned, but did not scream.

Gulgarin was not about to let up. He ran as best he could on his injured leg and leapt to tackle the she-elf again. This time, the assassin escaped. She fled out from the tent. Gulgarin called out for the guards.

"Assassin!" he yelled. Shouts rose up through the camp. Gulgarin tore his tent down around him in anger rather than take the time to exit through the flap. Still, he was far too late to catch the she-elf. Several orcs mounted goargs and went after her. "Bring me her head!" Gulgarin shouted.

*****

Lady Arkyn ran for all she was worth. Arrows streaked near her. She could hear the goargs' hooves thumping against the ground chasing after her. The orcs shouted and grunted, but she didn't bother to turn around. She pushed on, her feet barely lighting upon the ground before propelling her forward. She had prepared for this.

Lady Arkyn circled around a mark in the ash she had left before entering the camp. Her lips stretched into a smile when she heard the tell-tale *schnap!* A goarg screeched in pain and an orc's shouts turned into garbled mumbling. She glanced back to see the pair of spikes jutting up through their bodies. The trap had worked perfectly.

The pursuers redoubled their efforts, closing in on her. She sprinted between two darkened, burnt trees, careful to run over the tripwire without springing it. She ran straight as fast as she could. None of the orcs could have known what was about to happen. She didn't hear the tripwire snap, but she heard the groans and grunts as the several dozen spikes she had set up in two columns behind each burnt tree erupted out from the ash and tore into their targets. She stopped and turned to see her improvised traps in action. Only one orc survived the onslaught. All the others were caught in vital areas and either died upon impact or would soon bleed out.

"Okos borszorkany," the orc grunted. He pulled his battle axe free and motioned for her to come to him.

"Eager to join your comrades in death?" Lady Arkyn asked. She sneered wickedly and beckoned the orc forward with her hand. "Catch me if you can," she taunted.

The last foe glanced at the fallen orcs and then started to run after her once more.

Lady Arkyn spun around and ran away. Her feet were so light that she ran over the final trap she had prepared, a pit covered loosely with small branches and ash, without falling through. Her smile widened. She hadn't succeeded in killing the chief, but she had wounded him. She had also humiliated his army. It was an act sure to sow the seeds of discord and doubt throughout the camp. Better still, she had managed to escape. Only a few more seconds and her final remaining pursuer would lie impaled by spikes in the bottom of a pit, and she would be free to return to Stonebrook.

Unfortunately, she was too busy congratulating herself to notice that her pursuer had stopped running. Her ears missed the ceasing footfalls, and they also failed to catch the warning sound of a whirling axe spinning through the air.

A sharp point tore through her armor and cut through her skin. Her eyes went wide. Something snapped. A rib maybe, or perhaps two. Her breath left her with such force that she wheezed and gasped for air. She didn't realize that she was flying forward until her upper body tilted toward the ground and her face crashed into the layer of ash covering the hard ground beneath. Her legs flopped over her back and pinched her spine at the waist. Her body twisted and contorted unnaturally under her momentum, spinning and sliding through the ash for several feet before coming to a stop.

With great effort, Lady Arkyn managed to raise her head so that her right eye could see over the layer of ash. She choked and sputtered, still unable to suck in air. Her vision blurred, but she could see the orc running toward her again. She couldn't think. She couldn't react. Her fingers trembled and her lungs burned. Her back would not respond to her mental commands. She was helpless.

The orc shouted something and pulled what looked like a long knife, or perhaps a short sword, from his belt. He raised it high above his head and then disappeared. A horrible howl rose up from where the orc had just been. Only then did Arkyn realize he had fallen into the pit and met his own end.

Khhhhhugh! The air rushed in and she immediately choked and spat out a mouthful of ash that had entered with the air. Her lungs begged for breath, but the broken ribs burned and cried out against any movement. Finally, overcome with pain and shock, she lost consciousness. The darkness swept in over her and she went still in the ash.

CHAPTER NINE

Gilifan sat in his soft chair that had been brought in by the mercenaries some time ago and placed next to the blood-stained altar where the many victims had been sacrificed and their energies used to speed the egg's hatching. He looked up when he heard the heavy footsteps echoing into the chamber where he sat. The gray haired, wide-shouldered man strode up to him confidently. It struck Gilifan how different Bergarax was from his half-brother, Governor Finorel. There was hardly an ounce of fat on the soldier, whereas Gilifan doubted he could find an ounce of muscle on the governor. One of them had the brawn to compel, while the other had the brain to control the populace.

Gilifan chuckled to himself then, thinking that if he could somehow merge the two into a single being, they might prove useful. Still, he had to acknowledge that they were upholding their end of the bargain. The necromancer had already lost count of the sacrifices they had brought to him for his rituals.

"Sir," Bergarax said with a slightly bowed head. "I thought I should tell you that the snow has come."

"Yes, that usually happens when autumn gives way to winter," Gilifan said with a derisive snort. "Have you come empty handed only to tell me that snow falls upon Pinkt'Hu?"

Bergarax shook his head. "No. It appears that this winter has come early, and is much more severe than usual. The docks are now inaccessible due to ice forming in the shallow waters. Trade has been halted, and we will be reliant upon the storehouses for food."

Gilifan smiled. "Well, then I suppose it will also help keep the citizens from buying their way aboard the trading vessels and escaping. That should help with the collection efforts."

Bergarax frowned. His eyes flickered toward the altar and he sighed. It was a slight movement, but the necromancer noticed it. He knew the sacrifices made Bergarax uncomfortable. He also knew there was nothing the muscle-bound soldier could do about it.

"How many more do you require at this time?" Bergarax asked dutifully.

"How many do you have in the holding cells in the fortress?" Gilifan inquired.

"About thirty," Bergarax answered.

"Bring me half," Gilifan said quickly. "And make sure the chains are tight. I don't want any of them trying to escape and being killed in the attempt by one of your mercenaries. If they die anywhere but the altar, I cannot capture their energy as it leaves the body."

"Of course," Bergarax said.

Gilifan twitched when he heard a slight *crack*. He held his hand up, motioning for Bergarax to remain still. Then he moved a single finger to cross over his lips. Bergarax nodded his understanding. The necromancer pushed up from his chair, wincing when the furniture creaked under the shifting weight. He softly walked toward the large egg which stood at the opposite end of the altar, nestled snugly in a concave half bowl of stone so that the top of the egg pointed slightly toward the flat of the altar. The river of blood from the numerous sacrifices had run down a trench in the stone to flow out over the egg shell so that now it appeared to be mostly brown and burgundy instead of showing the crowning spot over the top of the eggshell.

Gilifan hovered his hand out over the egg. A warm, vibrating force rose up to meet his hand.

"Will today be the day?" Gilifan whispered.

A throaty growl sounded in the distance. The necromancer couldn't see his spirit, but he knew that Tu'luh was near as well. He smiled and turned his attention back toward the egg.

Click-click-crack!

Rapid tapping created a split in one side of the egg. A bright light flashed from within and a wisp of smoke snaked out through the crack.

"It is strong," Gilifan commented. "The souls have fed it well." He turned around to Bergarax. "On second thought, go and fetch all thirty. Then go out and find me a few hundred more."

"A few hundred?" Bergarax repeated. His spine stiffened and his eyes went wide.

Gilifan ignored the man's reaction and nodded. "The host will need to be strengthened quickly if it is to be fused with the master's spirit." He waved the soldier away. "Go, leave me to this. The dragon will be wild when it comes out, and I shall need to subdue it."

Gilifan didn't bother watching for Bergarax to leave. He turned his attention back to the egg. Another crack ruptured through the shell. This one was nearly as long as Gilifan's hand. He would have to hurry.

The necromancer began weaving a powerful ward around himself. Bands of red and gray encircled him and created a large sphere that was impervious to fire. Next he cast a net of lightning over the sphere. The crackling bolts flashed across the sphere every which way in a raucous, chaotic pattern. This would protect him in case the hatchling thought to make a meal of him. It wasn't enough to kill the young dragon by any means, that would be counterproductive, but it was enough to stun the beast if needed.

Next he turned back and enclosed the chamber with a wall of lightning. Around that he created the illusion of a stone surface. He knew it wouldn't hold up to a mature dragon's keen mind, but a hatchling didn't have the awareness to dispel illusions yet.

Another crack appeared in the shell. This time a fracture crossed horizontally across the shell. Time was running out.

Gilifan muttered an ancient spell, one shown to him by Tu'luh himself, back when the egg was entrusted to him. A golden orb appeared over the egg. A loud sound, like that of a constantly ringing gong filled the chamber, drowning out the lightning and even Gilifan's own voice. The necromancer shouted as wind rushed through the chamber, whipping up dirt and dust around the magical spheres in the room.

The golden orb then flattened on the bottom and stretched until it resembled a great bell of brass.

A piece of shell the size of Gilifan's face fell from the egg and split upon the stone floor. Inside the shell a yellow eye flashed across the opening, followed by a mass of silvery scales. A great light erupted from within the shell and then out came the hatchling. It roared mightily as the shell shattered around it. The fragile, leathery wings expanded out from the sides and a column of blue flame spewed upward from the hatchling's throat.

The magical bell grew large enough to encapsulate the

hatchling and then fell down to trap the beast.

Koorrrrrrrrrrrringgggg!

The hatchling didn't even flinch. Instead, it immediately lunged at the inside of the magical net. Gilifan smiled as he watched the golden shape vibrate against the hatchling's attack. Keeping his personal ward up, he waved his hand and turned the golden prison into a translucent bell so he could inspect the hatchling. It spun and wheeled around, attacking the inside from every angle. Claws, teeth, and fire assaulted the magical prison, but it was futile.

"Imagine the power the men of Kendualdern must have had once they created this spell," Gilifan whispered to himself. The constant ringing died down just as soon as the dragon became still. It's yellow, angry eyes turned to the necromancer. Gilifan cocked his head to the side and grinned. "If the master didn't need you, I might have made you my own."

The man dropped his ward, but kept the magical wall in place behind him. He wasn't worried that the hatchling would escape, but he had no patience for intruders at this time. He wanted this moment to himself. The power he felt conquering a dragon was more ecstatic than any other he had known. Even raising the dead had not brought thrills like this. Inside of a translucent bell sat a live dragon. The spell, Gilifan knew, was used to not only to capture dragons, but to imprison their minds before they could develop. It would enslave them.

"The men of Kendualdern had no idea what greatness was theirs," Gilifan whispered. "If they had, they might have saved their world." The necromancer bent down and placed a hand on his side of the bell. The hatchling snarled and shot a puff of flame at him. Instinctively, Gilifan jumped. He laughed at himself afterward. He knew the spell would hold, but that hadn't lessened the sudden fright.

"So," Gilifan said as he locked eyes with the dragon. "Shall we begin?" He rose up and stretched both hands out to the top of the bell. As he had been instructed by Tu'luh, he began the chant. He wasn't sure the words were pronounced exactly as Tu'luh had shown him, but they were close enough. He began to feel the bell vibrating underneath his hands. The dragon shivered and curled into a ball as tendrils of golden light flashed down time and time again. The hatchling cried out and attempted to cover itself, but there was no escape. The tendrils continued to fire down rapidly, pinning the beast to the stone floor and beating its will into submission.

Gilifan continued the chant for perhaps half an hour before the last tendril flashed and then exploded into a cloud of what looked like gold dust. That, Tu'luh had told him, would be the sign that the spell was complete and the dragon had been tamed. Gilifan stepped back. His body was noticeably weaker. His hands trembled and his feet were numb. His head ached in the front and he struggled for breath. Goosebumps rippled over his entire body. Placing one hand upon the bell, he lowered himself down to his knees.

The dragon came to the edge of the translucent bell and sat upon its haunches expectantly. Gilifan smiled at the beast.

"Lie down," Gilifan commanded.

The dragon dropped to its belly.

"Raise your tail," Gilifan said.

The dragon lifted its silvery tail and held it as high as it could.

"Stand and roar," Gilifan said.

The hatchling sprang up and roared as mightily as it could.

"So that is what it feels like to control a dragon," Gilifan chuckled to himself. "Lie down, now we rest," Gilifan said. The dragon dropped back down and closed its eyes obediently. A pair of fierce eyes stared at Gilifan from the other side of the bell. The necromancer's heart nearly stopped until he realized he was seeing Tu'luh in spirit form.

A low throaty growl filled the chamber, reminding Gilifan that the hatchling belonged to the master.

*****

"Another game of cards?" Maernok grumbled when he saw Salarion take out the well-worn deck of playing cards.

"We have enough food for today, and Tu'luh's spirit is still near. We can't make ourselves known until his spirit has been fused with the new body."

Maernok moved to the window and looked down. "The soldiers are gathering more than usual today," he commented. "Are you sure they won't come in here?"

"They can't see this building," Salarion replied. "To them it looks like a burnt shell of stone without a roof and filled with rubble on the lower level. My spell will keep them out."

"I hate magic," Maernok groused.

Salarion shuffled the cards. "If you want to run out and meet Gilifan's army head on, be my guest."

"This doesn't feel right," Maernok said. "Hiding in here while others flee and are rounded up."

"I told you before, only after the spell is used will Gilifan be weak enough to vanquish."

"You sure we can't sneak in and kill him before?" Maernok pressed. "If your spell works on the guards down below, then we can get close enough to kill the meddler. Let's end this madness!"

Salarion shook her head. Her raven hair fell over her brow and covered one of her purple eyes. "I told you, Tu'luh can see through any illusion I could create. He would alert them and then we would find ourselves fighting an army of hundreds with no escape."

"Sounds more honorable than this," Maernok spat.

"The mission is to kill Gilifan. Doing so will save thousands more than will be lost here in Pinkt'Hu. Though I must say I admire your consistent concern for the humans."

Maernok's eyes flashed with anger and he folded his muscular arms over his thick chest. "I have no love for the creatures," he snarled. "I am not accustomed to hiding in the shadows when there is glory to be won."

"You are not so different from the humans," Salarion said. "You both have this delusion that glory will grant you immortality. Tell me, what good does it do you for strangers to sing songs of your deeds around a campfire you will never see? Does it ease the suffering you will endure in Hammenfein?"

"Watch your tongue, drow. I shall be a captain in Hammenfein. I will lead legions."

"Again," Salarion began as she reshuffled the deck. "What good will that do you? You will still be cast out and imprisoned in a fiery realm bereft of beauty and pleasure. What difference if you are a captain of slaves when neither are free?"

"You wouldn't understand," Maernok replied.

"That is exactly my point," Salarion said as she dealt three cards to each of them. "I don't understand why the armies of Hammenfein don't rise up and conquer Terramyr. An army of immortal orcs crushing every living thing on the surface would be quite the campaign."

"You mock us?" Maernok asked. "You elves are supposed to possess wisdom unmatched and yet you don't grasp something as simple as the rules that bind us to Hammenfein?" Maernok shook his head and sat at the table opposite Salarion to take his cards. "Without bodies, we can do little in the realm of the living. The gods that rule Hammenfein are not able to give us our bodies back, otherwise we would have spilled out from Hammenfein ages ago to avenge our ancestors."

"Hatmul and Khefir are the current lords of Hammenfein, yes?" Salarion asked.

"Yes, the sons of Khullan, our Creator."

"Why not send the valiant orcs down to liberate Khullan? Surely he could resurrect you into your bodies," she pointed out."

"Bah," Maernok groused. "Khullan is bound in Vishnull, with a limb lashed to each pillar of Hell. Not even Hatmul could survive a descent through the lower levels of Hell. Only Icadion has the power to do that."

"Which brings me back to my original question," Salarion said. "If there is nothing you can do to change anything on a lasting scale, then why try to seek glory?"

Maernok growled and tossed a card onto the table face down. "What do you fight for elf?"

Salarion placed her card down on the table. "I say my card is high."

Maernok reached over and the two flipped their cards over. Salarion's card was indeed higher and she took both cards. "Answer my question, drow," Maernok pressed. "Tell me what you fight for. Show me the fabled wisdom of the elves."

Salarion placed another card down on the table. "High," she said. Maernok placed his card down. She watched the orc overturn his card and then hesitated on hers. "I fight for those who cannot. I fight to keep the world alive."

"That's it?" Maernok said. "You fight to save the world?" Maernok chuckled and shook his head. "If other elves are half as idealistic as you, then the wisdom of elves is foolishness."

"Is it?" Salarion asked as she overturned her card. She won the round and stuck a finger on her card to accentuate the victory. "What else is there to fight for but the world? Nothing else we ever do will mean anything to anyone else on any realistic level. You can keep your songs of bravery and greatness. I fight so that others will live to sing those songs. They need not know my name. It is enough for me that they will have breath."

CHAPTER TEN

Erik sat in his glass room. His eyes stung, his stomach growled and churned, and his head ached. He could only manage to focus on his training until the Immortal Mystic would send him back to his room at the end of a day. Then the shadows and nightmares found him. Voices of enemies and fallen friends haunted him. He should have felt safe in the palace. He should be expanding his power. Instead he felt numb at best. When he wasn't dead to everything he was cold and empty. He lost hold of the hopes for saving the world. Those thoughts drowned in the sea of doubts that pummeled him with unrelenting waves.

He leaned his head back against the cold wall and then he felt a slight breeze. He turned his head to the right and saw the Immortal Mystic standing in the doorway.

"You don't truly believe I haven't noticed the ghosts that torment you, do you?" he asked pointedly.

Erik didn't know what to say. He sat and shrugged.

"I have seen them, but you have to know something." The Immortal Mystic walked in and sat cross legged on the floor in front of Erik.

"You're going to tell me it is good to face my fears?" Erik asked dryly. "Or are you going to say that only by vanquishing my doubts will I finally come into my power? Whatever it is, I don't think it will help."

The Immortal Mystic frowned and sighed. "Your heart is closed. I cannot help you unless you open it."

"Ah," Erik said with mock surprise. "That is a great pearl of wisdom. I am honored to be here to hear it."

"Erik—"

"No," Erik said, cutting the man off. His voice wasn't raised, but the tone was decisive and curt. "I have been here for months. I see the snow falling outside. In training I can only think of my friends who are out fighting a battle that I caused. When I am not training, and my body begs to sleep, I am visited by nightmares that burn me to my core. You say you have *seen* the ghosts? You saw my father? Did you see Tatev? Or did you see Janik and Tukai? Tell me why you let them in this palace if you can see them?"

The Immortal Mystic shook his head once. "Specters cannot enter here of their own accord. They must be brought by someone else. They hang around you, like familiars. Until you banish them, there is little I can do for you."

"Some sage you are," Erik snapped. "I traveled the world to find you. I lost..." Erik's words trailed off and he closed his eyes.

"Erik, listen to me and I will offer you the best help I can," the Immortal Mystic said.

Erik opened his eyes and raised his brows at the man. He didn't say anything, he just stared with a clenched jaw and unrelenting, fierce blue eyes.

"You didn't cause this war," the Immortal Mystic said. "You see your father's ghost and see your own faults, but you fail to see the whole picture. You are looking at a single thread in a tapestry and wondering why it touches neighboring threads the way that it does, but what you need to see is the overall design."

"I don't believe in fate," Erik said. "I was supposed to be a prophesied champion, but instead I find out that I don't fit any description that you have seen of the champion. I am a mistake."

"No, it isn't that way, Erik."

"Then tell me I am wrong," Erik pressed. "Tell me that your visions showed me to you. Tell me that you saw me destroy Nagar's Blight. Tell me that everything I have lost is actually worth it. Tell me that we haven't fouled everything up by wasting time on me when we should have been looking for someone else."

The Immortal Mystic sat silently, looking back at Erik. His emotionless features rested on his face as though he were chiseled from stone. No words emerged, nor was there any smile of comfort. There was only the silent stare.

"You can't, can you?" Erik asked. "I figured it out, you know. Only, it's too late to fix it. I don't know who the real champion is, and we don't have the time to find him."

"Visions are not without faults. There are mistakes, and misunderstandings."

"Don't do that," Erik said. "That is what Marlin would say. I expect you to be straightforward. Just tell me the truth."

"Very well," the Immortal Mystic said with a nod. "You are

not the champion I saw in visions."

Erik's head dropped backward to thud against the glass wall.

"That doesn't mean all is lost," the Immortal Mystic continued.

Erik shook his head. "Really? You know who I should find? Do we have time to train him?" The Immortal Mystic held up a hand. Erik felt a tingling sensation fill his mouth. No matter how he tried, he was unable to speak.

"Forgive me, but lessons work best if the student is listening," the Immortal Mystic said. When Erik stopped squirming, the man continued. "Despite all the visions I have had, and all the books of prophecy that we have written here and given to Valtuu Temple or other orders, I also do not believe in fate. The visions show me what can be, given a specific set of circumstances. Usually they are highly accurate, but there are always minor inconsistencies. However, I was never surer of my visions as I was with those concerning the Champion of Truth.

"You were never seen as the champion in any of my visions. You come from a different lineage, and were destined for a much darker path. I will speak plainly." The Immortal Mystic cleared his throat and tears came to his eyes. "You are the son of a powerful shadowfiend named Dremathor. Your mother died in childbirth. You were destined to follow in your father's footsteps. I am not privy to all the details, so I can't explain everything that happened to change your course. However, I believe Dimwater will have answers for you."

Erik's eyes widened and he opened his mouth to ask questions, but the words didn't come out.

"There are other factors as well," the Immortal Mystic said. "Some of them remain clouded, even to me. Whatever happened, it set you on a different path. You were able to grow without the shadow of your father. Then, you were adopted and your course was changed even more so. You may not have been the champion I saw in my visions, but I need you to hear me now. You *are* the Champion of Truth. You have every potential to end this terrible plague and remove Nagar's Blight from this plane. Tu'luh seeks to enslave the realm, but he fails to understand that a world darkened by slavery and despotism will also bring about the end he is trying to avoid.

"The four horsemen are real, Erik." The man rose to his feet and waved a hand. The glass wall opposite from Erik became colored with the scene of a beautiful valley. Trees swayed in the wind and flowers dotted the green valley as far as the eye could see. Then, off in the distance, a great fiery cloud fell from the sky. It was soon joined by three more. They crashed far from the vantage point Erik was watching from. The sky grew dark. The waters turned red with blood. Veins of brown and black ripped through the green valley. Trees died and turned to dust. The sun ceased to give its light. Finally, a great wall of fire rose in the distance and ravaged all that Erik could see.

A chill ran down Erik's spine.

"This is no vision," the Immortal Mystic said. "It is a memory. It happened much slower than the way you just saw it, but time is relative when looking through the eyes of a dragon."

Erik wanted to ask whose memory it was. He wanted to know where it had happened, but his mouth was still sealed. The Immortal Mystic turned to Erik and placed a hand on his shoulder.

"When your eyes are fully opened, you will know where that memory came from, but until then you must continue your training." The Immortal Mystic placed his other hand on Erik's other shoulder and looked deep into Erik's eyes. "You must understand that you can succeed. There is no fate. There is only us, and the moments we have been given to use. Do you understand?"

Erik nodded.

"I will tell you one more thing," the Immortal Mystic said. "Dremathor was the son of Allun Rha. That means you are the grandson of the great wizard who defeated Nagar and Tu'luh in Hamath Valley. So, when I tell you that the power to be victorious flows in your veins, you had better believe that I mean every word of it. If I didn't, I wouldn't waste time with you, and neither would your friends. You have lost friends and family, so have I. This is a war that has been dragging on longer than I care to think about any longer. It is time to end it."

The man pulled away from Erik and then folded his arms. "After we win, I can also show you how to defeat the four horsemen."

Erik's eyes nearly popped out of his skull. His mouth opened and had he not been silenced by magic he would have shouted his excitement.

"It will not be easy, but it is possible. They will come eventually, that much is certain. The only question is whether the greed and envy of men is what will bring them down on Terramyr, or the corruption that Tu'luh would force upon the world. Both are equally unacceptable to the four horsemen. They are powerful beings, but they can be stopped, *if* you are able to finish your training."

Erik nodded his head quickly.

The Immortal Mystic waved his hand and Erik's mouth was freed.

"What do I do?"

"You leave," the Immortal Mystic said. Erik's face went from one of excitement to one of confusion in an instant. The Immortal Mystic smiled and continued. "To finish your training you need to banish these ghosts that plague you. To do that, you need to help Tatev's soul find rest. He wanders the plains, looking for the Eyes of Dowr. Go out and find them, then come back here and your eyes will be free of clouds and you will finally be able to see."

Erik couldn't believe what he was hearing. "Won't that take a long time?" he asked. He wasn't trying to be argumentative, but he was more than a little worried by the proposition.

"It will take as long as it needs to. When you have finished, return to complete your training."

"Then I should go now," Erik said.

"I have already prepared a pack for you with food and water."

"I'll get Jaleal," Erik said.

The Immortal Mystic shook his head. "No, this is one journey you make alone."

Erik's mouth fell open.

"Trust in who you are," the Immortal Mystic said. "You come from a noble, powerful heritage. You have been trained well, and you have more potential locked away in that small frame of yours than you can possibly fathom."

"I have never been alone," Erik said.

"This is the best way for you to chase away your ghosts. They won't come near you while friends guard you, but when you are alone they perceive your fear and will plague you. That is when you will battle them and conquer them. Remember, you have more power than they do. Focus on who you are and what your mission is, and you will succeed."

Erik took in a deep breath and ran a hand through his hair.

"I have something for you," the Immortal Mystic said. He reached into a fold in his robes and pulled out a blue crystal. "You may not have noticed, but your birthday passed a few weeks ago. This is my gift."

"What is it?" Erik asked.

The Immortal Mystic smiled. "Some answers you must find on your own," he said. "Go on. When you need the crystal, you will know."

CHAPTER ELEVEN

"The orcs are falling back again. The sun has fallen below the horizon and they have had to turn back. First time I have wished for the sun to drop during a battle," Commander Nials said as he entered the room. They keep going after our catapults much longer and we will not be able to hold the line, though."

Lepkin nodded. "I have never known them to be weak minded, but this is far beyond the tenacity I have ever seen from them before," he said.

"It's their chief," Lady Arkyn said. Her hand reflexively went up to caress the healing wound on her shoulder. "He won't stop until we are all dead. Worse than that, I think they have reinforcements coming."

"How can you tell?" Commander Nials asked. "None of my scouts have reported anything like that."

"They also haven't been as close as I have," Lady Arkyn replied. "I spent the last several weeks evading them behind enemy lines, remember?"

"With broken ribs, no less," Lepkin put in for good measure. "If you say you saw evidence of reinforcements, that is good enough for me."

"Well, I am afraid I have good and bad news," Commander Nials said.

"What more is there?" Lepkin asked.

A scream from the room behind them halted the conversation.

"If it wasn't for her, we might not have any catapults left," Commander Nials said with a nod to the door. "Dimwater has been extremely effective."

Lepkin nodded. "Marlin is in with her, he says everything is going fine."

"I have seen it many times, the screaming is normal," Lady Arkyn said as she reached out to put a comforting hand on Lepkin's arm.

"As I was saying, I received word from King Mathias. There

aren't any more soldiers to spare for us. He says that he had to divert significant resources to the north where the Tarthuns were trying to invade."

"What of Grand Master Penthal?" Lepkin asked.

Nials shrugged. "It didn't mention anything bad, so I assume he still lives."

"So what are we to do without reinforcements?" Lady Arkyn asked.

Nials smiled. "I also received an advance letter from an army of dwarves."

"You received word?" Lepkin asked.

"Well, King Sit'marihu received it, but he relayed the message to me as well." Lepkin nodded his understanding then and Nials continued on. "Apparently they collapsed some sort of underpass in the east and vanquished a large Tarthun army. The dwarven force split after the battle. Half went north to help Grand Master Penthal, and the other half will arrive to our position tomorrow. Beyond the extra soldiers, they are bringing carts filled with provisions to help us wait out the winter."

"That is great news," Lepkin said with a smile.

Another scream erupted from the room behind them.

"Do you need to go in there?" Commander Nials asked. Lepkin regarded the man curiously. The commander's face wore a somewhat disturbed expression, as if the next room held a caged demon or some sort of abomination. Lepkin had not expected to see the man so uncomfortable with the idea of childbirth.

"She asked me to remain out here," Lepkin said.

Another scream.

"Push, woman, push!" Marlin commanded.

"I'm… I'm going to go," Commander Nials said. "I have to settle the casualty count for the night and make sure everyone is accounted for."

Lepkin nodded.

"I can go in," Lady Arkyn offered.

Lepkin shook his head. "She said she didn't want anyone in there who didn't have to be. Told me not to come in until it was over."

Lady Arkyn nodded. "Then I am going to turn in for the night. I'll be upstairs if you need me."

Lepkin offered her a smile and then began pacing back and forth before the door. His mind raced in a million directions as he listened to the commotion inside. Doubts and fear crept into his mind, but he managed to shrug them off. Though he wasn't sure if it was denial or actual confidence that forced the fears out of his mind. The battle raged in his mind until at last he heard the distinct cry of a newborn baby.

"Hawwwwah! Huh-hawwwaaaaah! Hawah-wah-wah! Waaaaaaah!"

Lepkin could wait no more. He burst in through the door. His eyes wide he spied a messy pile of blood-soaked rags next to a basin of steaming water. He then looked beyond that to see Marlin placing a small, wrapped bundle into Dimwater's arms. She was crying and smiling at the same time. Sweat soaked her face and blood stained the sheets below her. The small infant in the blanket started grunting and snorting as she held him close to her.

Marlin stepped away and finished covering Dimwater with a clean sheet. He looked up and smiled at Lepkin. "Everyone is doing just fine," he said. Then he turned to the two mid-wives that were with him and he dismissed them to the hallway.

"Come here," Dimwater said with a weary smile. "Come see your son."

Lepkin shuffled near the side of the bed and peered over the soft, blue blanket to see a red-faced baby boy. He was blinking hard against the light in the room, with little dark eyes grabbing onto both of their faces and his brow furrowed into a cute little scowl.

"Judging by his face, I don't know that he was ready to come out," Lepkin joked.

"I was more than ready," Dimwater said. Lepkin bent down and kissed her forehead.

"Is there anything I can get for you?" he asked.

Dimwater shook her head. "Just be here with us."

Lepkin smiled and pulled a stool close so he could cuddle next to them without causing Dimwater any discomfort. The two of them spent the next few hours watching the infant as he learned to eat and then fell asleep.

*****

Erik trudged through snow that was knee-high. If not for the thick furs that the Immortal Mystic had given him, he was certain he would have frozen to death by now. Even with the furs, his nose and eyes felt as though they were turning to ice. Every breath in his nostrils stuck together. Every breath out melted the scarf over his face only to have the fibers refreeze to his skin. Even his eyelashes stuck together when he blinked.

If only the blue crystal could make fire, that would have been useful! It didn't, though. Erik had tried that the first night after leaving. Not that that was so important though, considering his sword could help him create a fire. It was more that he wished the crystal could warm him while walking. It couldn't though. In fact, it didn't seem to do anything. The second night, after making a campfire, he had tried to use his power on it, but nothing happened. For all he knew, it was just a blue crystal that sparkled nicely in the sunlight.

The thought of the sun made him glance up to the west. The sun was already dipping behind the mountains in the distance. It would be dark soon. He began looking around for a place to settle in for the night. He moved toward a large, thickly branched pine and pulled his sword free. He climbed up into the tree and began cutting some of the lower branches off. He left those that hung the lowest, he would use those as a wind buffer. He spent the remaining daylight clearing snow from the boughs he cut from the tree and then arranging them into a heap near the trunk of the tree. Then he took his rope and tied the lowest branches in such a way that he created a veritable wall of pine branches. It wasn't perfect, but he was shielded from snow fall and most of the wind was blocked as well. He then pulled two blankets out from his pack. They were both made of a thick canvas, though one was definitely softer to the touch than the other. The soft one he stuffed into the center of the pile of branches. The coarser blanket he draped over the pile. Then he burrowed into the branches he had cut.

His workmanship kept him warm through the night without the need for a fire, though he certainly did his share of tossing and turning. He was more than happy when the sun finally peeked its light into his shelter. He repacked the blankets and stuffed the rope back into his pack and continued on. He ate while moving. His pack was filled with enough bread to feed twenty men, so his stomach never went hungry for want of food.

As he made his way down into the valley, the journey became easier. The snow was not as deep as it had been farther north. There were even occasional streams that were not entirely frozen over and provided him the opportunity to restock his water supply.

He had expected to see Tarthuns along his journey, but he never saw so much as a footprint. It was as if they had all disappeared. He couldn't say that he actually was displeased by that fact though. The last time he had had a run in with them, he and Tatev had been kidnapped and Tatev was murdered after the barbarians had tried to burn the Infinium.

Erik's heart felt heavy then as he recalled Tatev. If only he had done something. If he had used his power to scare the Tarthuns, or maybe if he had been faster when they were first kidnapped. If he could have stopped the man with the bone necklace, maybe Tatev would still be alive.

"No I wouldn't," a familiar voice said.

Erik jerked his head to the side and saw Tatev standing next to him. The librarian was smiling, with his red, curly hair bouncing slightly as they walked. "Am I dreaming?" Erik asked.

"Not this time," Tatev said.

"So you are real?" Erik pressed.

There wasn't anything you could do," Tatev said. "It was my time."

Erik stopped walking and looked at the man. "I don't believe in fate," he said defiantly.

"Whether you believe the sky is blue or not is irrelevant. The sky is blue. Fate may not exist in its purest sense, but I had a meeting with destiny. It was my time."

"Why?" Erik asked. "What possible purpose could that serve?"

Tatev smiled. "Have I ever told you about the Eyes of Dowr? They were created by…"

Erik reached out to grab Tatev's shoulders but his hands went through the image.

"You can't grab a spirit," Tatev said. "It is widely known that a spirit holds the intelligence from life but not the physical body. It only retains a likeness of image, in those rare instances when a spirit can be seen by mortal eyes. Which, by the way is a rare trait. It usually happens in times of great need, or when a person has developed the skill to see those that have passed on." Tatev raised a finger. "This skill by the way is not to be confused with clairvoyance, or mediums. Many of those people are nothing more than swindlers who use..." his words stopped and he looked at Erik. "Where are my glasses?" he asked.

Erik sulked and shook his head. "They were lost."

"I see. Well, then we must find them. I can't go on until we do."

"What do you mean?" Erik asked.

Tatev's spirit began walking. His head was focused on the snow covered ground and he muttered something to himself that Erik couldn't hear. Erik watched the apparition search the snow for a few moments, wondering if his mind was playing tricks on him or if Tatev actually stood before him. He called up his power.

Tatev stopped and went rigid. He turned back to Erik with a curious look on his face. "I am real, Erik."

Erik's mouth fell open. He had gotten so used to his hauntings that he hadn't actually expected Tatev to remain after he called up his power. "Tatev..." Erik's sentence fell away in his mouth. He wasn't sure how to say what he wanted to say. "I'm sorry," he finished under his breath.

Tatev smiled and gave a quick wink. "Help me find the Eyes of Dowr."

Erik nodded and then Tatev's image faded away. Tears came to Erik's eyes, but he was quick to wipe them away with his gloves before they could fall and freeze on his cheek. He then pushed on, travelling westward and hoping to find the large brook where he and Tatev had been kidnapped by the Tarthuns. He walked for days, stopping just long enough to find or build shelter as he made his way across the wintry valleys.

Tatev's ghost came and went on occasion, but Erik was unable to hold a conversation with him again like he had before. Now when he saw Tatev the ghost was completely engrossed in searching for the Eyes of Dowr. His head was always down and he seemed not to notice Erik at all. Erik was unsure if it was Tatev's sudden silence as compared to his former talkative nature, or if it was the utter hopelessness he saw on Tatev's face that bothered him more. Erik couldn't help but wonder if his friend was trapped in a kind of hell, unable to move beyond the last thing that occupied his mind upon death. This thought only served to magnify the guilt and shame he felt. Every day he failed to reach the brook and find the Eyes of Dowr he felt less and less capable of anything. Some mornings he struggled to rise from his sleep, secretly wishing that a beast could have found him during the night and ended his own suffering.

In those moments he tried to focus on Lepkin. He tried to force himself to push on and act more like he knew Master Lepkin would in his place. It didn't make it easy, but it made it possible for Erik to continue putting one foot in front of the other.

Then came a day he hoped would not come. His wanderings had somehow taken him back to the place where Tatev had been killed. The camp and all of the structures were gone now, save for the pit and the large timber that jutted up out from the pile of ash like a grotesque monument to Tatev's murder.

Erik surveyed the area and saw that each of the more permanent buildings had been razed by fire. There was nothing left but ash and snow. The young man walked toward the fire pit and looked down. His eyes could see only a dip in the snow where the pit went down into the dirt, but his mind replayed the entire scene for him in every vivid detail. The men chanting and gyrating as Tatev was bound and sacrificed to some pagan god. Erik drew his sword and moved toward the standing pillar of burnt wood. In his anger and grief he hacked at it with his sword.

Charred bits of wood exploded out from the pillar in clouds of black ash and soot. Erik put more and more effort into each swing until finally the pillar cracked and the top half broke and fell to the ground.

"Does that make you feel better?" Tatev asked from behind.

Erik turned and nodded dumbly. "A bit, actually," he said. He stabbed his sword into the pile of frosted ash and folded his arms. "I am sorry," he said.

"I told you before, Erik, it was my time." Tatev offered that reassuring smile of his and at last Erik could see that Tatev held no ill will toward him. There was no blame in the ghost's eyes. There was only compassion. "Before we found you at the mouth of the cave, I had a vision." Tatev shrugged. "Visions are usually reserved for others in the order, not for the librarian. Still, I know what I saw. I knew I would die along our journey."

Erik ripped his sword free from the ash only to sheath it and walk up to Tatev in a huff. "Then why come with me?" he asked incredulously.

Tatev smiled wider. "Because my vision was two parts. One showed me my death was sure if I traveled with you, but the other part was worse. It showed me that if any other besides me went with you, or if you went alone, then you would die. I could not let the Champion of Truth fall. The whole world would then be at the mercy of that wretched book!"

Erik shook his head. "You died for nothing!" Erik screamed. "I am not the champion. I am just a boy."

Tatev shook his head. "No you aren't," he said adamantly. "You are the champion."

"You don't understand," Erik continued. "The Immortal Mystic said I am not the one he saw in the prophesies. I am an imposter."

Tatev shouted, "No!" and a great burst of thunder shook the sky. "You are the champion!"

"How can you not see it?" Erik asked in a whisper.

Tatev moved in close. "If you are to win, there can be no doubt left in your heart."

"How do you propose to fix that?" Erik asked.

Tatev pointed to Erik's pocket. "You have the Tear of Goresym in your pocket, I can see its energy radiating out from within your clothes."

Erik reached in and pulled the blue crystal out. It still appeared to him nothing more than a sparkly bobble. "You mean this?"

Tatev nodded. "It is a powerful relic, I assume the Immortal Mystic is the one who gave it to you, am I correct?"

"Yes," Erik replied.

"I told you that ghosts appear infrequently yes, that they only can be seen in times of great need or if one has developed the skill. Well, this is a time of great need, Erik. You are the champion and yet it is *you* who are blind. You are letting your doubt and grief defeat you before you have even set foot on the field of battle. This is unacceptable."

"You don't understand," Erik interjected.

Tatev cut him off. "It is *you* who does not understand. Give me the crystal." Tatev held out a hand.

Erik shook his head. "You can't hold it," he said. "You are a ghost, remember?"

Tatev stepped forward and reached out so quickly Erik couldn't react. The ghostly hand whiffed through his own, leaving a cold feeling as it passed through. Then the crystal was taken from him and Erik gasped when Tatev held the blue crystal and a great light started to grow from deep within it. "Now you will see the truth."

A great cloud formed overhead as a blue streak of lightning shot into the sky from the crystal.

"What are you doing?" Erik looked up to the sky and put an arm up to shield himself from a sudden burst of wind that flurried the snow and nearly hid Tatev from his view.

"Prepare yourself, Erik!"

A black bolt of lightning crashed down to the ground. Tatev disappeared, leaving the blue crystal hovering and spinning in the air. Another form stood nearby, laughing and holding an axe.

"So, we meet again, young Erik."

The voice was familiar. Erik peered through the snow to see Janik. The man was standing confidently, smiling and twirling his axe.

Erik looked to the man's wrist and noticed it was no longer disfigured. When Janik stepped forward, he didn't limp either.

"What is it, Erik? Nothing smart to say?"

Erik drew his sword. Flames covered the black, Telarian steel with hardly a thought from the young man.

"You have no dwarf here to protect you today," Janik said. "Now I will finish what I started.

The two ran toward each other. Janik sent a powerful spell at Erik, but Erik dodged left and then came in with a horizontal chop of his sword. Janik nimbly flipped over the swing and countered with his axe. Erik jerked his arms back and managed to catch the axe with his blade. Erik had no way of understanding why it was happening, but the shock he received when the weapons collided told him that this was a real battle.

Erik sprang away and readied his sword. Janik laughed and

pressed the attack. He swung downward in a diagonal chop, then reversed his swing and drew his blade out to the side. Erik managed to escape both and then countered with a quick jab. The point of his sword tore into Janik's flesh, but Janik recoiled before the sword could do more than cause a minor gash. The flame from the blade left a smoldering mark on Janik's tunic and chest, but the man didn't seem to notice.

"You have improved," Janik noted. "But you are no match for me."

Erik saw through the man's lie. The champion's gift told him that Janik was lying. Erik's confidence soared. He stepped forward, careful to note each of Janik's movements. Janik swung furiously, but Erik parried every strike. Then, after he pressed in close enough to force Janik to take a couple steps backward Erik launched into an attack. He jabbed forward, then swept his sword at Janik's stomach. Janik smacked down with his axe and shot his hips out behind him, exactly as Erik had hoped. The young champion sent a savage snap kick to Janik's face. The man's head jerked upward and his nose leaked blood. Erik then plunged his sword deep into the man's chest.

A flash of lightning struck Janik and he cried in agony as his spirit disappeared.

Another bolt struck the ground nearby.

A man with a dark, hooded robe stood and smiled. A bony, pale hand reached up and pulled back the hood to reveal Tukai, the warlock.

"A most impressive display, but you are a fool to summon me here, boy," Tukai said. "Your sword will do you little good here." Tukai sent a fireball hurtling toward Erik, but Erik raised his sword and cut through the spell as he had seen Lepkin do in the previous battle with Tukai. "Try this one, then," Tukai taunted. He clapped his hands together and a massive wall of air slammed into Erik, flipping him end over end to land several yards away. When he shook his face free of the snow he realized that his sword was nowhere near him.

Erik pushed himself up quickly and dodged another series of fireballs that sailed at him.

"Dance little champion, dance!"

Erik's mind raced. He couldn't see the sword anywhere. He

had no other weapons on him. Then, a moment of calm clarity overcame him and he smiled at the warlock. He didn't need to have a weapon *on* him. He had one *inside*. Erik sprinted straight for Tukai. The warlock laughed and gathered a massive, green ball of flame between his hands.

"Time to send you to meet your father, boy!" Tukai shouted. The fireball flew on its trajectory, spinning and crackling as it soared ever closer to Erik.

Erik ran on, undaunted. He gathered his power and let it build within his chest. The fireball came within ten feet and then Erik released his power. A column of bright, white light streamed out from Erik's mouth. It pierced the fireball and blasted it apart before continuing on to strike Tukai in the face. The warlock flipped over backward and landed face down in the snow. Erik continued sprinting toward the warlock and before the foe could clamber up to his feet Erik was upon him. The young champion leapt atop Tukai's back and drove a furious fist down into the base of the warlock's neck. Tukai's head snapped down to slam into the ground. Erik continued beating on him relentlessly as he gathered his power for another shot.

A sudden burst of energy knocked Erik to the ground and Tukai rose into the air.

"Clever, but that will not be enough!" Tukai shouted.

Erik didn't hesitate. He sent another column of light at the warlock, striking Tukai in the center of the chest. The warlock shouted out in pain as Erik poured all of his energy into the light. As he focused his power, the light burned bright orange and within seconds it had bored through Tukai's chest and shot out into the sky behind the writhing warlock.

"How?" Tukai asked as his face drained and his limbs went limp.

Another bolt of black lightning came down, removing Tukai.

Erik shut off his power and pushed up to his feet. He was breathing heavily now, and his senses burned with the heat of battle. No longer did doubt swirl in his mind. He was wholly in the moment, prepared to handle whatever was to come next.

A thick bolt of gray lightning struck the ground twenty yards away, but with enough force that the ground shook.

"Erik, has it been so long?" A man stepped out from the

smoke wearing white robes with purple stripes around the sleeves. It was the warlock Gondok'hr, the fiend who had masqueraded as Senator Bracken and was responsible for Erik's father's death. "You struck me down in my sleep," the warlock said. "I won't be so easy this time around."

The warlock transformed from his human body and took on that of a fiendish demon with spikes like granite jutting out from his shoulders, terribly long talons extending out from his fingers, and wicked fangs protruding out from the grotesque mouth. "Now you must fight me in my true form."

If Erik had felt any fear while watching the warlock transform, it was dispelled as soon as he heard those words. "Then I shall take on *my* true form," Erik said. He didn't think about what he was saying. He didn't think about the ramifications of shifting earlier than his time. He made the choice, and transformed as was natural for any Sahale.

A great ball of fire encircled him, shielding him from the warlock's attack while his body shifted and changed. His bones snapped and elongated. Pain rippled through his body, but so too did power and strength. Great wings developed over his widening back and he let out a mighty roar that shook the ground and caused the warlock to tremble before him.

When the fire dissipated, Erik stood high over the puny warlock. He looked down at him through wise eyes the size of shields. A puff of smoke flew out from his slender snout and he flicked his forked tongue out over his sharp fangs.

"I can taste your fear, warlock," Erik said.

The warlock sent spell after spell, but Erik leapt this way and that, dodging each with blinding speed. He then sprang into the air and whipped his tail under his body to slam into the warlock. The frail creature was sent sailing through the air to land nearly one hundred yards away in a crumpled heap. Erik then sent a gargantuan sphere of fire to consume the warlock's body. It had barely reached the creature when the tell-tale black bolt of lightning struck and the warlock was gone.

Erik turned to regard the blue crystal again. It now looked so tiny to him. With his dragon form he could hear the crystal emitting a sweet melody along with the light. At once he understood the magic that had formed it, and he comprehended its purpose. In an instant he transformed back into his normal body. The blue crystal ceased to glow and it fell to the ground. Erik pulled his clothes tighter around him.

Had he not understood that the Tear of Goresym had transformed him and sent him to a plane between the realm of the living and the dead, he might have been confused that his clothes were still intact. Even still, he knew the battles were no less real.

"Now do you see?" Tatev asked as he returned to stand before Erik. "You are the champion. There is nothing that you have done with help that you couldn't do on your own now."

"The crystal didn't let me fight Tu'luh again," Erik pointed out.

Tatev nodded. "His spirit is highly guarded. The Tear of Goresym was not powerful enough to summon him. Still, this should open your eyes and broaden your understanding."

Erik nodded. "Let's go find those glasses of yours. You have helped me find peace, so let me return the favor."

Tatev smiled. "Let's get the book first," he said wryly. "It's just a short walk to the south."

Erik returned the smile. "Lead the way."

CHAPTER TWELVE

For the next several weeks, Erik carried the Infinium in his pack while he and Tatev walked through the land to find the Eyes of Dowr. With the blanket of snow fallen over the ground it was hard to recognize where they had been on their journey into the Eastern Wilds. Eventually they came to the brook where they had been captured and Erik spent several days digging through the snow.

As the days wore on, Erik built a lean-to and dug a fire pit. The search for the glasses was fruitless and frustrating. The days turned to weeks. Two months passed and Erik was out of ground to search. The only place left was the brook itself, but it was far too cold to wade into the water.

Tatev grew quiet again, pacing in circles around the cleared camp and dragging his feet.

Erik ran low on food, and soon had to start foraging around. Erik fashioned several snares and managed to catch a couple of snow hares. One of them was dismembered by a fox before Erik could get to it, but the other was whole and would supply meat. He stopped looking for the glasses long enough to stock up on food. Soon he had several hares. He skinned them and fashioned a tight string from their sinews. Next he cut a long branch and trimmed it into a smooth pole. He bored a hole through the top end and tied the string through it. He then tied a loop on the other end of the string. He took the pole to the brook and used the thick end to smash up the bits of ice that covered the water. He inserted the end with the string and began fishing along the bottom of the brook for the glasses.

"That won't work," Tatev said as he appeared next to Erik.

Erik jumped. Tatev hadn't spoken to him since they arrived at this spot. Any previous attempt to get Tatev's attention had been fruitless. He wasn't sure if Tatev's sudden change in behavior was a good or ill omen. Either way, he wasn't about to lose the opportunity to enjoy some company. Erik shrugged. "I have looked everywhere else. The glasses have got to be in the water."

Tatev frowned. "You'll never find them like that."

"Well I can't very well go into the water and spend time swimming around for them." Erik then stopped and looked at Tatev. An idea came to him and he grinned. "Why don't you go in the water?"

Tatev looked at Erik with a curious expression and then wrinkled his nose. "I can't swim."

"You're a ghost," Erik pointed out. "You don't need to swim. Just go in and look around." Tatev frowned. Erik grinned wider and motioned to the water. "You can follow the pole and look along the bottom."

Tatev arched a brow and shook his head. "I don't like this, not one bit." The ghost moved toward the water and walked out over the surface. "I don't see anything," he said.

"Go down," Erik pressed. "You can't possibly see the bottom from there. Go in the water."

Tatev mumbled something and then drifted down into the water. Erik soon lost sight of his image. The minutes passed. After a while, Erik was sure that Tatev was either pacing along the bottom uselessly or had gone back to wherever he went when he disappeared. Erik continued raking the bottom with his improvised tool. Whenever he felt a snag he would carefully pull the pole up to reveal his prize. After an hour and a half he had collected three sticks, countless patches of algae, and a large bone from some sort of animal.

"Tatev was right. This is stupid." Erik walked a ways down the bank and began raking a new patch of brook bed. Then he heard a sharp whistle to his left. Erik turned to see Tatev rising above the water some sixty yards away.

"I found them," he said with a great grin. "I remembered that the glasses would have been carried by the current, so I started to walk downstream after I searched the area you are looking in and I found them tangled in a patch of algae down here."

Erik could hardly believe his ears. "Are you sure?"

"Well of course I am sure. They are *my* glasses after all. Don't you think I would know the Eyes of Dowr when I see them? Come on, get them out of the water. I can't pull them out."

Erik rushed down to where Tatev hovered over the ice and broke through the frozen layer with his pole. He started to slip his pole in but Tatev shook his head.

"You'll need to go in after them. The algae has grown around them and entangled them pretty securely."

Erik nodded. He tested the depth with his pole, but failed to touch the bottom. "It's pretty deep," Erik said.

"We are too close to stop now," Tatev said.

Erik went back toward the camp and began cutting branches and logs into a pile. "I'll need a strong fire as soon as I come out if I am going to survive this."

No response.

Erik turned back around and saw Tatev kneeling over the spot in the brook where the glasses were. Erik sighed and went back to work gathering wood. He spent the rest of the day creating a fire pit near where he would enter the water and piling the wood tall and wide in the pit. He would wait until the next morning, to maximize the time he would have in the sun to dry out and try to regain his warmth.

When morning came he laid out his two blankets near the bank as well. One he planned to use as a towel, and the other he would wrap around himself after he dressed, assuming he could dress again after diving into the water.

He looked to the brook and already his bones felt cold.

He used his flaming sword to set fire to the great pile of wood. Once the flames took hold he moved to the bank. With the sword still burning brightly he stabbed it into the dirt. Then he extinguished the flames and slipped the looped end of the string around the handle. He undressed and placed his clothes on the second blanket. The cold air tightened his skin and caused him to shiver. He kept telling himself that it wasn't cold.

"It's warm outside," he said. "The sun is soooo hot."

Neither his mind, nor his body bought into the lie.

Feeling the urgency as the heat left his body he grabbed onto the pole and tested the water with his right foot. Cold didn't even begin to describe it. Still, spring was several weeks away. That was time he didn't have to wait. He ran into the water, splashing and falling in as he gasped for breath. All of his muscles contracted simultaneously and he nearly turned back, but by the sheer power of his will he continued on.

The air in his lungs felt as though it was going to explode out of him as the water enveloped him and he swam down toward the bottom. With his right hand he held the pole, knowing he would need it to help pull himself up with once he had the glasses.

His legs curled up under him and his torso shuddered and quaked. His shoulders barely responded to his commands. His body started to drift with the current, and then Tatev appeared before him.

"This way," Tatev said as he pointed toward a patch of green at the bottom of the brook. At first, Erik was surprised he could hear Tatev speak, but then he realized that Tatev also didn't appear wet either. The ghost occupied an existence that was not bound by the same restrictions placed upon a mortal body. Erik pushed on, encouraged by his friend. He stopped and looked back when he reached the end of the pole. He was still several yards away from the glasses and he could feel his strength leaving him.

"Call upon your power, Erik," Tatev said.

Erik summoned his power as though he would release the great column of light from his mouth. The warmth it created in his chest wasn't much when compared to the crushing cold of the water all around him, but it gave him enough courage to move on. He released the pole and fought against the current. He swam to the glasses and ripped the whole patch of algae free. The glasses tumbled out and started to drift away, but Erik managed to catch them. Then he turned back for the bank.

He saw there was little point going for the pole now. The wood had floated up and now was slapping against a patch of ice near the bank as far downstream as the tether would allow.

Erik clutched the glasses in his left hand while he used his right to climb up the sloping bank and emerge from the water. He managed to pull himself half way out of the brook, but then he collapsed and gasped for breath. His body shivered uncontrollably. His fingers curled painfully and he pulled his arms in close to his chest. His teeth made a chattering noise that would rival any woodpecker he had ever known in terms of speed.

The bonfire wasn't far away, but it did little to help him. He felt as though he had not the power to even crawl to his blanket.

"Put on the glasses, Erik," Tatev said.

Erik scrunched his brow and tried to tell Tatev how stupid that sounded, but his jaw wouldn't hold still long enough for him to gain control of it.

"Put them on."

Erik fumbled with the Eyes of Dowr for a few seconds and then finally managed to get them onto his face. No sooner did he do that than he saw several others standing around him. There were dwarves and soldiers standing around that he did not recognize. Tatev stood in their midst and held out his hands to them.

"There are many who have fought and sacrificed in this effort. They are all pulling for you. They didn't come this far just to watch you freeze to death."

Seeing the scores of people around him, Erik felt a mix of embarrassment and courage at the same time. He slowly pulled himself out of the water and crawled to the first blanket. He began to towel himself off and scoot closer to the fire. The warmth pierced his shivering skin and assuaged the cramps in his body.

As he looked around, still wearing the Eyes of Dowr, he saw Master Orres standing on the opposite side of the fire. The large man was smiling at him, but he didn't say anything. Then, out from the crowd came Al's apprentice. The young man smiled and nodded to Erik approvingly. Erik felt no blame coming from anyone there, only love and compassion.

"Erik," Tatev called out as he stepped up next to him. "My time with you grows short. Now that the Eyes of Dowr have been found, I can complete my mission."

"Your mission?" Erik echoed. "I thought finding the glasses was your mission."

Tatev shook his head. "My mission is to dispel your doubts. I am, and always have been, helping you to fully understand your potential and your role. As my last lesson, I will leave you with this." Tatev smiled and stepped back to reveal Lord Lokton standing behind him.

Erik's mouth fell open and tears filled his eyes.

Lord Lokton stepped forward and stopped only inches before Erik. He knelt down and looked up to Erik's eyes. "You must know how proud I am of you," he said. "Remember your duty. You took an oath at your Konn Deta. You live to defend the realm, and our house."

"Our homes is destroyed," Erik said tearfully.

"No," Lord Lokton said. "The building was destroyed, but that can be rebuilt. Our house consists of all the people we serve. House Lokton still stands. We are diminished, but we are not all gone. Keep fighting for us, Erik. Keep pushing through."

"I am sorry I couldn't save you," Erik said. He dropped down to his knees and the glasses almost fell from his face. He caught them and pushed them back up on his nose so he could see his father. "I did everything I could."

Lord Lokton nodded and smiled. "That is all anyone can ask, of a man, and that is why I am proud of you. Now, rise up, and finish your training. You have an oath to fulfill."

"You don't blame me?"

Lord Lokton smiled and shook his head. "One cannot blame the candle for the shadows that dance upon the walls. Be that light, Erik. Chase away the darkness. That is what House Lokton stands for. That is what Master Lepkin fights for. As for me, I am, and always will be proud to call myself your father. Know that we are watching you, and there are far more of us than will ever stand with the likes of Tu'luh the Red."

"I love you, father," Erik said in a whisper.

"And I love you, Erik," Lord Lokton replied.

"Our time is up," Tatev said. "We must go now."

"Where? Why?" Erik asked.

Lord Lokton stood up and smiled wide. "Who do you think helps the Immortal Mystic see his visions of the future?" he asked. "The good and just that have passed on try to gather the bits of wisdom they can and help him make sense of the world. Until the rainbow bridge is reestablished and the path back to the Heaven City, Volganor, is open, it is the best we can do."

"You help the Immortal Mystic?" Erik asked incredulously.

"And others, in times of great need," Lord Lokton replied.

"Then I will see you back at the palace?"

Lord Lokton smirked. "Perhaps from time to time. I am going now to look in on your mother."

A great wind picked up and then the many spirits vanished as if nothing more than wisps of smoke. Erik stood there in front of the fire for a long while. He no longer felt the chill of the water. In fact, he no longer felt anything other than warmth and courage. The ghosts that had haunted him were now at peace. No more screams. No more nightmares. His mind and soul were clear. He dressed and began the long trek back to the Immortal Mystic, securing the Eyes of Dowr safely within his pack.

CHAPTER THIRTEEN

Aparen sat at a small, rectangular table staring at the pile of grapes next to the pair of rolls on his plate. He hadn't touched them. He just looked at them. He wasn't hungry, hadn't been all day, or the day before for that matter. Njar had shown him so much over the last several months and it was only just now beginning to sink in.

All of his fantasies of being some great warlock seemed so laughable now. Nothing he could ever do would change the course of events in the realm half as much as one satyr had done. More than that, he could feel *his* insignificance as well. Whether he lived twenty, one hundred, or even a thousand years, nothing he did would ultimately matter. He would die sooner or later, and the world would go on without him just the same as if he had never been.

The only thing that seemed to make any sense at all anymore was the idea of balance that Njar was showing him.

He reached for the glass of wine in front of him and took a drink. He hadn't been hungry, but he *had* been thirsty, especially for wine. He rose from the table and started to move to the cot he had been given when a knock sounded at the door. Aparen waved his hand and the door opened.

He stiffened when he saw Silvi standing there. He hadn't seen her for a long time. In fact, not at least for a couple of months, and the last time he had seen her was only in passing.

"May I come in?" Silvi asked.

Aparen looked at her raven black hair and her supple features, then he nodded as he took another drink of his wine.

"I don't suppose there is an apology I can make that will help things between us," she started. "But I wondered if we could start over?"

"Start over?" Aparen asked.

Silvi walked into the room, her hips swaying slightly under her form-fitting dress. She closed the door behind her and moved to sit upon the table. "I have been watching you," she said.

"I know," Aparen said. "Njar has told me."

Silvi nodded and smoothed a lock of hair back over her ear. "Are you still interested?"

Aparen pulled his brow together and looked at her. "Are you here to charm me again?" he asked.

Silvi shook her head. "No, I promised I would never try that again."

"How can I be sure?" Aparen asked.

Silvi shrugged. "I would imagine you would be able to detect a charm spell if I tried," she pointed out. "You have progressed along extremely quickly, and with the additional power given to you, I don't see how I could be much of a threat to you anymore."

"What do you propose?" Aparen asked.

Silvi smiled and bit her lower lip before answering. "I want to know if the man who fought a vampire for me still lives, and if he does, I want to ask if he still wishes my hand. I did promise it to him some time ago."

Aparen set the goblet down and moved toward her. "You also told me that you had to be sure I was thinking above the belt."

Silvi blushed and nodded. She folded her hands into her lap and took in a breath. "I would understand, especially with all that you now know, if that man has changed his mind."

Aparen moved in close enough to smell the perfume she wore. He couldn't deny she was beautiful. His heart thumped within his chest as he took it all in. "I am still interested," he said in a whisper.

Silvi's eyes darted down to Aparen's lips and then back up to his eyes. She started to lean in. They both began taking shallow, quick breaths as their faces neared each other. Silvi's lips parted slightly and her eyes closed.

At the last moment Aparen slid a firm finger up to press against Silvi's lips, stopping her instantly. "First I will have to see that you want me for more than just my power," he said.

Silvi blinked and grinned, narrowing her eyes on him playfully. Aparen stood stoic, his face expressionless. Silvi blushed and turned away. She pulled at her dress when it snagged on a bit of wood from the table and made quickly for the door. She paused only when her hand touched the knob.

"I am still interested," Aparen said again. "But the moment

may have passed."

Silvi turned her head slightly to talk over her shoulder. "It isn't too late now," she said.

"You wanted to make me a powerful warlock, and now I am," Aparen said. "The only trouble is now I have something I must do. My focus needs to be solely upon my task. If I complete it, and live through it, then perhaps we can resume this conversation."

Silvi turned all the way around to face him. "You have matured much these last few months. In part that makes me proud of you, but I have to wonder if your ego hasn't grown too large for you." she commented. "I won't promise to be here if you take too long."

Silvi then left and slammed the door behind her.

Aparen smiled and nodded. "One should always be careful what they wish for," he said at the door. "You may not like it in the end." Aparen recalled the lessons about the many Cursed Races. Never had the age-old saying had more impact or meaning for him than it had when he had learned of Khullan's failings after creating the Cursed Races.

He wondered if Silvi would come to regret helping him achieve his great powers. Or perhaps she would wish to have the younger Aparen back, the one that, as she put it, couldn't think fully above the belt. He smirked to himself and turned away from the door. He moved toward his cot and decided that he no longer cared what Silvi thought. If she was around when he returned, then perhaps they would pair off and continue on some other adventure. As he dropped down onto the cot and stared up at the ceiling he thought of Erik Lokton.

With all that he had learned over the course of many months while under Njar's tutelage, he still couldn't shake his hatred of that boy. True, Njar had shown Aparen the meddling witches and their roles in his life, but it was still Erik who broke Timon's hand. It was still Erik who took the horse from his family. Now it seemed as though Erik was about to take a heroic destiny that had been meant for him as well.

The witches may have set the course, but Erik had never been bound by a charm spell.

Aparen knew that Njar would be displeased, but he was happy that Erik's real father was a shadowfiend. A grin of sick, twisted satisfaction stretched his lips as he thought about how fitting it was that Dremathor's powers would soon be given to him. He would honor his word to the shadowfiend, but he would also relish the knowledge that he had gained something of far more value than a simple coven hiding in an underground cavern.

Now he had the power to create his own destiny. Perhaps he could even use it to shape future generations of Erik's own family. After all, he never promised not to interfere with Erik's descendants, and a shadowfiend can live for a very long time.

*****

Grand Master Penthal of the Lievonian Order looked out across the field. The defenses had fallen, and the pass had been claimed in whole by the Tarthuns. Their horses now spilled into the snow-covered valley like wine spilled over a stone floor. Their organization was messy. There appeared to be no order whatsoever. The mounted idiots whooped and hollered as their horses galloped down toward Master Penthal's men.

Master Penthal surveyed his own men. Neat, orderly rows and columns of pikemen hemmed in the valley. Archers stood at each flank, and in two rows behind the main formation of footmen. Swordsmen stood behind the archers, ready to rush in should the Tarthuns blast through the pikemen and get to the archers. The Lievonian knights sat upon their armored horses behind Penthal, waiting for his command. If the battle tipped in their favor, then Penthal would lead the knights personally in an assault as a terrible force. If, on the other hand, the Tarthuns appeared strong, then Penthal would dismiss the knights to lead each of their own men. This type of autonomy had its risks, but the Lievonian Order consisted of the keenest minds, and their ability to quickly respond on the field without waiting for Penthal's own analysis followed by a delayed relay of orders outweighed the risks.

Penthal also had another surprise waiting for the Tarthuns.

Up until this day, the Tarthuns had only faced men conscripted by the Lievonian Order. Despite the fact that Penthal had lost several battles, notably along the walls and towers built in the mountain pass itself, each victory brought only a false confidence to the Tarthuns that would hopefully goad them into making a dire mistake.

Just below the hill less than a quarter mile behind the very spot where Master Penthal sat stood a fierce army sent by King Mathias. There were thousands of soldiers. Pikemen, swordmen, archers, cavalry, and even a few berserker units. If this wasn't enough to send the Tarthuns running, then the several hundred dwarves would be. Unfortunately, their cavedogs would be of no use in this bitterly cold environment, but the dwarves themselves would still send a crushing blow through the Tarthuns' ranks.

The Tarthuns continued to whoop and shout. Penthal smiled at them. "They have absolutely no idea," he reassured himself. He turned back over his shoulder, eyes still glued to the battlefield as he shouted out the order. "Send in the pikemen to plug the gap," he instructed.

One of the knights pulled a horn and gave two quick blasts.

Immediately the several hundred pikemen moved in. They didn't rush or charge. They moved methodically, together. It was a wall of spears, pikes, and pole-axes closing in on the narrow neck of the valley at the base of the pass.

"Let's show the Tarthuns what a real bow can do," Penthal ordered.

Another knight pulled a horn and gave a long, two-toned blow of the horn. Three hundred archers pulled their bows, leaned back to get the greatest range, and then let the black arrows fly through the wintry sky. Scores of Tarthuns fell to the ground. The horse-archers galloped in quickly to answer with their own arrows, but the shafts fell short of the mark.

Penthal smiled. "The horsemen may have us in agility, but they will find our bows can reach them anywhere in the valley, and in order to close off our archers, they will have to break through a wall of steel."

He continued to watch as the pikemen closed in. The galloping horde thundered toward them. Horse-archers fired arrows at the pikemen, but their armor was so well built that only a few unfortunate souls fell at the tip of a Tarthun arrow.

The wave of rampaging hooves crashed into the silvery wall of armor and spikes. Horses cried out, men shouted, and the metal rang out through the valley. Row after row of Tarthuns fell at the point of a spear or pike. The pikemen were vigilant, turning to protect their flanks as the Tarthuns tried to gallop around their sides. The archers continued to thin out the Tarthun flanks, forcing them to face the pikes head-on.

The pikemen formed a perfect crescent, effectively sealing off the narrow neck of the valley and creating a living, ferocious fence around the Tarthuns. Master Penthal smiled. The battle was tipping in his favor. Still, it was too early to call it for the day. He knew all too well that the mounted warriors were not likely to lose their strength as quickly as the pikemen might.

"Sir," someone called from behind.

Grand Master Penthal didn't recognize the voice. It wasn't one of his knights. He turned to see a man wearing a gray robe.

It was Master Cagen, one of King Mathias' mages that had been sent to bolster the eastern defense.

"What are you doing up here?" Penthal growled. "If the enemy sees you, they might turn and rethink their strategy."

"I-I-I know, sir, forgive me, but I thought you would want to know that I have perfected the spell."

"What spell?" Penthal hissed. Then he smiled and held a hand up. "You have figured out the invisibility spell?" he asked enthusiastically.

"No sir. That still eludes me. I don't think we can create an invisibility spell for the army. It is beyond us."

"Well then what do you have to offer?"

"The cavedogs can ride in the snow now," Cagen said with a self-appreciating grin. "I fixed their blood so that they will be just as agile and fast as if they were in a desert cave."

Penthal cocked his head and his eyes nearly fell out of his head. "That is impressive," he said. "Good, have them suit up. When they are ready, we will form a proper cavalry and we will move in to the enemy flank upon my command."

"The others want to know what we should do," Cagen pressed.

Penthal looked to the knights around him and then out to the field. He analyzed the shifting movements of the battle. The center line, where everything was a chaotic mash of bodies and blood, was tilting slightly. He pointed to the point where the enemy had been pushed back the farthest. "You will tell the others on foot to circle around there. Come up behind the archers, then bolster our forces and push the enemy farther back. Your goal will be to pinch the enemy force so that we can trap a significant number of them in a vice while the rest scatter before my charge with my knights and the cavedogs. Wait for my signal. When you hear three short trumpets followed by one long, then you will march at full speed."

Cagen bowed and made his way back down the hill.

"Send the cavedogs up closer, we will attack soon." He watched the field and then his eyes drifted up into the pass. A singular doubt crept into the back of his mind. What if the Tarthuns had more in reserve as well? Could it be that they had a similar plan to his? He shook his head as he went over the notion again in his mind. No. That was not the Tarthun way. They relied on sheer numbers and surprise to gain their victories.

Grand Master Penthal sat atop his horse watching the battle for another ten minutes before the cavedogs were in place. He knew it would take another ten or possibly even twenty minutes before those on foot would be able to reach their position.

The clanging steel continued to drum out across the snowy valley. The archers worked steadily on squeezing the Tarthun flank and keeping the horsemen trapped face to face with the pikemen. However, the pikemen were losing ground now. The sheer numbers and power of the Tarthun horde far outmatched the wall of spears. Far more horsemen were falling by the second, but the actual group of pikemen was being pushed back as the Tarthuns continued a relentless press.

He knew he could wait no longer.

"Knights, this is it." Grand Master Penthal drew his sword. The bright sun glinted off of it and seemed to infuse his very soul with courage. The frigid air filled his lungs, burning slightly, as he pulled in a breath before he shouted the command. "Charge!"

The seven knights of the Lievonian Order galloped down the hill. Their heavily armored horses tore at the snow as they gained speed and became an unstoppable avalanche of steel and fur. One of the knights blew the warning on the horn as they came near to their pikemen. The soldiers immediately parted, allowing the charging knights a direct path into the horde.

Penthal glanced over his shoulder to see many cavedogs only half a pace behind him. A smile crossed his face and he dropped the visor on his helmet.

The world seemed to slow as he galloped atop his horse between the pikemen. Three Tarthun raiders were galloping toward him and the other knights. In that moment he studied each of the Tarthuns' tanned, weathered faces. The scowls and grimaces they wore only accentuated the blood streaked across their weapons and armor. One of the raiders looked back at Penthal and the two locked eyes. They charged directly toward one another. Neither of them flinched. Penthal's horse, being much larger and covered with armor, bowled the Tarthun's horse backward as they collided. At the same time, Penthal brought his sword down low and jammed it through the Tarthun raider's chest. He barely managed to yank his sword free before his horse finished trampling the fallen Tarthun and horse and quickly pressed onward.

Time sped back up to its normal pace again, seeming almost as though it moved faster now than it ever had. The knights slammed into the mass of horsemen. Neighing and screaming drowned out all sound around them. Then came the shrieks and groans as cavedogs fanned out around the knights and started ripping into the Tarthun horses. Penthal was nearly stunned when he saw a cavedog bite off the front leg of a horse as it streaked past. Others darted under and between the enemy horses, giving the dwarven riders ample soft targets to work on with their axes and swords.

The only way Penthal could describe it was to compare it to a sudden earthquake that dropped the first several ranks of Tarthun raiders. All around him the pikemen were able to stand still and breathe for several moments while the cavedogs and knights shocked the enemy force, driving back a whole third of the army.

Grand Master Penthal's horse, however, was not stunned by the carnage. It galloped onward, and Penthal was forced to return to his own defenses when he collided broadside into a large raider. He reached out with his left hand and pulled the Tarthun back enough to run his blade through the man's right side, up between the ribs and into the soft tissues behind them. The Tarthun's eyes went wide and his body stiffened just before Penthal pulled his sword out and let the body drop.

Penthal looked up to notice that the Tarthun horde was recovering. They were shifting their force to deal with the knights and the cavedogs. This is what Penthal had hoped for. The

Pikemen were able to squeeze the flanks even sharper now, and the reinforcements would have a chance to seal off the enemy from behind if they were quick enough.

"Call in the others," Penthal shouted.

Three short trumpet blasts were followed by one long one.

Penthal went back to his deadly work, trusting that Cagen had relayed the appropriate information so that the others would do what he wanted. Still, after the several hundred footmen blasted into the enemy, it came as a bit of a shock when a large serpent made entirely of ice rose up from the midst of the Tarthun horsemen. Horses shied away and men faltered as the magical beast crushed and chewed its way through the enemy force. Penthal only slightly caught a glimpse of Cagen and a few others standing off behind the battle. They were moving their hands and focused intently.

"Gotta love magic!" a dwarf cavedog rider shouted up from below.

Penthal nodded and continued to press into the fray.

Before long, the Tarthuns broke off. Those who were not directly embattled retreated up the sharp slope back toward the pass. The cavedogs, being much more nimble and quicker than the armored horses, gave chase. The savage lizards ripped limb after limb off the fleeing horses and the dwarven riders were quick to finish off each Tarthun that fell to the ground.

Penthal stood in his stirrups and shouted at the Tarthuns, cursing them as they fled the field. The other knights remained silent, but the pikemen joined in the victorious shouting.

A large cloud formed over the mouth of the pass. Its dark, rumbling form grew in less than a second to cover the entire entrance to the pass. Great crackles and snaps were heard as flashes of light sparked within the dark mass. Then a series of purple and gold lightning blasted down at the rock and ice near the top of the slope. The mountains groaned in protest, but the lightning did not stop its relentless assault. Even when gargantuan hunks of granite and ice exploded from the mountainside, the lightning continued. The debris shot out and landed in the retreating Tarthun horde, crushing many in the first wave. Then, as the lightning persisted, a great wave of snow and ice broke free and began to slide down the slope.

Grand Master Penthal glanced back to the wizards. He didn't have to hear their spells to know it was they who controlled the avalanche. He looked back to his men. "Sound the retreat. Fall back, men, fall back!"

Each knight pulled their horns and signaled the retreat, though the pikemen had already started sprinting back toward the safety of the hills where they had started the day.

"Sir, the wizards are in danger!" one of the knights called out.

Penthal looked out to see a sizable group of Tarthuns galloping toward Cagen and the others. Penthal knew that if the Tarthuns reached Cagen, the lightning and the avalanche would be stopped. He also knew that if he intercepted the Tarthuns, there wouldn't be time to escape the avalanche. He didn't have to think about it. He turned his horse toward the Tarthuns. The other knights followed him.

Grand Master Penthal smiled when he saw several rows of his archers also standing their ground to help the wizards. Arrows flew dangerously low over the wizards to pierce the charging Tarthuns and slow their advance.

The growing, thunderous wall of white and gray snow shook the very ground more and more with each passing second. Penthal could see it out of his peripheral vision as he locked his eyes onto the Tarthuns. A few moments later he and the other knights crashed into the enemy flank. The Tarthuns were forced to stop and engage.

After the space of fifteen seconds, Penthal dropped two Tarthuns before taking a heavy blow to the back that lifted him up from his horse. He flew several yards in a blink of an eye. Only when he crashed down to the frozen ground did he realize what had happened. A flash of white was followed by darkness as a cold wave crushed him into the ground. His head rang and he couldn't see anything. At first, he was more aware of the weight than the cold. His armor bent inward in places, making it difficult to breathe. He couldn't move his arms or legs. His lungs struggled against the pressure to draw breath, but there was precious little air to be had.

A bit of snow dropped in through his visor. His nose chilled as the snow melted and ran down his face. His last thought was one of conquest. He knew that if he was at the bottom of this frigid tomb, then so was the entire Tarthun army. He had led a great battle, one that should ensure the Middle Kingdom's safety from the eastern savages. His only regret was that none of the Lievonian Order would live through the ordeal. He could only hope that the footmen and dwarves were able to escape.

CHAPTER FOURTEEN

Gulgarin pulled the brown fur cloak over his shoulders and fastened the chain in place with a brooch in the shape of a rearing stallion. Next he slipped his hands into his thick gloves and then placed his conical helmet with horse hair sticking out from the top onto his head. His armor, consisting of small, oval plates of mithril woven together over a shirt of chain mail jingled slightly with each movement. The leather hauberk underneath it all lent him some protection from the cold, but not the stares he was sure to receive when he stepped out from his tent.

"I am chief," he said aloud to himself. "*I* am chief." He clenched and released his fists, taking in a fresh breath and exhaling slowly. "I am *chief.*" He reached down to his belt and slid his sword up slightly before dropping it back down into the scabbard.

He turned and exited the tent as if he was about to slay a dragon. The two soldiers nearest the tent nearly tripped over themselves scampering out of his way. Gulgarin paid them no attention. He moved on holding his head high, simply expecting others to create a path for him. His destination was the council, which was already sitting at a large fire under the shadow of three pines that although burnt, retained their overall shape.

The five officers watched him carefully. Gulgarin was sure to study each face in turn. He could see the mixed emotions on their faces. Anger, resentment, even contempt stared back at him. Those emotions he could handle. He understood them. Then his eyes settled on Fenerik, a young captain who was related to one of the late chiefs that had been sacrificed to create the battering ram at Ten Forts. His face wore an unacceptable emotion painted across it.

Fenerik's eyes were slightly wide, darting from side to side and averting to the ground whenever they happened to hit upon Gulgarin's steely gaze. His hands we folded into his lap, thumbs twitching and twirling. Then there was the foot tapping.

Gulgarin could almost smell the orc's fear. He snarled at the young officer and stormed right up to him. "You have something you want to say?" Gulgarin snarled.

Fenerik shook his head and glanced to the others. "No, chief."

Gulgarin reached down and snatched Fenerik by the front of his armor, lifting him up to eye level. "I *hate* fear," Gulgarin said. "It is exactly what makes an orc weak. To fear is to let yourself be conquered by shadows. You are not fit for this council." Gulgarin shoved the young officer back down and then pointed out to the side. "Get out."

Fenerik scrambled out with hardly more than a timid squeak.

"That wasn't necessary," one of the others said.

Gulgarin turned on the others and let his anger at Fenerik play to his advantage. Now was not the time for counsel, it was the moment for him to solidify his power over the tribes. "His weakness will kill our spirit. This campaign is going to be difficult, even for us, but we are going to win, Khullan demands it!" Gulgarin turned his head to the side and narrowed his eyes on the four before him. "I know you doubt me. I know you have anger at the losses we have suffered, but I never said it would be easy. Think back to Ten Forts, did I ask for this?" Gulgarin made a show of turning around, indicating the surrounding camp with his arms. "I assumed command only after Maernok failed to lead us. Do any of you remember why he left? Because he was WEAK! He chose to pursue a personal vendetta instead of leading the united tribes on a glorious conquest to reclaim our homeland."

"The winter will drive us back," Lorik said.

Gulgarin pointed at Lorik and shook his finger in the orc's face. "We will march on. We have come too far now to go back. For the glory of Khullan!"

The others did not join in with him.

Gulgarin let out a sigh that sounded like a feral growl. "Khullan has chosen us," he said. "He has opened the way to our enemy and now he demands courage. Only those who are worthy will survive. This campaign will reclaim our homeland while also culling the weak from our midst. Those who will die will die. Some will win glory and honor, while the others who are afraid and too pathetic to honorably claim the right to walk among us will be stripped from us. Like a herd of deer that is thinned by the wolves, it will only serve to make us stronger in the end. Can you not see?

This is the glorious battle that our sons, and their sons and their sons will sing of for centuries after we have gone on to claim our glory in Hammenfein. You are angry? Good! Now turn your anger toward those who deserve it. Let us stop quibbling amongst ourselves and go out and face down the dogs that steal from our tables. Let's crush the humans and wring their blood out over our land to replenish it and make it vibrant once again. For the glory of Khullan!"

This time the others joined in. "For the glory of Khullan," they said. Three of them seemed genuinely convinced, while Lorik appeared only to be somewhat deferential. Still, as long as he had the council in agreement, Gulgarin needed only one solid victory to solidify his rule. If he could push them through the winter and overtake the human settlement, they wouldn't be able to refute him as the rightful leader.

"These are the orders I wish disseminated," Gulgarin said as he pulled out a single parchment rolled and sealed with a thin string of red silk. "I want these preparations seen to immediately. As soon as it is complete, we march against the humans."

*****

Several days after the council met, Gulgarin woke well before the sun rose into the sky. He stepped out from his tent to address the ten groups before him. He surveyed them once more, ensuring they were ready. Each group had five orcs, and each of them were dressed in white furs. Their faces and any other bits of visible skin had been covered with a whitish gray paint. They were armed extensively with swords, axes, and javelins. Additionally they had each been given tinder boxes and several small vials of oil.

These ten groups were his answer for the enemy catapults.

"Khullan smiles upon you," he said. "While the slothful humans lie asleep in their warm cottages, you have persevered and endured the elements for this moment. There is no shame in cunning and stealth. We may not employ assassins or wizards, but the employment of smaller groups of berserkers is an honorable tradition. The few go out to meet the many on the field of battle. Once you have destroyed their catapults, you will have to fight those that discover you. Kill as many as you can with each breath

Khullan grants you. Your legends will be sung for generations. For the glory of Khullan!"

"For the glory of Khullan!" the groups echoed in unison.

Then they ran off into the darkness. Gulgarin watched until the last of them disappeared from his sight before he moved back into his tent. He moved in and grabbed his warhammer, the fabled, elegant Rombolo. He then moved out to mount a goarg and follow the berserkers.

He found Lorik already atop a goarg and waiting for him. "My soldiers are ready and in place," he said.

"Good. The others should be ready shortly," Gulgarin said referring to the soldiers under the direction of the other officers. Gulgarin had personally taken command of Fenerik's forces and Fenerik had been forced to join the rank and file for his cowardice.

Gulgarin and Lorik walked their mounts out to the edge of the burnt forest. They passed by their waiting troops and stopped just before they emerged from the forest. They stared out blankly into the darkness. From this distance, it was impossible to see the enemy forces. Even the catapults were hidden by the night's shroud. All he could do was hope that the berserkers would set fire to the catapults and sew discord among the humans. If they could destroy the catapults, even just a few of them, it would open up corridors through which the orcs could reach the settlement without being obliterated by raining stone.

They waited for what seemed like an eternity. All was still and quiet. No fires. No sounds. Nothing.

"Maybe they are having trouble finding the catapults," Lorik said. "They do have magic on their side."

Gulgarin nodded. "If they cannot find the catapults, then they will enter the town and slaughter the fools in their beds," Gulgarin assured him. "Either way, there will be blood before the sun rises."

Another hour and a half expired before the first flame was born far off in the darkness.

"Look there," Gulgarin said. "One is down." The chief caught the hint of a smile on Lorik's face as the officer nodded and silently clapped his hands together.

"If they take out the others, we can roll over the humans, just like you said," Lorik commented. "For the glory of Khullan," he added.

"For the glory of Khullan," Gulgarin replied. Two more fires went up. The flames rose high into the darkness and the orcs watched the machines crumble. When another couple of fires began, Gulgarin turned back to the army behind him. "Now is the time to bathe our souls in human blood. Let tonight wash from us the guilt and shame of our ancestors' defeat. For the glory of Khullan!"

Shouts and hollers went up through the ranks and every soldier jumped up and started running across the field. Gulgarin let a couple of rows pass him by before he urged his goarg forward. He was not about to let anyone steal his glory from him this night.

The goarg responded eagerly, leaping and dancing between the orcs until Gulgarin was out ahead of everyone once again. He kept his eyes on the fires ahead, trusting his goarg to maneuver in the darkness. When the large animal approached the chasm it sped up and leapt across. The orc chief held tight with one hand on the reins and his hammer poised for a strike in his other. The firelight from a nearby catapult illuminated the spot where he would land, showing him the petrified face of a human soldier that stood still, staring up at Gulgarin.

The hammer came down and the soldier crumpled to the ground.

Gulgarin's senses came alive. Now he could hear fighting nearby. He urged the goarg in the direction of the noise and found two berserkers fending off a dozen humans. Three berserkers and nearly a score of human soldiers already lay upon the ground in heaps. Gulgarin laughed maniacally as his goarg lowered its head and crushed seven men with its horns and hooves. Gulgarin dropped another three humans and the two berserkers killed the rest.

Gulgarin turned to direct the berserkers, but they were already sprinting north, intent on finding the town and wreaking as much havoc as they could. A smile crossed the orcs face and he moved along the chasm, heading for the next fire. No one was there. Corpses, including four orcs, littered the ground around the burning catapult but no one was nearby. The machine collapsed and cracked like thunder as Gulgarin rode past, showering him with red sparks and hot embers. He didn't bother to brush them away. He let the night's cold air take care of them for him.

He focused on the next catapult. He rode for a couple of minutes before finally reaching it. This time his heart sank when he saw five dead orcs. There were only a few dwarven corpses, and there were about six of the half-pint demons left. The survivors were busy trying to heap snow onto the fire, or smother it with blankets. They never saw Gulgarin coming.

The goarg trampled two dwarves and Gulgarin took the head clean off of the one nearest him. The other three turned to fight, but just at that moment a wave of orcs clambered up out of the chasm. The army had reached the front. The dwarves were overwhelmed and cut down in seconds.

Gulgarin roared mightily, holding his warhammer high above his head. He turned to the north, shouting for his army to continue their slaughter and conquer the city. He pressed on, keeping his pace more or less equal with the soldiers around him. Now he saw torches coming from the north. The enemy was awake.

The orc chief had no way to command the entire army, he had traded that for the opportunity to launch the surprise attack under the cover of night. Now there was only fighting. It didn't matter how many orcs survived. It only mattered that Gulgarin kill all who approached him.

He and the soldiers nearby collided with the humans and dwarves with a thunderous explosion. Time after time his hammer came down to crush foe after foe. Helmets collapsed, men crumpled, and bones shattered under Gulgarin's fury. The orcs around him were no less effective. Their swords hacked the enemy down several at a time. For a moment, it seemed as though it was going to be a wholesale slaughter.

Then Gulgarin saw several hundred dwarves. They stood just on the edge of his visibility, half hidden in the darkness. By the time he realized what they were doing, it was too late. Crossbows clicked into place by the hundreds. The rushing wave of orcs was cut down. A couple of bolts bounced off of Gulgarin's mithril armor. The orc chief grew furious. He let out a feral yell and charged on. The orcs who had not been killed by the volley sprinted faster, weapons ready and anger flowing out from them in their grunts and growls.

The dwarves fired another volley. This time several bolts struck Gulgarin, but his armor held true. His goarg, on the other hand, was not so lucky. The beast collapsed to the ground and threw Gulgarin to the ground. Heavy boots stomped the ground around him as he rolled to a stop. He had managed to tuck his hammer with him when he landed, but he had lost all his momentum.

The orcs and dwarves clashed. Swords and axes rang out in the night air. Neither side appeared to have the advantage. The orcs were much larger, but the dwarves were just as fierce and powerful. The battle turned into a bitter hack-fest. Each side beat on the other, with rows and rows of eager warriors growling and snarling to get their chance at the line.

Gulgarin waded through the orcs, in some cases literally throwing his own troops out of his way to get to the line. As he broke through to the front, he saw a stout dwarf with a dark beard. The short warrior's eyes sparkled from the many fires around. Gulgarin brought his hammer down onto the dwarf's right shoulder. The dwarf was crushed downward, but the blow didn't kill him. He countered with an upward swing of his axe. The blade was stopped by the mithril armor, but Gulgarin felt the weight of the swing and was moved to the side a few inches.

The large orc pulled back and rammed the hammer into the dwarf's stomach as he was trying to clamber onto his feet. Short arms and legs kicked out like an overturned beetle. Gulgarin sucked in a breath and brought the hammer down once more. This time there was a distinct crunch of bones beneath the armor as the metal gave way and caved in.

There was no time to celebrate the victory. Dwarves moved in to fill the void almost before Gulgarin could reset his hammer.

The battle turned extremely bitter. The orcs clawed inch for inch, paying for every step forward with blood of their kin. The dwarves fought valiantly, slaying many of the larger orcs, but they were ultimately outnumbered.

The orcs pushed through the ranks until the golden sun came over the horizon and shed its light on the battlefield. Had Gulgarin not been embattled with three dwarves at his front and a heap of corpses under his feet, he might have had the time to see the devastation around him. With the benefit of the light he would have seen that two catapults had survived thus far, and they were punishing the orcs. He also would have seen a great ring of warriors protecting those catapults. He didn't see any of that. Nor could he count the thousands of bodies covering the ground. He pressed on, leading his surviving warriors toward his goal.

As he finished off the three dwarves with the help of several other orcs that surrounded them, he realized that he had cleared a path toward the city. He looked back to encourage those around him, but saw only a couple dozen still standing. There were many other orcs, but the unit that he had led had been demolished.

Those who still drew breath were covered in so much blood it was impossible to know whether the blood came from them or from vanquished foes. For a moment he thought of calling for a retreat, but he knew that the orcs would all have to cross the chasm again. It would expose them to the humans in an unacceptable manner. So, he turned to the east and saw Lorik still fighting along with soldiers from his unit. Gulgarin broke into a run and his unit followed him.

They made their way over the many corpses as best they could, but they never reached Lorik.

A wall of fire rose up before them and then turned eastward to sweep into Lorik's unit.

"Wizard!" Gulgarin called out.

"Sorceress!" a woman's voice answered.

Gulgarin looked up and saw a woman with dark hair riding upon a cloud over them. "Find a crossbow or something to shoot her with!" he shouted at his troops.

Something moved a few yards away, but Gulgarin couldn't see what it was. A moment later, two of his orcs screamed in pain. He turned to see a massive wolf tearing into one of the orcs. When the warrior fell, the wolf moved to the neck and snapped it like a twig. It looked up and growled with a blood-soaked maw. The other orcs moved in to engage it, but then another movement caught Gulgarin's eyes.

The large orc turned just in time to see a man appear out of thin air. He was a large man with salt and pepper hair. He wore the black, Telarian steel armor of a dragon slayer, but did not use a helmet. It was then that Gulgarin remembered seeing this man before, along with that she-elf that had tried to assassinate him. He took up his hammer and started for the human.

Before Gulgarin could reach him, the man dropped seven

warriors. Tendrils of fire streaked through the air, catching others that the wolf wasn't able to bring down. Gulgarin lifted his hammer to strike and cried out for Khullan's blessing.

He swung, but the man dodged underneath and came up with a hard shoulder, knocking Gulgarin backward three paces. The spikes on the man's armor poked into the mithril and dented it, but they did not manage to pierce Gulgarin. The orc looked down for a moment, shocked that the mithril had nearly failed. The man lashed out with a stab. Gulgarin moved to parry, but the man retracted and then spun around backward, gathering momentum to put into a horizontal swipe at Gulgarin's neck. The orc ducked and then struck out with a jab of his hammer. The man kicked the hammer to the side and then came down hard with an overhead chop.

A flash of burning pain ripped through Gulgarin. He stumbled back and looked down his arms at two stubs. His hammer now lay upon the ground, with both hands and forearms still clutching the weapon. The sword, made of the same hardy metal as the man's armor, had cut clean through the chainmail sleeves and severed Gulgarin's arms just above the elbows.

"You haven't seen the last me of," Gulgarin snarled.

"Then let me tell you my name, so we can dance again," the man replied as he stepped in slowly. "I am Lepkin, and the orcs stop here."

Gulgarin felt a rush of ripping run through the front of his neck, piercing downward through his body. He convulsed and choked as his life force left him. As his last breath escaped, he whispered Lepkin's name over his lips and looked into the man's eyes.

Everything went dark.

Gulgarin twitched. His eyes opened some time later. No one was near him. He sat up and looked around. The field was nearly still. His heart sank when he saw a number of humans combing through the dead, tallying the numbers. Where were the other orcs? Why had they left him there to die?

Then he looked to his hands. As he saw his arms intact, that is when he realized the truth of it. He turned around and looked down. He saw his own face, twisted in a grotesque display of pain and horror. No one had left him for dead. He *was* dead.

He rose to his feet and looked around again. If he was dead, then why couldn't he see other fallen orcs?

Gulgarin froze as a black hole ripped through the air only three yards away from him. Through the hole stepped an immensely large figure. His feet were shod with burning coals. Ash fell from his feet as he walked, but the being showed no sign of pain whatsoever. His legs were massive, muscular limbs that were each as thick around as Gulgarin's waist had been in life. A decaying left hand reached through and grabbed onto the edge of the hole. Skin hung loosely from the exposed finger bones. The arm itself was still encased in skin, but it was pale and gray. A hooded vest covered the creature's head and torso.

The orc knew who it was. "Khefir," he said in a whisper. "Son of Khullan and collector of the damned and accursed."

"I have come for your soul, Gulgarin," Khefir announced in a clicking voice. Khefir reached up with his rotting hand and pulled back his hood. Black orbs looked out from Khefir's yellowy skull as long, coarse white hair hung around the sides. The jaw bone moved when Khefir spoke, but it hitched and clicked with each word. "Hatmul, my brother, will judge your deeds and see whether you have earned your place among our army in Hammenfein. If not, then you shall spend eternity in torment along with every other cursed soul that I collect."

"I have fought valiantly," Gulgarin whispered.

Khefir laughed. "You have betrayed your own kin in order to advance your position in life. You used subterfuge and magic to gain the advantage over others. You sent two chiefs to die and be sacrificed for a weapon."

At that moment, several black tendrils came through the hole and stretched out for Gulgarin. The orc panicked. The tendrils snaked around him and started to constrict. He didn't bother struggling. There was nothing he could do about it.

A spark of lightning streaked in from the west and shot through the black tendrils. The appendages shriveled away into nothingness and Khefir turned to face a pillar of silvery lightning that seemed to stand still as though it were a tree. Then a voice came out from the lightning.

"Khefir, I have need of this orc," a large, very deep voice said. "I cannot let you claim him."

Khefir waved a bony hand and dispelled the lightning. "Show me who dares interfere with my duties."

The lightning morphed into a dragon's head. There was no body, but the head spoke as though the whole dragon were there. "You know me, Khefir," the voice said. "I mean you no harm."

Khefir cackled and pointed at the image. "Tu'luh the Red," he said. "I thought it was you. Tell me, what does a dead dragon need with a dead orc?"

The dragon snarled and hissed. "That is for me to know!" Tu'luh's voice was so forceful that Khefir winced and shied away. "I have claim on him, and that is all you need to know."

Khefir snapped his fingers and a trio of burning, black dogs appeared next to Gulgarin. "Icadion has not given you dominion over the dead. Your claim is void."

Tu'luh turned around and appeared to say something, but Gulgarin didn't hear any words.

In the next moment, a small imp appeared in the air, preceded by a ball of yellow fire.

"My master has sent me as an emissary," the imp snarled. "There is a wizard who works with Tu'luh and Gulgarin. This wizard has the power to resurrect Gulgarin and restore his body."

"I forbid it," Khefir said. "The orc is mine."

The imp smiled wickedly and flew closer to Khefir's face. "The power is facilitated by a powerful artifact. Whether you take him now or not, the wizard can raise him again. You could burn the body and throw him into Vishnull with your father, and he would still be raised up to life."

"If that is so, then let me take him, and prove your power," Khefir replied.

"Take this imp," Tu'luh cut in. "He will make a great addition to your collection."

"You wish to trade me the soul of an imp for the soul of an orc?" Khefir asked. "Hardly an equal trade."

A bolt of lightning struck out and froze the imp in the air. "Take the imp. Use him as a familiar, or destroy his soul, whatever you wish. Consider it not a trade, but a payment for additional time. When the orc has run his natural course, I will forfeit his soul back to you."

Khefir reached out and touched the imp. A black spark leapt

from the imp's head to Khefir's finger. Khefir waved the imp away and the still body floated back toward Tu'luh's head of lightning. "Tell me what you want with the orc, or else I will destroy his soul."

Tu'luh laughed. "You have not the power to destroy a soul such as his. Lesser demons and animals perhaps, but nothing so large as an orc. It isn't a power you can possess unless Icadion were to grant it to you. Still, so that you may know I strike an honest bargain with you, listen to the words I will say next. This orc leads the united tribes. I am using them to cleanse this land in an effort to keep the four horsemen at bay. You would not wish for your world to be destroyed as mine was, would you?"

Khefir cackled again. "I am a god," he said. "Whether Terramyr remains or passes away, I shall live on so long as I fulfill my duties to Icadion."

"So there is nothing I can offer you then?" Tu'luh asked.

Khefir moved to Gulgarin and bent down to look at the orc's soul and body. "I have already collected the other orcs," he said. "Do you seek to raise them as well?"

"I am only asking for Gulgarin," Tu'luh said. "He has reinforcements coming. If I resurrect him, he will be hailed as a true hero, and the orcish tribes will unify in a way that has not been known upon this land. Think of Khullan. Imagine his pride if he knew that one of the races he created had finally set up a kingdom of their own that would last indefinitely. They would even be responsible for protecting Terramyr. Perhaps Icadion would allow the cursed races to earn their way into Volganor." Tu'luh paused and then smiled with his crackling lightning-like face. "Maybe I could even convince him to release Khullan from his prison."

Khefir stopped and looked back to Tu'luh.

Tu'luh smiled wider. "I have your attention now, do I not?"

"Do you jest?" Tu'luh asked. "If you betray me, I will collect your soul and feed it to the leviathan. I may not have the power to destroy souls, but I could bind even one such as you."

"Leave me this orc, and I will fly to Icadion and ask for Khullan's release just as soon as I have fended off the threat of the four horsemen."

Khefir reached out and a black spark leapt out from his bony index finger to seal itself into the space between Tu'luh's lightning eyes. "So it is agreed." Khefir turned and walked through his portal again, but not before he grabbed the frozen imp as a prize. Then the black hole resealed.

Tu'luh turned to Gulgarin. "Wait here. Gilifan will come shortly."

"How do you know I have reinforcements coming?" Gulgarin asked.

Tu'luh smiled. "Gilifan placed a few spells over you and your cousin before he left the caves. We have some limited visibility on the events that happen around you. Your cousin is secure back in Ten Forts, and he just received word that the tribes can send another five thousand warriors. I do not know whether the survivors from this battle have regrouped at camp, or run for Ten Forts, but I have sent a messenger to your cousin. He knows that we are going to raise your body again. You will yet lead the orcs in great battle."

"What do you ask in return?" Gulgarin asked.

Tu'luh chuckled. "Your loyalty. Clear the Middle Kingdom of the humans. They are a troublesome lot that will destroy Terramyr. Destroy them. Take your glory as an orc king, and receive my boon in return for your service to me."

Gulgarin nodded. "Yet when I die, I am still going back to Hammenfein. You saw Khefir, I was to be judged and found without honor."

"You knew that when you struck your deal with the necromancer," Tu'luh said. "But, perhaps there is a way we can preserve your soul after you have lived your natural life. Just, do not disappoint me."

Gulgarin looked down to his body. "When will Gilifan come?" he asked.

"When the humans have finished their tally and returned to the city. Unlike myself, he cannot come without risking being seen. You only see me because you are also dead, and I choose to show myself to you."

The orc looked to the north. "How could the humans have won?" he asked. "We should have crushed them.

"Never underestimate the power that comes from fighting for your home."

"It isn't their home, it's *ours*."

Tu'luh grinned and started to fade away. "Then I suggest you help the other orcs understand that. Perhaps then they will have more strength to fight. Either way, there are only a few hundred humans and dwarves remaining. Kill the dwarf king, and the dwarves will fall into chaos. Kill Master Lepkin, and many others will lose their will to fight."

"Lepkin," Gulgarin repeated. "I know him." He recalled the image of the man who killed him. "He will die by my hands," Gulgarin promised.

"Wait for Gilifan, and then make haste for Ten Forts. Your cousin will prepare the forces there to receive you. He will claim he has seen a vision granted by Khullan. When you arrive at Ten Forts, tell the orcs that Khullan sent you back."

"They will not believe," Gulgarin said. "How can they believe that he has any power when he is chained to the pillars of hell?"

"Just say it, and everything will fall into place."

Then Tu'luh was gone.

*****

Tu'luh pulled his mind back into the present, ending his astral projection. Gilifan was standing near him, looking into a scrying bowl and studying the images there. When the dragon moved, the necromancer looked up from his magic and stared at Tu'luh with a confused look on his face.

"Master, why should I waste energy raising Gulgarin from the dead? He has failed his duties. I would not reward him so handsomely. Let Khefir take him."

Tu'luh breathed out a long, slow wisp of black smoke and emitted a throaty growl. "The orcs are a fickle bunch, they always have been. They speak of honor and brag about their great deeds, yet if you slay their leader, those who follow will scatter. That is how the humans beat them and swept them from the Middle Kingdom to begin with. So it will be once they hear Gulgarin has perished. The tribes have a precarious treaty. If they believe that the last of the chiefs has been slain, they will take it as an ill omen and they will retreat from Ten Forts."

"But then we can use the spell to subjugate them. It doesn't matter," Gilifan pointed out.

"It is a matter of time," Tu'luh said. There are those that will resist the spell. Do not forget about Hamath Valley. Even with the spell, there will be pockets of rebellion that must be dealt with. If I let the orcs flee, it will take that much longer to gather them again. So go, raise Gulgarin and send him to Ten Forts. After we are done, I will go there and claim my army of orcs with which I will sweep northward. Those who have not fallen to the spell will be slaughtered, until we come to the tower in Drakei Glazei."

CHAPTER FIFTEEN

Gilifan stepped out from the portal and entered the chamber. The hatchling in the transparent shell looked up at him with wide eyes. Gilifan took in a breath and walked toward the altar. There were several new crimson stains running over the side of the stone. The necromancer moved to the chair near the altar and turned to drop himself into the seat. He let his mind drift and closed his eyes, but the peace was not to last.

"Is it done?" Tu'luh's voice called out from the void.

Gilifan opened his eyes but didn't rise from his chair. "The orc lives again. His body is repaired and he is on his way to Ten Forts now. Everything has been saved."

A throaty growl of pleasure was the only response Gilifan heard. A few moments of silence ensued and then the dragon spirit spoke again. "The hatchling is ready," Tu'luh said. "He is not as large as a fully mature dragon, but he is large enough to survive the fusion."

Gilifan glanced over to the dragon and studied the hatchling. It was true. In the time since he was hatched, the new dragon's growth was accelerated by the constant sacrifices provided from Pinkt'Hu. The white, leathery skin had formed silvery scales over the top, creating formidable armor. Great horns grew out like a mane around the dragon's head, and its fangs were exceedingly sharp and strong. Instead of the small hatchling he had seen the day he trapped it, the dragon was nearly sixty feet in length from snout to tip of the tail. It would be three or four times that at full maturity, but that would take too long. Tu'luh grew restless, and so did Gilifan for that matter.

Having the orcs beaten in the valley south of Stonebrook was an unforeseen event that begged Gilifan to hurry as much as he could. Procrastination now could tip the entire effort so that the enemy would have the upper hand.

"Very well," Gilifan said. "I will need to prepare another sacrifice. The ritual will take hours, maybe even a day to complete. Let me gather a few things so that I am sure to keep up my strength."

"Go, make the preparations."

Gilifan left the chamber and found Bergarax.

The brawny man turned and regarded the wizard with a sharp eye. "More sacrifices?" he asked.

Gilifan nodded. "This will be the last one," the necromancer said. "This is the night we have been working toward."

Bergarax seemed to take heart at those words. A ghost of a smile crept onto his features. "How many do you need?"

"We will need to make sure there are ample in reserve. There is no way for me to know exactly how many I need, and it will not be possible for anyone to enter once I begin. So, better to have more than less."

"So, a hundred?" Bergarax asked. "That would be double the last few orders."

Gilifan shook his head. "Double that," he said. "Make sure they are chained, unconscious, or both. I don't care how you get them, just get them. Bring them in and place them around the altar. I will also need ten or so of your strongest men. They will help me walk the sacrifices to the altar."

"Will you need anyone for cleanup?" Bergarax asked.

Gilifan shook his head. "This time, the corpses that remain will be used as food once the ritual is done. I will need their souls for the ritual, and the Master will need their flesh once he is reborn."

Bergarax turned away and walked off. "Glad this is the last one," the man grumbled to himself.

Gilifan smiled. *If only the fool realized that all of the Middle Kingdom was about to be under Tu'luh's rule. I bet he wouldn't rejoice then.*

Gilifan turned back into the chamber and went to sleep. He would need his rest.

Several hours later, after all of the sacrificial victims had been captured and hauled into the chamber, Bergarax woke Gilifan.

"It is done," the big man said.

"Good," Gilifan said. "I will begin."

Bergarax pointed to a dozen large mercenaries. "They will do whatever you need them to do."

"You aren't staying?" Gilifan asked.

Bergarax shook his head. "I have my limits," he said. "I think

I am going to go for a walk."

Gilifan sneered and shrugged. "Suit yourself."

As soon as Bergarax had exited the chamber, Gilifan wove a powerful ward spell over the opening. He was not about to let anyone in or out.

He pointed to the altar and the mercenaries tied down the first victim, a young woman no more than twenty with golden hair and fair, smooth skin. Gilifan pulled his amulet out and moved it to a small socket in the altar. For this ritual, he would divert most of the energy collected from harvesting the souls into the amulet. The part that remained he would use to strengthen the hatchling's body in preparation for the fusion with Tu'luh's spirit.

Out of the corner of his eye, Gilifan saw that the dragon hunkered down as far away from the altar as it could get within the confines of the translucent shell.

Gilifan spoke the words that Tu'luh taught him, bringing the dragon's consciousness into line with his own. Then he switched into his own language and began the ritual of capturing souls. As it had on countless nights since the egg was brought into the chamber, the whole mountain seemed to vibrate with energy. A rushing wind swirled inside the chamber and the ground trembled. Lightning flashed down from the top of the chamber to hit part of the altar. The first victim cried out in fear just before Gilifan pulled her life force from her. Black lightning shot down and split the woman's life force while Gilifan guided the bigger portion of the energy into his amulet and the smaller portion into the young silver dragon.

The mercenaries were quick to toss the corpse aside and tie another sacrifice onto the altar.

Gilifan repeated the steps. He first called the dragon's consciousness, connecting it with his own before severing the life force from the sacrifice and placing it into the appropriate places. Over and over he continued the sacrifices. With each one, he could feel the force building within the amulet. He could also smell the tension in the air. The hairs on his arms and neck stood on end and his skin felt tiny shocks as the lightning struck each new victim. Soon, he would have enough power to move on to the ritual that would fuse Tu'luh with the young hatchling's body.

*****

"What is that?" Maernok asked as he stared out the window.

Salarion rose up from her bed. Her bare feet touched the floor and made no sound as she moved to the window. Her eyes saw a bright, violet glow to the east. "That is what we have been waiting for," she said. "Tonight is the night that Tu'luh will rise again."

"Then we should move now," Maernok said.

Salarion shook her head. "Not yet. We have to wait for the ritual to be complete before we attempt to enter the mountain."

Maernok clenched his fists. "I am not accustomed to waiting. I think I have had my fill."

Salarion placed a delicate hand on his shoulder and pointed out to the street. "I have something else that will take your mind off of it," she said.

Maernok turned a questioning stare to her. "We go for the governor?" he asked.

Salarion nodded. "Let's go stick ourselves a pig."

Maernok slammed his left fist into his right palm and moved quickly to gather his weapons. Salarion gathered her clothes and changed into her armor. Her daggers and sword slipped into their places with hardly a sound and then the two exited the building.

They stole their way across town. They slipped into alleyways and stuck in the shadows to avoid detection. The few guards they did encounter in the streets were so preoccupied with the growing light in the east that they hardly noticed anything else. More than once, Salarion had to stop Maernok from openly challenging the guards and remain focused on the task at hand.

Each time, Maernok would explain that he was accustomed to slinking even less than waiting.

They soon reached the governor's manor. They circled around to the north side. Salarion picked the lock on a drainage grate and Maernok carefully pulled it free from its place. The hole was not large enough for Maernok, but Salarion was able to slip into it. The orc was forced to wait in an alley behind a large oak tree while Salarion moved toward the inside through the drainage tunnel. Salarion had told Maernok that it would take her roughly an hour to crawl through the tunnel and find the materials necessary to create a rope and toss it over the wall for him.

In reality, she had no intention of using the orc's help on this mission. A blunder at this point would disrupt their plans to slay Gilifan. That was a risk she could not accept.

She kept herself steady with her palms as she slid upon her back, driving with her feet through the drainage tunnel. She knew it wouldn't get her inside the actual manor. The governor's sewer drainage was far below ground and would never be large enough for her to crawl through. This one however, was part of the drainage for the governor's bath house.

She snaked her way through the large pipe and then had to wiggle into a smaller section that curved ninety degrees upward. Her hands trembled as she maneuvered her arms upward. They came to rest firmly against an iron plate. She worked her fingers around the edges until she managed to tilt the plate. She slid a dagger free and pried against one side. The plate shifted, and after a few minutes it came loose. She use her left hand to guide the plate down to rest below her as quietly as possible. Then she squeezed herself up through the section where the plate had been. Once she was up, the pipe became a kind of bowl-shaped space just big enough for her to lay in if she curled around the edges. In the center of the bowl was another plate. This one was not going to be as simple as the first, however. It held the water for the bath. She gently placed the back of her hand to the plate. It was cool to the touch. That was a good sign. Had anyone been using, or planning to use, the bath it would have been hot.

She worked her daggers around the plate-valve and managed to pry it open. The water coursed down into the drainage pipe below. Luckily, since she had removed the second plate, the bowl she was hiding in didn't fill with water as it normally would have down before the weight of the draining water had opened the second valve. She still got plenty wet, but she could breathe while she waited.

Ten minutes later, the bath was empty. She broke the top valve free, destroying both of her daggers in the process, and slipped up into the bath. The room around her was dark and smelled of cedar and sweat.

She clambered out of the bath and exited the small building. It connected to a solarium that also served as a hallway joining the bath house to the main manor. She moved quickly through the hall until she found herself at a large, wooden door.

She bent down and picked the lock. She moved in through the door and crept up a stone hallway. There weren't as many guards inside as she had expected. She did have to duck into a doorway to avoid being spotted by a servant carrying a tray of food but otherwise there was no one to be seen.

Guessing that the servant was taking dinner to the governor, she followed him. She was careful not to make any noise as they turned through several corridors and then made their way up two flights of stairs. When the servant disappeared in a room she heard a voice call out.

"Did you bring me my spiced wine?"

"Yes, my lord," the servant replied.

Salarion crept up near to the doorway and waited. When the servant came out, she sprang into action. Her right hand shot backward and caught the servant in the nose. The bone broke, snapping the man's head back. Her left hand came in quick and hard in a knife-hand strike to the servant's throat. The man fell to the ground.

"Guards!" the governor shouted. His bulbous belly caught on the table when he tried to stand and ultimately knocked the goblet of wine onto the floor. The look of fear on his face only lasted for the two seconds it took Salarion to cross the room. Then she plunged her sword into his chest and the governor's face twisted into one of pain.

She ripped the sword free. She glanced to the other side of the room and saw a closed window. Salarion severed the man's head and carried it by the hair with her as she ran to the window. She could hear shouting from out in the hall. She may not have seen the guards before, but they were coming swiftly now. She opened the window and checked her surroundings. She had hoped the wall would be close enough to jump over, or perhaps there might be a tree nearby, but there was no such luck. She could either climb down to the ground or up to the roof.

Seeing as she had no idea how hard it would be to escape the gatehouse, she opted for the roof. Even carrying the severed head in her left hand she made easy work of scaling the side of the building. Once on top of the roof she ran to the opposite edge and then spied a large oak tree that might allow her to escape.

Guards were shouting all around the grounds now and someone began ringing a bell. She would soon run out of time.

Salarion ran toward the oak tree and leapt through the air. She landed lightly on a branch and gracefully rolled along the limb as only an elf could. Then she sprang up, circling the trunk and running out across a thick limb to leap onto the outer wall. Then she sat, flung her feet over the edge, and lowered herself down with one hand before dropping to the street. None of the guards ever caught so much as sight of her backside as she sprinted off to find Maernok.

When she found him in the alley where she had left him, the scowl on his face was not a little intimidating. He looked down to the head and sneered wickedly.

"You ever going to tell me the truth?" he asked.

Salarion nodded. "We need to move, that is the truth."

Maernok grimaced and the two ran down through the alley. By the time they exited into another street, the city warning bells were ringing loudly. The turned around to the left and bowled right into a trio of guards. Salarion stuck one with her sword, and Maernok roared happily as he slammed the other two together to stun them. Then he kicked down on left guard's knee, breaking it out backwards and punching the throat of the guard on his right. To finish it off, he drew his sword across them.

The two continued running onward as some people began to look down from windows above and shout at them. Salarion threw the head into an open window and pulled on Maernok's arm.

"Why did you do that?" he asked.

"We have friends there," she answered.

The door burst open within seconds and a score of armed men rushed out.

"Fathers of victims?" Maernok asked.

"And brothers too," Salarion confirmed.

They wound their way through the streets as bugle blasts sounded in several different houses.

"The bugles mark our friends," Salarion said.

"When did you arrange that?" Maernok asked as they sprinted back to their hideout.

"An elf has her ways," she replied cryptically.

CHAPTER SIXTEEN

Erik made his way back to the Immortal Mystic. The snow was still all around, like a great blanket had been thrown over the realm, but it had ceased snowing at night so the snow that remained formed a crunchy crust. It made the trek much easier than it had been on the way down, not to mention warmer. Each day was a little longer than the last, bringing additional warmth and light. Not only did it help his body, but it lifted his spirits as well.

It took several weeks, as it had before, to find the palace. As he rounded the narrow path around the mountainside he was struck by how different it all looked to him. Without the green grasses around, it almost appeared as though the palace itself was made of ice. It sparkled and shone bright in the sunlight, and was actually difficult to look at from some angles. He took a moment to admire its beautiful simplicity, and then he broke into a run.

Jaleal was waiting for him at the door, grinning ear to ear and looking stronger than ever before.

"What took you so long?" Jaleal asked.

"It was harder than you might think," Erik shot back.

Jaleal grinned even wider. "*Maybe for you*," he teased.

The two went inside and Erik saw the Immortal Mystic standing before him. He pulled the Eyes of Dowr out and unwrapped them. "I found these," he said. "They were trapped at the bottom of a brook, but Tatev helped me retrieve them."

"Tatev helped you?" Jaleal echoed quizzically. His bushy, white brows scrunched together.

"What of the Infinium?" the Immortal Mystic asked.

Erik smiled wide and slung his pack around his body. "I have it here as well. He reached in and pulled the thick book out from the other things he kept in the pack.

"Have you tried to read it?"

Erik shook his head. "Tatev was only able to read part of it, and he warned me about its dangers. If he couldn't do it, then I figured I shouldn't try."

"Let me see the glasses for a moment," Jaleal said. He put out his small hand expectantly. Erik glanced to the Immortal Mystic and then offered the glasses to the gnome. Jaleal put them on and looked around. He started giggling softly to himself and then handed them back to Erik. "Put them on," he said.

Erik shot a puzzled look at Jaleal and slowly turned the glasses around to place them on his face. When he placed the magical glasses on his face, he staggered backward and would have surely tripped had he not backed into the door.

The three of them were not alone. There were many people around them. They were all dressed in fine silk robes of white, red, green, blue, and yellow. Feeling Erik's stare, many of them turned to greet him with nods or simple waves. None of them stopped to talk with him though. They were all busy walking through the palace. Erik couldn't be sure what each of them were doing, but it was apparent that they had places to go and tasks underway.

"What do you see?"

Erik wasn't listening. He walked farther into the palace to get a better look at things. Not only could he see men and women, but he was starting to see that the palace was not as empty as he had first thought. There were bookshelves, filled with books and scrolls, lining the walls of several rooms. There were pedestals, tables, chairs, and large carpets and tapestries throughout the inner palace. As he watched some of the people gather inside of a small room and grab a couple of books from the shelves, something strange happened to the walls themselves. A light blue energy flowed through the glass, humming sweetly and creating additional light within the room where they were reading from the books.

A gentle hand fell upon Erik's shoulder. It wasn't so rough that it broke his focus as he watched what was happening, but it was hard enough so that he was not startled when the Immortal Mystic spoke to him.

"They are studying," he said. "The energy that comes to the room helps them to be prepared for further enlightenment."

"But, are they dead?" Erik asked. "Why can't I see them without the glasses?"

"They are spirits," the Immortal Mystic replied. "As for why you cannot see them, well that is because your mind is weak. With your dragon blood, you have the ability to see not only the auras of living things, but the spirits of all that have passed on."

"But what of the books?" Erik asked. "Furniture and books have no spirits, so why can I not see those things without the glasses?"

The Immortal Mystic laughed softly. "All that exists physically, also exists spiritually. It is something you will get used to as your mind expands. "Come, I have something to show you."

Erik moved to take the glasses off, but the Immortal Mystic told him to keep them on. He then led him down the first corridor on the right. They walked for several hundred feet, passing chambers and rooms on either side of the hallway. Erik would look through the glass to see groups, or sometimes individuals, deep in study. At the end of the hallway, the Immortal Mystic opened a door that led to a stairway spiraling down into the ground.

As they descended the stairs Erik realized that the light was coming from the light blue energy flowing through the walls, the stairs, and the ceiling above. It was almost as if the palace was not made of glass, but of this energy and that the glass was a covering for it.

They descended deep into the mountain. The air remained warm and dry, but they walked downward for nearly thirty minutes before they finally reached the bottom. The Immortal Mystic put his hands on the door, which even though it was also made of the same glass as the rest of the palace, had so much energy flowing through it that it appeared nearly solidly blue in color.

"What I am about to show you may come as a bit of a surprise," the Immortal Mystic said.

The door moved silently as it glided open.

Erik's eyes were assaulted by an exceedingly bright light, far whiter than anything he had ever seen before in his life. He raised his arms up to shield himself from the brightness while at the same time he felt an inviting warmth wrap around him. He felt a gentle push from behind.

He walked through the doorway and heard a powerful roar. He moved his arms enough to peer around them while still trying to adjust to the light. The room, if it could be called that, was so large that Erik could not see any walls except the one behind him. About thirty feet in front of him stood a massive dragon. Its legs were blue and gray. Its snout was covered in shiny scales that only accentuated the sharp fangs protruding out from under the lips. A thick pair of horns grew up and back from the rear of the skull, ending in sharp points that would put any spear to shame.

The dragon growled, but not in a menacing or threatening way. Then it turned aside and let Erik take in the full sight beyond.

There were dozens of dragons. All shapes and sizes mixed in together in a giant chamber that seemed endless. There were blue and red skytes darting about through the air like sparrows. There were wingless drakes that walked upon all fours and breathed fire and wisps of smoke. There were greater drakes that had wings, larger dragons, and then there was a group far in the distance that appeared to be as large, or much larger, than Tu'luh the Red.

"What is this place?" Erik asked.

"Behold, the true source of knowledge and wisdom of the mystics!" The Immortal Mystic stepped around Erik and gestured out to the dragons. "This is where the prophecies originated. The dragons can read the very threads of time and fate, and they interpret them and pass them out as dreams and visions. Sometimes they also personally speak of their insights to the mystics."

"How many are there?" Erik asked.

The Immortal Mystic smiled. He took Erik's hand and the two floated up into the air as if upon a large platform. As Erik was lifted up, he saw not dozens, not scores, but hundreds of dragons.

"There are more dragons here than can be counted by a mortal. They use their combined wisdom in an effort to guide the mortals of this world. They all seek the same thing as you." The Immortal Mystic turned and pointed to the Infinium. "They wish to stop the four horsemen from destroying this world."

Erik's mouth fell open. He held the tome up and looked at it. "Tatev said that this book came from a different world, and that it was written with a powerful magic. Was it written by dragons?"

The Immortal Mystic shook his head. "It was not written by dragons," he said. "It was written by *the dragon*. Or, more appropriately, the father of the dragons."

"Hyasintar Kulai," Erik whispered. "I read about him at Valtuu Temple."

The Immortal Mystic shook his head impatiently. "No, not him. Hyasintar Kulai is not the father of dragons. He is the presiding dragon over the Ancients, but that is not the same thing.

The father of the dragons is known as the Aurorean. He is a dragon composed entirely of light that shifts and changes always. The Aurorean held the total sum of wisdom and knowledge known by any being in the universe. He is the one who wrote the Infinium. That is why its magic can drive morals to madness. Most do not have the strength of mind to withstand its power. It is best compared to a beetle that tries to understand fire by crawling into one. At best, he will be burned but a small amount. At worst, he will be consumed by a power far greater than himself."

Erik nodded and then looked up to the bearded man. "If it was so dangerous, why did the father of dragons write it?"

The Immortal Mystic returned them both to the floor and then gently took the book from Erik's hands. "He wrote it so that others might know the secrets of the universe. How it works, how it can be controlled, and how it can be saved."

"You mean from the four horsemen?" Erik pressed.

The Immortal Mystic nodded. "Among other dangers," he answered. "I will take this, and we will probe its knowledge. I must warn you, that even with our combined knowledge and power, it may take some time to tease out its treasures."

Erik nodded his understanding. Then, he looked out to the dragons and a sudden realization hit him. "They are all dead, aren't they?" he asked.

The Immortal Mystic nodded silently.

"Why are they all here?"

"Erik, I will tell you now the genius, and the truth of Nagar's Blight." The Immortal Mystic folded his arms and tears streamed down his cheeks. "The spell is so powerful that any dragon upon the Middle Kingdom is subjugated to its tyranny. Some dragons on far away continents have escaped its power, but even they are somewhat warped. They have become a feral and dangerous breed. Instead of helping the children of the gods, as we had promised to do, they are violent and subject to greed and jealousy. Worse than that, is the fact that Nagar's Blight stretches its evil hands out to corrupt dragons even after death. It ensnares the very soul of a dragon, even if it is already free of its mortal shell. In this way, Tu'luh can command a host of dragons even in death."

"Why?" Erik asked. "The spirits cannot harm people can they?"

The Immortal Mystic shook his head. "Not directly. But, by ensnaring them in death, he would deny them the ability to give dreams and help the mortals of this realm. He selfishly controls and hoards their collective knowledge and wisdom in order to discover secrets and remain ahead of his enemies. That is why he must be stopped, Erik. You see, his treachery and despotism does not end with death. With the spell he created, he will rule and conquer all who live, and all who are dead. This goes far beyond the dragons. With the help of a necromancer, he can resurrect other mortals and then capture their souls with Nagar's Secret as well. Nothing will escape his rule. With such power, he may not only enslave the world, but he may actually hasten the destruction of the four horsemen." The Immortal Mystic smiled and shook his head slowly. "Ironic, that in trying to save the world he may actually destroy it much more completely and quickly than if he had done nothing at all."

Erik thought for a few moments and watched as the Immortal Mystic unfolded his arms carefully so as not to drop the book. The tall man then opened the cover. The blue light in the room intensified even more, sending actual tendrils out to flow into him as he scanned the first two pages. All of the dragons nearby stopped and watched him. Erik didn't move or make a sound as he watched.

A green vapor rose up from the book and then formed into a thin, string-like column of light that waved and danced under the Immortal Mystic's breath. The Immortal Mystic suddenly dropped to a knee and bowed his head.

He whispered something in a language that Erik could not understand. All of the dragons also dropped down reverently.

A spark emerged at the top of the string of light. A second string, this one of violet light, extended out. A third one soon appeared and glowed bright orange. Erik watched in wonder as four more limbs grew out from the spark. Each of the limbs was a brilliant color, and they shifted and danced in a slow, methodical rhythm.

Erik watched for several more moments, and then the Immortal Mystic unexpectedly closed the book.

The room shook terribly as every dragon in the chamber roared with their might. Erik fell to the ground and barely managed to balance upon all fours. When the roars ceased, the Immortal Mystic helped him to his feet.

Erik then looked to the Immortal Mystic and pointed at him. "You said 'we' when you spoke to me," he said. "When you talked about promising to guard the mortals of this realm, you didn't say 'them' or something else, you said 'we' like you were there."

The Immortal Mystic turned and sighed. "I was among them when the promise was made," he said. "Can you not see it, Erik?"

Erik reached up and pulled the Eyes of Dowr off his face. He wasn't sure if it was the power in the room that aided him, or if he was finally progressing in his abilities. He could still see the other dragons around him. He looked deep into the Immortal Mystic's eyes and saw in them a golden color that spoke of an unnatural depth and wisdom. It was then that he broke through the mental barrier that had remained with him. He saw the truth, not with his natural eyes, but with his heart. The man standing before him was no man at all. It was a dragon, and not just any dragon, but an Ancient.

Erik dropped down to one knee and bowed his head. "Hyasintar Kulai, the Father of the Ancients."

The Immortal Mystic walked farther into the room. As he did so, a golden light grew around him and he transformed into a mighty dragon with golden scales. He stood proudly at the front of the chamber. He let out a blast of fire in a deep, rumbling roar. The other dragons answered with their own roars.

"I have kept my children safe here, in this palace, since I discovered Tu'luh the Red's treachery. It is here that I have sought to discover all of the secrets of the universe. Chief among them was how to defeat the four horsemen."

Erik dared not look directly into the dragon's eyes. His body trembled slightly. His heart told him he was safe, but his body felt fully aware of its insignificance before the dragons.

"The four horsemen destroyed my home," Hyasintar Kulai said. "When Icadion fashioned this world, I came to him with my family. We sought refuge from the four horsemen, and a place to live in peace. In return for allowing us to live upon Terramyr, we promised Icadion to guide his children. We would strive to give wisdom to the children of the gods so they might avoid the fate that doomed our home. It was Tu'luh, my own son, who betrayed me in the end. He was disheartened by the growing corruption in the world. After the War of the Gods, when the rainbow bridge was sealed off from Terramyr and the Gods ceased working with their children upon Terramyr, there was a rampant increase in corruption. After many eons, Tu'luh became convinced that the only way to save the world, was to enslave it. He would take freedom in order to secure the world's future because he was too afraid to fight the good fight and let people have their choices. This was a path I forbad him to follow. He was exiled. For centuries there was no sign of him. Then, he found Nagar. You know the rest."

"How do I stop Nagar's spell? What is it about Nagar's Secret that protects the book?"

"The blight will die when Nagar's Secret is destroyed, but to do that, you must have the power that Allun Rha created. For only when you drop water on a flame will it submit. However, in doing so, the water will too be destroyed as it turns to steam. In the end, neither power will remain."

"I understand," Erik said. "I am willing to use the power to destroy them both."

"Are you?" Hyasintar Kulai asked. "For Allun Rha was unable to do precisely that. He too fell victim to the promise of power. Tu'luh and Nagar created a power that would corrupt the souls of all living and enslave them to do their bidding. It would create mindless monsters that would serve only them. However, Allun Rha created something very similar, albeit on the opposite side of the spectrum. His magic would compel all living to become as angels, never choosing corruption. They would still be enslaved, though. Neither method leaves enough room for life as we know it. Whether a mindless monster or mindless angel, both are robbed of their individuality. They are bereft of the very soul that makes them unique."

"I will not fail," Erik said. "I will destroy both spells, and vanquish the knowledge that would threaten the realm."

"But you are not the chosen champion," Hyasintar Kulai said forcefully. "I have seen the visions myself. You are the son of a shadowfiend, born with a corrupt soul that will succumb to the lure of power. In the visions fate showed me, and the other dragons present today, you have ever been identified as one who would steal Nagar's Secret as well as any powers you could before submerging our world in an endless night."

"If it was power that I sought," Erik began. "Then I would not have given you the Infinium."

The golden dragon laughed and set the book on the floor. With a single talon he slid it across the glass to rest at Erik's feet. "Go on," he said. "Take it."

"What good would it do to lose myself in madness?" Erik said. "I don't seek power, I seek answers." He pushed the tome back toward the dragon with his foot. "You said you will find the answers to the four horsemen. Just promise to tell me how I can help after you find the answer."

"But what of the power of Allun Rha?" the dragon asked. "You saw the peace in the village before you came here."

Erik shook his head. "I saw only slaves. I saw shells of people. I saw no lasting happiness." Erik stood firm and held his hands relaxed at his side. "Give me the Exalted Test of Arophim," he said. "Let me prove that I will not succumb to the allure of power."

Hyasintar Kulai extended his other foreleg and when he lifted it there was a golden book sitting upon the glass floor. "This is the Illumination," he said. "This is the power that Allun Rha created."

"What about the test?" Erik asked.

"Pick up the book, and the test will begin. However, before you do so, let me warn you that this temple not only protects us all from the effects of Nagar's Secret, it also guards against the Illumination. Should you succumb to its power, we will destroy you."

Erik nodded. He looked down to the golden book and took in a deep breath. Doubts began to swirl in his mind. What if he failed? Then he thought back to Tatev and the others. No. He wasn't going to fail. He could not let them down.

Erik stepped forward and bent down to take hold of the book. The binding was thick, yet soft leather. He opened the cover and felt an immense heat as a golden light poured out from the book. He began to read the words silently, sliding his right index finger along the page.

A strength flowed out into him. He hardly noticed the blue light extending out from the wall to wrap around his body, mixing with the golden light from the book. He didn't notice the heat surrounding him, nor the change in air pressure. He continued to read the words until all at once a force leapt out from the page and slammed into his forehead. His skin held firm, but the sensations of thousands of needles pierced through into his mind. His whole body trembled and he cried out in agony. He closed his eyes, but the light around him was so bright that his eyelids offered no protection. It was as if he stood inches away from the sun. The heat and brightness were so intense that he fell backward to land on the floor. That was when the sharp sensations rippled like pulsing spikes through his veins to every part of his body.

He writhed on the ground in terrible pain for a long time. Sweat poured out from his skin. Blood coursed out from his nostrils. His toes and fingers felt fat and swollen, as though they would soon explode. His stomach twisted and turned and his heart felt as though a great vice had set upon it.

Then a singular pain stabbed him in the chest.

"Erik, let it go," Hyasintar Kulai said. "You are not strong enough."

"No!" Erik shouted back. "I can do this!"

"Why force it, Erik?" the dragon asked.

"They need me," Erik said. "They're counting on me. I…I have to help them."

The pain in his chest grew hotter and Erik cried out in hellish agony. His tears dried upon his skin only a second after they fell from his eyes. The blood from his nose dried and cracked, breaking into reddish brown flakes and lifting away as a column of invisible fire began to ravage Erik's body. He could smell his hair melting and burning. His lungs began to fail, drawing in only half-breaths every few seconds then expelling it quickly as the heat scarred the inside of his body. Then it was as if a giant boulder fell upon his stomach. His torso was flattened to the ground and he had neither breath nor strength left. His eyes shot wide open, bulging from their sockets.

"Let it go Erik!" Hyasintar Kulai roared. "Let it go!"

The weight was too much. Erik couldn't respond. Still, he would not give up the fight. His mind refused to surrender. He passed out only to wake again with a terrible heat upon his face. His lips and mouth dried and cracked. He closed his eyes again, but the heat pried its way in. He could hear the dragons all shouting at him now to give up, but he would not heed their warnings.

Then it was over.

Erik rose to his feet. He wasn't gasping. There was no pain. It was as if it had never happened at all. He looked back to Hyasintar Kulai and smiled. "Am I ready now?" he asked.

"You are dead," the dragon replied. A single, golden talon pointed to the floor behind the young man. Erik turned around and to his horror saw the grotesque remains of his body. As he studied every wound, cut, crack, and mark he recalled with devastating clarity the pain each moment had brought him.

"But, I am the champion," Erik said. "I *am* the champion."

"I tried to tell you that you were not," Hyasintar Kulai said sorrowfully.

"No, this is a trick. You are showing me an illusion," Erik said.

The dragon slowly shook its head. "I am afraid not. The Exalted Test of Arophim destroyed your body."

"But…" Erik stared down at the floor and dropped down to his knees. He wanted to cry, but he couldn't.

"Tears are a part of a mortal body," the dragon commented. "They serve no purpose to spirits."

Erik shook his head. "But my friends," he began. "They need my help."

Hyasintar Kulai lowered his massive head and moved in close. "I am sorry, Erik, but this is the end of your story."

Erik reached out to place a hand on the dragon in order to steady himself. His hand went through the golden scales and he felt nothing. It was then that Erik realized he was in fact dead. He was nothing more than a spirit.

"I am sorry," Hyasintar Kulai said. "I had hoped to give you the power. Truly, I did."

Erik shook his head and rose up to his feet. "No," he said. "This isn't over."

"You can't have the power now," Hyasintar Kulai said. "You have no way of using the magic without a body."

Erik shook his head and held up his slightly transparent hand. "I don't need to use it," he said. "You said I was not the one from your visions. So tell me who you *did* see. You and the other dragons may be trapped here by Nagar's magic, but I am not. I am a human spirit. He cannot lay claim to me. Send me out to get the real Champion of Truth. Tell me who it is."

Hyasintar Kulai raised his head and stared down at Erik for a moment. "Erik, I can help you with that, but it will be more painful than dying was."

Erik stared confused. "But how? I can't feel anything right now. You tell me where to go, and I will just go. It's that simple."

"No," the dragon said. "Now that you have begun the Exalted Test of Arophim, you are bound to this palace. To leave the walls will most certainly destroy your very soul."

"You mean I can die again?" Erik asked.

The dragon nodded slowly. "Only this time you will be destroyed altogether. There will be no remainder of you or your spirit. It will be as if you never existed at all."

"But we are running out of time," Erik said. "Let me try."

"Perhaps we could send Jaleal," the dragon spoke. "I can tell him what I know of the prophesied champion and the gnome can go and fetch him."

Erik shook his head. "It would take months to reach anyone not inside the eastern wilds. I am faster as a spirit right?"

The dragon nodded. "You could be there in the space of a single thought, but you will not survive. I am sorry."

"What about Tatev?" Erik asked. "Or Master Orres, or my father, they could go."

Hyasintar Kulai shook his head. "I cannot summon them here. I have no connection to them. I was only able to grant rare visions to Marlin and others at Valtuu Temple because I created a magical connection before I fled to this palace for safety. You yourself saw how fragile that connection was. Tu'luh was able to sneak into the temple and usurp the order for his own bidding while I am a prisoner here. I cannot summon any of them."

"What about Marlin then?" Erik asked. "Can't you give him a vision with the real hero's identity?"

The dragon shook his head. "It doesn't work that way. I have to send impressions, thoughts, and symbols. To send too much information directly to another being is dangerous. It can result in madness. If Marlin had died in the physical world, then perhaps I could summon him, but even then it wouldn't help. A spirit must have a personal connection with the mortal it intends to visit. For instance, Tatev could come to you because he knew you, and he had something that would help you. The others that came all had a connection with you, even Tukai and the others that had opposed you in life."

Erik thought for a moment. He turned and looked at his body. He thought to ask about being restored to life, but then that would not solve the problem of time. How could he run fast enough to fetch the true Champion of Truth? Then he turned back to the dragon. "Wait, you said a spirit must have a connection with the mortal it intends to visit, right?"

The dragon nodded.

"But you didn't say *I* couldn't go for that reason. You only said that leaving this palace could destroy my soul. Do I know the true champion?"

"You do," Hyasintar Kulai said. "You have met him only a few times, but your lives have crossed each other's paths numerous times."

Erik shook his head and shrugged. "Who is it?"

"To tell you would only aggravate you," Hyasintar Kulai said. "You would either live here knowing the truth but unable to do anything about it, or you would try to leave, and risk being destroyed."

"Then why let me try to take the test?" Erik asked. "Why not tell me in the beginning who it was? I would have gone right away to find the right person. I don't need the power myself, I just wanted to help!"

The dragon sighed. "I see that you are almost as stubborn as the Keeper of Secrets," he said.

Erik shook his head. "I am *more* stubborn," he assured him. "Lepkin would tell you that himself."

A slight smile appeared upon the dragon's features. "Very well. If I cannot stop you, then attempt to go outside. If you survive, then I will give you the name you seek, and where to find him."

Erik didn't hesitate. He ran to the wall and thought of getting outside. As his body pressed through the blue energy, it was as if he was being scalded by boiling water. The pain was so intense, far beyond what he had just experienced, that he was knocked back to the floor.

"I tried to warn you," the dragon said. "You won't make it through."

Erik didn't listen. He stood again and approached the wall. He extended his hand to the blue light. It sizzled and cracked as his hand neared. The pain returned. Erik pressed on. His fingers penetrated the wall, but then they faded away, as if ripped from his soul altogether.

"Erik, please stop!" the dragon said. "It isn't worth it. There is nothing to gain from this."

"No," Erik said. "There is everything to gain. It will work. It has to." He pushed farther in, the pain ripped his arm away from his spirit. He yelled and then ran toward the wall and jumped in. The heat tore through him. He flew upward through the wall to get out of the mountain. His legs began to fall away with every passing moment. His soul was diminishing. He focused on Lepkin and the others. He could still hear the dragon shouting for him to return, but Erik pressed on instead.

His spirit melted away. He looked down at himself and found that the part of him that remained was nearly faded out of existence entirely. He doubted anyone would recognize him if he made it out and managed to appear to anyone, but he knew he had to try. The orcs were pressing from the south. Tu'luh was going to be reborn. The Middle Kingdom needed a champion.

At last he saw daylight. He pressed against a tremendous force that fought to keep him inside the palace. Other spirits gathered around, shouting and screaming for him to come back. The dragons roared from far below the surface. Erik didn't care.

If he could only make it out.

His left hand was barely visible at this point and burned with such ferocity that Erik was sure he would be nothing more than a floating head even if he managed to escape. Still he pushed it out toward the light.

Suddenly the Immortal Mystic was behind him, calling out to him. "Erik, why are you doing this?"

Erik glanced over his shoulder to see that Hyasintar Kulai had returned to his human form. "I have to try," Erik said. "I have to find the champion. He can save everyone."

"But you'll die! You will be forever gone!"

Erik didn't care. His left fingers finally poked through the wall and he grabbed hold of the outside to pull himself through. He screamed out as he struggled. The heat pulled and tore at his back and chest. His legs burned away below the knees. His right arm was now entirely gone, and part of his right side was melting away as well. The essence of his spirit turned to golden flecks of light and then disappeared into nothingness.

I don't need all of me. Erik thought to himself. *I just need enough to send a message.* He pulled with his left hand and finally managed to squeeze his head through what felt like a pinhole in a wall of brimstone. Most of his body disappeared as he pulled. Then his left arm disintegrated. The golden flecks jetted away from him as if propelled on a blazing breeze outside the wall.

"Erik, I can't save you unless you turn back!"

Erik wasn't listening. He willed himself forward. *A ghost doesn't need arms or legs. I just need my thoughts. That will be enough of me to find the champion. Then I can be done.* He willed himself farther and farther through the wall. The fiery pain swirled all around him, evaporating his soul with every second, yet somehow he persevered. The thoughts of his friend and their peril compelled him onward.

At last he made it out. He was aware of what was around him, but he could see no part of himself remaining.

"I did it!" he shouted. He looked back to the palace and saw the spirits smiling inside. "Tell me who it is, I will go and find him."

The Immortal Mystic smiled wide, tears streaming down his face. He put his palms on the glass wall and came in close, leaning his forehead on the wall.

"Who is it?" Erik asked again. "We have no time to lose."

"Erik, my boy," the Immortal Mystic said in muffled whispers. "It is you. You are the Champion of Truth."

A flash of red and golden light enveloped Erik. He was ripped back through the wall, down to the great chamber, and shoved into his mutilated body. Every pain he had felt left him now as he was restored in full. His body was healed and his soul was returned to its whole state. Within moments he felt a tingling sensation, as though his whole body had been numbed and was now coming awake again. It was painful, but not nearly so much as it had been before. Moreover, it was over in a matter of seconds.

Hyasintar Kulai was standing before him, again in his dragon form. He scooped a talon beneath Erik and helped the young man sit up. "You have passed the Exalted Test of Arophim," he said. "You passed through pain, the temptation of power, and the danger of eternal destruction. You are the Champion of Truth."

All of the dragons roared mightily.

Erik managed to stand on his feet. He looked to Hyasintar Kulai and then he too let out a terrible roar that shook the very palace as he emitted the burning white light.

"Come, now you must rest, and then you shall have the rest of the power you need to vanquish Tu'luh, and to destroy Nagar's Secret."

Erik didn't complain about the test, nor did he ask about why it had been so terrible. He didn't care. He had one singular mission now, and his whole soul yearned to complete it.

CHAPTER SEVENTEEN

Gilifan woke to find Tu'luh, reborn in the silver hatchling's body, staring down at him. The beast was now probably one hundred feet long from snout to tail, and every bit as muscular as Tu'luh had been in his first life. A keen, cruel wisdom sat in those gray eyes of his, hinting at the danger should Gilifan cross him.

The necromancer rose to his feet. "You look strong," he said.

"I am strong enough," Tu'luh replied. "It is time."

Gilifan stretched his back and then nodded. He bent down and pulled the book from under his mattress. "Let's take it to the altar."

"We don't need sacrifices for this," Tu'luh said.

Gilifan nodded. "I find it more appropriate to perform the ritual here is all," Gilifan said. "Besides, I will be momentarily weakened when the spell is completed. I will need something to lean upon."

Tu'luh growled as a pleasured grin stretched his silvery lips over his sharp, curved fangs. "I will complete my portion first, and then I will retreat into my den," Tu'luh said.

Gilifan set the evil book upon the altar and opened it to the first couple of pages. A black vapor rose from the book and the light in the chamber seemed to be sucked into the tome slightly. Tu'luh moved his head down low to the altar as Gilifan pulled out his amber amulet and set it beside Nagar's Secret.

"Kom bela muoch de sent'tei," Tu'luh said aloud. He placed a talon upon the page and pressed it into the book, not enough to tear the sturdy paper, but just enough to indent the page. He closed his eyes and a column of smoke rose up from the book. A sickly green light swirled up around the shadowy smoke as though it were a great snake entwining itself around a black tree trunk. The chamber shook and trembled, but neither Tu'luh nor Gilifan paid any mind to that.

"Kos de alem beaoch con mes te'la," Tu'luh said in his thunderous voice. The green light struck out like a lightning bolt, attaching to Tu'luh's talon. The great silvery dragon trembled and quaked. He groaned in pain as the spell pulled some of his energy into it. The green light spread out thinly over his silver scales, as if he were being swallowed by bright pond scum. Tu'luh repeated the first two phrases over and over until his entire body was enveloped in the green light. Blood seeped out from under a few of the scales on his head and rivulets dripped from his nostrils. Still he did not stop.

He roared mightily, fire blasting the ceiling above and scorching the stone. When he took a breath, the light surrounding him infiltrated his body, running into his snout and throat. He swallowed the light down and fought against it as pain gripped him from the inside. It was a strange sensation, for a dragon to feel as though it was burning. Yet, that is exactly how it felt. His insides squirmed and convulsed as the heat ripped through every inch of his humongous body.

He continued chanting the two phrases for his part of the spell for over an hour. Then the light emerged from him, although now it was much brighter and infiltrated with veins of scarlet. The light pulled itself back to the column of smoke, wrapping tightly around the blackness.

Tu'luh looked down to Gilifan.

The necromancer nodded. Now it was his turn. Tu'luh turned and limped slowly toward a den he had created for this day that was several hundred yards away from the altar. The mighty dragon would rest there for a day to recoup, Gilifan knew.

The wizard placed a hand on either side of Nagar's Secret and began his own chant.

*****

Salarion watched the fighting in the streets below. This had been part of their plan, to draw out as many of Gilifan's goons as they could. Hopefully that would make it simpler. Even she doubted that it would. She glanced toward the east and the hairs on her neck stood on end. She didn't see anything, but she could feel it. She turned around to see Maernok sharpening his dagger and staring at the blade intently.

"Maernok, it is time," Salarion said.

"Are you sure?" the large orc asked.

The dark she-elf rose to her feet. "Remember, my magic will make you invisible for only a few hours. It should be long enough to find Gilifan and kill him, but don't waste your time."

"What about you?" Maernok asked.

"I will come with you for as long as I can, but you must promise to kill me when I turn."

"*If* you turn," Maernok said. "Maybe we can get to them fast enough that you—" Salarion cut him off.

"That isn't likely. I will go as far as I can, but I can see a dark cloud rising in the east even now. It will take some time to get there, and then if any portion of the inner caverns are locked down we will be delayed."

"Then let's move."

Salarion pulled out the box that held her father's essence.

"What is that?" Maernok asked.

"This will grant you immunity from the spell. It is my father's soul."

"His soul?" Maernok asked skeptically. "How could you have such a thing? It belongs in Hammenfein."

"No, I changed the spell when my father used it. I cursed it so that when he died his soul would be trapped in this artifact. This way, when the time came when Tu'luh had found a new champion, I could make myself immune to its power."

"So why not use it on yourself?"

Salarion smiled and shook her head. "There isn't time for questions." She reached into the cube and pulled a dark crystal out. She muttered something in Taiish, the language of the elves, and then she threw the crystal at Maernok. The orc flinched, but the crystal exploded around him and absorbed into his chest in a fraction of a second. Maernok grunted and rubbed his chest, then he grinned.

"I can feel the magic in me," he said.

Salarion smiled. "Don't try to use the power, you have no training and it will likely destroy you if you tried. At best, it would alert Gilifan to our presence if you used any magic."

"I prefer the blade anyway," Maernok said. He raised his left hand and a small, blue flame jumped up and then dissipated in the air. "Still, I suppose I can see why others become obsessed with the pursuit of magic."

Salarion nodded. "Now I will cast the invisibility spell and we will go." She chanted another spell in her language and then they departed, running through the crazy streets without turning a single head as they ran off to the east.

*****

Gilifan smiled as the clear orb floated up from the altar. He could see the soldiers and mercenaries in the cavern and old fortress ruins. Then he waved his hand to expand the view to include all of Pinkt'Hu. He wasn't surprised when he saw the townsfolk fighting against the soldiers there. It was an inevitable consequence for sacrificing so many of their kin. The necromancer sneered wickedly. He knew that none of it would matter in the end. All of the inhabitants of Pinkt'Hu would be under the control of the spell within the hour.

The ritual was close to completion.

Not only would the living obey him, but on the morrow he would use his enhanced powers to amplify his amulet. Then the dead would all rise and follow him as well. Gilifan glanced to the blood-stained altar and stifled a chuckle. All except for those who had their bodies *and* souls sacrificed would rise again. That would be enough. As the spell continued outward from the fortress, it would sweep over the whole of the Middle Kingdom. Victory was complete. There was nothing that pesky young hero could do to stop him.

He took in a breath, savoring the moment as he stared down at the last phrase in the book. He lifted his hands into the air and shouted the final words with all of his strength. Lightning ripped through the chamber. The ground shook and the walls cracked and fractured.

Gilifan kept his balance by holding the edge of the altar. He was spent now. His energy was depleted and he actually gasped for breath. It didn't matter. There would be no future threats against him. All were about to be his. His eyes moved up to the orb. He saw a great wave explode out from the mountain. As it stretched, he could feel the souls bending and bowing to the power of the spell. Some individuals fell immediately, with almost no resistance whatsoever, while others with stronger wills took as much as a minute or two to fully surrender to the spell's power. As each of them were dominated, Gilifan could use the power of the orb to see through their eyes, listen through their ears, and control their actions.

The necromancer tested his control of a large warrior by having him kneel before a thin man and commanding the thin man to take the large warrior's head. The warrior obediently bent his neck and even offered his sword to the smaller man. Gilifan smiled at his triumph.

He would raise the large warrior again later with his amulet.

For now he turned his attention back to the orb and watched in delight as the wave expanded out to cover all of Pinkt'Hu. His grin turned to a maniacal laugh as thousands of souls became subject to him. He knew he shared the power with Tu'luh, but what did it matter? He had done it. Victory was his. Despite the numerous setbacks and the meddling champions that had harried him along the way, he had overcome all.

Gilifan stretched his hands out to the orb, as if to hug the vision of conquest he saw before him. Then something went wrong. The wave stopped just beyond Pinkt'Hu and died in the sea. Panicked, Gilifan waved his hand to angle the orb and see where the wave was on the eastern side. To his horror, it too had faded only a few miles beyond the mountain.

The spell had failed.

"NO!" Gilifan shouted as he slammed a fist down on the altar. "This cannot be." He searched the orb again and again, quickly changing the viewpoint and searching for any shred of the expanding spell. There was none to be seen. He fell forward onto the altar and shook his head. His mouth hung open in shock and he stared blankly down at the pages before him.

That was when he saw it.

One of the Taish runes on the page before him had been added to. He picked up Nagar's Secret and inspected the rune closely. It had in fact been changed. He hadn't seen it before, but he could clearly see the newer ink now. He scanned through the rest of the page and found several more small, almost imperceptible alterations.

"Salarion," he said under his breath. She had to have been the one to change it. Then again, why alter the spell only to give it to him? Salarion had her father's soul, which she could use for immunity from the spell. Gilifan had always known she would use that to her advantage, but why change the spell? Surely there must have been a reason. Perhaps she was saving someone, or maybe she thought he wouldn't notice? Whatever the reason, Gilifan had to act fast.

If the spell was limited in range, then he would have to transfer the power into an artifact so he could use it on anyone he came into contact with. The longer he waited to transfer the power, the weaker the spell would be.

He glanced up and could already see the light and smoke fading away before him.

His eyes fell upon his amulet. It already contained a powerful spell to raise and control the dead. It was the perfect object to send Nagar's spell into. Gilifan went to work, weaving his fingers and chanting furiously. If he could finish the spell in time, then perhaps he could give the amulet a range of several hundred feet. It wasn't the world-conquering spell he had wanted, but it would still provide him with the means to perfect his vision.

*****

Salarion pulled Maernok into a corner of the cave. "The spell is completed," she said. "I don't have much time. Listen, we are close. Go around this bend to the left. It will open into a chamber. There will be two or three guards at the entrance. The rest of the chamber will be empty, save for the large altar. Slay him quickly. There is no way to know where the dragon is."

"I will slay them both," Maernok swore.

The invisibility spell that Salarion had enchanted them with dissipated and Maernok clearly saw the horror on her face. Trembling hands reached down and with one she handed her curved scimitar to Maernok. The other plunged a dagger deep into her chest.

"I won't let him take me," she said.

Maernok stood, holding her sword and watching her trembling body. Her skin began to lose its shine, and her eyes started to cloud over. Even without being well versed in the ways of magic, Maernok easily saw the spell's effects on her.

"You, are an honorable elf," Maernok said. Then he finished her with her own sword, as he had promised, so the spell could not take her.

From there he wasted no time. He ran with the sword in hand past the geysers on his right, ducking around a sharp overhang as the boardwalk slipped out to the left. The two guards stood near one of the geysers, not even watching the boardwalk. It looked as though they had been caught in the middle of a conversation when the spell had taken hold of them. Now they were little more than zombies, standing and staring at each other blankly.

Maernok gave one mighty swing, chopping through one and into the other. Their bodies tumbled from the boardwalk to land in the yellow, soft soil near the geyser. A moment later, one of the corpses slipped into the geyser, causing it to boil over and erupt.

The orc sprinted on into the chamber. It was not as open as he had thought it would be. There appeared to be a great energy barrier covering most of the entrance. He inspected the wall and found large hunks of rock that had fallen away, creating a small hole in the barrier. It wasn't large enough for him to fit through, but he knew that time was short. He went to work pulling heavy stones free from the wall until he had an opening large enough to slip through without touching the magical wall.

He crept quickly along the wall, keeping low to avoid any unwanted attention.

His eyes soon adjusted to the darkness in the chamber. He could see a strange black, red, and green light over an altar of stone. It was swirling in a column. The column then moved down, as if sucked into the altar. When the strange light had vanished, Maernok saw Gilifan standing near the altar. He was exhausted, his chest heaving for breath and his weight leaning upon his arms against the altar.

Maernok glanced around the chamber. He saw no sign of a dragon. In fact, he saw no one else in the entire chamber. The meddler was vulnerable. This was his chance.

The orc abandoned his silent approach and dashed directly for the altar. His footsteps resounded through the chamber and he lifted his sword into a striking position.

Gilifan looked up from the altar. His sweaty face turned into an angry scowl and he raised a hand. The hand lifted a yellow amulet. "You are mine, Maernok!" Gilifan shouted weakly.

Maernok ran on, unaware that the amulet was trying to seize control over him. The orc covered several yards before the necromancer set the amulet down and lifted his other hand. A blue fireball appeared and flew toward Maernok. The orc dodged it easily. Gilifan tried again, but Maernok easily out maneuvered the spell. Maernok leapt over the altar and landed a solid flying kick to Gilifan's chest. The necromancer flew back three yards and slammed to the ground, striking his head on the stone floor of the cavern.

"I told you I would kill you," Maernok growled.

Gilifan laughed. "I will be reborn, and I will have you anyway," he said. "You are too late to stop me."

Maernok walked up slowly. He drew his own sword and pierced Gilifan's right leg with it. Gilifan groaned and grimaced. His face turned into a snarl. "I want to hear you scream," Maernok said. "Come on now, wizard, give me a scream."

"You are a fool," Gilifan replied through gritted teeth. "It is over. You have sold your people for revenge. Nothing will save them from their fate. So tell me, great and honorable orc, which of us is the greater sinner now?"

Maernok flipped Salarion's scimitar upside down and held it over Gilifan's heart. "Salarion sends her regards," he said. The point of the blade came down, ripping through sinew and breaking bones apart until it stabbed through the back and blasted the stone beneath. "Now all is as it should be, and you are pinned like the spider you are," Maernok said.

He looked down and saw the yellow amulet lying on the ground. He bent down to pick it up. He turned the item over in his hands and felt a strange, entrancing power emanating from it. For a moment the thought came to him that he could use the power to subjugate the humans and reclaim the orcish lands for his own people.

No. His honor wouldn't let him do such a thing. Khullan demanded courage and honor, not subterfuge and cowardice. Maernok turned around to set the amulet upon the altar. If he could, he would shatter the gem and destroy it.

He barely saw the silver flash that came over the altar. Something warm pressed through his chest with a force so strong that it stopped him where he stood. With eyes wide he looked down to see the thick, silvery talon turning red with his blood. He followed the talon upward with his eyes, surveying the massive leg and shoulder of a great dragon. When he saw the gray eyes staring back at him, he knew his life was finished. His limbs began to feel cold and weak.

Maernok reached down, pulling his sword free from Gilifan's leg. He raised it up high and with his last bit of strength he shouted out and brought the sword down upon the talon. Sparks exploded from the blade when the steel connected with the dragon's talon. In the end, the dragon was stronger. The sword shattered and Maernok hung limply from Tu'luh's talon. The amulet fell to the ground unharmed.

"Foolish orc," Tu'luh growled as he flung the corpse aside.

Tu'luh slipped the amulet around his talon and set it upon the altar. It was then that his gray eyes noticed Salarion's sword. A wicked sneer appeared over his metallic features. "So the she-elf was the traitor to Nagar," he mused. "Interesting that she would risk so much to come back and try again." He turned his head to the entryway and with a single thought he dispelled the magical barrier. He then looked to the amulet.

Then he let his vision shift so that he could see the fallen souls in the chamber. Gilifan stood smug next to Maernok. The orc had his arms folded over his chest, obviously displeased at seeing Gilifan in the afterlife.

"Raise me again master," Gilifan said. "I will use the amulet to bring us glory. Salarion altered the spell, but I was able to save a part of it in my amulet."

Tu'luh shook his head. "You have served your purpose, Gilifan," he said. "I no longer require your service."

A grin appeared on Maernok's face. "Raise me, dragon."

Tu'luh turned to the orc. "I would raise you again, but I see that Salarion has imbued your spirit with that of her father. This gave you immunity to my spell. I do not care for rebellious soldiers. You shall wait here until Khefir comes for you."

Maernok stood firm. "Afraid of an orc?" he taunted.

Tu'luh laughed. "I like your tenacity, but I shall not be wasting my efforts on you, as fun as it may be to raise you and kill you again."

"I served faithfully," Gilifan screeched. "How can you betray me?"

Tu'luh bent his head low to address the ghost wizard. "You are also immune to the spell, since you are the one who enacted it with me. More worrisome than that is your propensity for seeking power. Better to have no friends at all, than a false servant who would stab at my back."

"But I haven't!" Gilifan screamed. "I have been faithful!"

"You are a schemer," Tu'luh replied. "Schemers are what will end the world. Each one tries to subdue the next, without any regard for order." Tu'luh shook his head. "You will also wait for Khefir. I am sure he will be quite pleased to take your soul down to Hammenfein."

Gilifan was silenced. He looked to the floor and shook his head.

Tu'luh came in closer. "I will tell you who will take your place, if you want to know." The dragon didn't bother waiting for Gilifan to respond. He grinned wider and whispered, "Salarion shall be raised up as my new servant."

The dragon then turned, grabbed the amulet with his teeth, and walked out of the chamber. He was still weak, and his body needed rest, but he was strong enough for this. It was the perfect solution. Each person who had, or would have, betrayed him was now conquered. The fact that Nagar's daughter would be raised again to serve under the influence of the spell as his right hand officer made the victory all that more delectable.

Tu'luh was now the undisputed king. He would rule the world by talon and fang. None could stop him now. Tu'luh walked down the corridor. The large dragon stepped over the geysers, feeling the heat and the moisture. When he saw the dark elf's body he smiled. Using the power of the amulet, he bent down and touched Salarion's body with a single talon. A ghastly green vapor emitted from the amulet sinking down through the air until it reached Salarion's nostrils. The green vapor moved into the body, calling back the spirit that had once inhabited the mortal shell. Salarion's eyes opened.

Tu'luh looked at the dark elf and smiled wide. His forked tongue flickered out as he tasted her fear when she recognized his face. He turned his head to the side and said, "I shall take great pleasure in having you serve me."

"Please don't," Salarion begged. Salarion squirmed before the dragon.

Tu'luh laughed, then he let the full power of the amulet take hold over Salarion's heart. The dark elf was now his. He delighted to see the single tear streaking down her face as her freedom, her very will, was stripped from her and subjugated to the mighty dragon.

CHAPTER EIGHTTEEN

Njar looked at the young wizard Aparen. Aparen sat at the table eating his breakfast. "Aparen, it is time. Are you ready to help me balance the realm?"

"I am ready," Aparen said. The young wizard stood from the table and pushed his plate of eggs and bacon away from him. He stepped around the table and moved toward the satyr.

Njar nodded. The satyr pulled a small box out of a pouch hanging from his belt. He put the box on the table. "There is no ritual here. All that you need to do is pull the obsidian vial out of the box and drink the contents."

As Aparen moved his hand toward the box his fingers trembled slightly. He could almost feel the power emanating from the box. He pulled a small pen made of bone out of a leather loop to unlock the lid. He opened the lid to peer inside. Nestled inside a bed of red velvet was a large obsidian vile. "Is this going to hurt?"

Njar sighed. He shrugged his furry shoulders and shook his head. "I don't think it will, but I cannot be certain. If you wish to seek balance you will need to drink the contents of this vile."

Aparen hesitated. He thought about opening the vile and drinking its contents, but he did not want to feel the way he felt during the ritual in the coven so long ago. The thought of stealing another's power now was not as tempting to him as it once had been. The thought of being pained to grow stronger was also a thought he didn't relish.

The satyr moved forward and placed a thick furry hand on Aparen's shoulder. "I know this is a hard thing, but there is no other way. We have trained for this. Dremathor believed you had the potential to complete this task. You should know that a great deal of planning and forethought went in to your selection. However, the choice is always yours, otherwise there would be no balance. If you choose to back out now, then I will not force you to drink the contents of this vile." Njar held up a warning finger and looked into Aparen's eyes sternly. "But know this, if you do not drink the vile no other is prepared to do so. Without you, this war cannot be won."

Aparen looked at the satyr and studied his eyes for a long time. He looked into the golden orbs seeking truth. Aparen was unsure, even now, whether the satyr truly had his best interest at heart. The young wizard knew all too well that this could also be manipulation. He was so very tired of being other people's pawn. Still, he could not deny the words that Njar had spoken. He knew this was going to be a monumental task, one that would possibly stretch him beyond his limits.

In that moment, his thoughts turned to his mother. What would she say? What would she advise him to do? The answer was already obvious. Though he had been raised in a proud house, his mother had taught him selflessness. Guilt crept into his heart then, for he knew that he had only been acting selfishly in the last many months. He could not remember the last time he had acted selflessly.

Today, he was going to become a new man.

He reached into the box and opened the obsidian vile. He pressed it to his lips and tipped his head backward so that the content spilled down his throat. The texture was like sand and the taste was far beyond bitter. He could almost feel the screams of the dying man whose power had been sucked into the vile. He felt both heat and cold spreading through his body. These two sensations rippled through him, battling each other and fighting for dominance of his veins, limbs, and organs. As the two sensations subsided, they were replaced with numbness. A feeling of utter deadness.

The light around him became dark. His head became faint and his vision blurred. The strength in his legs began to give out. For a moment he felt the sensation of falling, then he felt a pair of hands catch him from behind.

"This will pass Aparen," Njar said. "Now you will sleep, as your new power begins to take root in your body. I will return tomorrow when you are rested and you will begin your journey."

*****

Aparen opened his eyes and sat up from his bed. He felt the strange new energy running through him. More than that, he had a wealth of new knowledge and skills flooding his mind. As had happened before when he absorbed energies from other beings, he gained all of the abilities and experiences in this new gift of power. He was still himself, but it was as if he had also lived the life of each shadowfiend whose power had been captured in the vial. This new enlightenment brought him to a much higher level of understanding and empathy than he had ever dreamed possible.

It was Dremathor's experience that struck him most. He could see memories of Erik's birth, and shared in the feeling of loss that Dremathor had felt when the baby was stolen away from him. Aparen had to quickly take control over his thoughts and feelings, pushing the new memories aside and compartmentalizing them in order to maintain control over his mind.

It was as if not only his mind but his very body and soul had been expanded, strengthened. He stood up and pointed his finger at the table across the room. He did not speak any words, he only thought of a spell he wished to cast. The table ignited into green flames that danced high up to the ceiling scorching the room and sending smoke up into the air. Aparen waved his hand and the fire not only died, but the table was restored as if it had never been touched. Aparen grinned. He moved to walk toward the table, but instead he found his feet stepping upon air. He stopped moving his legs and instead used his mind to levitate and float over toward the table. He descended down with hardly a thought. "I could get used to this."

Njar opened the door. "I would appreciate it if you did not burn my furniture."

Aparen shrugged and laughed. "I didn't mean any harm, I just felt the urge to try out some of these new powers. Though the spells I know are all the same, they come to me much easier now and I can use them with more efficacy."

"Yes, that is the way it should be." Njar nodded and motioned to the door. "Aparen, it is time to send you on your way. Nagar's magic has been unleashed. The necromancer Gilifan and the dragon Tu'luh have ushered in an era of darkness that must be quenched. Tu'luh cannot be allowed to rule."

"Where shall I go?"

Njar spread a map over the table and pointed to an old city. "This is Pinkt'Hu. The dragon is there. However, by the time you reach them, Tu'luh will already be gone. From what I can see, the necromancer Gilifan, has been killed. The dragon now acts alone. Your job is to wipe the city and all of its inhabitants off of the map."

"Njar, that is not what I was trained for. I thought I was to bring balance to the realm."

Njar raised his hands, patting the air and shaking his head. "You do not understand. The spell has warped every living soul in that city. None of them have free will. They are all subject to the dragon under the curse that he and Nagar designed. To bring balance again, means that you must destroy the city and everyone therein."

"Is there no other way?"

"You do not have the magic necessary to reverse the curse. In fact, no such magic exists that would reverse the curse in full. All those who are under the spell must be killed. Even if they are allowed to live, they will die when the curse dies. Therefore, let the Champion of Truth perform his job, while you perform yours. By restoring balance, and killing those who have fallen prey to the curse, you will save many lives. The dragon would use these cursed men to fight in his army. If you destroy them, then his army is that much weaker."

Aparen nodded hesitantly. "I understand. How do I get there from here?"

Njar stepped toward Aparen and put a hand upon his shoulder. "If you are ready to go now, then I can send you through a portal."

The young wizard looked into Njar's golden eyes and placed his right hand upon Njar's left shoulder. "I will do what I can to restore balance."

Njar leaned in, placing his forehead on Aparen's. "May you have success, and find balance and peace for your own soul as you seek to restore balance to the Middle Kingdom."

Njar pushed Aparen away. In his left hand appeared his staff out of thin air. Njar tapped the staff on the floor three times. On the ground appeared a red circle. The circle expanded, humming and crackling as it moved across the floor, until it reached the size of a well. A column of yellow light rose up from the floor, stretching toward the ceiling. The yellow light hummed as it waived and danced before them. Njar then tipped the head of his staff to the column of light and a clap of thunder shook the room. Aparen could see the city of Pinkt'Hu through the column of light. A small hole appeared in the center of the column of light, roughly at the level of Aparen's head. The hole expanded, creating a large window that opened up onto the street near the dock of Pinkt'Hu. Aparen did not need to be told what to do. He took in a deep breath of courage, and stepped through the portal.

The wind rushed around him, both sucking him in and pushing against him as he passed through the portal. He could feel the cool air upon his skin as he stepped out of the portal. His skin felt the rain dropping from the sky and his nose smelled the scent of freshly wet stone and earth. He saw a score of people standing in the street. They looked at him, but they did not react immediately. The expressions on their faces were blank. They looked as though they were nothing more than shells of people. There was no anger, there was no fear, there was nothing. Aparen felt pity for these men from the depths of his soul, but he did not let that stop him in his mission.

Aparen considered for a moment as he took in his surroundings, and decided the best way to destroy the city would be in his shadowfiend form. He unleashed his power, transforming into the hideous, spiked monster that lusted for blood and power. Only this time, he felt much more control over the desires and the lusts that the beast created within him. Now he was the master, even in this form.

He spread his wings and flew into the air, raining fireballs from his hands and the sky. Out from his mouth issued a vapor of mist that poisoned and gagged all who were unfortunate enough to be caught in its wake. He then sent a fireball down to ignite the vapor. With a frightening whoosh, the flames roared up into the sky, ripping through flesh, objects and buildings alike.

The young wizard was startled by the lack of screams or shouts as his fire tore through the city. It seemed that not only did these zombies have no control over their willpower, they either felt no pain or their souls were already dead.

Soon arrows fired up toward him. Aparen could not know whether the zombies were defending themselves of their own choice, or whether Tu'luh had somehow commanded them to attack. Either way, it made little difference. Aparen created a shield around himself, vaporizing any arrow or missile that sailed toward him. In addition to the fires, he brought tornadoes from the East and cyclones from the West. The ships in the harbor cracked and began to sink while the city walls and the buildings within crumbled and were thrown into each other. Never before had Aparen felt such tremendous power. He felt unstoppable. Invincible. Now he had everything he had sought. He had the power to finally crush Erik. Still, he had made a wizard's oath, and he knew he couldn't do that.

Within minutes, all of Pinkt'Hu was ablaze. Aparen had destroyed everything within the city as well as anything within a four mile radius before the day was done. The fires rose high into the sky and the ash and smoke darkened the sun creating a night before the sunset. When it was finished, Aparen sat upon the mountain, the same mountain that held the orcish fortress within, and watched the burning fires. He wasn't sure what to feel, or what to think. He just watched the rising flames and let himself be lost in the pink and red firestorms.

He didn't expect Njar to appear next to him at that time, and startled when the satyr walked through a portal as calm and confident as he ever was.

"Your power is tremendous," Njar said, observing the scene below them. "It is far beyond even what I thought it could be."

"I have more still to use," Aparen said. "There is more to me now than fire or monster."

The satyr nodded knowingly. He pointed to Aparen's chest and tapped lightly on it. "There is one more thing that you should know."

"What else could there be?" Aparen sighed. He looked down to the ground and then up to the flames of the city far beyond the mountain.

"Have you heard of the Sahale?" Without waiting for an answer, he continued. "It is a kind of half breed. A mix of a dragon and a human." Njar tore his gaze away from the burning city to regard Aparen. "Erik is one of them. This is what grants him immunity from Nagar's Secret."

"Why find me to tell me this?" Aparen asked.

Njar fumbled for words. He cleared his throat and looked

back to the burning city. "You have an affinity for fire spells, it would seem."

"Don't try to change the subject, tell me what is going on," Aparen demanded.

Njar looked to the ground and sighed. "You are a Sahale, Aparen."

"What?" Aparen asked incredulously. "Why do you wait until now to tell me?"

"Let me explain," Njar said as he patted the air. "I wasn't sure your gift was intact. You see, this is something that is passed down in the blood from parent to child. Neither Lady Cedreau, nor Lord Cedreau held this gift, but now that you know you are not, in fact, their child, you should also know that Lady Lokton is also a Sahale."

Aparen shook his head. "No, if she was a Sahale, then why wouldn't she use it to protect her home?"

"The blood of the Sahale does provide some protection from Nagar's Secret, but it is dependent upon the purity of the Sahale blood within a person as well as their natural disposition. Some would say all Sahale are immune, but that is not entirely accurate. More to the point, Lady Lokton has a latent gift. It sometimes happens that the blood can be diluted to the point that the gift fails to manifest, or can skip a generation before reappearing. I doubt she actually can use the ability."

"But mine is stronger?"

Njar nodded. "Like I said, it can skip a generation sometimes and reappear stronger in the offspring than in the parent. Such is your situation, except you were put into Lady Cedreau's womb. Her blood mixed with yours before you were born. Normally this gift manifests itself on an individual's seventeenth birthday. I assume that your gift was delayed due to the magic which was used to manipulate your future when the witch coven stole you from your rightful mother, and placed you in Lady Cedreau's womb."

"Are you saying I can't use my gift?" Aparen asked.

Njar shook his head. "I spent the last several weeks working on this riddle whenever I had a moment to myself. I think I have figured it out, but I didn't bring it up before because I didn't want to disappoint you. I am still not sure it will work. That is why Dremathor traded his powers to Gilifan for immunity from

Nagar's spell, I don't know if your Sahale blood is pure enough to provide resistance to the curse once you take the form of a dragon."

"Then why tell me now?" Aparen pressed.

Njar closed his eyes for a moment and then he looked up into Aparen's eager eyes. "Because I have seen a future that shows you fighting Tu'luh directly. If you are to survive, even with your magical powers, you must be able to unlock it."

"How do I do that?"

Njar stretched out a thumb and pressed it to Aparen's forehead. The image of a bright, blue rune burned into the young wizard's mind. "Do you know what this is?" the satyr asked.

"No," Aparen replied.

Njar's voice turned cold. "Use your brain, boy," he chided. "Reach into *all* of your knowledge."

Aparen thought on the rune for several minutes. Something in his mind pulled at him, as if somewhere in the corners of his consciousness there was a key to the riddle. Aparen let himself entertain the thought, and a vision—no, a memory—opened up in his mind. In the memory, Dremathor was studying an ancient tome on dragons that spoke extensively about the Sahale. At once he had access to the knowledge learned from that book and he knew what the rune meant.

"I see it now," Aparen said. As he pictured the rune in his mind he could feel a fire burning within his chest.

"Continue to meditate upon this rune. Use your added knowledge to help you unlock its power. It is the key to your transformation. You will find that your strength as a dragon will far outperform your prowess as a shadowfiend.

Njar pulled his thumb away from Aparen's head and smiled at the young wizard. "I know this is a great and terrible thing that you have done here in the city, but you need to understand that it was for the best. We seek balance, Aparen. That is all we can do. Tu'luh seeks to destroy that balance. I have seen him. I beheld a great vision while you were here, and it showed me terrible things. The dragon has gone to Ten Forts and gathered a massive army unto himself that is like none other before. The living orcs he subjugated with the curse, while the dead orcs he raised using the necromancer's power." Njar looked to the ground, shaking his head. "Worse still, he raised the human dead, and they now serve in his army as well. They will march north, and they will destroy the army at Stonebrook. If Stonebrook falls, the Champion of Truth will not have enough time to return and fight. You must do everything you can to hold the dragon's army off."

"Are you saying that I should fight the army alone?"

"Of course not," Njar said.

"You want me to go back to Stonebrook and ask them to trust me?"

Njar nodded. "The only way this will work, is if you fight alongside the armies of King Mathias." Njar moved back toward the portal. "This is not a fight I can enter. This is a battle you must wage. Do not be afraid to search for, and unlock, your potential as a Sahale. The champion will be here soon, all you must do is hold the enemy army at bay."

"If the dragon can raise the dead, then how do I destroy his army?"

"You can't," Njar said. "The best you can do is hold them in place. Force the dragon to stop pressing forward and raise his army. This may mean that you have to fight to him yourself, but don't allow yourself to be killed. Engage enough to slow him, and then disengage. Keep the dragon far enough away that he cannot use his spell to conquer the living. Let Mathias' army fight the dragon's army." Njar stepped into the portal and the portal vanished.

Aparen sat still upon the mountainside watching the fires in the distance. A few moments passed and then he began meditating upon the rune again, hoping to find the answer to unlocking his potential as a Sahale. In the morning, he would travel to Stonebrook and find the king's army.

CHAPTER NINETEEN

Lepkin sat out on the terrace. He watched the sunrise in the East. He raised a glass of mulled wine to his lips and sipped it slowly. Lady Dimwater was still fast asleep after a long night of nursing their newborn. Master Lepkin had come to get some fresh air before the battle would start. His scouts had seen the signs of orcs sending smaller patrols to the north. None had gone so far as to reach the chasm where the brook was, but a few had gone beyond the burned forest. Lepkin knew the battle would not be far off. Perhaps a few days at most. While the main orcish army marched its way north, Commander Nials had the men preparing the field as best he could. With the reinforcements they had received they had decided to make a stand.

The snows had stopped falling some weeks ago and the winter was beginning to subside, giving way to an early spring. The ground was still frozen solid however, and the nights were still far too cold to travel openly. Still, Lepkin had sent the rest of Stonebrook's citizens north out of harm's way.

He had hardly seen Al over the last several days. The dwarf king was far too busy organizing his own soldiers. Marlin was busy too. He spent his time tending the wounded. A Hospital had been set up in a large manor. In the evenings, Marlin would return to Tillamon's house and help with Lady Dimwater and the newborn if he had enough energy. Lady Arkyn was out commanding the scouts as they hunted for orcs.

Lepkin watched a regiment of phalanx troops practice in the field beyond Tillamon's house. When he finished his wine, he rose to go into the house, but he was stopped by a sudden shout. He looked out to where the phalanx troops were practicing and saw that they had circled around something. He set the empty glass on the table, situated his sword on his belt, and ran out in a controlled fashion to see what the matter was.

When he arrived he saw a young man standing in the middle of the phalanx troops. Spears were leveled at his throat and chest, but he made no move to attack or to speak. Lepkin could not see the young man's face, as his back was turned toward Lepkin. When Lepkin pushed through the throng, telling them to stand down, he was surprised when he saw young Eldrik Cedreau standing there before him.

"Eldrik Cedreau, what brings you here?" Lepkin asked.

"I have come with a message, a gift, and help." The man stopped and smiled slightly. He looked at Lepkin, and Master Lepkin saw a confidence that he had never before seen in the young man's eyes. "My name is Aparen now," he added.

"Very well, Aparen, what is it you brought for us?"

"I have the book that you lost, Keeper of Secrets." Aparen pulled Nagar's Secret out from a small pouch at his belt and offered it to Lepkin.

Lepkin glanced around at the others before his eyes settled on Aparen. How had he found the book? More importantly, what was the price for which he was really offering it back now? Lepkin pulled a dagger and moved in quick, his left hand reaching out and seizing Aparen's wrist.

"Drop the book, and come with me."

Aparen smiled. "Dear Lepkin, I come with an offering of peace."

"Then drop it," Lepkin snarled. He pressed the blade to Aparen's skin and glared into the young man's eyes. "I will end you if you try anything." Without breaking his gaze, Lepkin called out to the soldiers around him. "Triple the guard, now!" The phalanx troops immediately broke into several groups amidst shouts and stomping boots.

"A blade is of little use against me," Aparen warned. "Put it aside."

Aparen's calmness unnerved Lepkin, but he was not about to let that show. He had known the boy as an Apprentice of the Sword, but he obviously had some sort of magic power now, otherwise he could not have teleported into the field amidst the soldiers. "I think you would find it hard to use magic if I slit your throat."

"I mean you no harm," Aparen assured him. "Remove the knife."

"How did you come by the book?"

"I found this yesterday in a cavern. A mountain near Pinkt'Hu had swallowed an old orcish fortress, and deep inside that fortress I found an altar that Gilifan used to resurrect Tu'luh the Red."

"And how did you get the book?" Lepkin asked. "How can I know that you are not in league with the dragon?"

"Dear Lepkin, if I were, what good would it serve to give you the book now?" Aparen dropped the book at Lepkin's feet. "I come to you with an offering of peace. I show you that I have destroyed an army the dragon was raising against you. Don't you understand? Gilifan resurrected the dragon. They used Nagar's Secret. They turned thousands into their mindless soldiers. Thousands more they raised from the dead as zombies, and I destroyed them. The dragon has now moved south, to Ten Forts. He is using his magic to build another army against you. This is an army unlike any other you have ever faced. There will be orcs and humans fighting alongside each other. Those who have not been turned to living slaves by the dragon will be raised as zombies. Is your army prepared to fight monsters that look the same as their comrades before they died?"

"How can you be sure of this?"

"I have spent a great long while studying the ways of magic. I have no way to prove to you that what I say is true other than to give you the book. I can say that I am on your side. I do not want Tu'luh to enslave the Middle Kingdom any more than you do. I am here to fight the dragon."

"How can you possibly expect to fight the dragon? And how can I believe that Tu'luh has been raised from the dead?"

"Let me go, and I will show you," Aparen offered.

Lepkin shook his head. "No, you will show us." He moved around Aparen, still holding his knife in place on the young man's neck. He slipped the toe of his boot under the large book and flicked the book up to his left hand. He slammed it into the young man's stomach. "Hold this with both hands," he said. Lepkin then urged him forward. "Let's go and have a talk with someone else. Remember, if you try anything, I will slit your throat."

They got as far as the table where Lepkin had been sipping his wine before Dimwater and Marlin emerged from the manor.

"Some of the men told me what happened," Marlin said.

"Read him," Lepkin told Marlin. "Do it now."

Marlin took one look at Aparen and then nodded and made a

gesture with his hand for Lepkin to move the knife away. "I see no deceit in him."

"Are you sure?" Lepkin pressed.

Marlin nodded. "He is strong, and has far more power than I would expect for someone of his age, but he is no threat."

"That isn't entirely accurate," Lady Dimwater said suddenly. She moved in close and smelled the side of Aparen's neck. "You are a shadowfiend, I can smell it."

"And you have demon blood running through you," Aparen countered. "Does that make you an enemy?"

Lepkin shoved Aparen onto his knees. "Hold your tongue." He looked up to Dimwater and then glanced to Marlin. "Why didn't you mention that?" Lepkin asked Marlin. "Surely you can see the difference in his aura enough to know what he is, just as you can with Dimwater."

The prelate sighed disapprovingly. "Assuming he could deceive me, I suspect he is strong enough that he would have already attacked if he had come to cause trouble. I say we let him speak."

Lepkin growled and roughly shoved the young man forward while yanking the book back. Aparen didn't show any sign of aggression or resentment. He slowly stood and then turned to Marlin. "I can show you something." Aparen brought a single hand up before the two of them. He muttered a word and then an orb of silver appeared in his hand. "I have not performed this spell before, but I believe it will give us some insight into Tu'luh's mind. I was just explaining to Master Lepkin that I found this book in an old orcish ruin buried in a mountain east of Pinkt'Hu. They have used the spell already, but I destroyed Pinkt'Hu and everyone in it, preventing that army from assaulting anyone in the Middle Kingdom."

Lepkin glanced to Marlin. Marlin nodded, showing that he thought Aparen was, in fact, telling the truth.

Aparen muttered a few words and the silver orb flashed yellow, then white. The orb then cleared of all color, allowing Lepkin to stare into it. Lepkin saw a large chamber, as if it were in a stony mountain. In the center of the chamber he saw an altar. Beside the altar he saw Gilifan and a large, silvery dragon.

"Tu'luh has returned," Marlin gasped.

"Tu'luh does not look like that," Lepkin argued.

Marlin shook his head. "A new body, but I see the same aura within. It is him. The beast has returned to Terramyr."

Lepkin was not overly convinced by the orb that Aparen used, but Marlin's word was good enough for him. He did not need to see anymore to know that Tu'luh was real.

"Does this orb show the present or the past?" Lady Dimwater asked.

"This orb shows the past." The orb melted into Aparen's hand. "Because I was inside the chamber, I was able to capture some of the past and put it into this orb. As I said before, I had never done this before, so, I was unsure it would work. That is why I grabbed the book. I want you to understand that I am a friend in this battle. I do not pretend that I wish to stay in the Middle Kingdom when this fight is over, but I do not want the dragon to win."

"How long do we have?" Lepkin asked.

Aparen shrugged. "I do not know. The master who taught me is Njar, a satyr. It is he who told me that Tu'luh has gone to Ten Forts to raise a large army."

"What did you say?" Lady Dimwater asked as she grabbed Aparen's shoulder and spun him toward her.

"I said Tu'luh has gone to Ten Forts to raise an army."

Dimwater shook her head. "No, the name of your master. Who did you say it was?"

Aparen frowned. "Njar, he is a—"

"I know very well who he is," Dimwater said quickly. She looked to Lepkin. "If Njar taught him, then we have nothing to fear."

"What is it that you suggest we do?" Lepkin asked. "I should trust him because you know his master and Marlin says his aura is clear?"

"I know Njar," Dimwater said.

"And since when have you ever doubted me?" Marlin cut in. "I may be blind, but my eyes see more than yours."

Lepkin stared hard at Aparen for a long while. He didn't like it. It all seemed too easy. "Why would Tu'luh leave the spell behind?"

Aparen shrugged. "I don't know," he said. "I only know what

I showed you."

Dimwater interjected, holding her hand out for the book. "Perhaps there is something wrong with the spell," she said. "If they have already used it, then it should have done more than conquer a city. Perhaps its reach was not what Tu'luh expected. If this is the case, then he would have transferred the power to some other artifact. Something that can be carried before him to dominate all that stand in his way."

"So, then back to my question," Lepkin said. "What should we do?"

"I suggest you run." Aparen said coolly. "I will stay here and fight the dragon."

"Where should we go?" Lepkin pressed.

"Go north. I have enough power that I can fight and hold the dragon and his army off. You should take your army and retreat northward until the Champion of Truth has met with you again. When he returns, then you will have the power you need to defeat Tu'luh and destroy the curse."

"How do you know of The Champion of Truth?" Marlin asked.

"We do not have time to discuss it all. I don't know why you chose Erik to be your student, but I have heard it was because you saw something in him that you had not seen in others. If this is true, and you have such a gift of discernment, then look at me now to see whether I am a friend. I am asking you to trust me."

Lepkin nodded. Despite the young man's history, Dimwater and Marlin both felt it wise to believe him. If they did, then Lepkin had to believe him too. "I imagine Commander Nials may wish to raze the city if we were to evacuate. We could leave you a house, if you wish," Lepkin said.

"Razing the city will make no difference. The army that comes here has no need of food nor shelter. The evil magic that the dragon uses will sustain all who have been raised from the dead. Even if the elements kill them, he can raise them again. We should save ourselves time." Marlin said.

"It isn't me we need to convince," Lepkin said. "It's Nials."

"Then let's go and speak with him now," Dimwater said.

"Gather what equipment and supplies you need, and then make haste to the north. I will do battle with the dragon as I can, and buy you as much time as possible."

Lepkin reached out to retrieve the book. "And what shall I do with this?"

"Give me a moment," Dimwater said. She closed her eyes and weaved a spell over the book. N orb of light, very similar to what Aparen had used, grew on the book and a flood of different colors streamed from the book into the orb. A moment later, Dimwater took the orb in hand and the energy transferred to her body. After a moment she opened her eyes. "From what I understand, the magic that has been enacted has been transferred to an amulet. It has no more power within itself than it used to. So, as long as you do not use your dragon form, you should be fine. However, the book still contains the actual text of the spell, so you should take it with you. Let's hope that Erik can destroy it when he finds us."

Lepkin offered a half smile and then he pointed to the house. "If you have some time, we have food if you are hungry."

Aparen shook his head. "I will begin going south. When I see the orcs, I will fight with them. I have enough food for what I need."

"Very well," Lepkin said. Master Lepkin clapped a hand onto Aparen's shoulder and nodded at the young man. "I wish you the very best of luck," he said. "If you get into trouble, then retreat northward. We will be ready to fight, so do not think you must do this on your own."

Aparen nodded and then he vanished with such blinding speed that Lepkin thought he had disappeared. It took Master Lepkin several seconds to realize that Aparen had not actually disappeared. He was traveling exceedingly fast through the air on a small silver cloud toward the south. Master Lepkin looked back to the house and thought of his wife and child. He turned and made haste to set the new orders.

It was not easy to convince Commander Nials, or Al for that matter. The two officers could not believe Lepkin's account of what happened, nor could they believe that Tu'luh had an army of zombies or had been resurrected from the dead. Al turned to Marlin and asked the prelate whether there was any way he could validate Aparen's story. Marlin, said that unless he could see the young man while he spoke, there was no way for him to know the truth of it.

In the end, it was lady Dimwater who convinced them all. She told them of her dealings with Njar years ago and explained that though he was not a well-known individual, he most definitely had the Middle Kingdom's best interest at heart. She convinced them that the mere mention of Njar's name was enough to show her that Aparen was in fact telling the truth. None of them would argue with her.

After the orders were set, soldiers went to work with haste. Whatever supplies they could fit in the wagons, they did. When they had no more wagons to fill, they filled backpacks and rucksacks. It took them two days to be fully prepared for the journey. As soon as everything had been collected and prepared they marched north.

CHAPTER TWENTY

After spending a night traveling and meditating, Aparen felt ready to do battle with the army. He wasn't entirely sure he could unlock the power of his Sahale blood, but he felt as ready as he could given the fact that he could already sense the army approaching. He stalked through the burnt forest, using his new skills and powers to feel the enemy army before his natural eyes could see them.

Aparen encountered the orcish army just two miles north of Ten Forts. He had never before seen such a large force in all of his life. By comparison, it made the battle at Lokton manor seem childish to him. There were easily twelve, or possibly fifteen-thousand troops marching directly toward him. He scanned the entire area, but saw no sign of the dragon. He knew there was only one thing he could do to draw the dragon out. He rose into the air, shielding himself with an invisibility spell, so he could gain a better vantage point over the enemy army.

He delved into his mind, focusing on the rune Njar had shown him. Thundering boots marched below him as he levitated invisible in the air above the army. The fire built within his chest again, as it had during the night meditations. The rune glowed brightly in his mind, and then it began to chime sharply. The melody it played called to Aparen's soul. He wasn't sure if he was unlocking the rune, or if it was unlocking him.

A good portion of the army had already passed under him when the transformation occurred. The transformation was far more painful than anything he had ever experienced while transforming into his shadowfiend form. His body grew to such immense proportions that he felt as if he had been ripped apart and rebuilt as a living mountain of granite. He could feel the fire burning within his chest grow stronger and hotter, waiting to be unleashed on the enemy army.

His arms became thick forelegs tipped with sharp talons and covered in large, black scales. Four horns grew from his head, two on each side that curled upward into sharp points. A ridge of bone formed over his snout and sprouted smaller, pointy horns. His tail grew long and slender, with a large, spiked ball on the end of it. His hind legs were thick with muscle, but also had horns poking out over the back of the leg, like dew claws made of black spears. He roared and unleashed a thick column of green fire.

His vision acuity was heightened so that he could see not only the physical aspects of each individual before him, but he could sense their very spirits. It was this that surprised him most, not because he could see their spirits but because their spirits were gray. Whether they were the living slaves or the resurrected zombies, they all looked the same. Their spirits were the color of ash. In that moment he knew he was not doing battle with any living creature in the sense that he understood. He was fighting animated shells, golems, and abominations. With a mighty roar he swooped down and unleashed his wave of fire, bathing the ashen snow-covered ground in a flood of flame. As had happened in Pinkt'Hu no one screamed or cried out in pain.

However, this army was not without reaction. Archers reached for their bows and unleashed a flurry of arrows into the sky, while spearman from below threw their spears and javelins and the sword men ran and spread out to avoid the flame. As before, Aparen called upon his magic, creating a shield around himself that devoured any arrow or missile coming toward him. There was nothing the army of zombies could do. Time after time he swooped in like a great raptor, burning the zombies with fire and using his tail spikes to destroy others. His magic was so powerful that none of them came close to striking his body.

Aparen dove down, swooping low and gliding upon his jet black wings just out of reach of the enemy spears. He spewed out his green flame and devoured hundreds in a single attack. The mindless soldiers were not difficult at all to fight. In his dragon form, Aparen likened it to stomping on an ant hill and then using a torch to demolish the angry little pests. With this in mind, and the fact that he had never before had any physical power that came close to what he now felt, he decided to experiment.

He dropped down after the second swoop with his fire. He crushed thirty warriors beneath his body and let them test their swords and spears against him. The weapons glanced off his scales harmlessly. Aparen roared in delight and swung his tail around his right side. Dozens of soldiers were caught by the move. Some were crushed while others were flung far away. Several bodies were impaled upon his spikes, but with his strength the extra weight didn't seem to slow his attacks at all.

Next he shot out with his claws. He had of course used claws before in his shadowfiend form, but these were very different. Each talon was the diameter of a small tree, and their points rivaled the sharpness of any javelin or spear he had ever seen. He punctured through armor and skewered enemies effortlessly. Aparen curled his right fingers into a massive fist and then brought it down like a great boulder upon seven warriors. Their bodies squished and gushed beneath his might.

He launched into the air again, blasting fire over the army and using each of his appendages as best he could to accelerate the battle's pace.

A goarg rider charged him once and he reflexively snapped down with his fangs, biting rider and beast in half. The blood rushed into his mouth. Aparen spat the bodies out in disgust, but he had not found the blood itself to have a bad taste. Rather, it was the idea of eating such creatures that had compelled him to spit them out.

As the battle raged on for the space of several hours, he saw reinforcements marching up from the south.

There were another five or six thousand souls, he couldn't be sure exactly how many. It didn't matter. He tore into them as he had the first fifteen-thousand. By the time the afternoon had finished the field was covered in bodies and limbs. Aparen had destroyed twenty-thousand troops without receiving a single scratch. He moved on toward the south after he had completed his attack and then he saw Tu'luh the Red. The mighty dragon was massive, much larger than Aparen was in his dragon form.

"Bow before your new master, wyrm!" Tu'luh roared.

Aparen felt the sudden, cold grip of terror seize his spine. He froze on the ground, standing and staring at the mighty dragon as it soared closer with blinding speed.

"Bow to me, or face my wrath!" The beast roared, emitting a column of fire and sparks.

That is when Aparen saw the she-elf upon Tu'luh's back. A bright yellow amulet hung from her neck, and he knew that was the power source. He made his way toward Tu'luh, unleashing fireballs, lightning bolts, and even great spears formed of ice in the air, but none of them struck their mark. Tu'luh was too powerful. He deftly dodged, swooped, and dove under each and every missile sent toward him and then he fired back a massive sphere of terrible fire. Aparen was not deterred by the fire. Instead he decided to fly directly toward it. After all, his magical shield had stopped every other attack that day. He paid the fireball no mind, barreling forward on a direct collision course, until he came within range for his magical barrier to dissipate the fiery missile. Instead of doing so, the fireball broke through his magical shield with an audible crash and a spray of sparks. Aparen was forced to take action quickly, diving down toward the ground in such a reckless manner that he actually crashed into the snow-covered earth below. As quickly as he had reacted, the fireball still grazed his tail. He wasn't injured, but he was shaken by the fact that the fire had managed to penetrate his magical shield.

The great silver dragon flew toward him, and Aparen knew he was outmatched. He looked quickly around the ground and saw that the entire army had been destroyed. He wasn't sure how long it would take, but he knew that Tu'luh would have to stop marching north in order to resurrect his army. So, in a moment of strategizing, Aparen decided to flee to the north as quickly as possible. Better to live another day and delay the enemy, than to die on this day. Perhaps if he continued to kill Tu'luh's army, forcing the enemy dragon to slow his pace in order to stop and resurrect his army each and every day, that would give Erik enough time to enter the fight and break the spell.

Aparen reverted into his human form, and then cast a very powerful transportation spell that sped him through the air at such blinding speeds that even Tu'luh the Red could not follow him. He retreated out toward the east, hoping that on the morrow he could flank the enemy. Even so, the army was many, many days behind Lepkin's army. Aparen only had to buy them another few days in order to win the battle.

CHAPTER TWENTY-ONE

After the abrupt disappearance of the strange dragon, Tu'luh surveyed the field of wreckage that only that morning had been a formidable army. Cursing the sudden appearance of a Sahale with powerful magic he called Salarion to him. He took the amulet from her and began the task of resurrecting his fallen army. He was chagrined to find that the dragon's fire had managed to damage some of his forces beyond the possibility of resurrection. So long as something remained of the body, it could be restored, but ashes were of no use to him. It took until the sun had fallen behind the horizon to complete the task of reclaiming his army from the muck and ash of the battlefield. When they were again prepared, he marched them through the night, with Salarion riding upon his back. The next morning, the strange dragon appeared again and attacked Tu'luh's army. This time, Tu'luh did not let the strange dragon kill so many of his soldiers. Tu'luh flew into the sky and attacked the smaller dragon. Lightning bolts and fireballs crashed down around Tu'luh, but the dragon did not stop. He broke through the young dragon's magic and pressed the attack, forcing the young dragon to flee.

Over the next several days, this pattern repeated itself. Tu'luh would circle around the army patrolling it and protecting it from the young dragon. The young dragon would appear, using magic and curses in order to destroy as many orcs and humans as he could.

Tu'luh had no chance to rest until he finally managed to escort his army into Stonebrook. There, the dragon was able to command his troops to take up proper defensive positions. They built ballista launchers from the wreckage of old catapults. They were also able to find more suitable armor to protect against a dragon.

Tu'luh took particular pleasure in pillaging Tillamon's house. He had heard of the dragon hunter many times, and relished the feeling of satisfaction as his own troops carried out the very weapons and armor that would have been used against dragons such as himself in order to prepare for the meddling, black dragon. This satisfaction was only heightened when Tu'luh burned the house to ashes in a single breath.

To his dismay, the black dragon did not approach Stonebrook. Tu'luh spent two days waiting for him to return, but the black dragon was nowhere to be seen.

The great dragon summoned Salarion to him on the third day. There was no need for words, her mind and will were connected to his, entwined with his desires. Still, she retained her body and abilities, which was more than useful. Tu'luh equipped her with a set of Telarian steel armor to protect her body from the black dragon's attacks. Without Gilifan, Salarion was the only talented magic user he had in his army. The other zombies were essentially walking swords.

After she was dressed and equipped to his satisfaction, Tu'luh compelled her to use her magic on him. His form shifted and changed. His body became pressed, squeezed from all sides, until he was no bigger than a large orc. His wings flattened to his body. His bones compressed. His fangs shortened into the characteristic orcish tusks. His silvery scale took on the appearance of a pale green skin. When the spell was complete, even he was almost fooled by the disguise. He now looked no different than any other orc in the army.

Next he compelled one of the orcs to come near. Salarion weaved a spell over him and transformed him into the exact image of Tu'luh's new body. The orc took up no more space than he had before in reality, but he now looked as large as Tu'luh had. Great silvery scales shone brightly in the sun, and he even breathed with the low, lumbering sounds that a dragon did. Soft tendrils of smoke snaked out from the illusionary nostrils and Tu'luh grinned.

He willed half of his army to stay with the fake dragon, including Salarion. The other half he commanded to march with him to the north. If the black dragon would not come to him, then he would hunt it down and flush it out of hiding.

The trap worked perfectly.

The following day as Tu'luh marched with the army northward, the young dragon appeared from the west just before sundown. The black scales reflected the last rays of the sun as it swooped down to attack. The young, four-horned dragon tore into the army laying waste to hundreds at a time. Tu'luh bode his time, making sure that the black dragon didn't suspect anything before he sprang into action. As the young dragon swooped down for a strike, Tu'luh leapt into the air and his real form became known just as he collided with the young dragon. He ripped at the young dragon clawing at his wing with his right foreleg and biting at the dragon's neck. His spiked tail whirled around fast and slammed into the young dragon's hindquarters. The black dragon fought back with all of his might, throwing spells and magic and curses at Tu'luh in rapid succession. Tu'luh felt the lightning course through his body. One of the ice spikes jammed into his hind leg, but it was not so deep to worry about it. The black dragon even managed to stab one of its tail spikes into Tu'luh's side, but the wound went only skin-deep underneath the scale it pierced. Tu'luh did not disengage from the young dragon. He answered each attack with one of his own, and very soon won the upper hand.

They tumbled down toward the ground spiraling in a death grip. Finally the young dragon was able to score a hit just under Tu'luh's eye. The large silver dragon recoiled just enough that the young dragon escaped. The young dragon immediately shifted form back to that of a human. A gash in his back dripped blood down his shirt, and just before he finished transforming Tu'luh saw the dragon had a broken wing. Tu'luh sent a whirling tornado of fire at the young dragon, but a portal opened and it escaped.

From that point on, Tu'luh knew the black dragon would not harass him again.

He flew back to regroup with Salarion and the others. Salarion wore the amulet around her neck and led the army forward. Tu'luh would let her dominate the enemy soldiers while he would remain in reserve in case the young dragon, or another threat, arose during battle.

Within days, Tu'luh and his army overran several small villages. Whatever stragglers they found, they either killed or turned. Using Salarion's skill as a stealthy scout, Tu'luh would send her forward into some villages alone. She could then sneak in and capture all of the inhabitants without a single blade being drawn or any alarm being raised. This saved Tu'luh the time of resurrecting dead bodies all of the time, which also preserved his strength. Tu'luh's army grew, albeit incrementally. Soon the massive army crossed to enter Grobung, a city, just south of Fort Drake.

When Tu'luh found the town, it appeared as though Master Lepkin had already evacuated the city. The stores were empty, some buildings were boarded and shuttered up, and the streets were void of anything save for a random gray cat. Tu'luh decided that he should send Salarion forward while he holed up in the city in case Master Lepkin had a surprise for him.

The dark she-elf approached Tu'luh. No words were spoken between them. Words were unnecessary as the power of the amulet connected each slave directly to Tu'luh's brain. In fact, the only reason Tu'luh brought Salarion to him was to give her better armor. He knew that the fight ahead of his army would be fierce. He gifted Salarion with a set of steel mail. Then, he sent her to the north.

*****

Lady Arkyn sat next to a smoldering campfire between two other scouts. She took the last morsel of bread, turned it over between her fingers and then placed it into her mouth and chewed. She kept her eyes toward the south. She could just make out the outlines of the buildings in the city of Grobung. Just before dusk she saw the first ranks of the army marching north on the road. She spied orcs and humans alike, wearing full body armor and heavily armed. It was a formidable force. On the flanks she even saw resurrected goargs with riders bearing spears and bows. She sent the other two scouts immediately toward the fort to warn the others. She, however, stayed behind and readied her bow that she had taken to replace the one that was broken when she had tried to kill Gulgarin.

She knew that if she saw the dragon, she would stand little chance of defeating him, but she hoped to find the source of his power. The amulet that Dimwater had spoken of was something that could be taken, or possibly even destroyed. The only question was whether or not she could get close enough to destroy it without falling victim to its curse.

Her hopes were dashed apart when she realized the one who wore the amulet was a dark elf riding upon a great goarg. The elf was heavily protected amidst ranks of orcs, and Lady Arkyn knew there would be no way to get close to the elf without being exposed to the amulet's magic. She turned northward and fled, hoping to warn the others before the army could reach Fort Drake.

*****

Marlin stood in a tower, watching all the soldiers stand and march toward the enemy army. This was not a plan that he had hoped for nor one that he was particularly fond of. Still, even Marlin had to acknowledge the fact that standing inside the fortress would afford the heroes little protection, if any, once the amulet came close enough to enslave them. Their choices were simple. They could run out to meet the enemy and hope that somebody stopped the dark elf who wore the amulet, or they could flee northward. The latter choice was not an option. The farther north they fled, the more innocent civilians would fall to Tu'luh's power. Marlin knew that Aparen would also join the fight. If the heroes could use archers to slow the enemy army, then perhaps Aparen could get close enough to take the amulet.

As the archers drew back their bows and catapults began to fire, Marlin scanned the enemy army with his special vision. He noted that his army, those fighting for the freedom of the Middle Kingdom, all had bright, colorful auras. The enemy army, on the other hand, had almost no auras at all. They were a pale, sickly gray. Marlin saw no emotion in them. There was no fear, no pain, and certainly no love or hope. It was as if they were nothing more than animated corpses. Marlin watch them fall as the missiles rained down, pummeling the enemy. Still, they came onward. Their marching footsteps thundered over the road despite the onslaught of their comrades. It did not matter how many fell before them, they continued to advance.

Out of the corner of his eye, Marlin saw Lady Dimwater. She was up on the fortress wall. Resonating within her aura was a strong, fierce anger that shone brightly in red hues. From her vantage point on the wall she fired spells to attack the enemy army. Scores of enemy orcs and humans fell, yet even the magic did nothing to slow them.

As the enemy closed within one hundred yards of the defenders, Marlin watched in horror as the enemy dead were raised again. Salarion carefully picked her way through the field and used the amulet to bolster the enemy army. The freshly raised zombies joined back in their ranks without hesitation. There was no shouting, there were no orders spoken, and there were no trumpets or bugles to sound their advance or their maneuvers. The enemy army acted by someone else's will. Marlin knew they were unstoppable. He could see no spell that could halt them, even those that were burned, unless they were completely disintegrated into ash, were resurrected only a short while later to rejoin the ranks and continue the fight.

At this sight many of the archers broke their ranks and fled Fort Drake. There was nothing any of the officers could do to save their faltering lines. Those men who were valiant enough to remain steadfast in the face of such formidable danger were soon taken over by Nagar's curse.

Marlin studied the battle scene. He watched the zombie Salarion carefully and soon discovered that the amulet had to be within fifty yards of a target in order to enslave it or resurrect it. He didn't know how, but he knew that he had to try and stop the amulet taking all of the people from Fort Drake. Luckily, at that moment he saw Aparen running out to the field. Before Marlin's very eyes the young man shifted into a grotesque figure, like that of a monstrous beast with spikes, horns, and demented wings. He leapt into the air over the enemy army and rained fireballs upon them. He called down lightning and even made the earth shake tremendously so that the enemy army could not keep their footing. He started to run towards Salarion. Marlin watched intently. When Aparen came within fifty yards of Salarion, Marlin thought for sure that Aparen would fall subject to the amulet, but he did not. Aparen ran directly toward Salarion.

A great flash of light struck out across the sky like a bolt of lightning, but it did not disappear or vanish. Instead the great light spread, flattening and broadening like a great blanket over the enemy army. The blinding light dropped covering the immediate area around Aparen, Salarion, and most of the enemy army. When the light faded Aparen was stuck. He stopped advancing toward Salarion. He cut down many orcish soldiers around him and flew into the air above the enemy army. He continued to rain fire and lightning down upon the enemy but he did not strike at the amulet or take it.

Marlin watched, confused for a moment why Aparen was failing to attack. Then he studied Aparen's aura and realized that Aparen was confused. Only then did Marlin understand that Salarion had used an illusion spell. She made it appear as though all of the soldiers around her were her. Now Aparen had to guess which the real Salarion was.

Marlin called out to Dimwater upon the wall, "Do you see Salarion, the dark elf?"

"There are hundreds of her," Dimwater replied

Marlin tried to shout to Aparen and identify the correct image for him, but Aparen was too far away to hear him. Aparen became locked in a great battle as the entire enemy army turned on him. Marlin knew that Aparen had been wounded in his dragon form when he had fought with Tu'luh, therefore he was not likely to take the dragon form again as it would leave him without the option of retreat. Marlin decided that he would lend a hand to Aparen, hoping that his magic would help the young warlock wade through the enemies until he finally found Salarion and could take the amulet from her.

Marlin caught a glimpse of something on the southern horizon. When he focused on it, his heart sank in his chest. Aparen would not have enough time to find the amulet, for Tu'luh was coming. Marlin could see the dragon's aura as clearly as if it had been the noon day sun. He glanced to the battlefield and saw that as quickly as Aparen slayed the enemy, the amulet resurrected them. The battle was all but lost.

Despite his best judgment, the prelate decided to act. He leapt from the tower and called upon the grasses below to catch his feet as he landed harmlessly on the ground. He ran forward, ignoring Lady Dimwater's shouts. Using his magic, he disguised himself with a spell that made him appear like a rabbit. He picked up a javelin on his way through the battlefield and ran for Salarion. Aparen was obviously not trained well enough to find the real Salarion, so Marlin would do it for him. He knew not to come too close to the amulet. He came within throwing distance and let loose with the javelin, using his magic to make it invisible and help guide its trajectory. The javelin struck true and Salarion took the point in the neck. She fell back off her mount crashed to the ground. Marlin watched as the energy in her aura faded and disappeared. Now, those who fell in battle, remained dead. The amulet still held the spell, but without either a slave or a master to direct it, the amulet neither resurrected the dead nor enslaved the living.

Marlin looked up to Aparen and shouted, "Do not let the enemy take the amulet."

Aparen dove down, bathing the area in brimstone and fire. Lightning crashed all around, thundering as it created an electrical cage of blue and yellow and white. The enemy turned from Fort Drake, concentrating fully on retrieving the amulet. Marlin and Aparen fought side-by-side as they kept the enemy at bay. Arrows and catapults continued to fire down upon the enemy. For a moment it looked as though they might succeed in destroying enough of the enemy army to capture the amulet.

Then there was a great thunder. The ground shook. Marlin lost his footing and fell. He looked up in time to see a massive, silver tail sweep through the electrical cage that Aparen had created and smack the shadowfiend through the air. Aparen sailed over the walls of Fort Drake and out of sight. Marlin stretched out his hand to grab the amulet, but it was too late. A silver talon slipped through the amulet's gold chain and picked it up from the battlefield. Marlin looked up into the great and terrible aura of Tu'luh the Red, and his spirit filled with dread. The dragon smiled and great pain crept into Marlin. The sensation of thousands of burning needles pierced through Marlin's head and heart. He fought the spell with everything he had in him, but it was no use.

"Don't do this!" Marlin pleaded. Marlin's gift of sight was taken from him as the spell ravaged his mind. In a fluttering moment, his normal vision returned. Instead of seeing Tu'luh's aura, he saw the silver scales on the dragon's snout. A strange numbness took hold of Marlin's legs and spread up through Marlin's body. The last thing Marlin saw before the spell completely captured his spirit was the evil grin on Tu'luh's wicked face.

A moment later, every corpse within a fifty yard radius was resurrected. The amulet was placed over Marlin's neck, and Salarion was commanded to guard Marlin as he wielded the amulet. Tu'luh used his fiery breath to destroy the arrows coming down toward his army. He used his claws and tail to bat away the large rocks hurled by the catapults. Tu'luh leapt into the air, sending a great wave of fire over the remaining few archers that had not fled. He did not bother to resurrect them. Instead he opted to turn them to ash.

"The fortress is mine," Tu'luh said. "I will give you two hours to surrender. Submit to me and there will be no more death. You know you are already defeated, but I do not wish to rule a graveyard. I want only to prevent this world from falling into the chaos that mine did, which led to its ultimate demise. The great prelate of Valtuu Temple is now fallen, never to be seen nor heard from again. I have taken not only his life, but also his soul. This is the end that awaits all who oppose me now. Join with me, and you shall live a normal life. Fight against me, and I will destroy body and soul."

Tu'luh watched as a large man moved on to the wall next to the sorceress, and waited for him to speak.

"You know me, dragon," Lepkin said "I am the Keeper of Secrets. There will be no surrender. Not to you, or to anyone else who wishes to use that despicable curse upon the Middle Kingdom."

Tu'luh snarled, wisps of smoke snaking out from his nostrils along with sparks of blue fire. "You are a fool. Even if you could defeat me, you cannot defeat what comes behind me. The life I offer is the only way to save this dying world. I will give you two hours to reconsider your fate."

"Come at me now dragon, and I will show you who will die."

The lady next to him gathered a great spell and sent it forward. Man and orc started to writhe in pain and agony as their bodies twisted and contorted. At first, Tu'luh was unaware of what was going on. Then he saw the truth of the dark magic that was being used. The sorceress had sent soul fire down to the army and it was devouring not only the enemy's bodies, but also their souls. It was a spell that would leave their souls and bodies unusable again. Not even the amulet would revive a body from such a spell.

Tu'luh did the only thing he could do, he reached out and snatched Marlin and Salarion into his talons as he turned and fled from the battlefield. Soul fire was as effective on dragons as it was on other creatures. The only way to escape it was to flee. He glanced over his shoulders and wings as the last several hundred soldiers were consumed by the soul fire, screaming in agony and dropping dead on the ground.

"That was clever, witch," Tu'luh snarled to himself. "But, I will be back. You need to rest for quite a while after such a spell, while I can return before the next sunrise with an army just as large, and ready to use my spell to ensnare you and everyone else inside Fort Drake. Even after you have recovered your energy, you cannot use that spell again for at least a week. "

*****

When Tu'luh arrived at the city of Grobung he took his two riders to the graveyard on the western side of the city. This is where the veterans of Fort Drake, as well as many other honored dead had been buried for centuries. Their bodies were in different stages of decay, but most were not beyond saving. The amulet could raise even the worst cases of skeletons or rotting corpses, so long as something remained of either body or soul. He sent Marlin out into the graveyard and commanded his new slave to raise another army.

A great, black cloud appeared over the land as the tombstones began to quake and tremble. Caskets cracked and corpses began to claw their way out of the dirt. Hands of bone ripped through the earth and pulled up skeleton bodies. Some wore armor that they had been buried in, while others wore nothing. The fresher corpses had skin covering their bones and other than their bloated faces and the pale green and purple coloring of their skin they looked fairly normal by human standards. They all bowed to their new master ready to do his bidding. Row after row came alive in the graveyard as Marlin walked through using Nagar's spell to wake all of the dead.

While Marlin worked to create an army of zombies, Tu'luh flew a bit farther to the south. He sought a secluded glade from which he could contact his other servants. He summoned imps, sending them out to Verishtang and having them call upon the drakes and other monsters that waited for Tu'luh's call. The monsters would fly with great haste, arriving before midday on the morrow. Tu'luh could wait that long. Then, he would have his victory. The Middle Kingdom would fall at Fort Drake.

CHAPTER TWENTY-TWO

Lepkin stood in the room, his arms folded and his head leaning against the doorjamb. He watched Lady Dimwater feed their newborn son. "I want you to leave," Lepkin said.

"And I wish to find that cabin in the woods, where everyone leaves us alone and we can live together in peace."

"I have to stay here, but you don't. Take our son, go north."

Lady Dimwater shook her head. She gently rocked their son back and forth as she sat on the edge of their bed. "In life or in death, I'm not leaving your side again."

Lepkin rubbed a hand over his face moved toward her. He knelt down in front of her placing one hand on her left knee and one hand on their son's back. "You saw what the magic did to Marlin," Lepkin said "He's gone. There is no way for us to make him come back. It is one thing to die, but it is another thing to lose your soul. I want you to leave."

"I said no." Lady Dimwater readjusted their son on her lap so that she could take Lepkin's hand in hers. "I can send our son away, but I'm not leaving."

"Where would he go?"

"I can send him to Njar, the satyr."

Lepkin stared at their child. He wasn't sure what he thought about that. He trusted Dimwater, but he had never heard of Njar before. Up until the time he saw Aparen in Stonebrook, he had no idea that any satyr existed within the Middle Kingdom. What he did know, was that he had no better ideas. "If you trust him, then I suppose I can as well."

"Doesn't really matter if you trust him. If we both die in this battle neither one of us are going to be having any say in what happens to our son." Dimwater offered a half smile. A flash of silver appeared in the room. The two of them looked over to see Silverfang, Dimwater's wolf, standing before them. "If you prefer I can send our son to Silverfang's realm." A sarcastic smile crossed her lips.

Lepkin shook his head "No, but perhaps you could send

Silverfang with our son to Njar."

Dimwater nodded her head. "That I can do."

The two of them watch their son for the next several minutes before Lady Dimwater finally opened a portal to a strange land inside a beautiful forest vale. She pointed at several cottage style houses in the vale and assured Lepkin that their son would be safe there. She explained that with the amulet's limited range, and the fact that Njar's home always moved and was covered by a magical spell that concealed it, it would be one of the last places Tu'luh could ever reach.

"Then let us pray that Erik is able to return and defeat Tu'luh before the dragon can find Njar." Lepkin frowned as he bent down to kiss his newborn son's forehead. Dimwater caressed Lepkin's cheek with her palm and then sent their son through the portal on a magical cloud. Silverfang also went through the portal and then it closed.

When the two hours was over, Lepkin bent over to kiss Lady Dimwater's cheek. "The dragon will return soon, and I should be out there to meet him. You should continue to rest until the last possible moment."

Lady Dimwater pulled on Lepkin's arm and struggled to stand on her feet. "I told you before, I do not intend to leave your side." Lepkin opened his mouth to chastise her for being pigheaded, but she flicked his nose with her index finger and then leaned into a hug. Her embrace took the fight out of him, and he agreed to let her come with him.

The two of them left their room, walking out through the courtyard and up the stairs onto the south wall. They saw their friend Al, the king of the dwarves, already standing upon the wall with Commander Nials. No one said a word. They stood in the night and waited for any sign of the dragon and his army. They waited for hours, but no sign came.

Sometime around midnight a young soldier came up the stairs on the southern wall and handed a letter to Commander Nials.

"This just came in by messenger falcon."

Commander Nials nodded, thanked the young soldier and then sent him back to his station. He opened the message and leaned to his right to get a better angle on the light from the torch nearby.

"What does it say?" Lepkin asked.

"I will be there before noon." Commander Nials looked to the bottom of the small message and smiled wide. "I found the Immortal Mystic. Signed, Erik Lokton, the Champion of Truth."

The four of them shared a smile, but none of them shouted for joy. Instead of yelling and shouting and cheering, their relief was evident in the silent tears that fell from their faces. Even Al was unashamed to let the water roll over his cheek and into his red beard.

"So, we only need to hold out until lunch tomorrow," Lepkin said.

"We can do that," Lady Dimwater said.

Al clapped his hands and looked down to the courtyard, filled with a renewed sense of hope. "I will see if my dwarves can't dig a few tunnels, traps, and surprises for the dragon. Maybe we can slow him a bit more." The others nodded and Al ran down the stairs on his short, stubbly legs. Lepkin watched him go down the stairs then turned to put an arm around his wife.

Commander Nials smiled, "go and get some sleep. Your wife needs her rest, for tomorrow we have a battle to win."

"And if the enemy comes tonight?" Lady Dimwater asked.

"Then the alarms will wake you," Commander Nials said. "Until then you should rest. You will be of more use to me after you have rested than if you were to stay up all night for nothing. Perhaps that is what Tu'luh had in mind -making us wait all night so that he could vanquish us in the morning when we are exhausted."

"That is an astute observation," Lepkin said.

"If he is to raise an army, it could take him a little longer," Dimwater said. "He won't be able to raise any of the men he brought against us today."

"Yes, I must say that I do not entirely approve of your method," Commander Nials said. Before Lady Dimwater could respond, Commander Nials put a hand in the air and smiled softly. "I understand it was likely the only way to save us in that moment. Had your spell been able to consume the dragon as well, then you would hear no complaints from me whatsoever. It is just that I knew some of the men down on the field."

"Those men were not the men you once knew," Lady

Dimwater said. "Their souls were already twisted and warped by the curse Tu'luh placed upon them. My spell only devoured that which was already corrupted beyond recognition and salvation."

Commander Nials nodded his head and ceded the point. He then gestured back toward the main keep. "Go, and get some rest. If the enemy arrives early I will sound the alarm."

Lepkin and Lady Dimwater nodded and left the wall.

*****

The warning bells sounded shortly after the morning meal. Lepkin looked to Lady Dimwater and they shared a somber frown. Erik had not yet arrived, but it was apparent that Tu'luh had. Soldiers ran to and fro, gathering weapons and armor as quickly as they could. Lepkin and Dimwater moved to their position on the wall, standing next to Commander Nials again.

The gates opened and the army marched out.

Within a few minutes Al the dwarf king bounded up the stairs and stood next to Lepkin on the wall. He reached up and smiled. "The enemy gave me enough time that I prepared a great welcome for them."

"What did you do?" Commander Nials asked.

"Just keep an eye to the south," Al replied.

The four of them watched as an army of skeletons and grotesque zombies walked forward over the road in the south. Master Lepkin and Commander Nials kept glancing to Al. The stocky dwarf grinned and fidgeted with his fingers, but he did not reveal what was about to happen. The farther the enemy army advanced, the bigger Al's grin became.

All of a sudden there was a commotion. The sound of breaking bone and clattering armor. Lepkin spotted an area where as many as a dozen skeletons had fallen into a large pit that had been covered loosely with straw and moss to appear as though the grass and ground beneath was solid. Several more pits opened underneath the army's feet.

"Those pits are fifty feet deep," Al said proudly. He put his hands on his hips and nodded with a great grin that stretched his mouth nearly ear to ear on his face. "I would love to see those zombies climb out of there anytime soon."

The enemy army maneuvered around the open pits, quickly discovering additional tricks and traps. Al moved forward on the wall and started fidgeting with his fingers again. The enemy army came in another fifty yards, and then a great trench, which must have been at least a quarter mile long, opened up and burst into flames. The flames swallowed several ranks of the enemy army.

"I noticed yesterday, that the corpses that burned to ash were unable to be resurrected by the curse," Al said. "So I devised a special pit for some of these abominations with that in mind."

"You are a devious one, dwarf king," Commander Nials said. "Devious indeed."

The enemy army was nearly halted by the great wall of fire. The force had to split in order to maneuver around the edges of the trench. Archers from Fort Drake assaulted the dividing army. Unfortunately, they found the arrows were not as effective against the skeleton warriors as they had been against the army the day before. The arrows either passed through the skeletons without harming them, or they would bounce off the bone without damaging them enough to stop them. The catapults, on the other hand, were able to hurl massive boulders that crushed many skeleton warriors beneath them.

A volley of arrows flew over the trench of fire from the enemy army toward the men of Fort Drake. Lady Dimwater acted quickly sending a whirlwind through the air to sweep away the missiles. On the whole, the spell worked rather well, but it did not divert all of the missiles. Many of the arrows fell down to find their mark, slaying several good soldiers.

Then a strange noise rose in the air, like that of a wailing banshee. The four heroes atop the wall strained their eyes to find its source. When they found it, they all gasped in unison. There were hundreds of creatures coming in from the southeast. There were gorlung beasts, fire drakes, and great tusked mammoths charging toward the fort.

Al reacted quickly, grabbing his battle horn and giving a long below. In answer, cavedogs emerged out of covered holes in the ground, with their riders atop them wielding bows, spears and axes. The dwarves charged out to meet the ghastly creatures while the humans continued to do battle with the skeletons and zombies. The fighting became fierce. The dwarves clashed against the great

236

creatures in a thunderous clap of metal, screams, war cries, and screeches. The mammoths trampled many of the cavedog riders, while the fire drakes blasted dwarves with fire. The dwarves answered by firing crossbows, hacking at their enemies' feet, and letting their giant lizards bite at the monsters' legs.

While the dwarves fought, locked in a bitter battle, the humans came face-to-face with their skeleton enemies. Swords and axes hacked through bone and rusted armor, beating out the strange, obscene melody of death and war. Lady Dimwater lent what aid she could by sending lightning and fire from the sky. Still, she was not rested enough to do much. Her spells managed only to slay a few dozen of the enemy skeletons.

Aparen moved out to help the dwarves. He ran toward the wall from inside the courtyard and shifted into his shadowfiend form, jumping into the air as he did so. He flew gracefully over the wall and down toward the battlefield like a great raptor hunting a rabbit. He tore into a fire drake with his talons and teeth, ripping the beast's right wing from its back while simultaneously biting its neck. He then flew on to save a pair of dwarves just before they were trampled by a great mammoth. A lightning bolt struck down from the sky, burning a hole through the woolly mammoth and dropping the beast to the ground.

"I do believe he is more powerful than you, Lady Dimwater," Commander Nials said.

"You may be right," Lady Dimwater agreed. They watched as scores of beasts continued to flood onto the field. The battle raged for more than three hours before there was any sign of Salarion or Marlin. When the four of them finally caught sight of the two that held the amulet, they wondered where Tu'luh might be. The dragon was nowhere near them.

"Surely Tu'luh would not let them come alone this time, would he?" Commander Nials asked

Master Lepkin shrugged. "I do not know." Master Lepkin moved to the edge of the wall and placed his hands upon the crenellation.

"What are you thinking?" Lady Dimwater asked.

"That maybe it is time for me to take my dragon form again."

"If you do that, you will be turned by the spell."

Lepkin nodded his head. "But maybe I will have enough time

to steal the amulet. If I can reach it, I can throw it back to Fort Drake and one of you could destroy it."

"Lepkin, if it was that easy, we would have destroyed the book that held the spell," Lady Dimwater said. "You know we won't be able to destroy the amulet if it has been imbued with Nagar's spell. We will have to wait until Erik arrives. Erik will be here soon, I know it."

"Perhaps not soon enough, look!" Commander Nials shouted as he pointed the two toward the north.

They all turned to see the great silvery dragon flying in from the north. He had circled around them for an attack. He blasted the northwest corner of the fortress with fire as he swooped down from the sky. Soldiers shouted and cried out for help as they died a terrible, agonizing death by fire.

"Man the ballistae!" Commander Nials ordered.

Soldiers fired from the towers with the great ballista launchers that had been erected as the fortress' defense. Tu'luh, the great dragon, dodged and evaded every missile that was fired at him. He swooped under, and spun over and around every missile. Soldiers lined the walls of the fortress, firing arrows at the silver dragon. The small shafts were nothing to the great, metallic scales of the dragon. They bounced and ricocheted off like rain on a metal roof. The dragon continued to dive and attack time and time again, forcing the heroes to turn their attention to him and forget about Marlin and Salarion.

Master Lepkin was about to transform into his dragon form and engage Tu'luh, when he saw Aparen fly back over the wall in his shadowfiend form. Aparen engaged Tu'luh, firing lightning and spears of ice through the air at the great dragon. Tu'luh roared, answering with fiery blasts and swipes of his sharp talons. Neither was able to land a hit on the other. Instead, they danced a fiery, electrifying dance in the sky over Fort Drake while soldiers died by the scores below on the ground.

Lady Dimwater kept her attention on Tu'luh, firing spells to try and catch the dragon off guard. However, she lacked the strength to make any of them very effective. A fireball she sent dissipated as it collided with his great scales. A lightning bolt she summoned from the sky missed Tu'luh and struck one of the towers instead. When she gathered a magical arrow and sent it at the dragon, Tu'luh was fast enough to evade the dangerous missile.

"Lady Dimwater, focus on Marlin. He is coming closer," Commander Nials said. Master Lepkin and Lady Dimwater turned to see Marlin walking near one of the trenches. The amulet swung from his neck as he walked. If he came much closer to the fortress, the battle would be over as all the living would fall victim to the amulet's power.

Lady Dimwater began chanting a spell calling a great arrow of blue fire into existence. She sent it streaking downward toward Marlin, telling herself that it was no longer her friend she saw in the body before her. The arrow flew straight and true, but it did not strike Marlin. In the last second, Salarion dove in front of Marlin and took the arrow in her own chest. Her body vanished into nothingness.

"They are coming too close," Lepkin said. "Get the archers to fire on Marlin."

A great howl rose up from the east and the four of them turned to see a massive pack of black wolves. The wolves chased the creatures that were battling with the dwarves, hunting them down and bringing them one by one to the dust.

"That would be a friend of mine, Rjord," Lady Arkyn said as she came leaping up the stairs with a bow in hand. "He said he would come after the snows had fallen. I didn't realize it would take so long, but better late than never I suppose."

"Well at least we have some help," Lepkin said.

Lady Arkyn strung her bow and went to the wall. In the space of three seconds she fired seven arrows down at Marlin. They were the last arrows she had in her quiver, so the heroes on the wall watched them fly toward Marlin's chest with not a little anticipation. Marlin must have seen them too, for he was able to evade them with his magic. The first three arrows disappeared as if they had never existed, and the last four were turned aside and fell to the ground.

Master Lepkin climbed to the edge of the wall prepared to leap over the side. "There is no more time. I must act now, or we will lose everything we have fought for."

In that instant a great and powerful beam of golden light shot into the battlefield from the west. It burned through the skeletons, turning them to gray ash in the blink of an eye. The zombies it caught in its path fell to the ground dead. The heroes turned to see a young man running toward the battlefield. Behind him were several thousand men clad in golden armor and wielding great spears.

"Is that Erik?" Commander Nials asked.

Lepkin nodded. "That is the Champion of Truth," he said.

The ray of golden light then expanded into a great wall. Crackling lightning blasted out each and every direction striking many people in both armies. Zombies and skeletons burst into flame, while the human soldiers of Fort Drake that were hit stood rigid and their skin took on a golden luster and their weapons shone brightly. The golden wall then morphed into a great dome, sliding itself over Fort Drake and protecting it from any further attack from Tu'luh. Aparen was knocked from the sky by a golden bolt of lightning, but he did not seem to be hurt or changed. Rather, the strike stunned him. He landed on the southern side of the fortress near one of the trenches the dwarves had dug

Tu'luh swooped down and cut Marlin's body in half with his claws as he ripped the amulet from him. The great dragon stood on his hind legs and swallowed the amulet. Large, black spheres with silver lightning streaking across their surfaces appeared in each of Tu'luh's giant hands. Again he was able to raise all of the fallen warriors from his army that had not been reduced to ash, but this time he could no longer capture new ones. He dropped down next to a squad of Fort Drake archers, but instead of bowing to his will, they continued to fire directly at the dragon. Tu'luh, enraged, slammed his tail down on top of the archers and crushed them into the earth, killing them instantly. He then sent his great fiery breath at the Fort, but it was stopped by the golden dome Erik had placed over it.

Tu'luh could see that he was beaten. Erik had only to point his sword and direct a golden beam to cut down the skeletons and zombies that Tu'luh raised from the dead. Each time Erik did so, those skeletons and zombies were not salvageable. Tu'luh was unable to raise them again. His army was diminishing faster than he could do anything about it, nor could the dragon attack Erik head on, for he was backed by the Golden Army, the very spearmen that had driven Tu'luh out of Hamath Valley. The Dragon blew fire in his rage at Erik, opening his mouth as wide as he could. In that instant, Aparen jumped up and into Tu'luh's mouth. All that was seen from Lepkin on the wall was a strange shell of white and gold around Aparen as he dove through the flames and down the dragon's throat. There must have been some other magic, for the dragon seemed not even to notice the intruder.

An instant later the Dragon roared terribly. He reared up on his hind legs again and clutched his stomach with his own talons, digging at his scales. The screeching talons against his metal scales made everyone nearby shake and tremble. Scales fell from his underbelly and blood burst out from a hole in his abdomen as Aparen clawed his way through the dragon in his shadowfiend form. In his hand was the yellow amulet.

*****

Erik saw the strange monster dive into Tu'luh's mouth, he was confused. Still, he continued to run toward the fight sending bolt after bolt of the golden energy at the dragon and all of the enemies around Fort Drake. When the monster emerged from the dragon's belly with the amulet in hand, Erik knew what he had to do. He commanded his soldiers with his mind to sprint as fast as they could. He led the charge heading straight toward Tu'luh.

Today everything was going to end.

The dragon clutched at the hole in his stomach. Blood oozed out onto the battlefield, but the dragon did not stop. To Erik's dismay, the hole in the dragon's stomach healed before his eyes. Scales didn't regrow to cover the wound, but new skin developed over it and closed the hole that had been there. The dragon smashed down with its great left foreleg to crush the strange monster that had entered its throat. The monster was able to survive the attack by creating another shield around itself, but it was obvious that it was horribly injured. The magical shell creaked and cracked under the weight of Tu'luh's attack. Erik called upon his power for the last time. He knew he was too young to change his form. He knew the dragon before him was far larger than anything he had ever seen before. The silvery beast was well over one hundred feet long from snout to tail. Erik was less than a third of that when he had used Lepkin's dragon form, and when he had used the special crystal to find his own form, he was still only slightly larger.

Erik also knew that he had not been the original prophesied champion. Doubts tried to remind him that he had a pattern of not fitting in well and breaking the rules, it seemed. Erik was not going to give any room in his mind for doubts, though. He embraced himself, and everything that he was and yet could become. He leapt into the air, summoning every bit of strength he had. He threw the flaming sword end over end to distract Tu'luh while his power enveloped his body and changed him into his dragon form. His bones snapped and elongated, while his muscles thickened and grew. The heat of anger in his chest burned and morphed into a roiling fire that he prepared to spew out over his enemy. While he finished his transformation, the thousand spears below launched into the air as the Golden Army clashed with Tu'luh the Red. They fought well, keeping his attention focused on them while Erik changed. Tu'luh killed them by the scores without even leaving the ground. He cut them down with his claws. He bit them in half with his fangs. He crushed them with his tails and legs, and he bathed them in fire until they turned to ash. When he was finally able to launch into the air, Erik was already diving for his neck. The two collided with the sound of great boulders clashing together and shattering in the air. They fell to the ground and shook it so much that a large crevice opened up in the ground beneath them stretching all the way to the fortress and breaking the southeast corner of the wall. All of the remaining humans and dwarves on the outside of the fort rushed in for the attack. The Golden Army continued rushing in as well. They hacked and slashed at the great beast while he thrashed his tail and swiped at them with his claws. Erik scratched at Tu'luh's underbelly, ripping open the hole that had healed already and then jamming his own claws up inside the beast.

Tu'luh reached around with his tail and smacked Erik's body, but Erik did not relent. He dug his talons deeper into the hole, reaching inside for any organs he could find. Erik pulled, scratched, and tore at his enemy, weakening him with every second. The Golden Army closed in around them chopping and slashing at the scales on the beast. A silvery talon exploded through Erik's left shoulder, nearly severing it from his body. Erik howled in pain, but he used his pain and channeled it into rage. The new rage he turned to strength as he pressed his taloned hand up into the hole and seized Tu'luh's heart. He grabbed the beating organ and pressed each of his talons into it as he turned and ripped his right forearm down and out through the hole. The heart beat twice in Erik's hand and then Tu'luh went limp.

Erik disengaged and tumbled backward to the ground in exhaustion and shock from the loss of blood in his arm. Without a thought he reverted back to his human form. The massive hole in his left arm remained and he could not move. As numbness took over his body he craned his neck up and around to stare at the disfigured monster that now held the amulet. Before Erik's eyes, the monster shifted forms to that of somebody he recognized. Whether it was from the loss of blood, or the frenzy of the battle, Erik wasn't sure, but he could not remember who the familiar figure was exactly. The young man, bloodied and battered from the battle, smiled at Erik and stretched out his hand with the amulet in it. Neither had the strength to complete the transfer. The amulet fell between them and both of them lost consciousness as the Golden Army, or what was left of it, sprinted in around them to give help.

CHAPTER TWENTY-THREE

When Erik opened his eyes again, he was in a well-appointed room. Tapestries and paintings hung over neatly organized bookshelves that lined the walls. The bed he was on was the softest he had ever felt. He tried to move, but a pain ripped through his body that originated from his left shoulder. He looked down see a large bandage covering most of his left arm and part of the left side of his chest. Jaleal was next to him.

"How did you get here so fast?" Erik asked "I thought you stayed behind with the Immortal Mystic so the spell would not affect you."

"I did, but I left the palace four days after you did. I knew I had to stay far enough away so your spell wouldn't catch me, but I wanted to be close enough to find you if you needed help."

"It is a good thing he did," Lepkin said from a chair on the other side of the room. "He was the only healer who could help you."

"Where is Marlin?" Erik asked.

Lepkin stood on his feet walked over to Erik. He took Erik's right hand in his hands and shook his head with a frown clearly painted across his face. "Marlin is dead. He died while trying to take the amulet."

Tears filled Erik's eyes and he looked to the wall.

"Leave us for a moment," Lepkin said. Jaleal left the room. "Tu'luh is dead," Lepkin said. "All that remains now is to destroy the amulet, and the two books."

Erik nodded. "I know how to do that."

"Can you also tell me, what happened to the men and dwarves who are outside Fort Drake when you arrived?"

Erik struggled to sit up and looked Lepkin in the eyes. "The Illumination is the opposite side of the scale. It is the light that banishes Tu'luh's night. Unfortunately, it is essentially the same type of magic. It enslaves whoever it touches. So, in a way I have given the soldiers of Fort Drake a similar death. Except, Tu'luh would have made them corrupted with evil, the Illumination overpowers them with good."

"So you are saying the only way to save the realm from slavery, is to enslave it with a different spell?" Lepkin asked.

"No. I am saying that it was necessary to use it on those close enough to Nagar's secret that they would have been enslaved anyway. In this way I was able to keep them fighting for our side until I could stop Tu'luh from using his magic. However, to save the realm, I must destroy both spells. There will be no slavery. Though, I am afraid that those already under the Illumination will die once the spells have been destroyed."

Master Lepkin moved to a desk and picked up a bundle wrapped in a black cloth. He turned and set the bundle next to Erik. "This is everything that is left."

"Can you tell me, where is my sword? I threw it on the field during battle."

Lepkin reached down to the floor and picked up the sword, placing it on the bed next to Erik. "After you lost consciousness, and the golden dome over the fort subsided, I retrieved the sword for you."

"Master Lepkin, this is something I need to do on my own. Please go out of the room, and I will tell you when it is finished."

The large warrior nodded his head and turned to leave the room. Erik watched until the door was closed and the latch was secured in place before he unwrapped the bundle. The two books were set one atop the other. The Illumination, which he had brought from the Immortal Mystic's palace, rested on Nagar's secret. Next to them was a yellow amulet with a golden chain. Erik placed the yellow amulet atop the Illumination. He then placed the bundle onto his lap.

Erik placed his hand over the amulet. He could feel the evil power emanating out from it. For a moment, he allowed himself to feel the fear and torment this curse caused. Then he called forth his own power, which was now augmented by the additional power he had been given at the palace before he left after he had passed the exalted test of Arophim. It was something very similar to what his grandfather, Allun Rha had used, but it was more pure, and it was stronger. Erik now held the power to destroy both spells.

He recalled the ancient runes that he was shown at the palace. He focused on them in his mind, but he did not speak them aloud.

He let his mind's focus course through his body until it streamed out from his right hand and into the objects on his lap. A red glow encompassed the books and the amulet. Waves of heat danced before him. Soon a white fire ignited within the ball of red and ate up the pages and the amulet. The flames did not destroy the artifacts however, it melted them together into one. Inside the glowing red globe a tempest of lightning and thunder erupted as both of the books and the amulet protested their destruction. They fought against him, trying to break his power and his concentration. Erik focused solely on the runes in his mind.

Within a few minutes the artifacts were melted together into one brick. It was not a solid object, but rather a gelatinous brick that waved and jiggled as the lightning continued within the red orb. Erik slid the brick and the red orb off of his lap and onto the bed.

He then took the flaming sword, holding it upside down as high as he could over the brick. He called to his mind a different rune, one that meant destruction or undoing, and he let that power course into the sword. The sword ignited as it always did when Erik took it in his hand, but this time the flame was black. He jammed the sword down into the brick. Lightning flashed out into the room singeing the walls and the bookshelves and even the ceiling. The sound of a strange, gasping scream was heard as the brick was pierced through. The black flame devoured the brick. The destruction of the artifacts not only drained Erik's energy but also began to eat away at the Telarian steel. The very metal that protected it from dragon fire was now melting away. In the end, a great white flash exploded in the room knocking Erik back to the far wall and opening his wound again. He held in his hand only the hilt of the flaming sword he had used before, as the blade was now consumed and gone. He did not need to look outside to know that all those who had been under the Illumination's control were now dead. The Golden Army, those who had been trapped as the slaves of Allun Rha since the battle of Hamath Valley, were now released from their prison and allowed to rest. Those who had been ensnared by the magic during this most recent battle at Fort Drake were also let go.

Erik fell asleep again.

He woke again shortly before dinner, with Lepkin and Lady

Dimwater in his room. He looked to his shoulder and saw that he had new dressings on his wound. He then looked to his bed and saw that the mattress had been replaced and the hilt of his sword had been placed on the pillow next to him. He sat up and looked to master Lepkin, he wasn't sure what to say. He felt at once a great wave of relief, but also a profound emptiness and confusion. Master Lepkin must have sensed this, for he spoke first.

"It is never easy for the warrior to return home after the war is done. It is not uncommon for someone in your place to lose themselves in the past, or to forget who they are in the present. Things that you have seen, and the things that you have done, are now a part of you forever whether you like it or not. Those friends and family members we have lost will also stay with you in memory."

Erik nodded his head and shifted to sit up. "Where will you go?"

Lepkin arched an eyebrow. "Is it so obvious that I am leaving?"

Erik smiled. "I am the Champion of Truth, Master Lepkin. It is hard to hide your feelings from me now."

Lepkin smiled wide and put an arm around Lady Dimwater. "A son was born to us while you were away." Erik's eyes went wide in surprise. "We hid him away before this last battle. We are going to go and get him back now."

"But you will not be coming back right away, will you?"

Lepkin shook his head. "No."

"The orcs have been beaten," Lady Dimwater said. "Not a single member of their army remains. Those who survived the battles against us at Ten Forts and Stonebrook were enslaved by Tu'luh. You destroyed the last of them with your army. I imagine there are still a few nobles who will scheme and try for the throne, but they will think twice before acting overtly."

"So you both have finished your duty to the Middle Kingdom then," Erik said. "I hope you both find peace."

"The dragon is dead, Erik," Lepkin said. "Your task is also finished. You destroyed the curse that threatened the Middle Kingdom. You also vanquished the king's most dangerous foe. I should also tell you that I can now take my own dragon form at will without fear of what might happen. If I can do that, then I suspect some of the Ancients, or any other dragons that remain, might return someday soon."

Master Lepkin and Lady Dimwater rose from their seats and moved toward Erik. They both smiled at him. Lady Dimwater bent down and kissed Erik's forehead.

"I have a present for you before I leave," Lady Dimwater said. "This is the spell I use to summon Silverfang. Where we go, I hope not to have need of him, but perhaps you can let him have some exercise from time to time."

"I would be honored to have such a companion," Erik said.

Master Lepkin bent in low and gave Erik a hug. "I am proud of you, as proud as if you were my own son."

Erik was not sure what else to say. His mind flashed back to his training sessions with Master Lepkin and he recalled the rigorous, strict lessons at Kuldiga Academy. He also remembered all of the times Master Lepkin had been short or ill tempered. To hear such an open expression of affection from Master Lepkin now seemed almost strange. However, as Erik let the words sink in, the sentiment felt entirely natural. It was as if Master Lepkin had never really been the gruff, stoic warrior he had portrayed himself to be. Erik was now seeing the man for the first time, for who he really was. Lepkin had the muscular appearance and the legendary traits any hero would desire, but he had a much softer side as well. Perhaps that was the real reason he was so legendary.

Erik understood then that only a warrior with a heart could rise to such a status as Master Lepkin, for they are the only ones who truly know what they are fighting for.

Erik nodded and smiled at them. He wished them goodbye as Lady Dimwater opened a portal and the two walked through it. The young champion looked down to the small rolled up piece of paper that held the spell for summoning Silverfang. He looked at it for maybe a minute or two before the door opened.

"Hey beanpole," Al said with a soft wink.

"Hi," Erik replied. Al's face smiled, but his eyes didn't. Erik knew why. All of the dwarves that had been without the walls of Fort Drake had been caught by his spell, which now meant they were all dead.

"I don't need an apology," Al said quickly, as if understanding Erik's mind.

Erik looked to the floor and sighed. "There wasn't another way," he said.

"I said I *don't* need an apology," Al repeated. "I know why you did what you did. Frankly, I am just glad you found a way to shield those of us inside the fort. I wasn't aware the magic of Allun Rha could be directed like that. I have known for a while now that using it would prove fatal to anyone caught by it." Al took in a breath and slipped into the room. "You must remember, the dwarves kept the most accurate history of all. I know the secrets of Hamath Valley, and I knew the price of being present in the final battle with Tu'luh."

"Then why did you come with me?" Erik asked.

"I couldn't very well let you come alone, now could I?" Al replied with a half grin. He clasped his hands together and the grin disappeared. "I had hoped we would find a way to get the dragon alone, or at least on an empty field surrounded by his own goons instead of my kin, but that is the burden of being king. That is my stone to bear, don't let it weigh you down. You did what you had to do, and there was no other way to stop him. Whether you came at that moment or the day after, my kin folk were already dead. Tu'luh was here, and he had the curse. It worked out as well as it could have."

Erik nodded. "I asked the Immortal Mystic how I could spare you," he said. "By the way, I should tell you what I found when I went to the immortal Mystic." Al stared at Erik blankly as he closed the door behind himself. He moved close and sat on the foot of the bed waiting for Erik to explain.

"The immortal Mystic is not a man."

"He is the Father of the Ancients," Al said.

"You knew?"

Al shook his head. "No, but after we found Tu'luh in Valtuu Temple, I hoped for it." The dwarf king smiled and then he rose from the bed. "I just wanted to check on you before I left."

"You're leaving now?"

Tears slid over Al's cheek, mingling with his beard. He opened his mouth to speak, but his voice cracked and nothing came out. His lower lip quivered and he wrung his hands for himself as he stared at the floor. He nodded and then finally found the words to speak. "I have many funeral pyres to build. My work outside the mountain is done. Now I must return and rebuild what is left of my kingdom. There is a bright spot on the wars, though. I received word that most of my warriors in the north who fought under Grand Master Penthal's command against the Tarthuns survived. Those horse-loving Tarthuns won't be back to bother the Middle Kingdom again any time soon." Al flashed his bright smile and nodded proudly. "We beat them twice, actually. Faengoril led a force of five hundred against seven thousand."

"He won?" Erik asked with eyes wide.

Al smiled wide. "He suckered them into a cave and then dropped it around their ears." His smile faded and he sighed then. "Unfortunately, he died there. I would have liked to see him again." Al became silent for a few moments and let his gaze drift to the floor before continuing. "The dwarves in the north fought well under Master Penthal. They will be hailed as heroes in Roegudok Hall."

"So will you," Erik said.

Al shook his head and then pointed a finger at Erik. "You remember one thing, beanpole," Al said is he regained his composure. "You always have a friend in the mountain. Never forget that."

Erik started to cry as he watched Al leave the room and close the door behind. Erik sat on the bed a long while, waiting for someone else to come in the room. It took him maybe an hour or two before he realized there was no one else left to come. He looked at the tapestries on the wall, realizing for the first time that there was no window in this room. He rose to his feet and went to the door. He exited the room and made his way down the corridor. He didn't get far when he heard a loud commotion.

He followed the sounds of shouting and yelling until he made his way to the inner courtyard of Fort Drake. Soldiers rushed past him, nearly knocking him out of their way as they streamed out into the courtyard. Erik stepped outside and saw the great golden dragon standing in the courtyard. The sunlight bounced off of his golden scales, and the men gathered around in a sense of reverence and awe. It had been a long, long time since the Middle Kingdom had been visited by a dragon other than Tu'luh. It had been longer still, since the dragon did not have to worry about Nagar's evil curse.

The Father of the Ancients quickly found Erik among the crowd and looked at him. Soldiers parted immediately, as if obeying some unspoken command from the dragon. Erik walked forward and knelt on a knee before the Father of the Ancients.

"Do not bow before me, Champion of Truth." The dragon's voice echoed in the courtyard. "It is I who should bow to you." The magnificent dragon bent down on all four knees, until his belly touched the ground, and his head rested in the dirt before Erik's face. Erik reached out with his right hand and touched the dragon on the snout. "Allow me to heal your wound." Hyasintar Kulai stretched forth a curved, golden talon and touched Erik's shoulder. Instantly the wound healed and the arm was usable again.

"Thank you," Erik offered.

"Climb onto my back," the dragon said.

At that moment a small figure came rushing out from the crowd. It was Jaleal, the gnome, and he was frantically trying to catch them before they left. He knelt before the Father of the Ancients and held his spear out reverently.

"Please, wherever you take him, allow me to go as well."

"Noble gnome," the dragon began. "Your place is with your kind. For now, your fight is done. However, there will come a time when you will need to take up your spear again. Go and prepare for that time."

Jaleal shook his head. "I cannot leave Erik's side."

"Where Erik goes, you cannot follow," the dragon said. "But you will not long be parted. Go back to your people now, and you will see each other again."

Jaleal nodded and remained in a kneeling position as he looked up to Erik and smiled his farewell.

"And what of me?" A female voice asked.

Erik scanned the crowd and saw Lady Arkyn standing there, looking at him with her beautiful eyes.

Erik felt a voice enter his mind. It asked him whether he wanted Lady Arkyn to accompany him. It reminded him of the time when he could speak with the dwarves telepathically, while he was in Lepkin's dragon form. He knew at once that the golden dragon was communicating with him in the same manner now. Erik looked at Lady Arkyn and did not have to think for long.

"There is room for you as well," Erik said. "Come with me."

Lady Arkyn quickly climbed onto the dragon and sat behind Erik. Without waiting a moment longer, the golden dragon leapt into the air high into the sky. He soared with blinding speed, much faster than Erik had ever been able to fly as a dragon, and faster than he had even seem Tu'luh fly. The golden dragon took him back to his home and set him down among the ruins.

They walked by the barn, or what was left of it after it had been burnt. They walked toward where the house had been. Erik looked down at the rubble at his feet thought of that battle when Senator Bracken, or more accurately the warlock that had masqueraded as Senator Bracken, had led an army against his home. "You knew then that I was not master Lepkin, didn't you?" Erik asked Lady Arkyn.

"I did," Lady Arkyn said.

"Thank you for not saying anything. If you had, the soldiers who followed me might have lost heart and fled."

Lady Arkyn shook her head emphatically. "No, not if they saw what I saw in you. There is a great strength in you, one that commands respect and speaks of a wisdom far beyond your years."

Erik smiled, blushing a bit in the cheeks, and looked back to the stones and bricks at his feet that had once formed his home.

The two of them walked in silence through the rubble for a few minutes before Erik turned back to the golden dragon and asked him a question.

"Why have you brought me here?"

"Your home is going to be rebuilt," the golden dragon said. "King Mathias has already decreed it. Your mother, and the servant called Braun, will leave the capitol city tomorrow morning. They'll be traveling directly here. I thought you might like to say goodbye."

"Goodbye?" Erik echoed. "Where is it that I am going?"

The golden dragon laughed a soft yet deep, throaty laugh. "I can see the rumblings inside your heart, young Erik. There is a wound - an emptiness that I believe only a new adventure will heal."

"So where are you sending me?" Erik asked. The golden dragon shook his head. "The tapestries of fate came undone after you destroyed the spells that threatened the Middle Kingdom. Neither I, nor the other dragons can see into the future with any degree of clarity anymore."

"Does this mean you cannot find the secrets inside the Infinium?"

"No, it only means that I cannot see whether you play any part in the Middle Kingdom's immediate future. We will continue to study the Infinium, and if we discover something of importance I will come for you."

Erik looked around at the rubble of his home and then he looked to Lady Arkyn. She smiled at him reassuringly. Erik looked back to the dragon and asked, "What will become of my mother?"

"Her heart is broken." A single tear emerged and fell from the golden dragon's right eye. "I have the power to allow her to reunite with her husband."

"You would kill her?" Erik asked.

"Now. I would transfigure her. Afterward, when the two have been reunited, I will personally carry their spirits to the heaven city, Volganor. It is something I can only do a few times before the journey would sap me of my strength and prevent me from returning to Terramyr. But, for your parents, I would be happy to make the journey."

Erik nodded. "Where should we go?" He glanced back to Lady Arkyn and her smile only grew brighter.

"The sea lies to the west, the wild lands are to the east, and there are orc lands to the south, with many rumored mysteries beyond that. I am sure we can figure something out."

"I like the sound of that." Erik turned and took a few steps back toward the Father of the Ancients. "If I leave, what will happen to the Middle Kingdom?"

"Now that I have returned, I will grant additional strength to King Mathias. When his body fails him, Master Lepkin will take his place as the king. I will work with Master Lepkin, and his posterity, to create a peaceful kingdom."

Erik was happy. He knew that Lepkin would make an honorable and just king. He only hoped that it would be far enough in the future that Lepkin could enjoy some quiet and peace before being called back to serve the kingdom again. For now, Erik was going to follow in Lepkin's footsteps. There was something he needed to find, and he could not find it in the Middle Kingdom. He turned to the west, and then the east, and finally to the south. Then he turned around and looked to the north. He wasn't sure where he wanted to go. He knew that he no longer had a home in the Middle Kingdom. It wasn't just the rubble under his feet. He had changed. He needed to find himself again. He turned once more and looked at Lady Arkyn.

He wasn't sure where he was going to go, but at least he knew who he was going with. Destiny may have finished with him for now, but he decided it was about time to write his own. Besides, he could do far worse than beginning that new journey with a beautiful woman.

CHAPTER TWENTY-FOUR

Aparen watched from the window as Erik and Lady Arkyn leapt atop the back of the golden dragon. He couldn't help but feel a little jealous. Erik had stolen the glory that should have been his. Then again, he now had a power far beyond what he might have had otherwise. He thought of Njar the satyr's teachings. Balance had been restored. The orcs had been repelled, the curse had been broken, and the Middle Kingdom was returned to its natural state.

He knew he could no longer find a home in the Middle Kingdom. He looked down at his left hand, seeing the horrible scars that were forming over his skin where the dragon's fire burned and mutilated his body. Now, even in his human form he was more monster than man. He moved to put on a long-sleeved cotton shirt, without regard for the pain as he slid it over his still open wounds. Then he exited the fort.

He walked toward the south, over the broken field, around the trenches between the pits. People were slowly making their way southward again, back to Stonebrook and the other villages and cities between Fort Drake and Stonebrook. Soldiers were on the move, transferring strength back to Ten Forts. Aparen intended to go beyond Ten Forts. If the orcish armies had been vanquished, then that meant there was a land to the south ripe for claiming. Who better to bring balance to a war thirsty horde than the greatest warlock in the history of the Middle Kingdom?

A great flash of lightning sparked in front of him. A silvery plate spun on the ground. The plate expanded to cover a large area in front of him and a great column of light descended down upon the plate. Within the light appeared his mother, Lady Cedreau. She stepped out of the light, followed by Njar the satyr, and Silvi the witch.

Aparen stood motionless. He had not seen his mother for quite some time, and certainly not since before he had led some of his retinue against Lokton manor.

The satyr was the first to speak. "Aparen, I found your mother. I have convinced her to stop hunting Silvi. In return, I promised to bring her to you so she could speak with you one more time."

"One more time?" Aparen glanced between his mother and the satyr. "What do you mean one more time?"

"Eldrik," lady Cedreau called out, using Aparen's birth name. "Njar has offered me a new life. He has found a place where he can send me, where I will be happy. He has offered to ensure that I have every need provided for me. I will have money, a home, and a place where people respect me."

"He told me of this plan before," Aparen said. "Where will you go?"

"That is why I have come. For this to work, the satyr is going to take my memories away and replace them with others. I will have a new family, and a new life."

"You would abandon me, my father, and my brother?"

His mother shook her head, with tears streaming from her eyes. She held out her arms to him beckoning for him to come to her. "No. I want you to come with me. He can make the same life with you in it if you choose."

"What do I give up in return?" Aparen asked.

The satyr stepped forward. "In addition to your memories, you will need to give up your magic. If you were to keep it, your memories would return and it would jeopardize you and your mother's happiness."

Aparen shook his head. "No. You ask too great a price." Aparen looked at Silvi. "Do you agree with them? Do you wish for me to give up everything that I am?"

"I wish for you to do whatever it is your heart desires to do. I also wish to go with you whichever choice you make."

"You will go with me whether I go with my mother or somewhere else?" Aparen clarified.

Silvi nodded in response.

Aparen moved in and gave his mother a hug. The two embraced for a long while, then he kissed her on the cheek. "I cannot go with you, mother. It is my memories that make me who I am, and it is my powers that make me who I will be."

The satyr came in close and put a hand on each of the shoulders. "If you choose not to go with her, you must forget about her. If you ever approach her in life, the spell will be broken and her memories will flood back to her. You would steal her happiness from her, and replace it with all the grief she has borne for this long while. You saw the vision of what the witches did. Your mother has suffered enough. I will not tell you where she is going, and you must swear in a wizard's pact never to look for her."

Aparen pushed his mother away, nodding slowly his agreement. "I wish for you to be happy, mother." He then looked at Silvi. "I am traveling south, through the orcish lands. Will you go with me there?"

Silvi smiled and rushed forward to embrace Aparen in a hug. She kissed him on his cheek and then let her head fall upon his shoulder. "I told you before, that I would be yours," she whispered.

The satyr summoned his staff and held it over them in the air. "This is where we all part ways," he said. "I wish each of you the best of fortune, and may Terramyr smile upon your days."

The satyr stamped the ground with his staff. A mighty whirlwind arose and each party was taken to their separate destinations to begin their new lives.

*****

Tu'luh floated toward the volcano Demaverung that he had once called home. His wings beat slowly, but he didn't need to move them. He was dead. His spirit would move with the power of will whether his legs or wings moved at all.

He studied the demolished volcano and his heart felt heavy. It wasn't the loss of the battle that weighed upon him. He had lost wars before. Hamath Valley had been a particularly humiliating defeat. Then there had been the time that the young boy and the gnome had cornered him inside Demaverung. At least he had destroyed Valtuu Temple before fleeing the battle there.

He looked to the sky and cursed it. "Fools!" he shouted. "You will all burn." His thoughts turned to Kendualdern, his former home world. Now it was nothing more than star dust. Terramyr was set on the same course, he knew. Without his guidance, there would be no redemption for Icadion's world.

The dragon roared mightily, but the ground did not quake this time. In spirit, his power was greatly diminished. He had to think of a way to reverse the events that had taken place. He had watched helplessly as his precious spell was destroyed. Erik had done a fine job of mucking everything up.

Still, he was never one to admit defeat. He had waited centuries before, he could do it again. He had only to find the right tool to bring his plan back into existence. There was always a human or elf that was seeking the darker arts. He was sure he could find someone to corrupt, eventually.

He snarled and stared at the ruined volcano before him. He knew that beneath the hollowed shell of the once mighty mountain was a great pool of lava building up. Whether in centuries or eons, the volcano would rise again.

"So will I," Tu'luh swore. "I will rise again. I have all eternity to find the way."

"Tu'luh, you broke our bargain," a voice boomed from behind, ripping Tu'luh from his thoughts.

The dragon wheeled around to see Khefir standing with a great scythe in his bony hands.

"Be gone, dog," Tu'luh snapped.

Khefir laughed, his jaw clicking and clacking with each chuckle. The god shook his head and pointed a single finger at Tu'luh. "You swore that when Gulgarin finished his life, I would have claim on his soul."

"Be gone!" Tu'luh repeated.

"I have brought a few visitors for you," Khefir said. He waved his left hand and a massive rift tore through the air. Burning, red lines ripped the very fabric of the air away to reveal an army of thousands of orcs dressed in blood-red armor. Each of them held halberds and swords at the ready. Flames of blue and white encircled each blade. Behind them was the abominable plane of Hammenfein. Waves of heat danced over the orcish spirit soldiers.

"You think to fight me?" Tu'luh mocked. "I am an Ancient. I am the son of Hyasintar Kulai."

"And I am a god," Khefir replied. "Let me introduce you to one of my newest generals. A fiery portal opened on Khefir's right-hand side. Through the opening stepped Maernok. The orc grinned wide and saluted Tu'luh.

"You should have resurrected me, dragon. Though it seems I

will have a more pleasing battle now."

Tu'luh growled. "I have a bargain," he offered.

"Enough of your schemes," Maernok said. "Khefir demands his soul," he shouted to the soldiers around him. "Attack!"

The orcish spirit warriors poured in from the underworld, flooding Terramyr like a great sea of brimstone. Tu'luh roared and lunged at them. Even though he was a spirit, he was not without power. He batted dozens away with his tail, swatted scores with his claws, and even devoured a few souls in his mouth.

Tu'luh could hear Khefir's laugh taunting him as the ever-charging ocean of orc spirits washed over him. It wasn't long before they subdued him with golden chains that bound his snout shut, and tethered his wings tight to his back. Even his powers could not break the chains that held him.

Maernok climbed atop Tu'luh and drove a long, golden spike though his head. The pain seared the dragon so that he collapsed to the ground and all of his strength left him. The orc bent low to his ear and whispered something that the dragon could not quite understand. Rattling chains were then attached to the spike and Maernok pulled on them. The pain forced Tu'luh up to his feet.

"Didn't you hear me?" Maernok asked Tu'luh. "Now you are *my* slave. I shall ride you into Hammenfein as my prize."

Tu'luh cried out in protest, but a quick yank on the chains attached to the spike in his head shut his mouth.

"That is right, General Maernok," Khefir said. "One must not let their steed have too much spirit. It is improper."

Maernok bent his head low, bowing reverently to Khefir. "I understand, my lord. I will be sure to break this one quickly."

Khefir laughed as the army pulled on the chains, dragging Tu'luh down to hell.

Epilogue

Jaleal stretched out his hand and grasped the brass knob on his door. The round, wooden portal squeaked as he pulled it out to him. The room inside was dark, and held a damp, musty odor inside. It seemed to the gnome that no one had bothered to air the place out during his absence.

That wasn't surprising. Most of his folk didn't even bother to welcome him back today either.

He entered and walked down the short flight of stairs to the main level inside. He lit the lantern hanging from the ceiling and then shook out the match's flame. He looked around his home, watching the shadows play off the lantern as it spun upon its chain. A thick layer of dust had gathered atop the small table and chair in his dining area. Mold had all but consumed a plate that Jaleal could only guess had once held bread.

"Well, ma always told me to clean up after myself," he said sarcastically as his eyes landed on the furry green and white glob growing on the table. "Guess she was right." He turned and gently slid his mithril spear into a set of iron brackets adjacent to the doorway. Then he moved farther into his home, heading for his green velvet arm chair.

Something moved in the darkness. At first Jaleal thought it was a shadow, but the more his eyes adjusted to the room, he realized it was not a shadow, but a black boot sticking out from the armchair and set upon the footstool.

Jaleal circled around the chair. How could someone have taken his home already? That was not the gnome way.

As he moved around the side of the chair he saw a stout gnome with a long, white beard. The intruder's hands were resting upon his slightly bulging belly and he was snoring softly.

Jaleal kicked the intruder's feet from the footstool.

The other gnome woke with a start, snorting and jerking his hands out to the side to catch himself.

"What, what? Who is it?" The gnome looked up at Jaleal and then he smiled. "Oh, it's you! I have ben waiting for you."

"Who are you, and what are you doing in my house?" Jaleal asked. Then he glanced over to the moldy plate on the table. Flustered, he pointed to it and shouted at the intruder. "And for Terra's sake, how can you invade my home without the decency to clean up such a disgraceful mess?!"

The other gnome frowned and looked to the table. He shrugged. "I have only just arrived an hour or so ago. I would have cleaned if you had taken longer to return, I suppose."

Jaleal grimaced and folded his arms over his chest. "Waiting for me? Why?"

The other gnome rose to his feet and bowed graciously. "I am Phinean, Sergeant of the Svetli'Tai Council of Svatal."

"Svatal?" Jaleal repeated as he drew his brow together. "But, Svatal Island is many months by sea beyond the Barrier Reef, what could you possibly be doing here?"

Phinean shook his head. "No, by sea it would take more than a year to get to Svatal, and it would only work if the Barrier Reef were not enchanted into a great ring of fire that blocks all ships from entering or leaving that entire area."

"You traveled more than a year to see me? Why?"

"Good heavens, no!" Phinean said quickly. "I used magic! I came as quickly as I could. It is a matter of the utmost urgency."

Jaleal narrowed his eyes on Phinean. "What?" he barked. The warrior-gnome was quickly losing his patience.

Phinean pointed to the small sack slung over Jaleal's left shoulder. "He said you would have it. The Goresym, do you have it?"

Jaleal thought of the magical crystal tucked safely into his sack. How could Phinean know of it? More importantly, what did he want with it? Jaleal held out his left hand and Aeolbani, his magical mithril spear appeared in his palm. He gripped the weapon and leveled the point at Phinean's throat. "You had better speak plainly, else I will end your nonsensical words."

Phinean blanched. "Quite right," he said with a slight nod. "Perhaps I should start from the beginning. I was sent to you by Jahre, he is the oldest and wisest of the elf sages on Svatal Island. He was there when King Lemork led a war to crush the Svetli'Tai race." Phinean paused and waited for a reaction. Jaleal stood stoic. Phinean frowned. "King Lemork was a dark elf, a Tomni'Tai, a sister race of the Sierri'Tai dark elves."

"I know who the Tomni'Tai are," Jaleal said impatiently.

Phinean nodded, glancing nervously to the spear's point aimed at his throat. "Well, did you know that King Lemork rode upon a black dragon in his war with the other elf races?" Again he paused, but again Jaleal didn't respond. Phinean stamped a foot in frustration. "Oh, must I spell it out for you?! King Lemork rode upon one of the Ancients, the black dragon who shall not be named! He wielded a great sword fashioned from that very monster and nearly consumed the Elven Isles of Svatal and Xlemt in his rage and bloodlust."

"When did this happen?" Jaleal asked, his tone now showing a bit more concern.

"Five hundred years ago," Phinean responded.

"So why seek out the Goresym now?" Jaleal pressed.

"Because we need it!" Phinean said impatiently. "The sage, Jahre, said that a great wrrior, named Talon, will come from the continent north of Svatal. This man is more than a simple warrior though, he is a cunning assassin and has great potential for either good or evil. Jahre said that Talon will come to Svatal looking for powerful artifacts that could disrupt the balance of Terramyr."

"How can one man do that?" Jaleal asked. In his mind he thought of each of the warlocks and wizards that Erik had fought with. Even they had to have the help of Tu'luh.

"Don't you see?" Phinean asked. The fear was evident in his wide eyes and nervous fidgeting. "The assassin now wields Lemork's sword. The black dragon is the Patron of Chaos. The sword is born out of the black dragon's bone and as such, the weapon itself has a mind and power all its own. It will corrupt the warrior, and he will turn to use the power he attains to destroy everything around him. If he succeeds in finding the other sacred relics, then he will be unstoppable."

"Why do you need me?" Jaleal pressed.

"Because, with the Goresym, we might be able to counter the sword's magic and restore balance. If we can do that, then there is still hope for him, and hope for us."

"And if we can't restore balance?" Jaleal pressed.

Phinean shook his head. "Then we must kill Talon before he finds all of the relics. Otherwise, he will set Terramyr on a collision path with a terrible and dreadful power known only as the four horsemen."

Jaleal stiffened. He had not expected that. He brought his spear away from Phinean and nodded slowly. "As a gnome, it is my duty to restore balance. More than that, as one of Terramyr's races, I am honor-bound to defend her against all calamity. I know of a great warrior who would be useful to us. He too is struggling for a way to stop the arrival of the four horsemen."

"Oh you can't prevent them from coming," Phinean said quickly. "But, if Talon succeeds in attaining all three relics, plus the sword, then they will come sooner, and we will never stand a chance. The world will be turned to ash, and Talon would help them do it."

"Then we must go and get Erik, we need his power."

Phinean shook his head. "There is no time! Talon may already have the Tomni'Tai Scroll, and if he were to get the King's Ring and the key as well, then it will be too late. Come, we must go now!" Phinean reached out and took hold of Jaleal's hand. A flash of blue and silver light washed over them, and then the room was empty again.

You can follow Talon's adventures in the Netherworld Gate Series:

The Netherworld Gate Series:
The Tomni'Tai Scroll
The King's Ring (Coming Soon)
Son of the Dragon (Coming Soon)

Other Books by Sam Ferguson

Tales from Terramyr

The Dragon's Champion Series

The Dragon's Champion
The Warlock Senator
The Dragon's Test
Erik and the Dragon
The Immortal Mystic
Return of the Dragon

The Dragons of Kendualdern
Ascension

Other novels:

Dimwater's Dragon

Jonathan Haymaker

About the Author

Sam Ferguson is a fairly average guy.
That's it.
No, really, that's it.
Oh- you are actually reading this?

Well… the truth is that Sam is a very *lucky* guy. He juggles work in such a way that he makes sure to spend enough time with his loving wife and six sons. His goal is to make writing his fulltime career so he can have even more time with them (assuming they can handle having him around that much every day…). If he can carve out an extra hour for himself during the day, he'll hit the gym to try and regain the body he used to have in his youth (but he eats too much junk food to ever accomplish that goal).

He spent nearly five years serving as a U.S. Diplomat and absolutely loved the experience, but decided to move back home. Outside of the U.S. he has lived in Latvia, Hungary, and Armenia. He speaks Russian, Hungarian, and Armenian. (He used to speak some Latvian too, but he has no one to practice with anymore…)

He also has two dogs.

He plays the Elder Scrolls series.

His favorite superhero is Wolverine, but Batman is a close second.

If the kids go to bed at a reasonable hour, he will cuddle up with his wife to watch Scrubs reruns, the Big Bang Theory, Castle, or Burn Notice.

See, really just an average guy after all.

If you enjoyed this book, then join Sam Ferguson's Facebook page, sign up for alerts on his Amazon page, and by all means leave a kind review!